Miss Etta

A Novel

Miss Etta

Copyright © 2018 Deanna Lynn Sletten

ISBN 13: 978-1-941212-38-7
ISBN 10: 1-941212-38-7

Editor: Samantha Stroh Bailey of Perfect Pen Communications
Cover Designer: Deborah Bradseth of Tugboat Design

Miss Etta

A Novel

Deanna Lynn Sletten

Novels by Deanna Lynn Sletten

Night Music

One Wrong Turn

Finding Libbie

Maggie's Turn

As the Snow Fell

Walking Sam

Destination Wedding

Summer of the Loon

Sara's Promise

Memories

Widow, Virgin, Whore

Kiss a Cowboy

A Kiss for Colt

Kissing Carly

Outlaw Heroes

Some of what you are about to read is true.

Prologue

San Francisco, CA
1972

Susan Sheridan hurried out of her car and headed across the street to the assisted-living facility where her grandmother lived. She checked her watch as she waited for the cable car to pass. As a reporter for *The San Francisco Chronicle*, Susan usually sprinted from place to place to catch a story for the paper. But today was different. Her grandmother had called and requested she come to see her. Susan loved her grandmother dearly, but she wished she could wait until the weekend to talk to her. But Grandma Em wasn't normally an impatient woman, so Susan felt she should at least check on her.

She entered the building and waved to the receptionist in the office near the entryway. As a frequent visitor, Susan was recognized and didn't have to check in. She slipped into the elevator and shared the ride up with Mrs. Jenkowski, who complained that her grandchildren never came to visit and proclaimed Susan to be a very good girl. Susan didn't feel like a good girl. She felt guilty about wanting to rush her visit with her grandmother so she could leave.

Susan walked down the plush carpeted hallway, and sure enough, there was her grandmother waiting for her in the apartment's doorway. The receptionist had obviously buzzed her to let her know her granddaughter was on her way up.

Grandma Em gave Susan a hug. "I'm so happy you could come by this morning." She turned and walked to her favorite rocker in the living room.

Susan noticed that her grandma walked a little slower these days. But at ninety-six years old, it was expected that this once lively woman would slow down.

Susan followed and sat on the sofa across from her grandmother. In-between them on the coffee table sat an antique carved wooden box with a tiny gold key. Susan gazed at the box, enchanted. It had intricate leaf detailing decorating the lid and looked to be made of very fine wood. She was surprised she'd never seen it before.

"That's for later, dear." Grandma Em settled back in her rocker. "For now, we need to talk."

Susan noticed that her grandmother sounded weary. Her long, silver hair was styled in its usual bun on the top of her head, a few loose tendrils framing her face which was wrinkled and soft with age. Her eyes were a beautiful lavender-blue that Susan had inherited. Susan thought her grandmother's eyes looked different today, though. They weren't just tired; they looked resigned.

"Is something wrong, Grandma?" Susan asked, beginning to worry why she'd been summoned here on such short notice. Was her grandmother ill? Her grandmother had always been the picture of good health. Susan hoped whatever was wrong wasn't serious.

Grandma Em shook her head. "No, dear. Nothing is wrong.

And I know you're a busy woman, but I have something I need to tell you. A story that's waited a long time to be told. Do you have that recording device of yours I asked you to bring?"

Susan nodded and dug through her purse for her small tape recorder. She used it on interviews to report quotes accurately. After checking to make sure the tape in it was new, she set it on the table in front of her. "Grandma, I'm sure what you want to tell me is interesting, but maybe we could do this on Saturday. I have two stories on deadline and one interview I still have to go to and…"

"Dear," Grandma Em interrupted. "I think you'll want to hear this. I'm not sure I'll ever be as ready to tell it as I am today."

Susan took a deep breath and nodded. She could never deny her grandmother anything. They had always been close, but after Susan's mother had died of cancer when Susan was fifteen years old, their relationship had grown even closer.

"Okay, Grandma," she said, resigning herself to staying put for a while. She clicked the tape recorder on. "Whenever you're ready."

"Susan," Grandma Em began, settling deeper into her rocker. "You know me only as your grandmother, the retired teacher. And your father knows me only as his mother and the wife of his stepfather, Edward Sheridan. But once, a long time ago, before I met your grandfather, my life was different. Very different indeed."

Chapter One

Pine Creek, MN
August 1911

E mily Pleasants stepped off the train onto the platform, scanning the small station with her lavender-blue eyes. It had been a long trip across country from California to Minnesota and she felt weary. The August afternoon was hot and humid, forming beads of perspiration under her corset. She raised a slender, gloved hand to smooth the back of her already perfect chignon, making sure her small hat was still in place, as she continued to scan the Pine Creek train station. She wanted nothing more than to find the gentleman who was supposed to meet her and be taken to her rooms.

From beside her came a soft sigh. Emily smiled down at the small boy standing there. Dressed in a brown suit and hat, he looked like a miniature adult, his gray-blue eyes staring up at her in question.

Emily lifted her gaze to the platform again, but the only people she saw were the ones who had also stepped off the train. At the far end, she caught sight of a man neatly dressed in a navy three-piece suit, impatiently staring at a gold pocket watch as if he was late for an appointment. He didn't look like a small-town school board member to her—he looked like a banker. Emily chuckled softly. She could spot a banker in a crowd any day. She'd had plenty of experience with bankers.

Sighing, she gave up waiting and decided to go inside the station's building. Perhaps the manager would know who was picking her up. Leaving her bags on the platform, Emily offered her hand to the boy beside her.

"Come along, Harry," she said, her voice gentle but authoritative. The little boy took her hand and followed her into the plank board building.

* * *

Edward Sheridan stood at the end of the platform studying his gold pocket watch for the hundredth time. He watched as the passengers disembarked and scattered, becoming impatient when he didn't see the new schoolteacher among them. A pretty, young woman with a small child beside her caught his eye, then he dismissed her immediately. He was not waiting for a young mother. He'd been sent by the school board to greet the new schoolmarm.

Edward watched the woman and young boy enter the station and turned his brown eyes again toward the train. No one else alighted from the passenger cars. Sighing, he contemplated what might have become of the woman. Perhaps she'd missed one of her transfers and would arrive on a later train. That wasn't entirely impossible, considering the distance she was traveling. His biggest fear was that she'd decided not to come after all. It had taken the board months to find a new schoolteacher and her references had been impeccable. Perhaps she'd decided Minnesota was too far a distance, the weather was too dreary, or the pay was too low for her liking. He truly hoped not. Finding a teacher for their small town was becoming more difficult with each passing year, especially with the larger cities paying higher wages and offering more opportunities for advancement. Small towns had so little to offer. They were lucky to keep a teacher for an entire school year.

The heat became increasingly unbearable and Edward felt trickles of sweat under his three-piece suit. He adjusted his vest over his waistline and studied his watch once more before deciding the train held no more passengers. Dropping the watch back into his vest pocket, Edward walked into the station to inquire about the next train.

"Well now, here's just the man you're looking for," Ernie Carlson, the station manager, blurted out as Edward entered the stuffy building.

Edward looked up to see the young woman with the child standing in front of the counter. The woman turned and stared at Edward, a look of relief on her face changing into one of confusion.

"Mr. Sheridan?" she inquired in a soft, yet purposeful voice. The boy beside her only stared.

"Yes, ma'am, this here's Edward Sheridan," Ernie replied as if the question had been directed at him. "This here's the new schoolteacher, Mr. Sheridan. She's been asking about you."

Now it was Edward's turn to be confused. He stared at the handsome woman before him, studying her with furrowed brows. She had hair the color of shining mahogany piled expertly upon her head and skin so smooth not a line showed on her face. Her traveling outfit and small hat looked to have been made of the finest materials and fit her slender figure as if cut specifically for her. Just above her left breast hung a lapel watch that glittered of gold with an intricate leaf design etched on its cover. This was a woman of substance and quality standing before him, not a woman of meager means, scratching her way through life on a schoolteacher's salary. Surely, there was some mistake.

"Mr. Sheridan?" the woman inquired again, this time her voice holding a more commanding tone. Realizing that his eyes were still upon the watch that hung above her breast, Edward snapped them up to her face, feeling his face flush all the way up to his hairline. A small chuckle came from Ernie behind the counter. Edward thought for certain he would perish from the heat rising inside him from his embarrassment than from the temperature outside. Anger at his lack of discretion caused him to draw his full lips into a thin line under his neatly trimmed mustache.

The schoolteacher, however, seemed unaffected by either Edward's rude stare or Ernie's chuckle. She crossed the space between them, offering her gloved hand in greeting. The little boy followed quietly at her side.

"Mr. Sheridan, I'm Emily Pleasants. It is so nice to finally meet you." She stood there, hand in mid-air for several seconds before Edward had the good sense to grasp it in his own. Her petite hand was practically lost in his large one.

"Miss Pleasants?" he asked, still not quite believing this was the woman they'd hired.

"Mrs. Pleasants," she corrected, returning her hand to her side and placing it around the boy's small shoulders. "This is my son, Harry."

Hat in hand, little Harry stretched out his other hand to greet Edward. Still somewhat dazed, Edward reached down and shook the tiny hand. Little Harry smiled up at him with shining eyes, his blond head bright in the dim light of the station.

"Pleased to meet you," Edward mumbled, and Harry only smiled then stepped back to his mother's side.

Silence filled the small station as the seconds ticked by. Outside, the train whistled in announcement of its taking leave, heading east to St. Paul.

The shrill of the whistle pulled Edward to his senses. He cleared his throat and focused on the woman before him, who continued to watch him in anticipation of his making the first move. Finally, he found his voice. "I'm sorry for my confusion, Miss, ah, er, Mrs. Pleasants. I wasn't expecting a married woman."

Mrs. Pleasants gazed calmly at him. "I'm a widow, Mr. Sheridan."

"Oh, yes, of course, er, I mean, I'm sorry." Edward stumbled over his words once again, feeling awkward, yet not understanding why. He was a successful merchant in town. Talking was as much a part of his business as selling. He was also part-owner of the town bank and held prominent positions on both the school board and town council. Yet, here he was, tongue-tied in front of this widowed schoolmarm while she stood there with perfect posture, looking in complete control of the situation. She had not a hair out of place, not even a bead of perspiration on her person from the extreme heat. And he, under his suit, was sweating like a farm animal. The lack of control he felt over the entire situation made his anger rise, and her complete coolness fueled it on.

Furrowing his brows, Edward blurted out in a razor-sharp voice, much louder than he'd intended, "Mrs. Pleasants. I'm afraid you've caught me at a disadvantage. I was expecting a single woman without a child. As you can imagine, I am shocked to find the situation different than anticipated."

Mrs. Pleasants straightened her shoulders and stood as tall as her five foot, three inch frame allowed. With eyes bright and blazing, she stared directly at him. "I see no problem here, Mr. Sheridan. I was hired to teach the children of Pine Creek. I intend to do just that."

Edward returned her intense stare only to find himself speechless once again in her presence. Her eyes completely distracted him. They were the most unique color he'd ever seen, not blue, but lavender-blue. Trimmed in thick, brown lashes, they were riveting. Absolutely beautiful.

Another chuckle from Ernie shook Edward awake. Bending his head close to Mrs. Pleasants, he suggested softly, "Perhaps we can discuss this outside."

Mrs. Pleasants tipped her head in agreement then turned back to Ernie. "It was very nice meeting you, Mr. Carlson," she said. "I look forward to having your son and daughter in my classroom."

"Pleasure's all mine, Mrs. Pleasants," Ernie said, tipping his cap.

Edward watched as Mrs. Pleasants took her son's hand and stepped up to the door. She paused in front of the unopened door for a moment before Edward remembered his manners and rushed to open it for her. Nodding her head in appreciation, she stepped outside with Harry, Edward close behind, as the sound of Ernie's chuckle followed him through.

Mrs. Pleasants walked over to her bags still sitting on the platform. There were only two, a large one for her, a smaller one for Harry. They looked well-worn and well-traveled.

"These are mine," Mrs. Pleasants told Edward, who still felt unnerved by the situation. "Will we be walking, or did you bring a carriage?"

Edward's mind drew a blank. Nothing about this situation was as he'd anticipated. He'd expected an older woman of single status, mousy, shy, and unsure of herself. Hadn't the last teacher been like that? Proficient at teaching numbers and letters but uncomfortable in social situations? Not that it mattered; she had been plain as a board and had no need for social graces. The only determined action she'd had in the year she'd worked there was to hand in her resignation. She had no liking for this small town on the plains of Minnesota and was homesick for her family in Illinois. Just as the schoolmaster before her had quit and just as the schoolmarm before him had left. Edward simply wasn't prepared for a self-assured woman like Mrs. Pleasants.

"Mr. Sheridan?" Emily said again to catch his attention.

"Yes?" he replied, confused.

"Walking or carriage?"

"Huh?" Edward squinted at her in the bright sun before realizing how stupid he must sound. Flustered, he tripped over his words again. "But we haven't settled our dilemma yet. I mean, we haven't decided what we're going to do about this situation."

Mrs. Pleasants sighed, her patience seeming to wane from the humid heat. Beside her, the little boy squirmed restlessly. Edward couldn't blame him. He was feeling restless in this heat too.

Mrs. Pleasants said in a steady voice, "Mr. Sheridan, I don't understand what there is to decide. The school board hired me. I have a contract for employment for the school year of 1911-1912. I've just spent four days shuffling from one train to another, making the trip from California to here. I'm hot, I'm tired, and I'd appreciate getting settled in my rooms."

Edward couldn't have agreed more. He was also hot and tired, and had to return to his store. Resigned that they were not going to resolve the matter standing here on the platform, Edward decided to let the school board deal with the situation. He'd finish what he came here to do—deliver the new school-teacher to her quarters.

Nodding his assent, Edward said, "Carriage."

Mrs. Pleasants looked puzzled. "Excuse me?"

Edward smiled a true smile for the first time since meeting her. "I have a carriage waiting behind the depot," he explained. "I'll take you to your room."

Looking relieved, she returned his smile. "Thank you."

He lifted her two pieces of luggage and led the way. Mrs. Pleasants reached her hand down to Harry, who dutifully took it and the two followed Mr. Sheridan to the open carriage.

Chapter Two

Pine Creek, MN
1911

Nestled one hundred miles northeast of Sioux Falls, South Dakota, and sixty miles southwest of Minneapolis, Minnesota, Pine Creek sat alone in the middle of prairie land. The Minnesota River flowed through the north end of town on its way to the southernmost part of the state. Named for the variety of pine trees that grew along the river's edge, the remainder of Pine Creek was open prairie, a small but prosperous town surrounded by fields upon fields of farmland growing hay, wheat, and corn.

From the simple beginnings of a single train depot when the Union Pacific first laid tracks through the area, Pine Creek grew from the need of nearby farmers for a place closer than Minneapolis or St. Paul for supplies. Zachariah Sheridan complied by moving his family from Illinois in 1881 and building the first dry-goods store in the fledgling town. It was a much-needed addition to the saloon, blacksmith shop and stable, and combination boarding house and restaurant that were already there.

Soon, several businesses sprouted up in the prairie town: a hotel, another restaurant, several saloons, a church, and eventually as more families moved there, a schoolhouse. Zachariah's son, Edward, continued the tradition by expanding the dry-goods store over the years, offering luxury items as well as staples to the growing population of townspeople. Whatever he didn't stock, he could order and have delivered promptly by train, making the need for trips to the big city unnecessary. He and two partners also opened the first area bank that sat adjacent to his store.

The town was a nice place to live and for area farmers to shop. With its neatly painted buildings, boardwalks, and cobblestone Main Street, Pine Creek showed its prosperity on its sleeve. Many lovely two-story Victorian homes were built on the fringes of town; green lawns sprawling toward the gravel roads and flowerbeds lining white picket fences that separated the yards.

This is what Emily saw first of her new home, the neighborhood of well-kept houses, for Edward had taken the west road into town, heading north to Main Street. She was confident he wanted her to see Pine Creek's best side. Emily had been in enough small but prosperous towns to know there was a seedier side to them as well, possibly a red-light district with questionable boarding houses filled with young, eager women and saloons that could become bawdy at night. But she said nothing as she surveyed her surroundings with a keen eye as they slowly rounded a curve to Main Street. The streets changed from gravel to cobblestone, much to her surprise. Of the many small, mid-western towns she'd experienced, she'd rarely seen one as refined as Pine Creek.

To her left, she noted a large building with a bell on top.

"That's the schoolhouse," Edward said, as if reading her mind.

"It looks like a fine building," she said, pleased to see its neatly painted exterior and well-tended lawn.

"Our town is very proud of its commitment to education," Edward told her.

The businesses ahead of her were built in an orderly fashion, as if the entire town was planned and constructed all at once. They passed Doctor Jenson's office, his gaily-painted sign swinging slightly in the gentle breeze. Next was a restaurant that emitted sumptuous aromas, immediately tempting Emily's appetite. They stopped at the building beside the restaurant, Sheridan's Dry Goods Store, which was attached to the First National Bank of Pine Creek. Emily found the proximity of the bank amusing.

Edward alighted the carriage with an agility that defied his stuffy suit. He came to Emily's side and raised a polite hand.

She accepted, stepping down beside him without a word. Next, he reached up and took Harry into his arms as easily as if he'd done it a thousand times before. Setting the young boy down beside his mother, Edward cleared his throat.

"Here we are." He raised his hand toward the store. "Your room is upstairs, over the store. I'm afraid it's not much, but it's what we've always given the teacher in the past."

"I'm sure it will be fine," she said, reassuringly.

He reached into the back of the carriage and pulled out the bags. Then, with a nod inviting them to follow, he led the way through the propped open door into his store.

Holding Harry's hand, Emily glanced around. It was one of the nicest stores she'd ever seen in a small town. The oak counter stood in the center. To the left of it were food supplies, and to the right, necessities for the home and of a personal nature. Bolts of fabric, sewing supplies, ready-made clothing, toiletries, pots, and kettles sat on shelving down tidy rows. Just about everything one might need was here. All items were neatly organized, displayed like the larger, big-city stores. Emily silently approved of Mr. Sheridan's store. It gave her a little insight into the man who owned it.

From behind the counter bustled a short, pudgy woman with graying hair piled askew upon her head, and a warm smile.

"Well, here she is, our new school mistress herself," the woman said, her bright blue eyes peering at Emily over gold-rimmed spectacles.

"Mrs. Pleasants," Edward began formally, "this is Gertrude McAffee, my assistant."

"Call me Gertie," the woman told her as she raised her hand to shake Emily's outstretched one. Her touch was warm and gentle. *Motherly,* Emily thought, as Gertie's friendliness touched her heart.

"It's very nice to meet you, Gertie," Emily said, their hands still clasped.

The small woman turned her eyes to the little boy at Emily's side. "And who do we have here?" she exclaimed. "What is your name, young man?"

The kindness in her voice made Harry smile up at her. "I'm Harry." He offered his small hand. A slight nudge from Emily reminded Harry to remove his hat indoors, and he did so promptly while shaking the older woman's hand.

"Well, well. Harry, you say? What a fine young man you are," Gertie said. "You look to me like a boy who would enjoy some licorice. Follow me and we'll find a piece."

For one brief second, Harry glanced up at his mother for approval, and with a nod of Emily's head, he dashed off behind his new friend.

Edward laughed at Harry's exuberance, making Emily smile also.

"That's very nice of her," she said. "I'll be happy to pay for it, though."

Edward shook his head. "Believe me, she loves giving candy out to the children. We both do. Sometimes, it's a contest as to who will get to the candy jar first when a child comes through the door." He chuckled and Emily liked the gentleness she saw in his face. "I'm sure Harry will be eating far more candy than you wish him to," Edward said, still beaming. Emily liked how his smile softened his features, making his face appear years younger.

As the silence grew between them, Edward soon appeared self-conscious again and his smile faded. Returning to the task at hand, his expression sobered, and he cleared his throat, returning to his position as Chairman of the School Board.

"Well, I shall show you your room," he said, all business now.

Emily found humor at his quick transformation, understanding, of course, that appearances were everything. If she'd learned anything in life, it was at least that. She nodded in answer, and he lifted her bags and carried them through the store as she followed. They caught up with Gertie and Harry, the latter sitting on the counter, gleefully swinging his short legs while chewing on a string of licorice. Gertie sent Emily a sweet grin.

"This young man tells me he's your son and he's all of three years old. What a pleasure it will be to have a young person around here." The excitement in her voice matched the gleam in her eyes. "Young Harry," Gertie said, turning back to the boy, "you come visit me here in the store often, you hear?"

Harry nodded enthusiastically, and Emily reached over the counter and grasped Gertie's hand affectionately. "Thank

you, Gertie. You've made us feel very welcome here." The two
women held hands for a moment longer, both smiling kindly
at each other, then Emily let go and stepped back. Out of the
corner of her eye, she saw Edward shuffle his feet in discom-
fort, embarrassed no doubt by the fact that he hadn't welcomed
them so sincerely.

She ignored his uneasiness, saying aloud to Harry, "Come
along, dear. Mr. Sheridan is going to show us our room."

Harry scooted off the counter and, without prompting from
his mother, turned to Gertie and said, "Thank you for the candy,
Miss Gertie." Plopping his hat back on his head, he turned to
follow his mother.

"You are ever so welcome, my dear." Gertie's words floated
to them as they followed Edward to the back of the store.

Edward led them to a storage room behind a velvet curtain.
There they found a set of stairs and they all walked up to the
second story. The steps curved as they ascended until they had
made a half-circle when they reached the top doorway. There
was only a frame, no door, and the three stepped through into
a long, narrow hallway. To the right stood a door and a small
window overlooking the back of the store's property. To the left
was only a long hallway with two doors, one on each side.

Emily and little Harry followed Edward down the hallway
and he opened the door on the right.

The afternoon sun poured in through both of the room's
windows, giving off a cheerful glow. The room was large, Emily
assessed as Edward placed her bags on the floor. It was wide and
long. She guessed it was the size of half the store below.

To her left, at the front of the building, there was a double
bed covered with a cheery patchwork quilt of blue, green, and
yellow. Beside that stood a nightstand with an oil lamp. A round

table with two chairs sat under one window, and at the other end of the room was a pot-bellied stove, a shiny copper tea kettle upon it. An oak armoire stood against the far wall, and a screen made of mahogany and bamboo sat in the corner for privacy while dressing. Oil lamp sconces hung on the walls to light up the room at night, and yellow calico curtains adorned the windows.

The room was large, airy, and gave off a comfortable, welcoming feel. Despite the hot sun outside, it felt pleasant in the room, an early evening breeze drifting through the open windows, caressing the cheerful curtains.

Emily smiled, pleased with the room, but Edward was immediately apologetic about it.

"I'm sorry it's not much. It will be cramped with the two of you here, I'm afraid. But it's the room we usually provide for the schoolteacher."

Emily turned to him. If he'd seen the small, sparse room she and Harry had shared at the convent over the past three years, he would not be apologizing. "This will do just fine, Mr. Sheridan. It's lovely. The coverlet and curtains brighten the room beautifully."

Edward's serious expression brightened. "That was Gertie's work. When she heard the new teacher was coming, she took it upon herself to make new curtains and a quilt. She said the room had become far too shabby over the years."

Emily watched Edward as he spoke, noting the admiration in his voice when he talked about Gertie. She wondered in what capacity were his affections for the kind woman. Perhaps he admired her like a sister, or a mother? Or as a lover? She tried hard to keep a straight face over this last thought. She couldn't imagine the two of them together.

"Please thank her for me," she said, erasing the last thought from her mind. It certainly was not a thought that should have been there to begin with.

Edward again cleared his throat. "Evy's Restaurant next door has always supplied meals for our teachers. The Townsend's own it, and they make delicious food and are very nice people. I eat there quite a bit myself."

"That sounds wonderful," Emily said. She stifled a yawn. The long trip and hot day were beginning to wear on her. Harry, too, was fading fast. Emily noticed he'd sat down on the bed and his lids were drooping.

Edward seemed to notice too. "I'm sure you're both tired. If you need anything, please don't hesitate to ask."

She pulled off her gloves and couldn't wait to slip out of her suit jacket. "Thank you, Mr. Sheridan, for seeing us here and showing us our room." She followed him to the door. Reaching up, she slid the pin from her hat, releasing it from her hair. Her long hair tumbled about her shoulders.

When Edward turned at the door, his eyes widened as he stared at her hair, seemingly entranced. Emily held back a chuckle over the dumbfounded expression on his face. Had the poor man never seen a woman's hair down before?

She smiled up at him. "Is that all?" she asked politely.

Edward regained his composure. "Oh, well, yes," he answered. "Good evening, Mrs. Pleasants." And with a final nod, he hurried from the room.

* * *

Edward stood in the hallway for a long time after Emily had closed the door, trying to compose himself before going downstairs. *What an idiot I must have sounded like,* he thought. *She must think I'm a complete fool!*

And what was all that throat-clearing about? As he'd spoken to Mrs. Pleasants, he'd noticed he'd done it several times. *What an annoying sound. When did I develop such an awful habit? She must think me a dolt!* Every time he'd spoken to her, he'd had to force himself not to clear his throat. What in heavens was wrong with him?

When she'd taken off her hat and her hair had fallen, it had completely unnerved him. He just stood there and stared. Her hair was the color of mahogany, gleaming as a table would after it had been hand-rubbed for hours. And her eyes. They weren't a color he'd ever seen before. Not blue, but lavender-blue. So beautiful, so intense, and yet so kind.

Edward had always prided himself on being professional in all situations. But for some reason, being around Mrs. Pleasants had turned him into a tongue-tied fool. And, if acting like an idiot wasn't enough to worry about, realizing that he cared what Emily Pleasants thought of him rattled him to his core.

Chapter Three

Pine Creek, MN
1911

Emily lay in bed, her mind swirling in the darkness that surrounded her. The room was quiet, even with the windows open to let in the cool night air. All the businesses were closed, the last street light extinguished, yet she was unable to sleep.

She'd been exhausted when she'd first entered the room. Gertie had appeared at the door soon afterward with a tray of food from Evy's Restaurant. The older woman had instinctively known the two travelers would be hungry but too tired to go out to eat. The creamed potato soup and fresh homemade bread had been delicious, and Emily was thankful that such a kind soul as Gertie existed in this new place they now called home.

Harry had barely finished eating when he crawled under the covers and fell fast asleep. Emily, too, thought tonight of all nights she'd fall soundly asleep when her head hit the feather pillow. She was wrong.

Night was always the most difficult time of her day. Or

the best, depending upon how she felt. It was when memories flooded back to her; memories that caused pain, but also reminded her of some of the sweetest times of her life. It was only when morning came that she had to face the cold reality of her life now and of her future without little Harry's father.

Emily glanced over at the small form sleeping beside her. Harry. What would she do without her precious reminder of the man she'd loved? Harry was the spitting image of his father in every way except one—he'd never grow up to live the life his father had lived. Emily would make sure of that.

She had come a long way since that first day she'd met her son's father. Many more miles than her trip from California to Minnesota. Miles that had taken her from west to east, north to south, stretching to the farthest reaches of another continent. And it all started with a simple meeting in Texas.

San Antonio, Texas
1895

Ethel Emily Pleasants walked hurriedly through the streets of San Antonio's red-light district. She had a piano lesson to give on the "proper" side of town in less than half an hour and she needed to pick up her music sheets at Fannie's.

The petite eighteen-year-old woman with shining mahogany hair pulled up in an unassuming chignon looked oddly out of place on this street of saloons and bordellos. Anyone watching her would believe she had lost her way from a church meeting or ladies' tea. But Ethel knew exactly where she was headed. She ducked into Fannie's Boarding House, a respectable name for a not-so-respectable business; a place that rented rooms by the hour and held far too many lady boarders who entertained gentleman callers.

It was just past noon when Ethel entered the quiet parlor and walked directly to the upright piano in the corner of the garishly decorated room. Daytime was rest time for most of the inhabitants, although an occasional gentleman caller might be lounging on the parlor sofa, enjoying a cigar or a bit of brandy, relaxing before the night's entertainment.

Ethel was used to such people lazing about and ignored the gentleman in the corner as she sifted through the sheets of music. She often practiced here in the early afternoon and occasionally met some of the customers, but everyone knew to keep their hands off Ethel. Although she lived in the apartment above the kitchen, she did not work here.

Feeling the man's eyes on her back, Ethel turned slightly and gave him a curt nod. He lazily tipped his hat and she returned to her searching, hoping her gesture would be enough to warn him off. To her surprise, he rose and stepped toward her. By the time she straightened, he was standing directly behind her.

"Morning, miss," he said softly. When she didn't respond, he continued with a grin, "Something I can help you find there?"

Ethel didn't know what to say. She wasn't sure of his motives, but in a place such as this, she could guess. She studied him a moment, trying to read into his gesture. He looked older than she, but not as old as many of the men who passed through this parlor. His hair, peeking out from under his short-brimmed cowboy hat, was sandy blond, as was the trimmed mustache that dressed his lip. He wore a respectable three-piece suit with freshly polished boots. His skin was deeply tanned, as if he worked out in the sun, and his eyes were a deep, steel gray.

He seemed comfortable in his suit, yet she couldn't help but think he'd be just as comfortable in work pants and a flannel shirt, riding astride a powerful horse. Yet, there seemed to be no coarseness about him. She could see that his eyes were kind.

"Now, Harry, don't you be bothering my young Etta here. She's not one of the girls." Fannie Mae Porter's voice boomed from the wide staircase in the hallway just outside the parlor. Both occupants beside the piano turned and looked her way.

Fannie stood on the last step of the paisley carpeted stairs, covered in a long black satin nightdress with a red satin robe thrown over it. She was a buxom woman, not overweight but big enough to handle any man who got out of control. Her thick, red hair was piled flamboyantly upon her head and even now, long before her workday began, she wore a heavy coat of face paint, her lips and cheeks a brilliant red.

Ethel could only smile at the 'Madame' who stood before her. Fannie was like a second mother to her, taking her in and watching over her after her own mother died.

"Didn't mean any disrespect, Miss Porter," the man Fannie called Harry said. "I was just offering this young lady my assistance."

Fannie stepped down off her perch and strutted over to Ethel. "Assistance my ass," she said, her eyes twinkling. "I know what kind of assistance you have in mind and it's not the polite kind. Now, take that hat off your head, boy. You're in the presence of ladies."

Harry obliged with a grin and a soft, "Sorry, ma'am." Although his words were directed at Fannie, his eyes were on Ethel.

Yes, Ethel thought. *His hair was highlighted blond by long days in the sun.* Harry grinned at her and Ethel dropped her eyes, embarrassed that she had been caught studying him.

His grin did not go unnoticed by Fannie. "Don't you get any ideas about my girl Etta," she said, her tone serious. "She's like a daughter to me and I protect her like a mother bear. She's from a good family and she has a fancy Boston education and a teacher's certificate. She's going places, places much bigger and better than here, and she's going to do special things. She's not going to get herself hooked up with the likes of you, son, so don't even think about it."

Harry seemed to contemplate this speech, all the while his eyes on Ethel. Finally, with a nod to Fannie, he spoke. "Sorry to have bothered you, miss. Good day." He turned and walked out the stained-glass door with Fannie hollering after him, "Come back later, Harry, and I'll introduce you to some of the other girls."

Ethel heard the door shut quietly behind him. The clock over the mantel chimed, reminding her of the appointment across town. She picked up the pile of sheet music and hurriedly gave Fannie a hug.

"I have a lesson to give. I'll be back in a while."

Fannie squeezed her back and waved goodbye.

Ethel had no sooner stepped outside when Harry matched her steps down the cobblestone sidewalk.

"Mind if I walk with you?" he asked.

She looked at him, wondering if he'd really take no for an answer. "Miss Fannie wouldn't be pleased if she knew you were following me."

Harry grinned. "I'm not following you, miss. I'm escorting you. Just want to make sure you reach your destination safely."

Ethel laughed softly. "Would you stop walking with me if I asked?"

"I'm hoping you won't ask." His eyes sparkled mischievously.

Ethel shook her head and sighed. What harm could there be in her walking down the busy street with him? Once she arrived at her appointment, he'd surely disappear and pursue a more willing woman.

As they strolled silently through the streets, the red-light district transformed into reputable businesses, then into elegant homes. Ethel kept up a brisk pace, eager to arrive on time, and Harry kept up with her at what seemed a leisurely jaunt. Although he was not overly tall by any means, compared to her five-foot, three-inch frame, he needed less steps than she to cover the same ground.

Occasionally, she glanced his way, curious about what he hoped to accomplish by accompanying her. But he only appeared interested in the neighborhood around him, seemingly unaware of her curious glances.

"Where, exactly, are we headed?" he asked.

"I give piano lessons. One of my students lives here."

Harry nodded, as if letting this information sink in. "You're a music teacher?"

"Yes, partially. I'm only doing this for the extra money. I'm actually a schoolteacher, but I won't be starting my new position until the end of the month."

Harry nodded again, looking as if he were forming his next question when Ethel stopped suddenly.

"Here we are," she announced. They stood in front of a large Victorian home with a steeple roof and gingerbread trim. "Thank you for your company, but I must go now."

"May I take you to dinner after your lesson?"

Ethel hesitated, unsure of how to answer. Could she trust a man she'd first met in a brothel?

Harry seemed to have read her mind. "My intentions are

completely honorable," he said, pushing back the brim of his hat and grinning at her.

Even though he looked older than she was, when he smiled, his face took on a boyish quality. Something about that face made her want to trust him. She decided that as long as they werc in a public place, it would be fine to go and eat with him.

"I'll be finished in one hour," she offered.

Harry nodded and slipped the hat from his head. "I'll be waiting," he told her with a slight bow.

Ethel headed up the brick walkway to the house, wondering if he'd really be there when she came back out. An hour later, to her surprise, he was.

Chapter Four

Pine Creek, MN
1911

Emily awoke early the next morning feeling more rested than she had since leaving California. She'd fallen asleep thinking of Harry's father, and it had comforted her into a peaceful lull. But daylight brought back reality. She had classes starting in a week, lesson plans to prepare, and a schoolhouse to organize. It was time to go to work.

Emily was cleaned up and dressed by the time little Harry awoke. Once he was ready, the two headed out in search of the schoolhouse.

In the hallway outside their room, the twosome stepped through the doorway at the top of the stairs that Emily had seen the night before. This led them to an outdoor porch that had steps going down to the alley behind the store. Emily and Harry followed the alley until they came to a road that led to the schoolhouse.

The town was just beginning to wake up on this early Tuesday morning. The smell of bacon, eggs, and homemade biscuits drifted past them as they strolled past Evy's Restaurant. A bell tinkled on the milkman's wagon as he made his rounds delivering fresh milk to the homes down the street from the schoolhouse. The iceman's horse whinnied as he, too, made his morning rounds to fill business and residents' iceboxes. Emily hadn't lived in a small town in a long time, and she savored the sights and smells.

The schoolhouse was set off a little from the town businesses, and also a distance from where the townspeople's homes stood. On its small patch of grassy land between the city and residential sections, it reminded Emily of an island, its own little world. Little Harry beamed and pointed to a tall oak with thick, rugged branches that held a rope swing with a wooden seat. There also stood a rustic tree fort set a few feet up on posts, and a girls' playhouse, painted yellow and white, with a porch attached and lace curtains in the windows. Emily appreciated these extras. It showed that the parents of Pine Creek cared enough about their children attending school that they even made recess play inviting. She hoped the school itself was equally equipped and cared for in the same manner.

Emily wasn't disappointed when she entered the building. They walked into the mudroom first, a small enclosed porch with hooks on the walls and benches along the sides to serve as a coat and boot closet. From there, they opened another door that led into the main schoolroom. She surveyed her surroundings, in awe of the room before her. The morning sun filled it with golden rays of warmth through the many panes of windows. Rows of oak desks were lined neatly upon a polished oak floor. In the back corner stood four large shelves filled with books for all levels of reading. Two small, round tables with chairs sat there too, like a miniature library setting. Short bookshelves lined the walls under the windows with textbooks of mathematics, history, spelling, science, and every other subject imaginable for all ages of study.

Emily was deeply impressed. She had taught in small-town schools before, but never one so equipped with tools of learning.

She and Harry walked between the rows of desks to the front. A heavy oak desk sat off to the left side, leaving the entire front of the room open, where a large blackboard covered the upper wall.

Emily found her desk also contained all the tools and textbooks she needed. This was a dream come true for her. If the parents of this town cared for their children's education as much as the supplies in this room suggested, then she would not disappoint them. She was willing to work hard for her pay, to prove to these people she was just as respectable as they expected her to be. With that thought in mind, she set herself and Harry to task, preparing for the upcoming school year.

* * *

That was exactly how Edward found them, two hours later, when he came to check on where the two had disappeared to. Poking his head through the schoolroom door, he saw Emily sitting at her desk, fast at work. Harry was bending over the smaller bookcases, cloth in hand, dusting. Neither heard him enter; neither saw him watching them. He took this inconspicuous moment to study the woman behind the desk, her graceful neck bent over the paper she was writing on. He imagined the script coming from the tip of her pen—it was neat and feminine, beautiful yet sensible. The sun shone over her mahogany-colored hair, painting it with luminous highlights, reminding him of the finest silk he sold in his store. She was the epitome of womanhood, so wonderfully petite and feminine in every way.

Edward sighed.

The sound apparently crossed the room, for both Emily and little Harry glanced up at him at the same time.

Edward felt his neck and face grow warm. What was wrong with him, thinking of the schoolmarm in such terms? His thoughts were like something from a woman's cheeky novel!

"Good morning, Mr. Sheridan." Emily smiled as she rose from her desk.

Edward watched her rise, her movements as graceful as a doe. He found his tongue. "Good morning, Mrs. Pleasants." He nodded over to Harry. "Good morning, young man."

Harry grinned up at him.

Emily drew nearer. The scent of lilacs drifted toward him. How could this woman always smell so fresh?

"What brings you out here so early?" she inquired.

Edward tried to remember his reason for coming to the schoolhouse, other than to look upon the teacher again.

"I, uh, I was wondering how you're settling in," he asked with effort. *Why did he become so stupid in her presence?*

"We're doing fine." She stopped a short distance away from him and folded her hands in front of her as if patiently waiting for him to speak. He noticed the white shirtwaist she was wearing tucked neatly into her gray skirt. Her waist was small, so small he thought his hands could easily encircle it.

"Are you always about so early?" Emily asked.

Edward's eyes darted up to her face and guilt rushed over him. Had she noticed he'd been staring at her waist? He took a deep breath to clear his mind so he could speak without stammering like a dolt.

"The store opens at eight. It's nearly that now. Gertie has everything under control so I was off to eat breakfast."

Emily's brows rose. "Is it really that late?" She snapped open the lapel watch clipped just above her left breast and studied the time. Edward did his best not to look at the watch, or where it lay. "Well, I'll be. Time has flown by."

"Have you eaten breakfast?" Edward asked.

"No. And I am sure Harry is famished."

Harry came to stand beside his mother and nodded at her words. "I'm starving."

Emily laughed. "I guess we're ready to eat also," she told Edward.

Edward hesitated a moment, the invitation to have them join him resting on his lips. He wondered at the propriety of the three of them sharing a meal. After all, he was not married and she was a widow. But then, just as quickly, he brushed that thought aside. He was a member of the school board, and she was the new teacher. Was it not his duty to make her feel welcome in this town? And it was only breakfast, not a candlelit supper.

His mind made up, he spoke quickly. "If you'd like, I'll wait for you and we can go to Evy's together."

She nodded. "That's so kind of you to ask," she said, her beautiful eyes sparkling. "We'll only be a moment." She headed back to her desk to put things away as Edward watched her.

He wondered if the sparkle in her eyes was caused by her being pleased, or if she was secretly laughing at his constant uneasiness around her?

Whatever reason, Edward didn't care once they were seated across from each other at a table in Evy's Restaurant. The place was busy, as most of the business owners ate there.

Many of them lived above their businesses and didn't have kitchens in their rooms, forcing them to eat out regularly, as Edward did.

Evy Townsend made a big fuss over the new schoolteacher, even bringing her husband, Arnold, out from the kitchen to meet her. Evy was a stout woman with a round face, dimpled cheeks, and a mass of red hair piled high upon her head. She appeared to be middle aged, but her energy was boundless. She immediately bonded with Emily and fell fast for little Harry.

"I just love children," Evy gushed, after asking Harry his name. "Arnold and I were never blessed with children, so I'm guilty of spoiling the little ones who come in here." She asked Harry about all his favorite foods and then took their order.

"Evy seems very nice," Emily said to Edward after she'd left.

"The Townsends are wonderful people. I'm sure you and she will be good friends. And she will also try to spoil Harry just like Gertie will." Edward grinned.

Evy proved him right when she brought Harry a fresh, warm cinnamon roll with his breakfast.

Over the meal, Edward learned that Emily was a light eater, she was an attentive and patient mother, and that she didn't easily give away too much information about herself.

Still, as he worked throughout the afternoon, he couldn't keep his mind off of her.

* * *

Later that evening as Edward sat outside, enjoying his pipe on the high back porch overlooking the alley, he realized Emily hadn't had much time to talk about herself during the meal. Between Evy popping by the table every few minutes, townspeople stopping to welcome her and Harry, and his own bumbling attempts at filling the silence with boring facts about his store and the community, she'd had very little opportunity to speak.

Edward drew deeply on his pipe and tipped back lazily in his chair as he stared out over the empty field. The sun was setting slowly, spreading long shadows over the land. He liked this time of day, when the town was settling down for the night. In the distance, the rowdy sounds of the red-light district drifted his way. As the night grew darker, the sounds would grow louder; rowdy men and bawdy women laughing and carousing over songs played on tinny pianos.

As Edward listened to the distant sounds, he suddenly felt lonely. While he tried to maintain an air of respectability in town, he, like all men, was not completely immune to making the occasional trip across the railroad tracks. But, more often than not, such visits only deepened his feelings of loneliness.

Edward had been alone for a long time. He sat there trying to remember the fair hair and porcelain skin of his lovely Lily. It had been twelve years since she was taken from him, and as each year passed, it became increasingly difficult to bring forth her face from memory. It pained him to think he might be forgetting her. They'd had five blissful years together, sharing a home, the business, their love. When she'd died, he'd felt he'd lost his entire world. It took years for him to accept she was gone from him forever, and except for his occasional visits across town, he'd never looked at another woman as he had his Lily. Not until Emily Pleasants arrived.

Edward closed his eyes and drew deeply on his pipe, thinking about the beautiful schoolteacher and wondering why she affected him so strongly. She was lovely, indeed, but she was also soft spoken, sweet, smart, and seemed to have a good sense of humor. All the traits Lily had possessed, yet there was something more. Something that shone in her eyes that he couldn't quite put into words. Something that made him crave to learn more about her.

Sighing, he opened his eyes and was so startled to see a figure standing in front of him that he almost tipped his chair over backward.

"Good evening, Mr. Sheridan. I'm sorry if I surprised you."

As if conjured up by his thoughts, there stood Emily Pleasants, smiling down at him.

Edward righted himself and stood quickly, dropping his pipe. He fumbled before catching it in both hands. "I didn't hear you come outside," he said, flustered.

"I didn't think anyone would be out here. Harry fell fast asleep after his long day and I thought it would be nice to get some fresh air. I hope I'm not disturbing you."

Disturbing him? Appearing in front of him as mystically as an angel? She stood there, her shirt still tucked in as neatly as it had been that morning, her hair still piled perfectly upon her head, her delicate hands clasped primly in front of her. Disturbing him—certainly not!

"No, no," he rushed to say. "No disturbance at all. Excuse me a moment." He brushed past her, careful not to touch her, and slipped inside the hallway, returning within moments with another chair.

"Please," he offered. "Do sit down."

Emily tipped her head in appreciation and sat, smoothing her skirt with her hands. The breeze drifted by, cooling the heat of the day, and now that Emily had joined him, seemed to smell refreshingly of lilacs.

"Did you have a good day at the store?" Emily inquired.

"Oh, yes," Edward answered, lifting his pipe to his lips and holding up a match up to re-light the tobacco. Remembering his manners a moment too late, he held the burning match away. "Do you mind?" he asked.

"No, please, go right ahead."

The match's flame had found its way down to his fingertips and Edward swore as he blew it out. He blushed when he realized what he'd said.

"Excuse me, please. I must remember my manners in front of a lady."

Emily chuckled, making his face grow warmer with embarrassment.

"Mr. Sheridan, I'm not laughing at you," she assured him. "While I appreciate the gesture, you needn't be so careful around me. I am not so delicate, nor so inexperienced, that a bawdy word will shock me."

Edward made a slight nod of acknowledgment as he once again attempted to light his pipe. He studied the woman sitting across from him, wondering just how much of life a woman such as she could possibly have experienced, especially considering she'd spent the last three years teaching in a convent.

"How are you settling in to our schoolhouse?" he asked, trying hard not to sound like an idiot.

Emily sat forward in her chair, her face lighting up. "Very nicely. I'm impressed by the schoolhouse and the many books and supplies available. And the teacher before me left excellent notes on all the children and their progress. I will feel very prepared by the time school begins."

Edward was delighted by her enthusiasm. "I'm happy you're pleased. We are such a small town and so far from any big cities that it's difficult to keep a good schoolteacher employed. I'd hate to see you high-tail it back to California." He laughed, a small chuckle, but when he looked up he saw that Emily had sat back in her chair and her eyes had lost the look of excitement.

"No," she said. "I won't be going back there anytime soon."

It was Edward who leaned forward this time, his expression full of concern. "I'm sorry. I didn't mean to say anything to upset you. Were you not happy living there?"

Emily shook her head slowly. "No. It wasn't that way. I appreciated living with the nuns these past three years and the chance to teach the children there. But..." She looked past him at the darkening horizon as if searching for her words. "But it was time for Harry and me to return to the real world again."

Edward wondered what she meant by the "real world," but he was too polite to pry.

"What is California like?" he asked instead, his curiosity rising. "Is it everything people say?"

This made Emily smile again, chasing the faraway look from her eyes. "That depends on what you've heard."

"I hear it's sunny and warm all year-round. The grass is always green and the vegetables and fruit trees grow in abundance. It's paradise."

"There is some truth in that description," Emily said. "The southern part of California is warm and beautiful, although along the coastline it can become very damp and cold. The convent I lived in was set high on a cliff above the ocean with a beautiful sandy beach below. We had our own small orchard and grew delicious, fat oranges, apples, pears, avocados, and plums. Our vegetable garden yielded the biggest carrots, squash, cucumbers, and strawberries you've ever seen. However, potatoes didn't necessarily do too well there."

Edward laughed. "Who needs potatoes when you have so

many other choices?"

"Very true," she conceded.

"I've always wanted to see the western states. They sound so different from here, so much more interesting."

"California is beautiful, in its own way. I think you would like the northern part better, though. It's a combination of wilderness and coastal cliffs. The trees are so tall they really do touch the heavens."

"You'd better stop," Edward told her. "You make me want to run away and go there."

"You should go. There's so much to see between here and there. Every new place is a wonderful experience."

"Well, if that's true, I'm probably the most inexperienced person you've ever met. I haven't been any farther west than Fargo."

"A lot can be learned in one's hometown, too," she assured him. "But if you ever get the chance, do go. You'll feel richer for it."

Just listening to Mrs. Pleasant's speak made Edward feel he could do just about anything.

Chapter Five

Pine Creek, MN
1911

The week was filled with little surprises for Edward. When Emily learned that the door in the hallway opposite her room belonged to Edward, she seemed almost relieved. He lived above the store too, even though he owned a nice house and property just outside of town. He'd worried that his living so near would make her feel uncomfortable, but she assured him it was quite the opposite. She said she was comforted there was someone else nearby, someone she already trusted. Edward was honored by her trust. He didn't believe this reserved woman trusted easily so it was a huge compliment to him.

He was also surprised to find himself seeking out her company often. He hadn't sought a woman's company in years but found that just the sight of her brought calm to his most hectic day. He'd thought he was past the age where a woman would bring joy into his life. But when he was around Emily, he felt alive again. It was remarkable for him to admit he was growing increasingly fond of her very quickly.

On Sunday the town planned a welcome picnic for Emily and little Harry on the church grounds after the service. Edward informed Emily of the plans and invited her and Harry to ride along with him in his buggy. He felt a tinge of embarrassment when she laughed lightly and said, "Couldn't we walk? The church is so close."

"The townspeople make a big to-do about Sundays," he explained, feeling foolish. "Everyone wears their best clothes and rides in their buggies and wagons. I guess it does sound a bit silly," he admitted.

"No, it sounds wonderful," Emily told him. "I'd like very much to ride to the church with you."

Edward's pride returned rapidly.

On Sunday morning, dressed in her finest suit dress and Harry in his traveling suit, they rode to the edge of town with Edward.

Edward tried not to look self-conscious about driving the schoolteacher and her son to church. After all, it was an innocent gesture, a polite offer from a school board member to the new teacher. It was his duty, he'd finally decided. It was his way of justifying his inviting her to ride with him. And, it was as fine a duty as he'd ever had, he thought, as he helped Emily down from the buggy, then little Harry. Emily looked lovely in her navy suit dress that accentuated her small waist, her gold watch pinned above her left breast. Dressed in his best navy suit also, Edward was honored to escort such a proper, beautiful woman and her adorable young child into the church. He could feel the eyes upon them as the townspeople craned their necks to catch a view of the new schoolteacher.

After the service, Emily was kept busy being introduced to the many townspeople and area farmers and their families.

Everyone was at the picnic lunch: Gertie, Evy and Arnold Townsend, Ernie Carlson from the train depot, his wife, Myrtle, and their two children. And there were so many other people to meet as well. The school board members, many of whom were also town council members like Edward, other shop owners, and several parents.

Everyone seemed pleased to have her and Harry join their small community. No one seemed the least bit shocked by the fact that she was a widow or a mother. Edward had also dismissed the idea that it was a problem now that he had come to know Emily better.

After an hour of being separated from Emily, Edward became frustrated by the many people who wanted to take up his time. Every few minutes he'd strain his neck to scan the crowd for a glimpse of her. When he'd catch sight of her, he'd long to stand beside her, laughing at whatever she laughed at, listening intently to whatever was being said to her. Once, over the sea of faces, she caught him looking and cast him a warm smile. That smile stayed with him for a very long time throughout several lengthy, boring conversations.

Much later, Edward found her sitting on a large blanket under a tree, eating the last remnants of a piece of apple pie that the pastor's wife had made. Harry had run off with some of the other children to play tag, and Emily seemed to be enjoying a peaceful moment.

"May I join you?" Edward asked, balancing his own plate of pie in his hands.

Emily swept the extra length of her skirt closer to her, allowing room on the blanket for him to sit down. "Of course." She moved to face him. The afternoon sun shone on her light complexion, her skin so flawless and fresh-looking.

Edward felt privileged to be allowed the space beside her, to bask in her glowing smile. She had been introduced to many younger, better-looking men today, yet her smile seemed only for him.

He sat, trying to behave casually, but how did one act casually in her presence? Although her demeanor was generally calm and collected, she caused his senses to run wild. He wondered, as he watched her take a small bite of her pie, if he was the only man who felt that way around her. Certainly not.

"Are you enjoying yourself?" Edward asked, pushing his pie about with his fork. He chanced a look into her eyes and was rewarded with seeing them twinkle.

"Very much. Everyone has been most welcoming."

Edward nodded. "Our town is filled with fine people. You'll find they are very interested in their children's education."

"I can see that already," Emily said. "It will be a pleasure working with their children this year."

Silence fell between them as they finished their pie and watched the people around them. It was a perfect day. Edward hadn't had many perfect days over the past few years, admittedly, maybe none at all. But this felt right, sitting quietly in the warm afternoon under a tree with a lovely, interesting woman. It felt comfortable.

Just as he was wishing the day would go on forever, their silence was interrupted by a young couple. Edward stood as the man lifted his hand in greeting.

"Edward, I see you are keeping our new schoolteacher company. I'm afraid we are the very last people in town to introduce ourselves."

"Hello, Ted. Mrs. Neilson." Edward nodded to the lovely young woman beside Ted.

Emily stood, raising a hand toward Mr. Neilson. "How do you do? I'm Emily Pleasants."

"Very nice to meet you," Ted said. "This is my wife, Allison."

Allison raised a delicate gloved hand to her in greeting. "It's very nice meeting you, Mrs. Pleasants," she said, a sweet smile on her full lips.

"And a pleasure meeting you too," Emily said.

"Ted is the town sheriff," Edward offered, standing up straighter, proud of the town's selection for sheriff. "He's been with us a little over a year and we're very lucky to have him."

"Now Edward, this is Mrs. Pleasants' day, not mine," Ted said, looking embarrassed by such praise.

"It's not every small town that can say it has a Pinkerton agent for a sheriff." Edward turned to Emily, who had raised her brows at this announcement. "He came to us from Chicago, finally ready to settle down to a quieter life after all his adventures."

"Ex-Pinkerton agent now, Edward," Ted said. Turning to Emily, he continued, "I'm very happy here as the town sheriff. I'm sure you'll enjoy living here, Mrs. Pleasants."

Emily smiled and nodded her agreement, then turned her attention to Allison. "And what of you, Mrs. Neilson? How do you like living in Pine Creek?"

Allison's blue eyes sparkled. "Oh, I like it here very much. I grew up on the outskirts of Chicago and I'm enjoying the tranquility of a small town."

Emily grinned mischievously at Allison. "Did you join your husband on any of his adventures?"

Allison laughed softly. "Oh, no, we weren't married then. Teddy and I were married just before moving here."

"I see," Emily said.

"I hear you came to us from California, Mrs. Pleasants," Ted said, staring at her intently with his gray eyes.

"Yes. I taught at a small convent there for several years."

"And you have a young son?"

Emily gazed steadily at him. "Yes. Harry is around here playing. He seems to have made some new friends."

"Oh, how old is your son?" Allison asked, delighted. Her hand went unconsciously to her mid-section.

"Three years old," Emily answered.

Allison moved closer to Emily and said in a discreet voice that hardly veiled her excitement. "We're expecting our first child. That's why we were so late coming here today. I've been feeling a bit under the weather in the mornings."

"Congratulations," Emily said in an equally quiet voice.

Edward beamed. "They told me their good news last week. I'm very excited for them."

Ted drew closer to his wife, placing his hand over hers. "Yes, we're very happy." His gaze fell again on Emily. "I feel as though we've met before, but I can't place where. Have you lived anywhere besides California?"

Emily remained composed. "I've lived many places in my life. I grew up in Texas and have lived in Boston, Wyoming, and Colorado. I don't believe we've ever crossed paths, though."

Ted scratched his sandy blond head and shook it slowly before saying, "Funny. Your face is so familiar."

"I'm sure there are plenty of women who look like me," Emily said casually, laughing.

"You're not interrogating our new schoolteacher, eh Ted?" Edward asked. "What could an educated woman like Mrs. Pleasants possible be guilty of? Reading too many books?"

Everyone laughed.

"No, no. I'm not interrogating her. I just feel as if we've met before. But then, I've met so many people. I'm sure I have her mixed up with someone else."

Emily smiled and nodded, but Edward noticed that her smile looked strained.

Chapter Six

Pine Creek, MN
1911

That night, as she lay in bed, Emily re-played the conversation with the sheriff in her mind, wondering if she'd said a wrong word or made a telling gesture. *Your face is so familiar,* Sheriff Neilson had told her, and suddenly her heart had begun pounding in her chest. What if today was the day? She lived in fear of recognition every day of her life—it would happen someday, she was sure. Staying calm was her only recourse at times like those. The sheriff had been a Pinkerton detective. Surely, he'd recognize her eventually. Then what? Would she have to pack up quickly with little Harry and flee? The thought of running again made her feel weary.

All because one warm day in Texas, she'd met a man who'd found his way into her heart.

It had begun so innocently and ended so quickly that Emily still couldn't believe how much her life had changed since leaving Texas. As she listened to the crickets sing and the breeze blew softly through the open window, Emily remembered those first glorious days when she'd fallen in love.

San Antonio, TX
1895

The two strangers assessed each other from across a table in a little restaurant in the proper part of town. Or, at least, Ethel was assessing Harry. She was still astonished that he had been waiting for her after the music lesson. Yet, for reasons unknown to her, she was equally delighted he had.

She was a pretty woman—she knew that in a non-conceited way, for she never thought of herself that way. But men had taken notice many times over the years since she had turned thirteen. She'd never taken their flirting seriously. Living around Fannie's house had taught her men weren't always sincere in matters of the heart. They'd say anything to get what they wanted. So, she'd ignored the men who made advances, and went about the business of her life. Even through her two years in Boston, she kept to herself at the all-girls finishing school. On weekends, the other girls met male friends and giggled about secret kisses and interludes they had, but not Ethel. Her upbringing, first on a cattle ranch outside of San Antonio, then at Fannie's after her father's death, had taught her what men were capable of, and not all of it was good. So she'd kept her heart guarded, as with all other parts of her, waiting for the right man to come along, if ever.

Now, she watched Harry across the table and wondered why he was different. Why had she accepted his invitation after years of refusals? There was something interesting about him, something mysterious and fascinating. She surprised herself by wanting to find out what that something was.

The restaurant was crowded, and they waited a while for their meal. Harry fiddled with his coffee mug, stirring the sugar and cream with a tin spoon longer than necessary. Ethel wondered about a man who used sugar and cream. She'd never known one who did. She also wondered at his sudden shyness after he'd acted so boldly earlier.

"We've never been properly introduced," Ethel said, staring straight at him. His gray eyes appeared both surprised and amused by her being the first to break the silence. "I'm Ethel Pleasants."

"Harry Longabaugh," he said, his voice rich and deep.

"Longbaugh?" Ethel tilted her head in question.

"Long-a-baugh," Harry pronounced slowly, then laughed. "Most people forget the 'A.'"

Ethel nodded her understanding, all the while wondering what to say next. But Harry spoke up instead.

"Ethel?" he questioned. His brows knit together, as if deep in thought.

She thought it made him look angry.

"That name doesn't seem to suit you," he finally said.

Ethel shrugged. "Sorry to disappoint you. But that's my name. My full name is Ethel Emily Pleasants."

"I'm sorry. I didn't mean to insult you," Harry said. "Emily is much prettier, if you don't mind my saying so."

This made Ethel smile. "I agree. That was my mother's name."

"Oh, I see." He tipped his head in question. "Seems to me Fannie called you Etta."

Ethel's eyes twinkled. "When I was younger, I couldn't say my name correctly. It came out as Etta. So that's how my family started calling me Etta." She thought back to her youth, her father and mother, and how happy they'd once been.

"Etta," he repeated. "I like that. It suits you better than Ethel. May I call you Etta?"

Ethel's brows rose. Propriety would dictate that he, still a stranger, refer to her as Miss Pleasants, not by her given name, let alone a nickname.

Harry seemed to read her thoughts.

"Of course, that wouldn't be proper," he said, acknowledging he understood good manners. "Could we bend the rules a bit and I'll call you Miss Etta?"

Ethel couldn't help but smile at this. Apparently, while Harry understood the rules of propriety, he liked to break them, too. She wondered how many other rules he liked to break.

"I'm sure that would be fine, Mr. Longabaugh," Ethel said.

They had a lovely meal and conversation flowed freely between them as if they'd been friends for years. She talked of attending school in Boston; he told her of being raised out east. She spoke of her family in Texas and the ranch they'd once owned; he mentioned how he had worked on many large spreads from Texas to Colorado. They had a lot in common. Both were educated, enjoyed reading, the theater, and opera, yet both appreciated the openness and freedom of living in the untamed west. And one detail they shared was that neither had family anymore. Harry was too far away from home and, aside from Miss Fannie and her girls, Etta had no one to call family any longer.

Harry walked Etta home as the sky turned to dusk.

"I had a lovely time," he told her. He studied her face a moment, then grinned.

"What is that smirk for?" she asked.

"It's not a smirk. It's an honest to goodness smile of delight. You have the loveliest eyes I've ever seen," he told her.

"Lavender-blue. So unique, like you."

Etta felt a blush rise up to her face. She'd never been left speechless by a man before.

Bowing over her hand, Harry bid her goodnight.

"Aren't you coming in?" she asked as he began to walk away.

Harry smiled wide—that boyish smile that lit up his face and made his eyes sparkle.

"I have rooms elsewhere," he said. With that, he jauntily walked down the street.

Fannie was furious when Etta stepped through the door. It was still early evening and the girls were just rising and preparing for the night ahead. By nine o'clock, the house's activities would be in full swing, but now everything was still quiet.

Fannie approached Etta in the hallway just as she closed the door. "May I speak with you upstairs?" she asked with measured patience, and Etta followed her up to her lavish rooms. She knew exactly what the older woman was upset about.

"What were you doing out with Harry Longabaugh?" Fannie questioned once the door to her private rooms was closed against prying ears.

Etta smiled patiently at the angry woman before her. She was not afraid of Fannie Porter, no matter what her demeanor, or the fact that the woman had been known to chase local police from her residence with a broom. Fannie wouldn't hurt a fly, let alone Etta.

"It was all very innocent," Etta answered in a calm voice. "We simply had dinner at the cafe and talked." Etta sat down on one of Fannie's purple velvet, tufted chairs, but Fannie was worked up, pacing back and forth on the room's plush rug.

Fannie's rooms were actually two bedrooms, one used as a private parlor; the other, her bedroom. Both were decorated garishly in deep purple velvets and satins with gold trim. Rugs, tasseled lamp shades, and gleaming mahogany furniture all added to the grandeur of her lifestyle as a Madame. Etta didn't believe that Fannie actually entertained guests herself anymore, so the rooms were for her pleasure alone.

But right now there was no pleasure in the woman's brown eyes. "Etta, you simply can't be seen with a man such as Harry. You do not know anything about him and his past. He's exactly the type of man I've been guarding you against."

Etta furrowed her brow. "How can you say that, Fannie? He seems harmless enough. He was a proper gentleman the entire time I was with him."

Fannie stopped pacing and let out a huge sigh. Setting herself into the chair opposite Etta, she held her hands. "Etta, dear. You know nothing of this man and his type. Yes, he's a good looking man and has gentlemanly manners, but he's not as he appears." Fannie took a deep breath, releasing it slowly. "He's an outlaw, dear. And he rides with others just like him."

"An outlaw?" Etta was shocked. Surely, Fannie was exaggerating.

"Yes, dear. An outlaw. Harry's been one of the main players in bank and train robberies throughout the west. He goes by the handle the Sundance Kid. He hangs out with a wild bunch of men who take what they want, when they want. Your mother would only want the best for you, dear, as do I. Harry Longabaugh is simply not the type of man for you."

The mention of her mother did bring a reaction from Etta, but not quite the one Fannie might have hoped for. Etta sat silently, thinking about all her mother had sacrificed to give her a better life. No, her mother would not approve of an outlaw for her daughter, but her mother did understand the desperate things people did when they were forced. Maybe Harry's reasons were legitimate, even justified, for why he lived his life the way he did. Maybe not. Etta had learned a long time ago not to judge a person so quickly. Understanding and trusting this woman before her, a known Madame, who gave her a home more than proved that.

Etta smiled warmly at Fannie. Gently, she said, "Don't worry, Fannie. Nothing will come of my knowing Harry Longabaugh. In another week, I'll be leaving for my teaching position in Durango. I'll never see Harry again."

Fannie continued to watch Etta with worried eyes, as if she wasn't quite sure this was true. This only made Etta laugh and say good-naturedly, "It's not as if I'm likely to marry the man!" But as Etta hugged her friend, Fannie said softly, "Let's hope not."

* * *

The next morning, Harry appeared at the door with an open carriage and fine set of horses, inquiring if the lovely Miss Etta would like to take a ride with him. Aside from Fannie's cook and butler, Etta was the only person awake in the household. Knowing Fannie and the girls would sleep until afternoon, Etta accepted his invitation, seeing no harm in a ride around town.

It was a glorious August morning—the air still holding the coolness of the night, and the sky was clear and bright blue. Etta settled beside Harry and off they rode down South San Saba toward the better, or at least more proper, part of town. Harry was not wearing his suit today but still looked appropriately dressed in trousers and a button-down shirt, a bowler hat upon his head, and of course, those polished riding boots he'd worn yesterday.

Etta wore one of her crisp shirtwaists and a navy skirt, a crochet shawl tossed over her shoulders, her hair piled high upon her head. But as they rode toward the outskirts of town, the warmth of the day made Etta shed her shawl and enjoy the sunshine on her shoulders.

They didn't speak for the first half-hour, there seemed no need, but as buildings turned to fields and an expanse of sky, Harry slowed the horses from a trot to a walk and grinned over at her. "Enjoying the ride?"

Etta smiled at him, as wide as the big sky, and just as lovely. Today was not a day for subtle hints or careful words. It was an honest, up front kind of day, where everything was no longer left to chance, but to be enjoyed freely.

"Oh, yes. It's so nice to be out of the house, out of the confines of town," she told him, and saw that he looked pleased.

As they came to a patch of trees beside a field of horses, Harry stopped the carriage and offered a hand up to Etta. She accepted, then strolled over to the pasture's fence and climbed the first rung to gaze at the beautiful animals grazing lazily. Harry did as she had and stood on the rung beside her.

"I miss owning horses," Etta said. "I miss riding them, caring for them, feeding them oats out of my hand and the feel of their soft, warm noses." She sighed, and Harry looked over at her, intrigued.

"Tell me about the ranch."

Etta's eyes lit up. "Our ranch was on the other side of town. My parents owned several-hundred acres and we raised cattle, sheep, and horses. My mother had chickens and a garden and canned delicious vegetables every year. My father and I would ride the ranch together to look for strays or broken fencing. It was a wonderful life." The memories of her childhood made Etta wistful for a life she no longer lived.

Harry chuckled. "You were a tomboy?"

"Yes, much to my mother's chagrin," she answered. "My father had no sons, only me, so he taught me to ride and shoot a gun and do all the things a son would do. I loved it." Her smile faded as she thought about her beloved father. She missed him greatly.

Harry seemed to pick up on her sadness. "What happened?"

Etta took a deep breath and let it out slowly, bracing herself to relive a tragic memory. She looked at Harry, a man who she knew must have had tragedies in his life too. Instinctively, she realized she could trust him with her memories.

"What happened is what's happening all over Texas. Big business ranchers taking over land from the private ranchers," Etta said.

"Big business ranchers," Harry said, venom in his tone.

Etta nodded. "One very rich rancher was buying up land all around our ranch. Slowly, we watched as our neighbors left, one by one. Ranches that had been in families for generations bought up for much less than they were worth. But my father refused to sell. He loved his life and the ranch he'd built up. He didn't care how much they threatened him. He wouldn't give in."

Etta paused a moment, then continued in the same quiet voice. "My father began watching the fences and cattle more frequently. Each trip out he'd find another dead calf or cut fence. He wouldn't allow me to come with him anymore. He feared for my safety. Then, one day, he didn't return home." Etta's voice turned into a whisper. "We found him, a mile away from home, his neck broken."

"I'm sorry," Harry said, sounding sincere. "I'm afraid I've heard of this happening dozens of times. What happened?"

"There was no way to prove it wasn't an accident, but no sooner had my father been buried, then the harassment to sell the ranch began. When my mother refused, our house burned to the ground—another accident," Etta said, bitterly. "My mother had no fight left in her. She sold the ranch for much less than it was worth and we moved into town."

"Is that how you ended up at Fannie's?" Harry asked.

"Not at first," Etta said, her tone softening at the mention of Fannie. "We rented a small house on the edge of town and my mother took in sewing to earn a little money. Fannie's girls brought her the most work, and soon Fannie was coming to my mother to sew her new dresses. But our money was running out quickly, and it was my mother's dream to send me to school in Boston. Fannie and my mother became close friends and soon Fannie offered us the room above the boarding house in return for my mother's expertise sewing for her and the girls. My mother also helped around the house and in the kitchen."

"Was that a difficult decision for your mother to make? I mean, she must have wrestled with the idea of you living in a brothel," Harry said.

Etta shook her head. "My mother did what she had to do. Fannie paid her nicely and charged us nothing to live there. It was a respectable living. My mother would say that with pride when her old friends turned up their noses at her for associating with Fannie and her girls. My mother meant everything to Fannie. Fannie looked up to her as a sister."

"Your mother sounds like an admirable woman," Harry said, looking impressed.

"She was," Etta agreed.

"What happened to her?"

Etta dropped her eyes. "My mother grew ill not long after we moved to Fannie's. She'd been tired and losing weight for a while, but she'd said it was because she was working too hard. Her strength slowly drained from her, and she coughed all the time. While I was away in Boston, she grew worse, but refused to let Fannie tell me. We couldn't afford for me to come back in the two years I was there, so I had no idea how unwell she was. When I returned, I was shocked at how ill my mother was. Fannie took very good care of her, though, and paid for all her doctor bills and medicine. Nothing worked, though. She passed away not long after I'd returned."

"That's terrible. I'm so sorry," Harry said, his face creasing with concern.

"The doctors said she had consumption. I blame her declining health on the stress and worry my father's dying placed on her. She was a good person, and a kind soul. She deserved so much better."

The pair sat quietly in the grass for some time, watching the horses in the field. Harry reached over and took Etta's hand in his. His hand was calloused from outside labor, but strong, and that simple gesture warmed her heart.

"Fannie says you're an outlaw. Is it true?" Etta raised her eyes to his.

Harry tilted his head and cocked one eyebrow at her, his surprise evident. But very calmly, he answered, "Would it matter if I was?"

Etta assessed him a moment, her fingers still entwined with his. In that moment, she saw everything she needed to know. Her heart trusted those eyes. No matter how dishonest they might be with others, she knew they'd always be truthful to her.

"No," she finally said. "Not really."

Harry leaned over and kissed her. A soft, tender kiss that made her heart skip. When he pulled away and smiled that boyish grin, she thought how empty she'd feel when she had to say goodbye.

For two days Etta didn't see Harry, then on the final night before she left for Colorado and her new teaching career, he showed up at the house and took her out for an evening meal.

"Will you come to the train station and see me off tomorrow?" Etta asked him hopefully.

Harry shook his head. "I'm not very good with goodbyes."

When he took her back to Fannie's, he kissed her softly and left without another word. Etta's heart broke. She'd promised Fannie she wouldn't fall for the outlaw, but she had, and it hurt knowing she'd never see Harry Longabaugh again.

The next morning was a blur of packing and tears and goodbyes, and true to his word, Harry did not come to the station to see her off.

With one last farewell hug to Fannie, Etta stepped up on the train and disappeared inside. She found her seat and settled in for the long ride, her eyes red and lashes still damp from tears. She sat quietly for a long time after the train had departed, staring out the window and thinking of what lay ahead of her. A voice beside her broke the silence.

"Is this seat taken?"

Etta turned and found herself looking up into familiar gray eyes. "Harry!" She jumped up and hugged him as the entire car of passengers watched.

"It was too soon to say goodbye, so I'm coming with you," Harry said, grinning devilishly.

Etta's heart filled with joy, and as she looked around her, she saw approving smiles from the ladies. Now, everything felt right and the adventure ahead of her would be even more exciting with Harry at her side.

Chapter Seven

Pine Creek, MN
1911

Emily and little Harry settled easily into their new routine. School began and Emily soon learned the names and abilities of each of her students. She had a variety of ages in the school, from five to sixteen, and she was delighted with the behavior of each student. Even the students from the surrounding farms attended school regularly. Emily knew what a sacrifice that was for their parents because their help was greatly needed for the fall haying and harvest. She appreciated the dedication of the parents and community. It made her job easier.

The younger children took to Harry immediately and he made several new friends despite being the youngest child in the classroom. Having grown up with the children at the convent orphanage, Harry had learned to make friends easily. Emily was relieved Harry was fitting in to their new environment so quickly. She also enjoyed her new surroundings and the friendly townspeople.

September sauntered in and the hot temperatures lessened

to comfortable days and cool nights. Emily's days were full. She woke early and breakfasted at Evy's Restaurant with Harry, and on occasion Edward joined them. Then she had school, and papers to correct afterward. Many times Gertie offered to watch Harry at the store while Emily worked after hours in the schoolhouse, or Harry spent an afternoon at a friend's house. Sometimes Edward, at Gertie's prompting, Emily was certain, brought soup or sandwiches to Emily at the schoolhouse if she had missed supper. She appreciated his company and thoughtfulness, but he was always the pillar of respectability.

Evenings was when she enjoyed his company the most, after Harry was tucked into bed and Emily would stroll out onto the porch for some fresh air before retiring for the night. Most nights Edward was there, pipe in hand, suit jacket discarded, his collar buttons open at the neck and sleeves rolled up. Here he was relaxed and open, and she relished their conversations. He soon lost his nervousness around her and insisted she call him Edward instead of Mr. Sheridan, at least when they were alone.

Emily liked her small life. After all she'd been through to get here, she was thankful she'd made it. While she knew she would forever be looking over her shoulder, as each day passed, she felt more comfortable and less fearful in her new situation.

Halfway through September, Edward offered her a part-time job at the store. "Other teachers have worked for me on Saturdays, and throughout the summer," he told her. "It gives Gertie a day off and will give you access to supplies you need at cost."

She thankfully accepted the opportunity to earn a little extra income. The discount on necessities was also a godsend. Harry was a growing boy and Emily could use all the help she could get to keep him in clothing and necessities.

The first Saturday that Emily worked, Edward gave her a

tour of the store and instructions on how to write up a sale. The majority of his merchandise was out on the crowded floor, but there was a little extra stock stored in the back room behind the curtain. After showing her where the backstock was kept, he stopped at a cabinet beside the curtained doorway.

"There is one more thing I should show you," he said as he reached high above his head and pulled a Colt .45 pistol from the top of the cabinet. "I used to keep this under the counter, just in case, but now that Harry is around, I thought it was safer to keep it back here." He opened the chamber to show her that it was loaded. "Do you know how to use a pistol?" he asked.

Emily stared at the familiar six-shooter in Edward's hand. Her husband had carried a pearl-handled Colt .45. He'd purchased a similar one for her, when he'd felt she'd needed a weapon. She was very familiar with shooting a pistol—more than she thought she should admit.

"I've had some experience," she told Edward.

Edward snapped the barrel shut and replaced the pistol on the cabinet. "I honestly don't see any reason why we will ever need to use it," he told Emily. "But it doesn't hurt to be prepared."

Emily nodded. She also hoped there'd never be a reason to shoot that weapon. She'd done that enough in her previous life.

Gertie offered to take Harry on the Saturdays that Emily worked. She adored the little boy and Harry enjoyed being with her, too. Emily couldn't have wished for a better arrangement. Gertie's motherly warmth was a welcome addition to her son's life.

Every Sunday, Edward drove Emily and Harry to church in the buggy, sometimes including Gertie when she needed a ride. It was on such a Sunday that Edward surprised Emily by inviting her for a drive after church. As they stopped to drop Gertie at her house, as if planned, Gertie invited Harry to spend the afternoon with her and bake cookies. Emily watched Gertie and Harry head into the house, hand in hand. Her attention was drawn back to Edward, when he cleared his throat, sounding for the first time in weeks as nervous as he'd sounded that first day they'd met.

"Since Harry is occupied, would you like to take a ride with me?" he asked as stiff as the starched collar around his neck.

"That would be lovely," Emily said, trying not to chuckle at the formality of his invitation. After all the evenings on the porch, and working side-by-side at the store, he still sometimes seemed as uneasy as a schoolboy.

Edward turned the wagon north of town and they rode in peaceful silence for some time. The day was warm, and the sun felt good on her back as they rode along. Emily discarded her gloves and laid aside her shawl.

Edward looked very proper in his suit, coat, and hat. From time to time he'd shift his eyes in her direction, not turning his head, and she'd smile, making him quickly avert his eyes. Emily wondered why he was so nervous.

At the edge of town, she finally gave up wondering and asked, "Where are we headed to? Anywhere special?"

Edward startled as if he'd forgotten he had a companion, and he cleared his throat again. "I thought, perhaps, I'd show you my house." He sounded uncertain of himself. Then he continued quickly, "I usually check on the place once a week and thought you might like to come along."

Edward had spoken of his house and land only briefly before, so Emily was curious to see it. "I'd love to see your home. Is it far?"

He relaxed a little. Emily saw his shoulders drop a bit and his hands loosened on the reins. "Not far. We're almost there."

Up ahead, Emily saw open pasture with a sprinkling of trees and white rail fencing marking off the land. Further in the distance stood a two-story Victorian house surrounded by a white picket fence. As they drew closer, Emily realized this must be Edward's home. It was painted canary yellow and white with gingerbread trim along the slanted roof. It was perfect and neat, just like its owner, and she guessed that the inside would be as nice as the outside.

"Here we are." They pulled up the narrow driveway at the side of the house.

She could tell he was proud of his place, yet she also saw a shadow of sadness darken his face.

Upon closer inspection, Emily noticed the window boxes and gardens that edged the brick walkway needed tending. Dried, dead flowers were hunched over, having never been pulled or replaced. And the white trim had grayed and was peeling in spots. But, overall, the house was just as beautiful as she'd first thought, only a bit neglected.

"This is very lovely," she told Edward, accepting his hand and alighting from the buggy.

"Thank you." He offered his arm. They strolled up the walk together. "I'm afraid I didn't tend to the flowers this season. Gertie would have done them, but I just never got around to asking." His tone was wistful as he gazed around.

Emily followed him up the front steps and through the glass-paned door he'd unlocked. She marveled at the interior the moment she laid eyes on it. Although everything from the oak banisters to the wooden floors was covered in a thin layer of dust, it didn't hide the beauty of the rooms. Sunshine spilled into the foyer through the beveled panes of the door. To her left, there was a large parlor, to her right, a formal dining room, both bathed in sunshine from generous windows.

"A bit dusty, I'm afraid," Edward said.

"That's to be expected," Emily said. "But it's easily fixed."

"I'll give you a tour, if you'd like," he offered.

"I'd like that very much." She followed him into the formal dining room, admiring its built-in oak hutch decorated with stained-glass doors in the pattern of roses. A chandelier hung from the ceiling, its crystal teardrops in need of polishing. The oak dining table was big enough to serve twelve people. Emily thought it would make a fine room for a family, but she kept this thought to herself.

He then showed her the parlor, where a sofa sat in front of a brick fireplace and a bay window had a padded seat so one could sit and enjoy the sunshine. Exquisite handmade tapestries decorated the walls, one still lying unfinished upon its frame. Emily noticed how Edward's eyes quickly passed over the frame, and he turned to show her the rest of the house.

It was obvious to Emily that a woman had lived here once, a woman of extraordinary taste and refinement. From the sofas in the parlor to the window dressings in the kitchen, everything displayed a feminine touch. She didn't ask who the woman had been. She knew Edward would share that information with her if he chose to. Understanding first-hand how private one's past was, she knew not to pry.

When they had finished the tour and made sure every door and window was secure, Emily turned to Edward in the foyer as they prepared to leave. "Your home is beautiful. Enchanting, actually. It's a shame you don't live here all the time."

"I'm pleased you liked it. It's a lovely home but I'm content living over the store for now," he told her. Emily sensed he wouldn't feel comfortable living here alone with whatever sad memories haunted him.

They stepped outside and he led her around to the back of the house where the pasture swelled out before them, spotted with several horses in the distance. They walked down a well-worn path and ended up by a corral fence where they stopped to gaze over the field. It was breathtaking here, and reminded Emily of happier times on ranches far away. She wondered what he'd think if she suddenly loosened her hair from her hat and climbed up on the rails of the fence. She smiled at the thought of it, remembering a similar buggy ride so many years ago that had also stopped beside a pasture fence. How different her life would have been if she hadn't fallen in love that day.

Emily pushed that thought from her mind, as well as any regret for how her life had turned out, and instead asked Edward, "Is this your land and horses?"

He nodded. "Yes. I have two-hundred acres and those are all my horses. I'm afraid I don't ride them much these days, though."

She shook her head sympathetically. "Such a shame. They look like wonderful saddle horses."

Edward raised his brows. "You're experienced with riding?"

"I've had some experience," Emily said, a mischievous smile on her lips. "I grew up on a ranch and my father had me riding practically before I could walk. And my husband worked on ranches and bred and trained horses, so I know a little."

"Ah." Edward looked amused. "So you are quite experienced. Perhaps you might like to go riding with me someday? I pay a couple of young boys to ride and care for the horses so they will stay tame. Having a riding partner might be enough incentive for me to go out again."

Emily could not imagine stiff and proper Edward on a horse. The idea of it almost made her laugh out loud. "You might be shocked to learn that I ride western style and I don't ride side saddle," she told him, glancing at his reaction from the corner of her eye. This time, however, Edward did not look surprised.

"Actually," he said, his eyes twinkling, "I wouldn't expect any different."

* * *

Sheriff Neilson sat at his desk contemplating his dilemma for the hundredth time. He would have welcomed a distraction from his thoughts, but Pine Creek was a quiet town and except for the occasional rowdy drunk across the tracks, there wasn't much else for him to worry about. Not that he minded the peaceful job; he loved living here and not having the worries or demands of a large city policeman. His position allowed him the chance to make lasting friendships and spend evenings at home with his beautiful Allison. But right now his mind was troubled with thoughts of another woman. He was sure he recognized the new schoolteacher from somewhere, even more sure since his wife had had Mrs. Pleasants over for tea twice since meeting her.

Allison was enchanted by Mrs. Pleasants. She looked up to her like a big sister, a woman she could share thoughts and intimacies with. Ted realized how important it was for his wife to have such a friend, especially now that she was expecting. But every time he passed Mrs. Pleasants on the street or saw her in the store, he couldn't stop the nagging feeling that came over him. Not only was her face familiar, but the name of her son, Harry, seemed to hit a nerve and it bothered him that he couldn't make a connection.

Ted sighed and ran his fingers through his hair. Ever since he'd first met her, his instincts had been pushing him to learn more. But he had to be discreet. The schoolchildren, townspeople, and his wife were enamored by the soft-spoken schoolteacher and her son. Even Edward, usually so careful and reserved, seemed smitten by her. Ted had no basis for his suspicions except his own instincts after years as a Pinkerton agent. He certainly couldn't risk alienating an entire town by accusing the new schoolteacher of causing some unknown injustice. He needed solid facts.

Finally, after much pondering, he decided to write to his former colleague and friend at the Chicago division of the Pinkerton Agency and describe a few details about Mrs. Pleasants. If his friend had anyone suspicious in mind with similar traits in his files, then perhaps he could send him more information.

Ted hoped he was chasing shadows for he also liked Mrs. Pleasants, but he had to satisfy his suspicions once and for all. So, with another huge sigh of resignation, he pulled a sheet of paper from his desk drawer and began to write the letter.

Chapter Eight

Pine Creek, MN
Autumn 1911

The first days of October arrived and Emily experienced her first harvest time in Pine Creek's farming community. With the harvests brought seasonal help to work the fields and traveling chuck wagons that parked at farms to feed the extra hands. Harvest also brought barn dances every Saturday night that both the town and country folks attended to celebrate their good fortune for the year.

With this influx of seasonal workers in the area, the stores, boarding houses, and saloons were bustling. Because Edward was busier at the bank, Emily helped Gertie for two hours each afternoon at the store after school let out. Harry entertained himself playing on the store's front porch or at a friend's home.

It had been only three days since Emily and Edward's ride to his home when, while closing the store, Gertie and Emily's conversation turned to Edward. He had peeked into the store through the connecting door to the bank to check if all was well with them. With so many strangers in town, he seemed worried about leaving the women alone. After returning to the bank, assured both ladies were fine, Gertie looked slyly at Emily who had been folding strewn pieces of fabric.

"He's quite smitten with you, you know," Gertie said, coming up beside Emily to straighten the bolts of fabric in the bin.

Emily smiled at her newfound friend. She adored Gertie. She was like a mother, sister, and friend all wrapped in one. Her forwardness sometimes reminded her of Fannie. "Now, Gertie, I'm sure his concern is just as much for you as it is for me."

"Oh, it's not just that. It's everything else." Gertie grinned. "It's not just anyone he'd take for a ride out to his place. As a matter of fact, he hasn't allowed anyone else there for years, except me, and that's because I make him take me there to clean from time to time." The older woman's expression softened. "You're special, Emily. You make him feel alive again. I can see it in his eyes every time you enter the room."

"Oh, Gertie." Emily felt embarrassed by Gertie's suggestion that Edward was sweet on her. "I'm sure you're exaggerating."

"No, dear. I see what I see. You're the first woman he's laid eyes on since his dear Lily passed away. And I think it's wonderful." Gertie tenderly placed her hand on Emily's arm. "I only hope you feel the same for him someday. He's a good, hardworking man and he already adores you and Harry. You both deserve a little happiness and I hope you find it together."

Gertie bustled off then to lock away the cash drawer, leaving Emily to contemplate her words. Emily had noticed that Edward was smitten by her and wondered if it was a good thing, or would prove to be an awkward inconvenience. She felt comfortable around him, and she did appreciate what a good man he was. His adoration for little Harry was obvious, which warmed her heart.

But it was too soon for her to know if her feelings of friendship with him could ever grow into something deeper.

That night, long after Harry had fallen asleep, Emily sat at the table in her room, staring out the window at the cloudless, inky sky. After her conversation with Gertie today, she'd avoided going out to the porch and seeing Edward. If he was truly infatuated with her, she was afraid of leading him on when she had no idea how she felt about him. Edward was a handsome man. He was also intelligent, hardworking, and successful, a combination that would please any woman. But was she capable of caring again for another man? She'd never imagined her life being this complicated after all she'd been through. Because with Harry Longabaugh, love had happened so easily.

Durango, Colorado
October 1895

Etta never realized love could be this beautiful. No matter that they'd only known each other for less than two months—she was completely enamored with Harry Longabaugh.

Her weekdays were filled with duties as the new schoolteacher. There were two teachers for the growing town. Etta worked with the younger children while Ida Cranston, a middle-aged woman, worked with the older children. Ida was a rather stern spinster, but she grew to like Etta and surprisingly approved of her gentleman friend.

Etta loved her teaching position and had also obtained a few students for piano lessons, which she gave at the local church after school. She had been given a nice room in the boarding house where Ida also lived, but she spent very little time there. Her free time was for Harry only.

Harry had lived in the area when he was younger and had family in Cortez, so he knew a great many people there. He found work on a local ranch, training horses. He was a natural with the creatures and Etta marveled at the control he had over them.

The couple spent whatever free time they had together, either in town or at the ranch. They loved going horseback riding on Sunday afternoons. Harry had his own horse, and would borrow one for Etta to ride.

It was on one such ride along the Animas River that Etta asked Harry about his life as an outlaw. It was a beautiful autumn day, the chill of the coming winter caressing the air, but the sun shone brightly on the winding river. Harry only hesitated a brief moment before answering.

"I'm sure you've heard a few stories about me already. There's no sense in my denying them."

Etta nodded. The people around the area knew Harry, or at least of him, and she'd heard stories about train and bank robberies and the Sundance Kid. It was time she heard the true story from him.

Harry motioned for them to stop and they tied their horses to a nearby tree. They found a sunny spot by the river to sit.

"You're so beautiful," he said, reaching over to caress her cheek.

Etta blushed and self-consciously smoothed out her riding skirt over her boots.

"I've never met a woman like you," he continued. "You're a lady through and through, yet you're tough, too. You ride expertly and shoot a pistol almost as accurately as I do. But you can dance a waltz with the grace of a butterfly and you're smarter than anyone I've ever known. I'm afraid if you learn the truth about me, the real me, I might lose you."

"Tell me the true story," Etta urged. "I want to hear it from you. Tell me about being the Sundance Kid."

Harry reached over and took her gloved hand in his. Leaning toward her, he asked, "If all the stories you've heard were true, would it make a difference between us?"

Gazing into his eyes, Etta couldn't imagine that anything he said would change how she felt about him. "Just tell me, Harry. Let me decide for myself."

"Fair enough," Harry said. As the river rippled beside them and the birds whistled in the trees above, he began his tale.

"Some of it is true. I am known as the Sundance Kid and I have robbed a train as well as a bank. But mostly I've just worked on ranches and rustled a few cattle and horses for the people I've worked for. One bank, one train, not the many that I've been accused of by gossipmongers. It's just that I'm friends with the men in the Robbers Roost area who make stealing their primary source of income, so my name is tied to all the crimes they commit."

Etta gave no reaction to his confession. What should have shocked her didn't. She just wanted to learn more, and why he felt he needed to do this. "How did you get the name, the Sundance Kid?"

"I didn't give it to myself; it was given to me. It's amazing how quickly a name like that sticks." He smiled one of his rare, boyish smiles and Etta couldn't help but lean in closer to him. He was handsome, kind, and polite, traits you'd never expect from an outlaw. She was undeniably drawn to him.

"When I was younger," Harry continued, "I'd purchased a

horse, saddle, and gun from a ranch hand at the VVV Ranch in Wyoming. I had no idea that he had stolen the horse and other items from the owner. I was charged with the crime and spent two years in jail in Sundance, Wyoming. The newspaper there had written an article about me and all my crimes, exaggerating immensely, and called me the 'Kid' from Sundance. After that, the Sundance Kid stuck."

Etta watched intently as he spoke, not judging, just curious. "If you were innocent of that crime, why do you steal now?"

Harry held no pretense in his eyes. "I could lie to you, Etta, and tell you how that experience soured me and turned me against the law, but that wouldn't be the truth. I enjoy the thrill of the chase, the risk of being caught, and the excitement of getting away. Pure and simple. I'm good with horses and better with guns. Maybe it was a combination of those things and meeting the wrong people at the wrong time, but I do it because I want to. No one is forcing me."

Etta's brows rose at his confession, but she continued to hear him out.

"I've always been restless and in search of excitement, and that's what I've found in being an outlaw." He reached for her and drew her near. "Do you think you can accept me as I am?" His face was so close she could feel his breath on her cheek.

Etta answered him with a question. "Do you think anyone could ever calm your restless soul?"

Harry brushed his lips over hers. "If anyone could, it would be you, Etta." He pulled her tighter to him and kissed her deeply.

To Etta, that was all the answer she needed. She would wait and see what the future held with Harry Longabaugh.

Pine Creek, MN
October 1911

Edward wasn't sure why Emily hadn't joined him on the porch in the evenings lately, but he missed her company. He'd played his last conversation with her over and over again in his mind but couldn't find any impropriety that might have chased her away. Neither did she act uncomfortably around him when their paths crossed, yet each evening she didn't join him for their usual conversations.

Gertie was no help either. When he broached the subject of Emily, Gertie only smiled slyly and giggled like a schoolgirl. *Silly women,* Edward thought. No wonder he'd stayed single so long. But he didn't like being single any longer. Everything changed when Emily stepped onto that train platform, and there was no going back for him now. So, with great determination, he decided to ask her to accompany him to the barn dance on Saturday at the Molby farm. He hoped she'd say yes. If not, he'd feel like a fool, exactly as he'd been acting since she'd arrived.

When Edward finally drew up the courage to ask her, Emily happily said yes.

"I haven't danced in ages. I'd love to go," she told him. Edward nearly floated away, practically giddy with happiness over her reply.

* * *

The night of the dance, Emily thought it was sweet how proud Edward acted to be escorting her and little Harry. Looking forward to a fun night, she'd shed her schoolteacher outfit for a dress with a full-flowing skirt, her hair half up, half down her back. Everyone commented on how lovely she looked, as a few men winked at Edward or patted him heartily on the back. Emily noticed that Edward tried to remain proper and dignified, but he still had a spirited spring in his step.

Emily found it all rather amusing. She was no queen of the dance. There were many prettier, younger girls present, but she found Edward's attention flattering. She would always love her husband but she'd been far too long without a man in her life. It felt good to have one compliment her as Edward was doing. Emily realized that there might actually be something between her and Edward, and she wasn't altogether against it.

The entire town had turned up at Frederick and Diane Molby's barn and as the fiddler and guitarist played, everyone danced to the lively tunes. With dancing came drinking, naturally, and the refreshments loosened lips and feet as people enjoyed the best part of the harvest season—barn dances.

Emily exchanged partners many times and they swirled and twirled about. The barn was filled to the brim with locals and the temporary farm help, adults and children alike. Emily had brought little Harry along, who was currently sitting off to the side with his school friends drinking punch and filling up on treats. She knew her son would suffer the consequences with a tummy ache later that night, but she didn't have the heart to stop him. He was having so much fun.

Whenever there was a break in the music, Edward was right at Emily's side to claim her, bringing her a fresh glass of punch. Emily had to smile at his constant attention. He looked happy and flushed, the warm barn turning his cheeks ruddy. People all around him were talking to him, patting him on the back, saying hello. He was well-liked in town and because of that, Emily was also accepted easily. It felt good to be accepted as one of their own now. Emily felt she could finally plant roots in this wonderful little town.

The music started up again and this time Emily found herself swooped up in Ted's arms for a lively spin around the dance floor. She'd noticed him watching her from the corner of the barn all night and knew that avoiding him was impossible. Allison sat with a group of women, evading the physical activity of dancing in case it made her swoon. That was what she'd told Emily when they'd visited earlier. So here was the sheriff, his intense eyes just inches from hers.

The tempo slowed, and so did their steps, giving Ted a chance to speak. "My wife approved of my dancing with you." He grinned. "She seems to trust you implicitly."

"Allison is a sweet and trusting soul," Emily told him. "We could all learn to be a little more like her."

Ted's brows rose. "So, who do you not trust, Mrs. Pleasants?"

"I could ask you the same question, Sheriff," she said lightly.

The music stopped and Edward was once again at Emily's side. She almost heaved a sigh of relief at not having to finish her conversation with the sheriff. Ted bowed slightly and walked back to his wife. Maybe it was her distrust of lawmen, or maybe she was simply paranoid, but Emily couldn't help but feel she was always under his scrutiny.

She and Edward walked over to the refreshment table to have a bite of food and found a spot to sit at one of the wooden tables. They strained to talk over the music. Nearby, a group of men were passing a bottle and getting louder with every swig. When Emily asked, Edward said he didn't know them and assumed they were temporary farm hands for the harvest.

"They're getting rowdy," Edward said, eyeing the men. "Should I ask Ted to remove them?"

Emily shook her head. "No, that isn't necessary. They're just having fun." She tried ignoring them, but every time she glanced their way, one man was leering at her. He was tall and scraggly looking, his dirty blond hair hanging down to his shoulders and his clothing looked dirty and disheveled, as if he'd slept in them.

The evening grew late and Emily decided it was time to get Harry and go home. She and Edward were having one last dance before leaving when the scraggly man came up to them and tried to grab Emily away from Edward.

"My turn to dance with the pretty teacher-lady," he said, slurring his words.

Emily backed away and Edward tried to get between her and the man, but the intruder lunged forward and gripped Emily's arms, hanging on to her tightly.

"Hey, what's the matter?" The guy glared at her, his balance precarious. "I been staring at you all night trying to remember, then it hit me. You're from San Antonio, right? You're that pretty lady from that house, the girl with the fancy education. The one no one was allowed to touch. That's you, right?" He swayed back and forth in front of her, his hands still grasping her arms.

Emily stared at him, horrified.

Try as he might, Edward couldn't eradicate the man's hands from Emily. After hearing his words, Emily knew she had to get rid of the drunken guy immediately.

"I'm not sure I know what you're talking about," she said. "I've never met you before."

"Course you do. You knew lots of men there. How could you not, living in that house?" He continued swaying on his feet.

"You have me confused with someone else," she insisted,

pulling away, but he held on tightly.

"Listen, mister, let go of the lady," Edward insisted. "She obviously doesn't know you." He grabbed again at his arms but the man had a vise grip. Their struggle attracted attention. Ted hurried across the room to help.

"Let go of the lady," Ted told the man, coming up behind Emily.

"Hey, what's the problem? Why can't we dance?" His eyes narrowed. "You think you're better than me, huh? You with your teachin' degree. Always thought you was better than everyone else. That's what that lady at the house told us. You was too good to touch. Better than the other girls, right?"

His words were slurred, but Emily understood him perfectly. Panic gripped her. She hoped Edward and Ted were too busy trying to get the man away from her to understand him. Soon, a crowd of people circled them. Finally, the offender stumbled and fell to the ground, angrily glaring at them. Ted didn't give him a chance to get up on his own. He dragged him up by the arm, pulled him to the door, and threw him out.

Edward was at Emily's side quickly, his arm wrapped protectively around her. "Are you all right?"

"I need to sit down," Emily said, suddenly lightheaded. Her fear that the drunken man might expose her past paralyzed her.

The crowd parted to let them walk to a table. By the time they'd sat down, Ted was back beside them.

"Okay, everyone," Ted told the crowd. "Let's get back to the music and dancing and give Mrs. Pleasants some room to breathe."

The band started up quickly and the crowd moved away. A fresh glass of punch appeared and Emily took a sip. Her hand shook.

Edward hovered over her, even more flushed then he'd been earlier. Little Harry had left his friends to stand beside his mother. Emily pulled him close and held him. He let her, seemingly sensing how upset she was.

"What a horrible, horrible man," Edward said with disgust. "Treating a lady in such a way. He should be thrown out of town!"

"I told him to go sleep it off and if he does anything like that again, he'll be in jail," Ted said. He studied Emily closely.

"I'm sure he meant no harm," Emily said, trying to make light of the encounter. "He was drunk." She was still shaking and she tried without success to control it. She was not a soft woman who swooned at adversity. The man physically accosting her wasn't what scared her—it was what he'd said. He knew her from a time best forgotten, and if anyone close by had really listened to him, her time here would be up. She couldn't bear the thought of leaving. Not so soon.

"You're cold." Edward took off his jacket and placed it around her shoulders. She was trembling despite the heat in the barn.

Ted sat down across from her. "What exactly did that man say to you? I heard something about a lady and a house full of girls. Do you know what he was talking about?"

"Sheriff, please," Edward interrupted. "Can't you see Emily's upset?"

Emily looked up at Ted. She knew if she didn't quell his questions now, she'd regret it later. "It's fine, Edward. I can answer the sheriff's questions." She kissed the top of Harry's head and told him to rejoin his friends. The music was still playing but not many couples were dancing. The enthusiasm of the night had been squelched after the disturbing episode.

Emily spoke quietly and directly at Ted. "I lived in San Antonio when I was younger. I grew up on a ranch near there and when my father died, my mother and I moved into town. My mother owned a boarding house, a legitimate boarding house," she added firmly. "Maybe that man knew me from then. I don't know. My mother was very protective. She may be the woman he was referring to." It was the best lie she could come up with on such short notice. She hoped it would be good enough.

"Well, that explains it," Edward said, looking relieved. "I think it's time I get Emily home. It's been a long evening."

Ted said nothing, and Emily could tell he wasn't completely convinced. His instincts learned as a Pinkerton agent wouldn't be satisfied with such a simple explanation. She knew it was only because he had great respect for Edward that he let it go. For now.

Chapter Nine

Colorado
1895-96

Life with Harry Longabaugh, Etta was learning, was quite exciting indeed. After that day at the river when Harry had bared his soul to her, the two were inseparable. If they had been in a large city, people would have talked mercilessly about the inappropriateness of their time alone together, but in the small town of Durango, no one paid attention to the young lovers. Etta suspected it was because most people knew and respected Harry. Whatever the reason, she was thankful they were free to follow whatever path their love took them.

Harry told Etta all about his life growing up out east in Philadelphia, and of his family, especially his favorite sister, Samanna. He said he hoped to take Etta there someday to meet them, as he knew they would love her. He also took her to visit his relatives in Cortez, a day's ride from Durango. Harry had moved from the east to Colorado with his cousin George and his family and still had close ties with them. They'd spend weekends with the family, and Etta got along well with George's wife and the children. Harry acted like a child himself there, playing on the floor with the young ones. Etta loved watching him play games with them and knew someday he'd make a wonderful father.

Their nights together, however, were for them only. There was a small cabin on the outlying property of the ranch Harry worked for. He'd asked the owner if he could live there instead of the bunkhouse. The owner was happy to oblige. Having Harry in the cabin would keep transients from squatting there.

The first time Harry and Etta were alone in the cabin he lit a fire and set out a lamb's wool rug in front of it. He held her in his arms and declared his love for her. "I was bewitched with you the moment I saw you that day in Fannie's parlor," he told her, his gray eyes intense. "I knew that day I would love you forever." He kissed her then, and Etta eagerly returned his kiss.

"I love you, too, Harry," she said between kisses and they made love right there, beside the fire.

Afterward, Harry teased Etta over her enthusiastic response to his lovemaking. "I thought I had to be gentle with you, but I see I'm the one who needs protection from you." He tickled her and laughed.

"You're stuck with me now, Harry Longabaugh." Etta pulled him close, her body pressed against his. "No matter what happens."

"No matter what," Harry responded, caressing her softly. "I like that."

After that night, the young lovers found any excuse to spend time alone at the cabin. Some weekends they'd claim they were going to Cortez, but spent the days in the cabin instead. Etta had to be careful to make her excuses plausible, despite people looking the other way about her relationship with Harry. The town would not like one of their unmarried teachers flaunting unsavory behavior. While she suspected most people knew she and Harry were close, as long as it looked respectable, they were left alone.

Harry talked openly now to Etta about his outlaw experiences and the people he knew. He told her about Hole-in-the-Wall, describing the beautiful red-rock cliffs of the secret hideout where he and others had stayed many times to escape from the law. He talked about Robbers Roost and Brown's Hole, showing her on a map where they were located. He spoke of Matt Warner, Tom McCarthy, Elzy Lay, Bill Madden, and Lonnie and Harvey Logan. There were other names as well: George Currie, Tom O'Day, Ben Kilpatrick, and many more. Etta couldn't remember them all. But the name that came up most was Butch Cassidy.

"You'll like Butch," Harry told her several times. "He's crazy and fun and there's not a mean bone in his body. He'll fall in love with you for sure."

Etta knew that Butch was in a penitentiary in Wyoming and wondered how a man in prison could have so many good qualities. But she also knew that there were two sides to every story. Ever since her father's untimely death, her views on good and bad were no longer black and white. Sometimes "good" people were the ones to fear, while "bad" people were just misunderstood. Wasn't Fannie a kind woman despite her occupation? Perhaps Butch Cassidy was also a kind soul. She chose to believe Harry because she trusted him completely.

The winter months passed quickly and happily for the young couple and soon the promise of spring filled the air. One Thursday, at the end of the school day, Etta rode out on her borrowed horse to see Harry at the ranch. Most days he worked well into the evenings and Etta stayed in town. But on Thursdays, Harry was off early and they usually spent time together at the cabin.

As Etta neared the cabin, she saw an unfamiliar horse tied up in front and the glow of a light through the window. She wondered who could be with Harry as she tied up her own horse, but her question was answered quickly when a strange man flew out of the cabin and hugged her, swinging her in circles and laughing loudly.

"So this is the beauty who's stolen Sundance's heart," he bellowed as he set her down and stood at arm's length to inspect her.

Etta stood there, dizzy and stunned, as Harry stepped out onto the porch and grinned. She studied the man in front of her. He was very close to Harry's height and had dark blond hair and a neatly trimmed moustache. His smile caused lines around his eyes and mouth, lines that looked warm and inviting, not hard. His eyes were bright blue and sparkled with excitement. Before she could say a word, he grabbed her again in a big bear hug.

"Miss Etta, you are the prettiest young thing I've ever seen. I wish I'd found you first," he said, his voice excited and teasing.

"Etta," Harry said from where he stood on the porch. "You've just met the famous Butch Cassidy."

Chapter Ten

San Francisco, CA
1972

Susan Sheridan sat on Grandma Em's sofa, her mouth agape, and eyes wide. Grandma Em had stopped telling her story only long enough to pour a glass of water for both herself and her granddaughter. Once settled back in her rocker, she urged her granddaughter to take a sip of the drink in front of her. But Susan was too stunned to drink. "*You* were Etta Place?" she asked. "*The* Etta Place?"

Grandma Em smiled and shook her head. "No, dear. I'm Emily Pleasants. But for a time, while I was with Harry, I was known as Etta Place."

Susan blinked. "And you were in love with Sundance? The Sundance Kid? An outlaw?"

Grandma Em sighed. "Yes," she answered. "But I preferred calling him Harry. Most everyone did, except Butch. He called him Sundance most of the time." She smiled as she spoke of Butch, her eyes soft with memories.

"Butch Cassidy." Susan shook her head, still stunned.

"Grandma, you're famous. Did you hear about the movie that came out a few years ago? *Butch Cassidy and the Sundance Kid?* It won awards! Everyone knows who Etta Place is. But no one knows what became of her. Grandma, do you know what this means?" Susan's excitement grew. The newspaper reporter in her was fueling up and her adrenalin was flowing. But in one quick moment, her exhilaration deflated as a thought occurred to her.

"Did Grandpa know?" Susan asked, her voice almost a whisper.

Grandma Em took a sip from her own glass of water. "There is more of the story to tell," she told her granddaughter. "Maybe all your questions will be answered when I'm finished."

Susan nodded emphatically. She was no longer in a hurry to leave. She had to hear her grandma's entire story now. After flipping the cassette tape over, she hit record and sat back for more.

Chapter Eleven

Pine Creek, MN
October 1911

Most mornings Emily sat at Evy's Restaurant for breakfast with Edward and little Harry. They had settled into a routine of meeting there, sharing the paper, and bidding good morning to the many residents who also ate there. It was comfortable and companionable, and Emily enjoyed the routine of it. There had been so much she couldn't count on in years past that this small ritual felt good, solid.

It was on such a morning that they were perusing the *St. Paul Dispatch* when a story caught Emily's eye. Her heart quickened as she read the small piece, then her eyes searched the top again to see when the article had first been printed. It was a reprint from an earlier article in the *Manti Messenger* dated January 20, 1911, ten months ago. Once again, she read the words:

Butch Cassidy Caught – Helena, Mont. – In John Davis one of two alleged post office robbers in jail at Bozeman the authorities believe they have Butch Cassidy famous as an outlaw. According to the statement of Glenn Henderson

the fellow prisoner of Davis the man is none other than the former bandit who operated in Montana, Wyoming, Utah and Idaho then or twelve years ago and who has been reported living in South America with Kid Curry.

Emily was stunned. Butch Cassidy. His name was appearing in the paper again. She knew his being caught was just as much a fabrication as the fact that he'd been in South America with Harvey Logan, alias Kid Curry. John Davis was lying about who he was, she was sure. But the fact that Butch's name had reappeared in the news meant he wasn't forgotten. Had he been seen again? Was he back? Emily was so absorbed in her thoughts she didn't hear Edward repeat her name for the fourth time.

"Emily, did you hear me? What's wrong? You look pale," Edward inquired from across the table. Even little Harry had looked up to see why his mother wasn't answering.

Dazed, Emily lifted her eyes. "What did you say?"

Edward frowned. "Is everything all right? Has something upset you?" He reached for the paper, but she quickly folded it and set it in her lap.

"I'm fine." She forced a smile. "I was just wool-gathering, thinking about the day ahead. I'm sorry I didn't hear what you said."

Edward didn't look convinced. "I was asking if you'd like to go riding at the ranch this Sunday after church. Hopefully, the weather will cooperate. I'm sure we can find a gentle horse for Harry to ride, or he can ride with me."

Young Harry nodded his head eagerly, his eyes bright with excitement. Emily and Edward had been to the ranch to ride twice already, but Harry had always been left with Gertie. Emily knew the little boy would enjoy joining them.

"That'll be fine." Emily glanced at the paper in her lap. She brought it with her to the schoolhouse after breakfast and kept it in her desk all day. Emily didn't open it again until that evening after she'd put Harry to bed but her mind had been spinning all day.

Butch Cassidy. Where Butch was, Sundance was also. It had been rumored for years that the pair had been killed in South America. As of yet, Emily hadn't been able to absolutely confirm or deny the rumor. She'd contacted a friend in Chile, Frank D. Aller, who was also a U.S. Vice-Council and helped Americans in trouble. For three years he'd tried to verify the deaths of Butch and Sundance in San Vincente, Bolivia. This past January he'd been sent copies of the death certificates of the two bandits who'd been shot dead. He'd sent those to Emily, but it hadn't been actual proof that the two men were Butch and Sundance. Aller had also told her that Percy Seibert, a former employer of Butch and Sundance at the Concordia Tin Mines, had stated the two who were killed that day in San Vincente were the American outlaws, Butch Cassidy and the Sundance Kid. Still, Emily had her doubts. They had all been good friends of Percy. He'd have easily lied to get the law off of Butch and Harry's back.

But now, someone was pretending to be Butch. What did that mean? How could she find out if he was really back?

Emily pondered this, realizing that any type of inquiry about either Butch or Sundance would only fuel Sheriff Neilson's suspicions about her background. She couldn't risk that, but she had to find out if anyone knew more about what had become of them. As she sat and thought it through, she realized it was finally time to go to the one place where someone might have information about Butch and Sundance.

* * *

Edward knocked softly on Emily's door, and she answered immediately. "Will you be joining me outside tonight?" he asked, hopeful.

Emily nodded and whispered she'd be out in a moment.

As he waited out on the porch, Edward felt relieved. Only once before had he knocked on Emily's door to invite her outside. She was always pleasant with him, but he didn't want to press himself upon her. They'd shared time alone together at his ranch riding horses, and once or twice he'd taken her hand in his as they sat together in church. She'd never rebuffed his advances and he was encouraged that perhaps their relationship might become something more than friends. He was head over heels in love with Emily. He couldn't deny it any longer. But he knew he had to tread lightly. He didn't want to scare her off before he could get closer to her.

Emily came out to the porch and greeted Edward with a warm smile. She sat in the other chair and gazed out at the open field that lay before them, pulling her shawl tightly around her.

"It's getting colder," Edward said, as he sat back and lit his pipe. "Soon, we won't be able to sit out here."

Emily nodded. "We'll have to find somewhere else to spend time together," she suggested.

He was pleased with her response, but noticed that she looked troubled. Edward set down his pipe and moved closer to her, clasping her hand in his.

"Something *is* wrong," he said. "It's been bothering you since breakfast. What is it? Can I help?"

"I've been worried about my husband's aunt," she said, her eyes not meeting his. "She's not well, and she has no family with her. I feel I should be there for her."

At the mention of Emily's husband, Edward slowly released

her hand and sat back in his chair. It reminded him that Emily did not belong to him and he shouldn't be acting so familiarly with her. "How long have you known?" he asked, returning to his pipe.

"I received a post from a friend of hers a few days ago. I've been trying to decide what I should do. I should be with her, yet I have school to teach. I'm so torn."

Edward hated seeing the strain on Emily's face. Her unhappiness was his also; he cared for her that deeply. "Where does she live?" He moved forward again, closer to her.

"In Wyoming, north of Cheyenne," she told him, raising her eyes to his. "It's a long way to go, but I think she needs me."

Edward nodded. Knowing how compassionate Emily was, he understood why she felt she had to go. "You could close school for a short time," he offered. "I'm sure the children won't object." He smiled and her face softened.

"What about the school board? Will they be upset with me? I don't want to risk losing my job."

"Then you will be coming back?" Edward asked.

Emily looked at him, surprised. "Of course I'd come back," she said adamantly. She placed one of her hands on his leg. "I love living here, and so does Harry. I don't want to risk losing this." She added softly, "Or being near you."

Her hand on his leg was more than Edward could bear. He wanted to touch her, pull her close, and hold her next to him. Without another thought, Edward dropped his pipe to the floor and placed his hands on either side of her face, drawing her to him and kissing her gently. He stopped for only a moment to look into her eyes, and seeing her consent, he kissed her again, this time with the passion of a man who'd been waiting an entire lifetime to find her. Emily didn't resist. She returned his kiss with equal desire.

When finally they parted, both were breathing heavily and it took Edward a moment to come to his senses. He dropped his hands to his lap, sorry he'd taken advantage of this moment and hoping he hadn't insulted her. He was about to apologize for his behavior when he saw Emily smile, then laugh lightly.

"You don't have to look so upset about kissing me. I'm glad you did." She bent forward and kissed him lightly on the lips.

Edward beamed as he clasped her hands in his once more. They sat there, holding hands and gazing in each other's eyes. Edward silently thanked God for giving him another chance at love.

* * *

Emily left on the train two days later. The school board appreciated her fine work and were more than willing to let her take some time off for a family emergency. She'd been quite successful with the children in the short time she'd been teaching and the board knew the time away from school wouldn't hurt the students.

Emily asked Edward if he and Gertie would take care of Harry while she was away. Edward consented cheerfully. "I'll care for him as if he were my own," he told her.

His words warmed her heart. She knew Edward had been nervous that she might not return, but by placing little Harry in his care, she was silently telling him she trusted him and would definitely be back.

Gertie was also thrilled to watch over Harry. Emily had a feeling the two adults would fight over who'd have Harry the most. That thought pleased her. She was so lucky to have found people in her new life who she could trust completely with her most prized possession.

Emily did feel guilty for lying to everyone about where she was going, but it was something she had to do. She had lived too long without answers about what had happened to Butch and Harry. She had to go back and at least try to find out. She thought for sure she'd find someone who might have news of the pair. It was time to go home to Hole-in-the-Wall.

Chapter Twelve

Hole-in-the-Wall
1896

Within a few months of Butch's return, the quiet life that Etta and Harry had enjoyed changed forever. After finishing the school year in Durango, Harry swept Etta away to join Butch and the other gang members at Hole-in-the-Wall in Central Wyoming. Etta didn't mind leaving her teaching position behind. Although she loved working with children, she loved Harry more and knew her place was wherever he went.

Hole-in-the-Wall was a desolate place, yet they were never lonely there. Several cabins spotted the landscape for outlaws and ranchers alike. The land hidden behind the red-rock walls was superb grazing pasture, and also a fine place to hide stolen livestock. Although Harry and Butch had rustled cattle in the past, now they were only interested in the big payoffs. And big payoffs they found, but with many risks involved.

Etta tried not to think about Harry's dangerous occupation. She hadn't yet had to wait for him while he was off on a job. She'd soon learn it wasn't easy to be the one waiting at home for her man to return.

While Harry was busy working with the horses they planned to use for their next job, Etta spent her time taking care of the small cabin the couple shared with Butch and visiting with the other ladies who had found their way to the Hole by loving outlaws. She also became friendly with some of the ranchers' wives. The ranchers didn't mind the outlaws being there as long as they behaved respectfully. In most cases, the ranchers and outlaws were friends who helped one another and socialized often by having barn dances and big outdoor suppers.

Etta felt a camaraderie with the other women. She was a hard worker and wasn't afraid to get dirty or jump right in to assist a friend. She quickly became a helper in someone's kitchen, a babysitter for another's child, or a shoulder for anyone needing to pour out their woes. She enjoyed being useful and feeling a part of this unique community.

One of Etta's favorite people in the Hole was a rancher's wife named Erma Hoffman. Erma was twenty years older than Etta, but the two connected immediately. Like Etta, she was educated and loved reading, owning several books that many of the outlaws, including Harry and Butch, borrowed. Erma and her husband, Joshua, had slowly made their way west from Ohio, stopping first in Illinois to farm, then heading on to Wyoming where they found the property in the Hole through a friend who had gone before them. Joshua liked working with cattle better than farming, so this was where they'd stayed. Erma was a great cook and baked the best pies in the Hole. But she was also a western woman who could ride the ranch with her husband, herd and brand cattle, and shoot with an eagle eye. Having no children of her own, she took Etta under her wing, making them fast friends.

Etta had other friends, too. Not many of the outlaws had women or wives along, but Elzy Lay, a longtime friend of Butch's and fellow outlaw, was married to a beautiful woman named Maude. Many evenings were spent on the cabin porch with Elzy and Maude, Harry, Etta, and Butch, joking and laughing away the night. Elzy was a quiet, polite man who took ribbings well from his old friend Butch. Etta adored him. Maude was madly in love with Elzy, and Etta suspected Maude chose to ignore the fact that her husband was a wanted criminal.

Etta, however, had no illusions as to Harry's profession and did not expect to change him. He was not a violent man, even though he could be moody at times, and he was kind to her. But he'd chosen the outlaw life, and loving him meant she'd chosen it also. Sometimes she struggled with her own feelings about it. She'd been raised to be honest. But since she was not going to give up Harry, she had no choice in the matter.

Butch was everything she'd been told about him. He was sweet, kind, and the biggest tease among them. He flirted with Etta relentlessly, which Harry took good-naturedly to a point but would sometimes tell Butch he'd gone far enough. Butch would just smile and wink and start up again later. Etta thought of him more as a brother than a rival for her affections, and told Harry that many times to ease his worry. Harry was much more serious about life than Butch, and while Etta knew Harry liked and respected Butch, he sometimes grew weary of Butch's lightheartedness.

In August, the Wild Bunch gang rode again after a four-year absence from the outlaw trail. The last heist Harry had participated in was a train robbery near Malta, Montana in 1892. Since then, he'd made his living working on ranches. But now, with Butch in charge, four of the men rode off to Idaho to rob the

Montpelier bank. While Butch, Sundance, Bub Meeks, and Elzy Lay headed west to Idaho, Maude and Etta were sent south to Robbers Roost, accompanied by gang members Bill Carver and Flatnose Currie, to wait for their return.

Etta waited impatiently in Robbers Roost for the return of her boys. That was how she thought of Harry and Butch now: *her* boys. She loved Harry, but she also cared about Butch.

She was frantic for news. A million thoughts ran through her mind of what could happen. They could be shot and killed, or arrested and sent to prison. What would she do then? And was the money worth the risk? Etta knew that by loving Harry, she'd also have to accept this lifestyle, but it didn't make waiting any easier.

Newspaper accounts of the robbery came to them long before the outlaws returned, and every moment was torture. When finally the group arrived at the Roost, safe and sound, Etta questioned whether she could ever live though such an agonizing wait again.

Hole-in-the-Wall
October 1911

The train ride to Wyoming was long, taking Etta down to Omaha, then west through North Platte and Cheyenne, then north through Casper up to the small town of Kaycee. As she gazed out the window at the passing landscape, Emily struggled with her feelings for the men in her life. She knew if she found Harry, she'd happily choose to be with him again. But Edward was a good man, and she hated the thought of hurting him.

Her love for Harry was one of passion and commitment, but for Edward she felt a warm, tender feeling. He was steady and honest, kind and hardworking. Edward would make a wonderful father for little Harry, and that was very important to Emily. But could she love him with the same passion as she had Harry? She doubted she'd ever love another man like that again. The hard truth was if she couldn't find Harry or Butch, life had to go on for her and her son.

She thought of the day she'd sailed away from South America, heavy with child, and watching as Harry's form grew smaller and smaller on the dock. It had ripped her heart out leaving him, but they'd both agreed it was best for their unborn child if she went home before giving birth. Harry and Butch were going to settle up their business and be only weeks behind her. But they never came.

It was late morning when Emily stepped off the train at the little station in Kaycee and made her way to the only blacksmith and livery stables in town. As she inquired after a horse from the owner, she noted the confused look on his face. Dressed in a traveling suit, her hair held up high in a bun with a small hat perched on top, she looked like she was ready to go to church instead of riding.

"You sure you're not looking for a buggy or wagon?" the man asked, rubbing his hand through his whiskers. He was short and dirty from working, and looked to be well into his middle years. Emily gave him her sweetest smile.

"I'm riding west of here to visit friends," she said. "I believe a horse would do much better than a buggy, don't you?"

The blacksmith wrinkled his face even more. "Out west of here? Ain't nothin' west of here 'cept a ranch or two and the old Hole," he said.

Emily nodded. "Maybe you know my friends. The Hoffmans? Erma and Joshua? They're still ranching in the Hole, aren't they?"

The man grinned. "So, you're a friend of the Hoffmans? Well, ain't that a treat. Nice people, they are. Don't know how much ranchin' they're doing out there anymore, not with Joshua's back all bent over, but guess he's got some help out there now. I'll get together a good horse and saddle for you." He smiled, showing missing teeth. "You ain't planning on ridin' in them fancy clothes, are ya?"

Emily looked down at her dress. Before she could reply, the man spoke up again. "My wife is at the house back behind the barn, here. You go on up there and she'll let you change your clothes."

Emily thanked him and did as he suggested. His wife was a small woman with a gray bun and pleasant smile. She let Emily change in the bedroom. Emily slipped on men's pants and a flannel shirt, wearing several layers, mindful of the cold weather. She pulled her Colt .45 from her bag and slid it into the pocket of her jacket. Emily didn't anticipate any problems, but as a woman riding alone, she knew she needed protection. She also knew it was a risk to ride into the Hole in late October. Winter storms had been known to blow in this early. But she was almost there and excited to see her old friends.

After paying for the horse and supplies, she took off. She had no need for a map or guide. She'd ridden these trails many times and could find her way into the Hole with her eyes closed.

All the tension she'd felt since leaving Pine Creek evaporated as Emily's horse trotted along the familiar terrain. She loved riding, had missed it dearly during the years she'd lived at the convent in California. She also loved these rocky plains, with their open grasslands and red rock buttes. It wasn't long before she came upon the rock formation that rose to the sky and was known to everyone around these parts as the Wall.

Urging her horse faster, Emily instinctively looked up as she crossed through the entrance 'V' of the wall into the Hole. In times past, there had always been sentries posted on the rocks high above to protect from intruders, mainly lawmen. But today there were none, probably hadn't been any in a long time since the outlaws had moved on or died.

As the sun lowered in the sky, Emily rode up to the Hoffman's ranch house. It was quiet all around, looking deserted. There were cattle dotting the landscape in the distance, but no noise to indicate anyone was here. As soon as she stepped onto the familiar plank porch, the door flew open and there stood Erma, squinting out at her, rifle in hand.

Emily approached cautiously. "Erma? It's Etta. Etta Longabaugh." She looked into the face of the older woman, hoping Erma would recognize her. Erma studied her for a very long time, but soon a smile of recognition lit up her face.

"Well, I'll be. Etta? Is that really you, dear?" Etta nodded and Erma smiled broader and threw her arms wide, embracing the younger woman with zeal.

Etta fell into her embrace, relieved her old friend was still here and still remembered her. Unexpected tears filled her eyes. She felt like she'd come home.

They both spoke at once, then laughed and did it again. Erma laughed so hard there were tears in her eyes. Grabbing Etta's hand, she led her into the dark cabin and quickly lit lamps that let off a gentle glow.

"Etta. Dear Etta. I can't believe it's you. I thought you were long gone." She motioned for Etta to sit and she did. After her long ride, sitting on a soft cushion felt good.

Etta looked around her, not surprised that nothing had changed since she'd last been here. There were three rooms: the living room, kitchen, and a bedroom at the back of the cabin. The hand-made furniture was still there, as well as the cushions and braid rugs made by Erma. The small windows were clean on the inside but covered with the dust blown around the dry valley on the outside. Over the fireplace mantel, Erma had re-hung the rifle Etta had been greeted with.

Erma bustled about and made tea, proclaiming a lady like Etta needed only the best while Etta unsaddled her horse and placed him in the fenced-in pasture. After she was done, the women sat. Erma took Etta's hands in her own and gazed into her eyes. "It's been so long I almost forgot you. And my, but you haven't changed a bit. You're still the prettiest girl in the Hole."

Etta shook her head. "I've changed but things still seem the same here."

"No, dear," Erma said sadly. "Things here aren't the same any longer. Most everybody is gone. Only us and a couple of big ranch holdings are here now. Everyone you knew from before have vanished."

"That's why I'm here," Etta told her, her voice solemn. "I was hoping you'd know where some of them were. I was hoping…" She stopped, afraid to ask about Harry and Butch. But Erma finished her thoughts.

"Harry and Butch?" she asked, her voice gentle. "You were wondering if they've been here?"

Etta's heart pounded as her eyes grew wide. "Have they?"

The older lady slowly shook her head. "I'm sorry, dear, but they've not been back since you all left. I thought you were with them."

A sigh escaped Etta, letting out the anticipation she'd felt seconds earlier. "I had so hoped they'd returned. But I suppose they wouldn't have come here."

"I'm surprised you aren't with Harry," Erma said. "You two and Butch were always together. But you aren't the only one to come asking about them. I guess a lot of people think they'll come back to the Hole."

Etta's eyes darted up. "What do you mean? Who's been asking after them?"

"Those Pinkerton men come here from time to time, asking questions and poking around. It's enough to make me want to shoot them. Every time I tell them we haven't seen hide nor hair of any of the Wild Bunch in years. But they are still looking, still expecting to find them. They still expect to find you, too, Etta."

"Me?" Etta was genuinely shocked. She'd never been wanted for any crimes in the States. "Why are they looking for me?"

"Why darling, they have a fancy photograph of you and Harry that they show around to everyone. Some photograph from New York City with you both looking so rich and dapper. You look just beautiful in it, sweetie." Erma beamed, as proud as if Etta were her own daughter. "But they have your name wrong and I didn't see fit to steer them straight. Called you Ethel Place. Of course, I acted like I didn't know either of you, and certainly no one named Ethel Place. I suppose they don't believe me. That's why they keep coming back."

Etta knew from a past encounter that the Pinkertons had the photo of her and Harry, but she was shocked that they knew she'd signed her name Ethel Place while traveling with Harry. She'd never felt completely safe, but now she knew she was even more vulnerable. If the Pinkertons were showing that photo around, she could be recognized. And if Sheriff Neilson had access to that photo, she hated to think of what might happen to her and little Harry.

Erma patted Etta's hand. "Now, now, dear. I didn't mean to upset you," she said, clearly worried about her young friend. "They truly don't know if you were ever here and they have no idea where you came from. They think you went to South America with Butch and Harry but have no proof. They are grasping at straws."

Etta nodded. She realized that this could be true, but her main concern was Sheriff Neilson.

The sun had set when Joshua came in from working in the barn, both surprised and pleased to see Etta. He was bent over from years of hard labor on the ranch and he looked so much older than Etta remembered, but his eyes were still bright and his humor was intact.

Erma lit more lamps around the cabin and began making supper. Etta helped her by slicing potatoes and carrots to serve with a hefty slab of steak. Over supper the trio reminisced about the old days and all the people who came and went over the years. Joshua and Erma had always been on the right side of the law, but they considered many of the outlaws and rustlers their friends. Often these men had helped them through tough times with a loan of money or help on the ranch. In exchange, the couple had provided them with shelter in times of need, and never repeated anything they knew about the outlaws.

According to the couple, none of the people Etta knew from the old days had returned for a very long time. "Heard the Logan boys were killed, each in a different place," Joshua told Etta. "And so were Flatnose and Will Carver. Elzy Lay was in jail, last we heard, and haven't heard a thing about Ben Kilpatrick. Their lives just caught up with them, I guess." He looked at Etta. "No word from Harry or Butch either," he added, his eyes sad.

Etta knew Erma and Joshua held a soft spot in their hearts for Butch and Harry. Of all the men who helped them, they had done the most and always were kind to the couple.

Etta told the couple how she, Butch, and Harry had gone to South America to go straight, and how things had not turned out as expected. They commiserated with her over having to leave Harry and Butch behind when she left for the states.

"You did what was right for your son," Erma told her. "Sometimes we have to make sacrifices for our children no matter how difficult it is."

Etta knew that was true, but she felt she'd made the biggest sacrifice of all. Losing Harry and Butch. And now, once again, her hope that they'd returned had been distinguished.

Etta fell asleep that night on a feather mattress in the living room by the fire, thinking of her past and everyone who was gone. More than anything, she'd wanted to find answers on this trip, but instead she was even more confused and upset. Not only hadn't she found Harry, but now she understood just how much the law knew about her. She wondered how long it will take for people to discover who she really is?

Robbers Roost
Fall 1896

After the Montpelier Bank holdup Butch went his own way while the others headed to Robbers Roost. Butch had taken a job as a ranch hand in Huntington, north of the Roost. A good portion of his money from the robbery had gone to Matt Warner's wife, a friend of Butch, who had been arrested and was currently in jail. That was one of the traits Etta loved about Butch—he was a loyal friend and gave away his money just as easily as stealing it. He might have been a criminal, but he was a generous and caring soul.

Harry and Elzy returned to Etta and Maude in Robbers Roost. It was one of the happiest days of Etta's life, having Harry back safe and unharmed. Everyone else was joyous over the money they had brought with them, but Etta was only thankful for Harry. After having waited for his return, fearing the worst, she would have given up everything the money bought to see Harry return to an honest and safe life. But Harry didn't feel that way, so she was resigned to loving a man she worried about every day.

Robbers Roost was located in the canyons of southeast Utah and consisted of many winding, twisting canyon trails that could confuse even the best tracker. Outlaws found it easy to hide there because no lawman would risk getting lost in the canyons or being ambushed by desperate outlaws. But Harry knew the territory well, having lived east of the Roost for many years. The rocky terrain was good for only one thing—grazing—so this was the perfect spot to raise cattle and horses. That was what the men planned to do: hide out in the safety of the canyons while training a new batch of horses to pull off their next heist.

Winter fell fast and cold in the Roost, snow so deep it separated the group from the rest of the world. Tents had been set up for the two couples, Harry and Etta in one, Elzy and Maude in another. They kept comfortable during the cold days and nights with woodstoves in their tents and cots covered with heavy wool blankets. Butch had rejoined the group before the snow fell and split the tent with Harry and Etta, hanging a sheet for privacy between their two spaces. Etta was no longer shy or self-conscious about Butch's presence. She'd grown used to him being around and didn't give a second thought to his sleeping only a few feet away from her and Harry.

Butch brought with him three powerful quarter horses that Harry was to work with over the winter. Harry had also obtained two more horses from a local rancher. The horses were to be used for the next planned heist with the outlaws' own horses waiting at a relay point, fresh and ready for the getaway. It was important that the horses were well-trained so as not to spook easily in case of gunfire.

Harry preferred quarter horses due to their compact size and great speed. Training horses was Harry's contribution to each robbery and he was good at it. He generally left the planning to Butch because he had a keener sense of what to anticipate. There was no doubt that there were two things Harry excelled at—a steady gun hand and controlling horses.

Etta loved watching Harry work with the powerful animals. She'd bundle up in long johns, trousers, a wool shirt, and sheepskin coat—she'd given up on all aspects of female attire while at the Roost, as had Maude, for warmth and comfort—and stand by the corral watching him work. He had a firm but loving hand with each horse and it was obvious that the animals respected him and willingly bowed to his command.

Daily, Etta and Harry would ride the horses through the open canyons, sometimes racing each other, sometimes just walking at a leisurely pace as they planned their future together and all the things they dreamed of doing. She was in such high spirits and so in love with Harry that it didn't occur to Etta then that those dreams might never come true.

Winter passed slowly at the Roost, but their days were filled with work and nights were spent in each other's arms. Butch grew restless, having no companion of his own, and sometimes became irritated at the two happy couples around him.

"Do you all have to be so lovey-dovey all the time?" Butch complained one evening as the five of them sat around the campfire drinking coffee after supper. "Can't you at least argue or something sometimes?"

Etta laughed and Harry nudged him with his elbow. "What's the matter, Butch. Aren't you enjoying this long, cold winter?"

"I'd enjoy it more if I didn't have to listen to you lovebirds cooing," Butch growled. He grabbed his mug and book and sulked off into his half of the tent.

Etta felt bad for Butch. Usually good-natured, she knew his loneliness was getting him down.

"Aw, don't feel bad for Butch, sweetie," Harry told her when she confided in him. "He's never had a serious relationship in his life. He'll feel better when spring comes and he can pull a job."

"Why do you think he's never had a long relationship?" she asked Harry. That puzzled her. Butch was so sweet to her, and kind to others. And he was a good-looking man, too. It seemed to her that women would flock to him.

Harry shrugged. "He doesn't stay in one place very long, and I guess he hasn't found the right woman yet." He kissed the tip of her nose and grinned. "Butch just isn't as lucky as I am."

Etta smiled and kissed Harry. She felt very lucky indeed.

They celebrated Thanksgiving and Christmas as best they could. Butch cut down a tree and brought it into the tent and they all decorated it with hand-made paper stars and pinecones the women had decorated. Their gifts were handmade. Butch had made a small wooden box for Etta with leaf carvings on the lid and a lock with a gold key. She loved it and knew she'd use it to keep her most precious possessions in. Harry gave her a gold bracelet he'd made by melting down gold coins and pounding it into shape. He'd carefully inscribed E & H on the front. She adored it, knowing that he'd made it just for her. She'd knitted warm gloves and hats for Harry and Butch, which they wore immediately. The group ate venison steak and potatoes from their supply and sang Christmas carols around the campfire. Etta felt it was the best holiday she'd ever had despite their meager supplies. She was with the people she loved most, and that was all that mattered.

In January, Maude confided in Etta that she was pregnant. She was ecstatic to be starting a family and Elzy was happy, too. Etta was pleased for her friend, but her own concerns were weighing heavily on her mind.

One night as she and Harry lay in bed, snuggled in each other's arms, Etta commented on Maude's pregnancy.

"It's exciting, isn't it?" she asked Harry tentatively. "By next summer they'll be parents."

Harry agreed, but added, "That's good for them, but I'd like us to wait until we can do it properly. After we're married and finally have a home of our own."

Tears filled Etta's eyes. She had little control over her emotions these days and couldn't seem to stop.

Harry sat up in bed, surprised by her reaction. "What's wrong? I love kids. I really do want to be a father someday. I promise we'll have children when the time is right."

"I think I'm pregnant," she said, sobbing.

"What?" he bellowed.

Her tears came faster. For several weeks she'd been afraid to believe it was true, but she couldn't ignore the fact she was carrying Harry's child any longer. She knew Harry loved her, but she was fearful she'd lose him if he didn't want a child yet. A child meant being tied down and that didn't follow suit with an outlaw's life.

"What in hell is all the noise in here about?" Butch growled, pushing aside the sheet and staggering into their side of the tent, a lantern in his hand. His undershirt was half-tucked into a pair of pants he'd carelessly pulled on. "What are you doing to my Etta?" he hollered at Harry. "Why are you making her cry?"

"Your Etta?" Harry yelled back.

"That's right, you oaf. You know I love Etta and I'll take her away from you the first chance I get." Butch came over and sat beside Etta in the bed, placing a protective arm around her.

"Now, what has this imbecile done to make my sweet Etta cry?" Butch asked gently, pulling a face at Harry.

Harry rolled his eyes.

Etta's sobs had slowed to sniffles. The way these two men were acting she didn't know if she should cry or laugh.

"*Our* Etta thinks she's pregnant," Harry said, calmer now.

Butch's eyes grew wide and he broke out into a huge grin. "We're pregnant?" he asked.

Harry glared menacingly at him.

"Oh, my Lord. I'm going to be an uncle!" Butch slung his arms around Etta and squeezed her tightly. Etta couldn't help but smile through her tears. Then Butch turned to Harry, frowning. "Hey, you were part of this, you know. So why aren't you celebrating?"

"I never got a chance to react," Harry said in his defense. "She just started crying and then you barged in."

Both sets of eyes turned to him, expectantly. Etta placed her hand over Harry's. He looked from Etta, to Butch, and back again.

"Does *he* have to be here?" Harry asked, nodding toward Butch.

In response, Butch clutched his arm tighter around Etta and sat up straighter. It was clear he wasn't leaving.

Harry ignored Butch as he looked into Etta's eyes. "I love you, Etta. Whether we have a child now or ten years from now, it doesn't matter. I plan to spend the rest of my life with you, and all our children."

Etta reached over and hugged Harry. "I love you," she whispered against his cheek.

"There we go. Was that so hard?" Butch asked from his spot on the bed beside Etta. When Harry glowered at him, Butch cleared his throat and stood. "My work here is done," he announced. He bent down to place a kiss on Etta's cheek. "Congratulations, dear. I hope you name your son after me."

By the end of March, as the snow began to recede from the canyons, making passage safe again, Etta miscarried. For Etta, it would be the first of many. For the trio of friends, it was the saddest moment ever.

Chapter Thirteen

Pine Creek, MN
1911

Edward and little Harry had enjoyed many adventures in Emily's absence, and Edward had relished every minute. During the day, Harry spent time either helping Gertie clean in the store, making a little pocket money for himself, or at a friend's house, playing. Evenings he spent with Edward, eating at Evy's, playing simple card games, or marbles. Edward read to him from *Tom Sawyer* at bedtime and tucked him into the little cot he'd placed in his bedroom. Harry was a happy, easy child to be with, and Edward was having the time of his life.

On Sunday after church, they had driven out to Edward's property and gone horseback riding. Edward had found a gentle mare for Harry and the boy took to it like he'd been born to ride. They'd had a wonderful time, exploring the fields as they walked the horses around.

At supper time, Edward felt as proud as a new father as he and young Harry walked down the street to Evy's. They filled up on biscuits, roast beef and gravy, and fresh green beans, then downed a piece of apple pie each at Evy's insistence. Evy hovered over Harry as much as Gertie did, each woman enjoying the sweet little boy. Although Edward knew that it was Emily who'd raised such a good child, he liked to think he had some positive influence on the boy, too.

One night, as the two were preparing for bed, Edward realized he needed to get the young child a fresh undershirt from Emily's room. Harry led the way with Edward entering tentatively. This was Emily's private area and he felt like he was trespassing. But Harry had no reservations as he urged Edward to come in and began digging through the bureau for his under things.

Edward glanced around the tidy room, marveling at how Emily had succeeded in making such a compact space cozy. He noticed a small photograph of little Harry on the bureau and picked it up for closer inspection.

"You're such a handsome boy," Edward said, smiling at Harry. "You must take after your mother."

"My mom says I look like my daddy," Harry told him. He found the items he'd been searching for, then glanced up at Edward. "Do you want to see a photo of my daddy? It's right here in this drawer."

Edward was taken aback, not knowing how to respond. He was curious about the man Emily had once loved, but he didn't want to pry. "Perhaps we shouldn't go through your mother's things," he told Harry, but it was too late. Harry had already taken out a small wooden box, a gold key inserted in the tiny lock, and was setting it on the bed. The box was beautiful, with intricate leaf carvings on the top. Edward drew in a breath at the sight of it, as if he were on the brink of a great discovery.

"Harry, I'm not sure..." he began to protest, but Harry opened the box and pulled out a photograph.

"It's okay. My mother lets me look at it anytime I want," Harry told him, innocently. He handed the photograph to Edward.

Edward stared at the picture in his hand. Emily was dressed elegantly in a lovely gown, her hair pulled up in a chignon, standing beside a handsome man in an expensive-looking suit, his top hat in hand. Edward immediately felt inferior. They were a beautiful couple, obviously very well-to-do. On the bottom corner the photo had the marking of a photography studio in New York City. Edward had never been there, let alone had his photograph taken at a studio as nice as this. Emily's life with Harry's father must have been exciting, full of adventure and travel. He couldn't offer Emily any of that.

Harry looked up at Edward, expectantly. Edward tore himself from his thoughts. "It's a lovely photo," he said. "Your father is a very handsome man."

Harry grinned. "My mother says it's their wedding picture. They took it right before they left for another country."

Edward frowned. Another country? Europe, perhaps? He sighed heavily, realizing again he could never give Emily the same things her husband had. He was only a small-town store owner. What could he ever possibly offer her?

Harry had already lost interest in the box and was searching under the bed for a ball that had gone missing. As Edward began to set the photo back in the box, he noticed that there were other photos, as well. Knowing he shouldn't, but unable to stop himself, he lifted those up for closer inspection. There were three postcard-style photos. One pictured Emily, her husband, and another man in front of a rustic log home. The men were sitting in chairs while Emily stood. This confused Edward. The ground around them looked rough, as if they were in the desert.

The other one showed several people in front of the cabin, Emily and her husband included, along with a few horses. The third was of Emily and her husband with their horses, looking as though they were ready to go riding.

There was nothing written on the back of any of these to tell him where they had been taken. They could have been living in Texas, as Emily had stated she'd grown up there. Or it could have been any number of places, he was sure. But little Harry's comment about them leaving the country made him wonder.

Deciding he'd pried enough into Emily's private things, he set to replace the photos. But as he looked into the box, he saw a gold stick pin lying at the bottom of it. He picked this up, noting the small diamond on the top. It was the type of pin a man wore in his necktie, and Edward wondered if it had belonged to her husband. Or maybe it belonged to the other man in the picture. Who was that man and what was his relationship with Emily?

Admonishing himself for thinking such thoughts of the sweetest woman he knew, Edward dropped everything back into the box, locked it, and returned it to the drawer. By now, Harry had retrieved his ball from under the bed and was ready to leave.

That night, long after Harry had been tucked in and Edward lay in his own bed, his thoughts continued to ponder the photographs of Emily's past. She'd openly admitted to him that she'd lived in many different places while with her husband, and he knew she'd gone to a teaching school in Boston. It shouldn't have surprised him that she would have a photo from out east. Yet, she'd also told him her husband had been a rancher, or ranch hand, and that was why they'd lived in so many different areas out west. The photo of them, however, looked like they'd had money. Edward wondered about a ranch hand who'd earned enough for expensive traveling. He fell asleep, finally, after deciding that Emily's past was her own and if he were lucky enough to love her, he would never pry.

Hole-in-the-Wall
September 1897

Harry was still fuming over the botched robbery in June at the bank in Belle Fouche. "How could we have done such a bad job of it?" he complained to Etta for the hundredth time as they sat in their cabin one evening. He had been cleaning his pistols and she'd been enjoying a new book he'd brought her.

Etta sighed and placed her book down in her lap. She'd heard the story of the botched robbery so many times she could recite it in her sleep. No matter how many times she told Harry that it wasn't his fault, or that he should put it behind him, she couldn't seem to keep him from obsessing over it.

She knew that Harry felt like an idiot for having botched the bank robbery just as he had his first train robbery years ago in Malta, Montana. When he worked alongside Butch, robberies went smoothly and the money was good. In April, Butch, Elzy, and Harry had successfully robbed the Pleasant Valley Coal Company in Castle Gate of over $7000: a fine take that was split three ways. But after the robbery, Butch had taken off down to New Mexico and was working for the W S Ranch near Alma. Harry hadn't wanted to leave yet, so he and Etta had stayed at the Hole. When Harvey Logan's cousin, Lonnie, and Flatnose Currie had come to him with a plan to rob the bank in Belle Fouche, Harry had thought it was a good idea. They'd all worked with Butch and knew enough to pull off their own job. Unfortunately, they'd only ridden away with $97—a measly amount for the risk they'd taken.

"That stupid Tommy O'Day and his drinking." Harry continued to rant. "If it hadn't been for him, we'd have had a successful take. He deserved to get captured after what he did."

"Oh, Harry." Etta shook her head. She knew he didn't mean it. But he ignored her and continued his tirade.

"We should never have brought Walt, either. It was a stupid thing putting a seventeen-year-old kid in danger that way. I shouldn't have let Lonnie talk me into it. I was so worried something would happen to the kid, I wasn't thinking straight."

They'd brought Walt Punteney along to be their lookout, but for whatever reason unknown to Etta, O'Day had ended up with the job. Etta had offered to go instead of Walt, but Harry wouldn't hear of it. She thought it had more to do with Lonnie Logan being along than the thought of her being in danger. Lonnie was much like his cousin, Harvey—mean and crude. Both men always leered at Etta, and Harry hated it. Yet, they were usually adept at robberies, so Harry put up with them. Personally, Etta could live without both Logans around. She had been happy to hear that Lonnie and Flatnose Currie had headed off in the opposite direction after the robbery. Unfortunately, Harvey was still around. He and Harry had been spending a lot of time together, which Etta feared was to plan another heist. She'd hoped that the botched attempt on the bank would keep Harry from any more jobs without Butch, but instead it seemed to have spurred him on even more.

"Harry, dear," Etta said in a soothing tone. "We have plenty of money left from the Castle Gate hold up. Why don't we head down to New Mexico and meet up with Butch? We could spend the winter there and the two of you can plan something together. Elzy and Maude are there too, with their new baby girl. It will be like last winter, all of us together, only warmer," she added with a teasing smile.

"Not yet," he replied harshly. "There are some things I want to do before we go on down there."

Etta knew those "things" were to prove he wasn't a total failure without Butch. Damn male ego! But they had more to worry about than that. "Honey," she tried again. "You know as well as I do about the price on your head for the robbery. If you're planning another one so soon, you're sure to get caught. No one will be looking for you in New Mexico."

"Damn wanted posters!" Harry barked, ignoring the rest of what Etta had said. "Paying over six-hundred a head for us and all we got away with were a few measly dollars. Hell, why don't they just give me that money and I'll leave them alone?"

"Or I could just turn you all in and make a hefty profit," Etta joked. "Then I could help you escape."

Harry narrowed his eyes at her. "Very funny."

The sound of boots reverberated on their front porch and a hearty knock shook the door. Harry opened it, letting Harvey in a moment later. Harvey nodded and tipped his hat to Etta, but she didn't like the sly grin on his face. His black hair and thick eyebrows made him look menacing. Or maybe her view of him was biased because she knew the evil he was capable of. He was a killer and made no apologies about it. If it wasn't for his respect for Butch, and for Harry, he'd just as soon kill everyone at a robbery than leave witnesses. Butch didn't allow for any unnecessary gun violence and Harry felt the same way. But if Harvey was left to his own devices, well, she didn't want to think of the consequences.

"We're going to check on the horses," Harry told Etta as he

slipped on his hat and headed out the door with Harvey.

Etta knew differently. More than likely, they were going out to share a smoke and make plans. Harry was being reckless with his life, and it worried Etta.

In early September, Harry, Harvey, and young Walt Punteney rode out of the Hole and up to Red Lodge, Montana to pull another bank job. Harry told Etta that Harvey thought the town marshal there could be easily bribed, and the job would be simple. He promised her that as soon as he came back, they'd pack up and go to New Mexico to spend the winter with Butch. But by the end of September, Harry still hadn't returned to Hole-in-the-Wall.

Pine Creek, MN
October 1911

The morning was crisp and heavy with frost as Edward and little Harry made their way along the boardwalk from Evy's Restaurant to the store. They marveled and laughed at their puffs of breath on the icy air, like two children in the cold for the first time. Edward would never have noticed the frost had it not been for Harry; instead, he would have walked swiftly through the cold, muttering at the early sign of the winter to come. But today, with Harry, frost was a whole new adventure of excitement and fun.

"It looks like you two are enjoying this brisk morning," Ted said as he came upon the pair in front of Edward's store.

Edward reached out and patted the sheriff on the arm in a friendly greeting. "We've had another delicious breakfast at Evy's and now we're off to work, right, Harry?" he said, directing his gaze to the little boy by his side.

Harry nodded his agreement, a broad grin on his face.

"Well, it's a fine thing seeing Pine Creek's businessmen going off to work," Ted said, winking at Harry. He turned back to Edward. "I assume Mrs. Pleasants hasn't returned yet?"

"No, not yet, but we expect her any day now," Edward replied, still cheerful and smiling.

"Hmm. A little odd, don't you think?" the sheriff asked, looking directly at Edward. "She's been gone for over a week now, hasn't she?"

Something in Ted's tone made Edward pause, the smile fading from his lips. He turned to Harry. "Son, why don't you go in and see what Gertie has for you to do today and I'll be there in a moment, all right?"

Harry nodded obediently, waved goodbye to the sheriff, and headed into the store.

"He sure is a fine young boy, isn't he?" Ted asked as he watched Harry go inside.

"Yes, he is." Edward focused on Ted. They had always gotten along well and Edward had never had any reason to think of him as anything but a friend. Just three weeks ago he and Emily had joined Ted and Allison at their home for Sunday dessert. They'd enjoyed themselves very much without any hint of tension throughout the evening. But the tone in his friend's voice just now told Edward something else—perhaps not all was well in the little world he was creating with Harry and Emily. He didn't like feeling that tiny inkling of doubt.

"Who did Mrs. Pleasants go to visit?" Ted asked conversationally. "I forget."

To Edward, however, the question didn't sound friendly. It sounded like the beginning of an interrogation.

"Her husband's aunt. She's ill, and Emily felt she should go see her."

"Ah, yes, of course. Her husband's aunt," Ted said, nodding agreement. "I remember now that Allison told me that. Where does her aunt live?"

Edward bristled and lifted his chin, his gaze on Ted turning hard. "Does it matter?"

"No, not really." Ted cocked one eyebrow at Edward's sharp tone. "Just wondering, that's all."

The two men stared at each other in silence for a moment before Ted smiled warmly and placed his hand on Edward's shoulder. "There's no need to get defensive, Edward. I was only asking, as a friend. You seem to have grown quite fond of Mrs. Pleasants and little Harry. I don't want to see you get hurt."

Edward continued to study the sheriff as he tried to unravel what his friend was really trying to tell him. His thoughts went back to the photograph of Emily and her late husband and the uneasy feeling he'd felt while looking at it. Did Ted know something he didn't? His irritation increased.

"Why would you think I'd get hurt?" he asked, his voice barely disguising his irritation. "If you know something I don't, why don't you just tell me?"

Ted maintained his calm demeanor as he removed his hand from Edward's shoulder. "I'm just looking out for a good friend, that's all," he said calmly. "I didn't mean to suggest anything other than concern."

Edward took in a deep breath and tried to relax. He wasn't sure why he suspected Ted meant more by what he'd said, but the thought lingered long after he'd stepped into the store and even after he'd gone to bed that night.

Chapter Fourteen

Pine Creek, MN
1911

Emily returned to Pine Creek feeling more unsure than when she'd left. She had thought she'd find answers at Hole-in-the-Wall, but instead, she'd learned very little. Butch's name resurfacing in the news told her that the Pinkerton men were still looking for the three of them. But if Butch and Harry had died as everyone believed, why would a detective agency as distinguished as the Pinkertons' still be searching for them? And there had been no real sighting of Harry or Butch. She was desperate to find answers. She had been living her life on the edge, constantly wondering what had become of the two men. It was time for her to know the truth, so she could move on.

Emily realized it would be difficult for Harry or Butch to find her. Harry's brother, Elwood, had known she was at the convent, but she hadn't written to inform him about her move to Minnesota. It would have been too risky. She knew that his mail was sometimes seized by the Pinkertons, so there was no way she could communicate with him. The nuns were the only people who knew where she'd gone. She could only hope that if either Harry or Butch were alive, they'd do everything possible to track her down.

Emily was tired of running. She wanted to settle down and live a quiet life. She could do that in Pine Creek. But knowing that the Pinkertons were still showing the photo of her, and actually searching for her, made her even more uneasy, especially with Sheriff Neilson acting suspicious. She'd have to be even more careful about everything she said and did.

Winter arrived and the days grew shorter as snow fell on the plains. Emily threw herself into her life in Pine Creek, teaching, working in the store, taking care of Harry, and spending time with Edward. Now that it was too cold to sit on the porch in the evenings, they had taken to sitting around the pot-bellied stove in the store. They would talk about their day or sometimes play a hand or two of cards. Emily was a mean poker player, as Edward soon discovered, and they had great fun playing for pennies. Since Emily had returned from her trip, there had been no moments like the one they'd shared on the porch before she'd left. They enjoyed a comfortable companionship together, but with no intimate gestures. Edward hadn't initiated a kiss or even holding her hand, and Emily wasn't sure if she was relieved or disappointed. She had reservations of her own for starting a serious relationship. Yet, she was attracted to Edward. She wished she could have been honest with him and explain her situation. He may not have understood, but at least it would be out in the open. The unspoken truths were what held her back from letting him know she would accept his advances.

Emily also visited with Allison as much as possible. She was growing larger each day and was experiencing a difficult pregnancy. The baby was due in February, but Allison continued to have morning sickness and Dr. Jenson insisted she rest. Even though many of the town women visited to keep her company, it seemed Allison enjoyed Emily's company the most. Emily brought her treats she thought would settle her stomach and they drank tea and knitted or worked on needlepoint if Allison felt up to it. Emily always made sure to visit right after school before Sheriff Neilson returned from work for the day. The less she encountered the sheriff, the better.

One Saturday afternoon in early December, Gertie, Emily, and Edward were working in the store. There had been a heavy snowfall earlier that week, but the past two days were sunny and warmer. Many of the families from the surrounding farms had come into town to shop for necessities and to visit among friends. Despite the cold days and abundance of snow, customers seemed to be in high spirits, perhaps anticipating the upcoming holidays or because the fresh snow always looked beautiful on the plains. The harvest season had been a good one and money was plentiful, allowing the farmers to indulge in purchases they might otherwise not have been able to afford.

All the children, Harry included, were at the church with Pastor Johnson and his wife preparing for the holiday play to be performed the Sunday before Christmas.

All day Emily and Gertie bustled about the store helping women pick out fabric for new winter dresses, staples for their larder, and special gifts for their children. Edward worked hard too, helping the men with such necessities as razors, new winter caps and gloves, and ammunition for their hunting rifles. It had been a prosperous day and the till was full of cash. As the afternoon slowed down, Emily went to the back room to find the broom to sweep the store while Gertie helped the last of the customers.

Hearing the bell on the front door jingle, Emily pushed aside the curtain that separated the back room from the store to see if Gertie needed help. What she saw turned her blood cold. Gertie was standing behind the counter looking directly at two young men who had pistols trained directly at her. Emily quickly closed the curtain, then inched it aside to peek out and see where Edward was. He was standing next to the door between the store and the bank on the far left of Gertie. One of the men had turned his pistol in Edward's direction.

"Don't either of you move or you'll both be dead," a scruffy, dark-haired man said. The scraggly-looking blond man standing next to him snickered.

It only took an instant for Emily to recognize the second man as the same one who had accosted her at the barn dance a few weeks before.

"Give us the money from the drawer, old lady," the dark-haired man said to Gertie. "Then you," he motioned to Edward, "will take us through that door to the bank and give us what you have in there."

Gertie glared at the man and didn't move. Edward told her to place the money into a bag and give it to them.

Emily watched the scene as she contemplated what she should do. She could run out the back door and go in search of the sheriff, but that might take too long. The two men looked nervous and were certainly not experienced. Emily knew robbers, and these two didn't look like they knew what they were doing. They were acting cocky, but they were also sweating and fidgeting. They had even been so stupid to not cover their faces. If she waited too long, they might shoot Edward and Gertie out of fear of being recognized. But if she approached them, they might shoot just the same.

After contemplating the predicament, Emily made up her mind. She quietly reached up to the top of the cabinet and took down the Colt .45 pistol that Edward had shown her on her first day of work. She clicked open the cylinder to make sure it was loaded then quietly snapped it shut. Steeling herself, she stepped through the curtains, the gun behind her back.

The two men saw her instantly but didn't move. They looked slightly amused.

"Well, if it isn't the teacher lady," the scraggly blond man said as Emily slowly made her way toward the front of the store.

Edward's eyes grew wide as he watched Emily approach the front counter. "Emily, no. Stay back!" he yelled.

But she continued to walk slowly up toward the front.

"What's going on here?" she asked, looking directly at the men. "What do you want?"

"Stay where you are," the dark-haired man yelled at Emily.

Emily continued to move toward the counter. If she could get there before they realized she had a gun, she and Gertie could use it for cover. Edward was far enough away to have time to duck behind one of the shelves if gunfire erupted. She prayed it wouldn't come to that.

"Aw, it's only the teacher lady," the blond guy said, as if her presence wasn't anything to fear. "What's she going to do, throw a book at us?" He laughed at his own joke but his partner didn't join in.

Emily made her way to the counter and stopped. Gertie looked over at her, then she gave Emily a slight nod. She had seen the gun in Emily's hand. Unfortunately, Edward had seen the gun, too.

"No, Emily," he said quietly, shaking his head.

"That's enough!" the dark-haired man yelled. Sweat dripped

down his face. "Give us the money now!"

Slowly, Emily raised the pistol in front of her, pointing it at the blond man. "I don't think so," she said. "Leave now and I won't shoot your friend." She nodded to Gertie, who seemed to understand and dropped behind the counter for protection.

Both men gaped at Emily. Neither seemed to know what to do until the blond man began to snicker then break out into laughter. "Oh, please," he bellowed. "She's a teacher, not a gunfighter. We got nothing to be afraid of."

The dark-haired man relaxed enough to snicker too. It was in that moment that Emily aimed and fired. In an instant, the pistol was shot out of the blond man's hand and Emily's gun was pointing directly at his partner's heart.

"Drop it!" Emily said, deadly serious.

His eyes grew wide and his hand was shaking.

"She shot me! The teacher lady shot me!" the blond guy yelled as he grabbed his hand and jumped up and down. "She shot clear through my hand," he whined to his friend. He seemed so dumbfounded by the fact that Emily had shot the gun out of his hand that he didn't even think to pick it up off the floor.

He wasn't the only one who was startled. Edward stood rooted to his spot, his mouth hanging open.

"Shoot her!" the blond guy cried. But his friend didn't look too confident that he could shoot her before she killed him.

"Drop it!" Emily ordered again, this time pulling back the hammer. That single click echoed throughout the room.

The dark-haired man glanced sideways at his friend, then back at Emily. What he saw in her eyes must have made him believe she would shoot him without regret. He dropped his gun on the floor and raised both of his hands. "Okay, okay. Don't shoot."

"What the hell are you doing?" the blond guy yelled. "What's wrong with you?"

"Shut up," his partner yelled back.

"But she shot me," the blond man whined.

While the two were arguing, Emily quickly walked around the counter and kicked their guns away, then headed back behind the counter again.

"Gertie, will you please get Sheriff Neilson?" Emily asked softly.

Gertie, who'd been behind the counter the entire time, stood up and nodded. She looked at the men in front of her, then back at Emily and grinned, but said nothing as she stepped around the counter and hurried out the front door.

"Edward, would you please pick up their guns?" Emily asked, her eyes never leaving the two men in front of her.

Edward moved forward slowly, still looking stunned by what he'd witnessed. He picked up the guns and went to stand beside Emily. The blond man was still whining about his hand and the other man was telling him to shut up.

"Here," Emily said to Edward, handing him the Colt. "I think it would be better if you were holding this when the sheriff comes in."

Edward took it, still looking confused.

Emily turned and walked stiffly to the back room, disappearing behind the curtain. Once out of view, she collapsed into a chair, relieved that all had ended well.

* * *

Emily calmly sat across from Sheriff Neilson in his office. The sun was down, and evening had settled in as the sheriff stared at her from behind his desk. Dr. Jenson had already come and gone, having cleaned and bandaged the young man's hand as the would-be robber complained the entire time about being shot by the teacher lady. Emily had walked in as the doctor was leaving and he'd winked mischievously at her while tipping his hat in greeting. Sheriff Neilson had frowned and once again reminded the doctor not to repeat that Emily, not Edward, had been the one who'd shot the man.

"I'm no gossip," the doctor had shot back, indignantly, but the smirk on his face told Emily that he'd found great pleasure over her shooting the robber.

Gertie and Edward had been in the office first, repeating their stories of what had occurred in the store. Then the sheriff had asked Edward to send Emily over. Harry had returned from the church by then, so Gertie offered to take him home for a late supper, much to Emily's relief. Now she sat, stiff-backed, her hands folded in her lap, waiting for Sheriff Neilson to speak.

From inside the cell room, separated from the office by a closed door, she could still hear the blond guy whimpering. His partner kept telling him to shut up. Sheriff Neilson had told them both to settle down and be quiet before he'd sat down.

The sheriff cleared his throat and finally looked her in the eyes. "I'm told you fired the gun at the robber." He didn't look as amused as the doctor had been.

"Yes," Emily answered.

"That was a mighty good shot, considering the circumstances. Weren't you afraid?"

She gazed calmly at the sheriff. "No."

"I didn't think so." He picked up a folder and placed it on top of the pile of papers on his desk. He opened it and lifted out a photograph, setting it in front of her.

"I know who you are," Sheriff Neilson stated. "I thought I recognized you, but now I have the proof." He lifted another sheet of paper from the folder and placed it beside the photo. It was a wanted poster with three smaller photos and descriptions on it of Butch Cassidy, the Sundance Kid, and Etta Place. "Do you recognize these?"

Emily stared down at the photo, and then at the wanted poster. A chill crept up her spine as her past stared back at her. She'd known this day would come, had known it for a very long time. Yet she was still not prepared for it. Remaining calm was the only way she knew how to get through this. She looked up at the sheriff. "I'm not that woman."

He raised one eyebrow. "Then, who are you?"

"I'm Emily Pleasants, teacher, mother, and widow. Nothing more."

Sheriff Neilson's face creased. "How can you tell me you aren't the woman in this photograph? Do you honestly think I believe you?"

Emily's heart was racing and her mind was too. *It can't end like this*, she thought. *I'm not the same woman who posed for that photograph. I can't lose everything now, not after all I've been through.* Yet, on the surface, she remained calm. She sat silently, not answering the sheriff's question. Her silence seemed to irritate him more.

"Don't tell me you aren't this woman," he repeated, pointing to the photograph. "You were younger, yes, but you've hardly changed at all. This is you, standing next to Harry Longabaugh. And it's a known fact that he's the Sundance Kid. You're a wanted criminal, just for your association with him. Don't deny it."

Emily remained silent, neither admitting to nor denying his words. She didn't know what to say with the evidence sitting right in front of her.

Sheriff Neilson shook his head. "I received this information a few days ago and wasn't sure how to approach you. But now, what happened at the store today is even more proof to me that you are Etta Place. No regular proper, widowed schoolteacher could have so accurately shot a gun out of a man's hand like you did today."

"As I've said before, I was raised on a ranch in Texas and my father taught me to shoot…" Emily began calmly but was cut off by the sheriff.

"Oh, yes. I've heard this all before and I'm not buying it. You seem to have a good explanation for everything. Like why that man in there recognized you a few weeks ago, and now why you're capable of shooting like a gunslinger."

"It's all true," Emily said quietly. "As I keep saying, I am exactly who I say I am."

Sheriff Neilson stood, kicked his chair back, and began pacing behind his desk. After a moment he stopped and looked down at her.

She was looking straight in front of her, head held high, her hands folded primly in her lap. With her hair pulled up on her head and her starched shirtwaist tucked neatly into her skirt, she looked exactly like the picture of innocence she wanted him to believe she was.

"I should arrest you right now," he stated. "I should handcuff you and take you on the next train to Chicago and turn you over to the Pinkerton Agency where they can question you about your activities over the past few years. According to this poster, I have the right to do that."

Emily lifted her face and looked into his eyes. "It would accomplish nothing. There is nothing I can tell them that they don't already know."

"Then you admit you're Etta Place?" he asked, looking surprised.

"I admit only to the fact that I'm Emily Pleasants and I'm exactly who I've said I am. I've never once lied about where I grew up. I've never lied about where I've lived or that I'm a widow and a schoolteacher. There is nothing more to tell."

Sheriff Neilson sighed. "Emily, you named your son Harry. Is that after his father? And what is little Harry's middle name? Robert, after Butch Cassidy? Or maybe LeRoy, Cassidy's middle name. You didn't do a very good job of covering your trail if you were trying to hide from your past."

Emily knew silence was her only salvation. One wrong word and it was all over.

Sheriff Neilson sat again and stared across the desk at her. "I know what I *should* do. As a lawman, and an ex-Pinkerton detective, I should turn you in. Unfortunately, it isn't as easy as that."

Emily glanced up at him, puzzled.

"My wife, bless her heart, thinks the world of you," he continued. "She actually believes you were sent from Heaven to help her through this difficult time. And Edward, my closest friend, is in love with you."

Emily's eyes widened at the mention of Edward.

Sheriff Neilson continued speaking. "Don't look so surprised. I can see how he feels about you. It's written all over his face. Then there's Gertie and Evy, who both treat you like a daughter, and the pastor and his wife, who are both charmed by you, and the students and their parents. Good God, even Eb the blacksmith thinks you're a saint just because you smile and wave at him every morning when you pass his shop. How the hell am I supposed to arrest you when everyone in town adores you?"

Emily controlled her expression even though she was

astonished by what he'd said. She hadn't expected this. Lawmen almost always did what they were sworn to do. Could she actually believe he might not arrest her?

After a moment's pause, the sheriff sighed. "It would break Allison's heart if she knew who you really were, and there's always the chance she just wouldn't believe it. In her delicate condition right now, I can't risk upsetting her. And Edward, what would I tell him? He wouldn't believe it either. Hell, the entire town wouldn't believe it. So, where does that leave me? And then there's your son, Harry. What would happen to him if I suddenly arrest you and you ended up in jail for years? I may be a lawman, but I'm not heartless."

Emily's heart ached at his mention of little Harry. It had always been her greatest fear, being recognized and losing Harry. That was why she'd moved halfway across the country to a place where she was sure the names Butch Cassidy and the Sundance Kid were not as familiar as they'd been throughout the western states. Yet, by the most horrible twist of fate, she had ended up in a town where the sheriff was an ex-Pinkerton agent. She could only pray that her actions since coming to town were enough to save her and Harry.

She watched as Sheriff Neilson seemed to struggle with his decision.

"I can't arrest you," he finally said.

Emily let out the breath she'd been holding but remained composed.

"But I'm not forgetting who you are, either. If I suspect for one moment that something isn't right, I'll arrest you on the spot."

Emily dropped her eyes to her lap, afraid he'd see her relieved expression.

Sheriff Neilson watched her a moment before adding, "I don't suppose you'd voluntarily answer any questions about your past so I might share information with the agency?"

Emily lifted her eyes to his. "As I've told you before, Sheriff, I don't know anything that would be of any help."

He sighed. "I figured you'd say that, but it was worth a try. Also, I told Gertie and Edward not to spread the word that it was you who shot the robber. I figured it might upset some of the parents if they knew you were such an expert gunslinger." He actually grinned at this as Emily nodded agreement. Then, looking more sternly at her as she rose to leave, he added, "Don't try leaving town. No more secret trips off to see some supposed relatives. I'll keep your secret for the time being as long as you remain in town, but if you try to escape, the deal is over."

"I've nowhere else to go, Sheriff," Emily told him honestly. "Pine Creek is my home now."

* * *

Emily felt weary as she stepped quietly out of her room and closed the door. After speaking to the sheriff, she'd gone to Gertie's to pick up Harry and put him to bed. Gertie must have seen how exhausted Emily was so she didn't ask how the meeting had gone. She'd also had the good sense not to mention the shooting in front of Harry. Emily thanked Gertie for taking care of her son and the two women hugged, no words necessary.

Now, with Harry tucked safely in bed and sound asleep, Emily walked down the hallway with the intent of speaking to Edward. She had hardly gone two steps when he appeared at the top of the stairs and stopped short, obviously surprised to see her standing there.

"I was just on my way down to see you," Emily said, noticing the frown on Edward's face.

"Oh, well, I was just about to retire for the night." He walked past her toward his door.

Emily reached out and touched his arm. "I thought you might want to talk about today."

Edward's eyes went to her hand on his arm and back to her face. "I'd rather not. It's been a long day."

Emily removed her hand. She couldn't tell if the look in Edward's eyes was contempt or disgust. Either way, she felt as if she'd been slapped. "I'm sorry if what I did today upset you. I didn't know what else to do."

A deep crease appeared between his eyes. "Who asked you to do anything? Why would you step in like that and risk everyone's lives? It was only money, Emily. Who cares if they'd taken it? You could have gotten us all killed."

"I was afraid, Edward. They might have killed you and Gertie anyway. I couldn't risk that. I couldn't stand the thought of losing anyone else." Emily searched his eyes for understanding, but all she saw was anger.

"When I saw you come out of the back room and walk up to the counter, my heart nearly stopped. I was so afraid of losing you. But then, when you shot that man, so steady, so precisely, I couldn't believe my eyes. And the hard, cold look in your eyes, that astounded me. I knew, in that instant, that you were capable of shooting the other robber dead without any qualms. I could hardly believe what I was seeing. I felt like I was looking at a stranger." He shook his head, his expression pained.

"Edward, please…" Emily began, but Edward stopped her.

"No, Emily." He looked her in the eye. "I thought I knew you. I even thought I might be in love with you. But today, everything changed. I'm sorry, but I don't feel as if I know you at all."

He turned away and opened his door, stepping through it without another word. And as the door closed between them, Emily's heart broke.

Chapter Fifteen

Hole-in-the-Wall
October 1897

Etta was scared. She hadn't heard a word from Harry or any of the group for over a month and she feared the worst. She visited her friends, Joshua and Erma Hoffman, who owned a cattle ranch in the Hole, to see if they had heard anything. The couple hadn't, but Joshua offered to ride into town and see if he could find out any information.

Etta loved visiting the Hoffmans and how warm and welcoming their home was. The older couple was honest and law abiding, but befriended the outlaws as long as they behaved themselves. Many of the outlaws, Butch and Harry included, helped the Hoffmans from time to time around the ranch. Everyone seemed to like the older couple and in return, they were always happy to offer a warm meal or some cheerful banter around the fireplace. The local outlaws would never think to steal from Joshua and Erma, nor would the couple ever betray them to the law.

Erma kept Etta busy helping her prepare supper then

showing her a new crochet stitch she'd learned from one of the other ladies in the Hole. They talked about past suppers and barn dances with the locals and how the Hole seemed to be less and less busy with activity. Etta appreciated Erma's attempt to divert her worried thoughts, but by the time Joshua came back, Etta couldn't contain her nervousness any longer.

"The shopkeeper in town had a recent copy of the newspaper from the Black Hills area. He let me have it." Joshua handed the paper to Etta. "I'm afraid there's no mention of any of the boys' names in it, but there is mention of some men being captured."

Etta searched the section of the paper where Joshua had pointed to and quickly read the print. The paper reported that three men had been captured north of Lavina, Montana and were suspected of being connected to the Belle Fouche Bank robbery in June. The men had been sent to Deadwood, South Dakota for trial. The names of the three men were reported as Frank and Thomas Jones and Charley Frost. They were being held with a bail of $10,000 each. Etta noted that the paper had been printed on October 13th, only a few days before.

"Does that tell you anything?" Erma asked, obviously seeing the crestfallen look on Etta's face.

Etta nodded. Harry sometimes used the alias of Frank Jones when he was in a situation where he didn't want to be identified. She knew now that all three men had been captured. What she didn't know was if any of them had been shot or hurt and when they would be tried for their crime.

Not wanting to involve the Hoffmans any more than she already had, Etta thanked them for their help and hurried back to her cabin. She needed time to think—to come up with a plan on how to help Harry. She didn't have $10,000 to bail him out, or the $30,000 it would take to bail out the whole group. Etta wished with all her heart that Butch was here. He would know exactly what to do.

She decided to talk with Flatnose Currie about their options. He had been involved in the Belle Fouche robbery but had been lucky enough not to be captured. She knew he was back in the Hole, so she rushed over to his cabin. To her surprise, Lonnie Logan was there, too.

Etta could handle Flatnose. He was always polite to her and she never felt threatened by him as she did with the Logans. He was taller than her by several inches, and would have been handsome if it hadn't been for his pug nose, thus the nickname Flatnose. Lonnie, on the other hand, was short with dark hair and piercing eyes that stared right through you. His upper front teeth stood out, making his already ungainly looks worse. Both men gaped at Etta as she entered the cabin.

Etta ignored their stares and squared her shoulders in defiance to the fear she felt in Lonnie's presence. She was thankful she was wearing pants and a flannel shirt instead of a dress. She rarely wore dresses while at the Hole because it wasn't practical. Today, it gave her more confidence being dressed like a man. She was also glad she'd strapped on her pistol before leaving the cabin.

She handed the newspaper to Flatnose. "Harry and the other men have been caught," she stated. "They're being held in Deadwood."

Flatnose and Lonnie quickly scanned the newspaper article before turning their attention back to Etta. "I know Sundance uses the name Frank Jones," Flatnose said. "But who are the others?"

Etta was stunned he didn't know who'd been with Harry, but

then again, Flatnose and Lonnie hadn't been in the Hole when the guys left. Since Lonnie was Harvey's cousin and Flatnose was a good friend of Harvey, she'd just assumed they knew he was with Harry. "Harvey is with them, and so is Walt," she told them.

Lonnie scowled and Flatnose's eyes widened. "They've caught Harvey?" Flatnose asked. "He wasn't even involved in the robbery."

Etta nodded. "I'm guessing they have him confused with Lonnie. There was a big reward on each outlaw's head, so I'm sure the men who caught them didn't care if he was the right man or not."

Lonnie glowered at Etta. "What do you suppose we're gonna do about it? Just walk in there and let them out of jail? We were involved in that robbery. We can't go anywhere near that place or we'll get caught, too."

Flatnose gave Lonnie a sideways glance and ignored what he'd said. "I'm not sure what we can do, Etta. I'd like to help the guys get out of there, but I'm not sure we can get away with it."

Etta spoke directly to Flatnose. "We have to try. We can't just leave them there. If Butch was here, he'd go help them."

"Well, Butch ain't here and we sure ain't going to help them," Lonnie said.

"Shut up, Lonnie," Flatnose growled. He turned back to Etta. "What do you have in mind?"

Etta sighed. She was thankful that Flatnose was on her side. "I don't have a plan. I was hoping you two could help me figure out what to do." Lonnie snorted and Flatnose glared at him.

Lonnie looked Etta up and down, a sly grin appearing on his face. "What are you willing to do for us if we help you?" he asked, his intentions obvious.

Her blood boiling, Etta scowled at Lonnie. "It's not me you're helping, you idiot. It's your cousin and your friends. You'd want them to get you out of jail if you were in there."

"Forget it." Lonnie turned away.

"I'm not sure we can do anything," Flatnose told Etta, though he looked regretful about refusing to help her.

"Fine, I'll get them out by myself." Etta spun on her heal and headed for the door. "I'll be sure to let your cousin know you didn't give a damn about him, Lonnie," she threw over her shoulder as her hand reached for the handle.

"Wait a minute, Etta," Flatnose called out to her. Etta slowly turned and faced the two outlaws. She knew that neither man wanted to face the wrath of Harvey Logan if he found out they hadn't at least tried to help him escape.

"We'll help you," he told her. "Right, Lonnie?"

Lonnie curled his lip up into a snarl. "Fine."

"Good." Inwardly, Etta was relieved she didn't have to go alone. "Be ready to leave tomorrow morning."

"Tomorrow?" Lonnie asked. "But you don't even have a plan yet."

"We'll come up with one along the way." Etta went out the door, a satisfied smile on her lips.

Deadwood, South Dakota
October 1897

The unlikely threesome left early the next morning. They brought along three extra horses, complete with saddles, bedrolls, and supplies, for the jailed men to use. Etta had learned from Harry the importance of being prepared. She hadn't wanted to leave it to chance that they'd be able to buy horses along the way.

Traveling was slow with the extra horses and it took them longer than they'd anticipated. Etta lifted the collar of her sheepskin jacket against the bitterly cold wind. They traveled the road to Newcastle, then up into South Dakota toward Lead and into the Black Hills. The scenery was beautiful, but frigid, with a threat of snow. Between Lead and Deadwood, the travelers found a ranch where the owner allowed them to camp on their property for a few days.

Etta was relieved when they finally set up camp—a small tent for her and a larger one for the men. She'd worn men's clothing, and had tucked her hair up under her cowboy hat so she could pass as a man from a distance. She was grateful that Lonnie hadn't bothered her during the trip and she knew that Flatnose was responsible for that. Harvey Logan looked up to Flatnose as a mentor and had even taken the name Kid Curry as a tribute to him. Because of Harvey's great respect for Flatnose, Lonnie also held Flatnose in high esteem. It also didn't hurt that Harry had a reputation for being highly protective of Etta. If anything had happened to her during the trip, there would have been hell to pay when Harry found out.

The threesome had already hit a bump in the road when they'd talked to the rancher about camping on his land. He mentioned that Deadwood's jail was holding four of the men involved in the Belle Fouche bank robbery. That meant Tommy O'Day was also in jail and they only had three extra horses. Somehow, they'd have to find another horse and saddle before they could get the men out.

Since Flatnose and Lonnie couldn't risk being seen in town, Etta was the only one who could scout out their chances of getting a note to the jailed men. Their plan was simple: they would leave the horses somewhere near the jail so the men would have them to escape on. The hard part was finding a way to get them out of jail, undetected.

Luck was on Etta's side when she rode into Deadwood on October 30th. She found the jail easily and the prisoners were outside, locked up in an exercise pen made of wooden stakes and heavy metal fencing. If they were out every day, it would be easy to pass a note to them.

She didn't make contact with the men, only watched them for a time to make sure they were all okay. They looked scruffy and dirty, but at least no one appeared to have been shot. She did notice a bandage around Harvey's left wrist, but that was the only markings of a wound that she saw. Relief flooded though her. Everyone was well and accounted for. Now, all she had to do was help them escape.

Etta made her way to the dry goods store and purchased a bedroll and food supplies. No one thought it was unusual for a woman to be dressed in masculine clothing, especially since one of their most famous residents, Calamity Jane, had often dressed that way. When the storekeeper asked Etta where she was heading, she simply told him that she and her two brothers were delivering trained horses to a rancher near Rapid City. It was a good story and explained why they had so many horses with them in case anyone became suspicious.

Etta returned to camp and explained the situation to Flat-nose and Lonnie. That evening, Flatnose purchased a horse and an older saddle from the rancher. He'd used the same story as Etta and explained they needed another horse to carry supplies. They all agreed that Etta should go into town the next day to find a secluded place near the jail to tie up the four horses and give a note to the men. This would give the men a day to figure out how to get past the guards.

In town the next day, Etta found a spot about a quarter of a mile behind the jail that would be perfect for posting the horses. After that, she tied up her own horse a short distance from the jail and casually walked over to the exercise yard. Just as the day before, the men were outside. Harvey and Harry were standing near the fence and the other men were sitting on a bench across the yard. Etta watched Harry, thankful he was unharmed. For weeks she'd worried he'd been shot, or worse, killed. But he was safe, albeit in jail.

As she stood there, trying to figure a way to casually walk up and talk to the men, Harvey yelled out to her, "Hey, mister. Got a smoke?"

Relieved for an excuse to approach the them, Etta lowered her head, shading her face with the brim of her hat, and sauntered over to the fence. When she drew close to Harvey, she tilted her head back a bit so he could see her. Her unique lavender-blue eyes gave her away instantly and he smiled wide with recognition.

"Frank," Harvey said, nodding his head in Etta's direction. "Someone's here to see you."

Harry, alias Frank, glanced over and stared directly into her eyes. "Etta," he whispered, looking startled. "What are you doing here?"

Etta didn't answer. She only grinned slyly and passed him a small, rolled up piece of paper through the wire fence. Then she quickly turned and strode away before anyone saw her.

On October 31st at 9:00 p.m. as Sheriff John Marshall and his wife were returning the prisoners from the exercise yard to their jail cells, the convicts knocked the couple down and locked them up instead. There were five inmates in all, the four bank robbers and another prisoner, who escaped. The four horses with supplies that Etta had posted a quarter of a mile away aided in their escape. Tom O'Day and Walt Punteney headed north toward Spearfish while Harvey and Harry rode southwest. Just outside of Lead, Harvey and Harry met up with Lonnie, Flatnose, and Etta.

Harry took a precious moment to pull Etta off her horse and swing her in circles in a bear hug. "You crazy woman! What were you thinking?" he asked, trying to look angry without success.

"I couldn't afford bail," she said, a wide grin on her face.

Harry laughed and kissed her with his scruffy, bearded face. But she didn't mind, she was happy to have her Harry back.

"Now can we go to New Mexico?" she asked, hoping he'd had enough excitement.

"Now we can go to New Mexico," he told her softly. They got back on their horses and headed out, an hour ahead of the posse. O'Day and Punteney were recaptured near Spearfish, but the posse never caught up to Etta, Harry, and the other men.

Chapter Sixteen

Pine Creek, MN
1911

E mily wasn't used to the men in her life treating her any other way than as an equal. Her father had taught her to ride and shoot, and Harry and Butch had included her the same as they would have any man. If an extra gun was needed, or another hand with a job, Emily had helped out. Even the other men at the Hole had treated her with respect. So the fact that Edward was angry because she had taken the initiative to stop the store robbery completely puzzled Emily.

Several times, she had tried to bring up the incident with Edward, but each time he found an excuse not to talk to her. He also made a point not to be alone with her. They no longer ate breakfast or supper together at the restaurant. Edward showed up for breakfast after she and little Harry had left for school in the morning and wasn't in the restaurant when they went there for supper. A few times, Harry asked why Mr. Sheridan no longer ate with them. The only excuse Emily could come up with was he was busy with his duties at the store and the bank.

She was hurt that Edward ignored her, but even more upset for little Harry. The boy had started looking up to Edward as a father-figure, and now he didn't understand why Edward didn't spend any time with him. Edward did continue to drive all of them, including Gertie, to church each Sunday, but the drives were filled with uncomfortable silence. Emily was at a loss what to do.

* * *

"Why are you still upset with Emily for shooting that robber?" Gertie asked Edward one afternoon when she'd cornered him in the back of the store. "It's over and done with. Don't you know how much you're hurting Emily?"

Edward looked down at his spitfire employee, surprised. He hadn't expected to be confronted about his relationship with Emily this way, especially by Gertie.

"Gertie, you don't understand…" he said, but she interrupted him.

"Yes, I do understand. I understand perfectly. You're letting your male pride get in the way of having a serious relationship with Emily." Gertie paused a moment and stared up into Edward's shocked face. "Oh, don't act so surprised, Edward. I've known you a long time and I've never seen you react to a woman the way you have to Emily. Yes, she shot the robber and saved the day and made you feel less than a man. You've had your time to pout and grumble about it and lick your wounds, but it's high time you stopped."

Edward stared down into Gertie's bright blue eyes that, at the moment, seemed to be spitting fire. All of his initial shock at Gertie's words vanished, leaving him deflated. "Gertie, it's not my ego that's in the way. That day showed me a side of Emily I didn't know existed. I feel as if I hardly know her."

Gertie's expression softened and she reached up and touched Edward's arm. "We all have sides to our personalities that others never see," she told him. "Accepting the whole person is what is important. Accepting the good with the bad. All I know, Edward, is that ever since Emily came to town, you've changed. I haven't seen you this happy in years. Not since before Lily died. Emily is good for you. Can't you see that?"

Edward knew her words were true and he nodded his head in agreement. But still, he was torn. "I just need some time to sort things out."

Gertie shook her head slowly. "Don't wait too long, Edward, or you may lose the best thing that has ever happened to you."

As Gertie walked through the curtain into the store, Edward pondered her words. And deep within his heart, he knew she was right.

W S Ranch, New Mexico
1897-98

As promised, Harry took Etta to Alma, New Mexico to spend the winter. Harry signed on at the W S Ranch to work alongside his friends, Butch and Elzy Lay, and Harvey Logan also came down to work that winter. The ranch owner, Captain William French, knew nothing about their outlaw history and trusted Butch with the hiring of hands because they were always good workers. When Butch and his men were working the ranch, they never lost any of the herd to cattle rustling.

The men used aliases while working there: Butch was Jim Lowe, Harry was Harry Place, and because Etta was believed to be Harry's wife, she was known as Etta Place. The owner offered Harry and Etta a small cabin on the ranch, and because he believed that Butch was Etta's brother, he thought nothing of the three sharing the space together. Etta and Harry shared the one bedroom while Butch slept on a bedroll on the living room floor. Elzy and Maude and their baby girl, Marvel, shared the cabin next door. Etta loved having Maude and the baby around. It felt like a repeat of the past winter when they'd all had such a good time together at the Roost.

The first few weeks were filled with settling in, get-togethers, and a lot of laughter. Etta spent time fixing up the little cabin, adding curtains to the windows, a soft coverlet for the bed, and rugs and pillows around the main room. All her little touches made it feel like a home. Harry had never been stingy with money and let Etta spend what she wanted on making the cabin cozy.

The men worked long hours each day and in the evening, Etta always had supper waiting for them. Many times, Elzy and Maude brought the baby over and the group enjoyed lively card games of 21, gin poker, and poker. Etta became especially competent in poker and often won the small pots of pennies that the group played for. Thankfully, Harvey kept his distance and lived in the bunk quarters with the other ranch hands and spent his free time drinking and gambling in nearby Alma. It was a wonderful time for Etta and she enjoyed the home-like atmosphere of being with Harry and Butch and their friends.

The more time Etta spent around Maude and baby Marvel, the more she longed for having a child with Harry. But when she brought up the possibility, Harry's answer was, "Someday, Etta. But not now." Although she understood their current lifestyle was not the best for raising a family, she hoped that one day that would change. Even though she'd willingly followed Harry, knowing he was an outlaw, Etta had thought that someday he'd grow tired of running and want to settle down. Unfortunately, that wasn't going to be anytime soon. As the months passed, Harry became increasingly restless and irritable. He began talking about planning a new robbery, but Butch wasn't ready to plot a new heist yet.

"It's best if we lay low a while longer," Butch explained. Harry was having none of it. When Elzy agreed with Butch, Harry began meeting with Harvey about planning a job. He spent more time at the bar in Alma, drinking and working on a plan. Etta tried to persuade him to wait until Butch was ready, but Harry wouldn't listen.

"I don't always have to do what Butch wants," he'd say angrily.

Etta was confused by Harry's sudden change in behavior. She knew he could be surly at times, but he usually didn't overindulge in alcohol or go against Butch. One evening, while she and Butch were alone in the cabin, she asked him if he knew what was happening with Harry.

"He's just trying to stretch his wings," Butch told her.

She knew Harry still smarted from the two failed robberies he'd pulled without Butch, but she didn't understand why he felt the need to prove himself. Butch thought of Harry as a friend and equal partner. It made no sense to her.

Etta also didn't like the dark side that came out in Harry when he drank. He hadn't drunk much in the two years she'd known him, so she'd had no experience with how harsh he could be.

One evening, he came home from drinking with Harvey and

scoffed at Etta and Butch, who were having a lively game of gin poker.

"You two are getting awfully chummy," he said, slurring. "Why don't you sleep with Butch since you're so close to him?" he threw out at Etta, his gray eyes cold as steel.

Etta had gasped, shocked at his words.

Butch ignored him and told Etta to do the same. "He's just being an old grouch," he said, trying to make her feel better. Even though Harry apologized the next day, she couldn't get his angry words out of her thoughts.

Another night Harry came in riled up about something. Butch was sitting quietly on the sofa, reading a book, while Etta did needlework. Out of nowhere, Harry took a swing at Butch. Etta jumped out of her chair and backed up against the wall in fear as Butch stood and blocked his swing, turning Harry around into a headlock.

"What the hell has gotten into you?" Butch yelled.

"You're trying to show me up to Etta!" Harry yelled back. "You sit here night after night pretending you're so damn perfect so she'll think you care more about her than I do. You're a scumbag, just like me, so stop acting like you aren't."

Butch threw Harry across the room and he hit the wall and fell to the floor. Harry righted himself but was swaying on his feet. He stood, facing Butch, his hand ready at his side as if to draw his pistol at the least provocation.

Etta watched, stunned. She'd seen the two men bicker, but never fight.

Butch didn't look afraid, he only shook his head. "You're drunk, you idiot. You're not going to shoot me. I'm not even wearing a gun. Go to bed and sleep it off before you do something you regret." Butch calmly ran a hand through his hair, smoothing it back into place, picked up his book, and sat down on the sofa to read again. After a time, Harry stumbled to bed, slamming the door.

Etta made her way back to her chair on rubbery legs and sat down heavily as Butch watched her, looking concerned.

"Why is he acting this way?" she whispered to Butch.

Butch reached over and clasped her hand in his. Rubbing it gently, he said, "I'd forgotten what a mean drunk he is. Something's bothering him, Etta, but I have no idea what it is. We're going to have to talk some sense into him when he's sober."

Harry apologized to Etta the next day, but he wouldn't confide in her why he was drinking so heavily. Butch told her that Harry sometimes went on binges like this then stopped as suddenly as he started. Etta hoped that Harry would stop soon.

The months moved on and summer came to New Mexico, hot, dry, and dusty. Etta worried increasingly about Harry's drinking and behavior. She knew deep in her heart that Harry loved her, but his tirades were getting worse. She wasn't sure how much longer she could take it. If it hadn't been for Butch's tender care, she probably would have been on the next train to San Antonio, back to Fannie's place. But she held on, because she hoped that Harry would come out of his dark mood and return to being the man she knew he truly was.

One evening, Harry announced to Etta and Butch that he was going to be away for a few weeks and he insisted Butch move into the bunkhouse while he was gone.

Butch chuckled. "Are you afraid I'll steal Etta away from you?"

Harry didn't look amused. "I'd feel better if you two weren't sharing this place while I'm away. You can move back in when I return."

Etta suddenly became furious. She'd been putting up with Harry's bad behavior long enough. He wasn't going to dictate what she or Butch were allowed to do. "This is as much Butch's home as it is ours," she told Harry. "Leave if you like, but Butch stays."

Harry stared at Etta, suddenly angry over her taking a stand. "This isn't a home—it's just a shit cabin sitting in a field in the middle of nowhere. Just because you've dolled it up, it doesn't make it a home. You've been living this vagabond life for so long now, Etta, that you don't remember what it's like to live in a real home."

Etta stood firm, glaring at Harry, but her eyes betrayed her and filled with tears.

Harry stormed to the bedroom. "Fine. Let him stay. I don't care." He slammed the door.

Butch reached for Etta and held her close as she cried. Harry left early the next morning without telling either Etta or Butch where he was going or when he'd be back.

* * *

On July 14, 1898, at 1:25 a.m., three men robbed the Southern Pacific passenger train #1 after it had left the station in Humboldt, Nevada. Fearing for his life, the express messenger was convinced to open the express car door after the outlaws attempted to dynamite the back door. The safe was blown open only to reveal about $450 in cash and some jewelry. The outlaws escaped. However, unbeknownst to them, the rear brakeman had fled as the train was stopped and returned to Humboldt where a message was telegraphed to Winnemucca. A special posse train car was sent their way.

Even with the posse's best efforts, they were unable to locate the outlaws. A one-thousand dollar reward was posted for the capture of the unknown men, but they were never caught. The outlaws suspected were Harvey Logan, Flatnose George Currie, and Harry Longabaugh, the Sundance Kid.

* * *

The news of the robbery came to Etta and Butch through the newspapers long before the outlaws returned to New Mexico. Etta was sure that Harry had been involved and she grew nervous when he didn't return home soon afterward. With only $450 taken from the train, she knew he would consider this robbery another failure. She thought he might be off licking his wounds somewhere before returning.

Etta and Butch spent their evenings in the cabin playing cards, reading, or talking. She and Butch grew closer and she learned more about his past. He talked about his childhood, living in Circleville with his large Mormon family, and about his siblings and his mother.

"My ma worked so hard to make our small cabin a home," Butch said. "And my father slaved away just so we could scrape by. I don't mind working, but what I saw was hard work didn't get you anywhere. I got into a bit of trouble as a young man and my father helped me out of it. That's when I decided it was time to leave home. I know it broke my mother's heart, but I couldn't stay. I wanted more from life than I could ever have there."

"That's sad, Butch. Have you ever gone home to visit your parents and siblings?"

Butch shook his head. "I can't go home. I won't embarrass them that way. They're good God-fearing people, and I'm their bad seed. It's better for my family if I stay away."

Etta could tell from the tone of his voice how much it hurt Butch to say that. If his family only knew the good he did also, maybe they wouldn't think too badly of him.

"Your past sounds so much like Harry's," she said. "He had a large family and his parents had to send him away just so they could make ends meet. He left at fourteen with his cousin to come out west. Like you, his life wasn't easy."

"That's why I turned to crime," Butch said. "It's more profitable than being honest."

Etta winced. While she understood how Butch felt, it was hard hearing him say those words. "But neither of you were brought up to believe that. And I wasn't either. Yet, here we are."

Butch gave her a tired smile. "I battled my conscience years ago, honey. I still try to have some morals. I've never killed a man, nor have I intentionally tried to hurt anyone. But I do realize that what we do is wrong. Men in suits ruin people's lives every day. But they are considered honest because they do it legally. At least I'm not pretending I'm something I'm not."

Etta knew that both men fought inward battles between the religious lives they were raised in and the criminal lives they now led.

One morning, after Butch had left for the ranch, Etta began cramping and bleeding. Etta knew she was pregnant, but had kept the news to herself. She'd hoped that by the time Harry returned, she could tell him the good news. But once again, she lost the baby. Maude had happened by to see her with Marvel in tow and she helped take care of Etta the day of the miscarriage. Etta swore Maude to secrecy about the lost baby. She kept her grief to herself.

Two weeks after the robbery, Harvey returned to the ranch

alone. Butch immediately questioned him. Harvey readily admitted it had been them and they'd walked away with very little for their trouble. "After the robbery, we went down to Eureka where Sundance's cousin, Seth, lives," Harvey explained to Butch. "Flatnose headed back over to Robbers Roost, but Sundance decided to stay in Eureka. His cousin is a barkeep there, so Sundance thought he might try his hand at cards."

Etta was relieved to hear that Harry was fine and staying with his cousin. She'd met Seth Longabaugh once before and had liked him. She hoped that spending time with family would help Harry settle down again.

Harry returned late one evening about two weeks after Harvey. He came into the cabin, swaying slightly and smelling of beer, but there was a smile on his face. "The prodigal son has returned," he announced to Etta and Butch, who had each been sitting quietly, reading.

Etta jumped up and ran over to hug Harry. He wrapped his arms around her and hugged her close, then dropped a kiss on her lips.

"Thank God you're home and safe," she said breathlessly after Harry let her go.

Harry dropped the saddlebags that had been slung over his shoulder onto the floor and they all heard the distinctive jingle of coins. "I may not be a great train robber like old Butch here, but I do play a mean game of poker," he said, his face still beaming.

Etta could tell he was drunk by the slur of his words, but she was still happy and relieved to have him home again.

"That's wonderful, Kid," Butch said. "Glad you had a successful trip."

Harry stared hard at Butch for longer than was comfortable,

but then he swept up the bags from the floor and took hold of Etta's hand. "Come show me how much you missed me," he told her, leading her to the bedroom.

Etta followed, but her face grew hot with embarrassment at the way Harry had talked to her. "Goodnight, Butch," she said hastily as she let Harry lead her away.

"Goodnight, darling," Butch replied, receiving one more glare from Harry before he shut the door.

The room was dark, so Etta quickly lit an oil lamp while Harry threw his saddle bags onto a chair and began unbuttoning his shirt. She pulled back the covers on the bed then stood there, nervously watching Harry. Never had she felt this uncomfortable with him, not even the first time they'd made love. Yet, it had been so long since he'd touched her, and his demeanor had changed so much, she felt as if he were a stranger instead of her beloved Harry.

"Come over here," he told her, taking off his gun belt and laying it on the table by the bed.

Etta did as he asked and trembled as she stood in front of him. His chest was bare and muscular and his waist narrowed down into the waistband of his trousers, so familiar it made her heart ache. He was exactly as he'd always been, yet his gray eyes held no warmth as they once had. Was he tired of her, or had the outlaw life finally turned him hard? Etta didn't want to know the answer to either of those questions.

She reached up to touch his cheek, but Harry quickly clasped her wrist and held it firm. Steel gray eyes met lavender-blue, and for a moment, fear coursed through Etta's veins. But then Harry slowly lifted her hand up to his lips and softly kissed her palm. Etta's heart melted with love.

That night they made love more passionately than at any

time she could remember. And although the words, "I love you," never passed between them that night, Etta felt sure she had her old Harry back.

Early the next morning, Etta awoke to the sound of heavy coins being dropped onto the bureau across from the bed. Groggily, she opened her eyes and saw Harry stacking them and then pocketing a few. He was fully dressed and she realized he was getting ready to go to the ranch and work.

"I'll make you some breakfast," she told him, getting up and tossing a white cotton robe over her. She saw Harry grin at her naked body as she slipped on her robe and she smiled back, remembering the passionate night they'd shared.

"Don't worry about breakfast. I'll eat with the hands at the ranch," he said, still eyeing her. "This is for you." Harry pointed to the coins on the bureau. "For the great night we had. Why don't you go into town and buy yourself something pretty with it?"

He walked out the door as Etta stood, frozen in her spot. She couldn't believe what she'd just heard. Was he paying her for sex? Was that all their relationship meant to him anymore? Anger raged hot inside her. She grabbed her Colt pistol and raced out of the room.

Butch was strapping on his gun belt as she entered the room. Etta looked out the window and saw Harry stepping off the porch and jauntily flipping a silver dollar up and down into the air as he walked toward the horse stalls.

"Etta? You all right?" Butch asked, sounding wary.

Etta swept past him and stepped onto the porch, raising her pistol. She watched the coin flip up, then land in Harry's hand, then flip up into the air again. She aimed and shot, hitting the coin in mid-air.

Harry turned quickly, pulling his pistol out of its holster in one smooth move, ready to fire at his attacker. When he saw Etta, his face paled. "What the hell's the matter with you?" he yelled. "I almost shot you."

Etta pointed the pistol directly at Harry's heart and narrowed her eyes. "Don't you ever treat me like a whore again, you son-of-a-bitch," she said, her voice low and menacing.

Harry stood frozen, looking unsure as to whether Etta would dare shoot him.

Slowly, she lowered the pistol to her side, turned, and stalked back into the cabin, brushing past Butch who had come up close behind her. Etta slammed the bedroom door shut as both men looked at each other, neither daring to say a word.

Inside the bedroom, tears filled Etta's eyes. She watched out the window as Harry holstered his pistol and turned, searching the ground as he walked away from the cabin. Finally, he found what he'd been looking for. Butch came up behind Harry and they both stared at the silver coin. It had an indention right in the middle where the bullet had hit it.

Butch let out a low whistle. "That's one hell'uva shot," he said to Harry. Harry nodded and slipped the coin into his pocket as the two men headed to the stables.

Etta made the decision right then that she'd had enough.

* * *

That evening as the two men were placing their horses in the stable, Butch pointed out to Harry that there was no smoke coming out of the chimney.

"Think Etta's so mad she didn't make supper tonight?" Butch asked.

Harry shrugged.

"Well, I hope not. I'm starved. She's mad at you, not me."

Harry glowered at him as they walked over to the cabin. When they were at the door, both men hesitated.

"You first," Butch said.

Harry shook his head. "You go. She doesn't want to shoot you."

Butch rolled his eyes and slowly opened the door. Inside, the cabin was quiet and there was nothing cooking on the stove.

"Etta?" Butch called tentatively. "Don't shoot, darling. I'm the one you like, remember?"

Harry gave Butch a shove on the shoulder. "Idiot," he said under his breath.

Both men entered the cabin and listened, but there was no sound. Harry went to check the bedroom while Butch walked toward the kitchen table.

"Uh, oh," Butch said. He lifted up a sheet of paper as Harry came back into the room.

"Her things are gone," Harry announced. "All her clothes, her gun, everything."

"She left a note." Butch handed it to Harry.

Harry read the note written in Etta's beautiful, perfect script.

I'm taking one of the horses and riding to Deming where I'll catch the stage to El Paso. I'm taking the train from there to San Antonio. I'm going home to Fannie. You can pick up the horse at the blacksmith's in Deming.

Etta

Harry stared at the letter in complete amazement. "She's left me. She's gone back to Fannie's."

Butch's eyes blazed at Harry. "You idiot! Look what you've done! We've lost Etta."

Harry felt stunned. "She's left, Butch. She doesn't want to be with me anymore. She doesn't want to be here with us."

"God, you really are a dolt!" Butch said. "She left because of the asinine way you've been acting all these months. Because of your drinking and whatever you did this morning or last night to make her mad enough to shoot at you. She's furious with you, you idiot, and she needs you to go after her and straighten things out. Dang it all, Kid. Don't you understand women at all? There's only so much shit they'll take before they've had it. Even Etta, who's put up with a lot of crap these past two years. You pushed her to her breaking point."

Harry was too shocked by Etta's leaving him to fight back. "She's better off without me." He sat down heavily in a chair. "Etta deserves so much better than I'll ever be able to give her. Maybe she'll find someone who can give her the life she deserves."

Butch crossed his arms. "You're right about one thing—Etta does deserve someone better than you."

"Hey…" Harry began, but Butch cut him off.

"But for some strange reason, she's chosen you, of all people, to love and you screwed it up. Etta is the best thing that has ever happened to you, and you let her get away. So, tomorrow we're going down to El Paso and hopping the train to San Antonio to get Etta back."

"We?" Harry asked.

"Hell yes," Butch exclaimed, grinning. "You don't think I'm going to miss a chance to visit Fannie's, do you? And this way I can make sure you behave."

"I don't need you tagging along with me," Harry grumbled.

"The way I see it," Butch said, "if you strike out with Etta then I'll be there to pick up the pieces. I love her. I know how to treat her the way she deserves."

Harry stood up and scowled at Butch.

"Don't be so touchy," Butch said, slapping him on the back. "Get some sleep and first thing in the morning, we're off to Fannie's."

Harry headed into the bedroom he usually shared with Etta. He stood in the empty room, rubbing the silver dollar Etta had shot between his fingers in his pocket. Butch was right—he'd screwed up with Etta. But he wasn't sure he could get her back as easily as Butch thought.

Chapter Seventeen

Pine Creek, MN
Winter 1911

Emily hurried along the streets of Pine Creek toward Allison's house, careful not to drop the packages she was carrying. School had just let out and it was late afternoon on a cold, December day. It had snowed the previous day, and while the effect was pretty, the reality was damp boots and wet skirt hems. Along the way she'd stopped at Evy's Restaurant to pick up supper for Allison and Rusch's Bakery where she'd purchased a special treat for her, too. As Emily balanced the items in her hands, walking on the wet, slippery street, she was happy that Gertie had offered to watch Harry while she went on her visit.

Emily finally made it to the edge of town where Allison and Ted owned a sweet Victorian house with gingerbread trim. Shaking the snow from the hem of her skirt as best she could, she stepped through the front door into the entryway. "Hello? Allison. It's Emily."

"I'm in the morning room," Allison replied in a tired voice.

"Just stay where you are. I'll be there shortly." Emily set her packages on the table and quickly undid the buttons of her boots to slip them off. She hung her coat on a wall peg and entered the hallway that led to the morning room, living room, and staircase. To her left, she saw Allison lying on the sofa in front of the fire, a blanket tucked around her. Emily quickly went over to Allison and gave the young woman a kiss on the cheek.

"How are you feeling today?" Emily asked her.

"Not too well, I'm afraid," Allison said. "I had hoped to feel better by this afternoon."

Emily nodded sympathetically. "Let me take these packages to the kitchen and I'll be back," she said. "Evy sent a pot of chicken stew for you and Ted." She hurried out to the back of the house where the kitchen was. "And I have a surprise for you," she called out as she went.

Emily set the pot of stew on the wood cooking stove and placed the other items on the kitchen table. She filled the kettle with water and set it on the stove, then quickly started a fire in the oven to heat up the stew and water. Finding the china teapot, she took a tin out of one of the packages she'd brought and carefully scooped out some of the special tea mixture, placing it in the teapot. From the other bag she took out two large muffins and set them on a plate near the stove to warm up. Quickly, she headed back to check on Allison.

"Has anyone been here recently?" she asked Allison, who was trying to sit up against the pillows on the sofa. Emily helped her and re-tucked the blanket around her growing belly. Allison was due in two months, but because she'd been so sick, she hadn't gained much weight. The baby was growing, but poor Allison was rail thin.

"The pastor's wife, Milli, was here this morning and Teddy came by earlier to fix the fire and check on me," Allison said.

Emily was relieved to hear the sheriff had already been by. That meant she probably wouldn't run into him before she left. She usually planned her visits to Allison's right after school because she knew the sheriff didn't come home until later in the evening.

Emily went to work setting logs on the fire. Noting that the basin beside Allison had been used, she picked it up to rinse it out.

"I'm sorry you have to do that," Allison said, looking embarrassed. "I couldn't keep any food down today and I feel very weak."

"Sweetie, that's why I'm here. To help out. Don't give it another thought." Emily went to the kitchen to clean out the basin. The women in town had been taking turns sitting with Allison and helping with meals and cleaning the house. Emily also tried to come over several times a week. Anne Rusch from the bakery often sent along bread or muffins, and Evy insisted on sending food for supper every night. Everyone in town adored Allison and had great respect for Sheriff Neilson and were more than willing to help out.

The kettle was boiling by the time Emily finished washing the basin so she poured water into the teapot and placed two teacups and the plate of muffins on a tray to take to Allison.

"I was walking by Rusch's Bakery today and the most wonderful smell wafted out, so I had to find out what it was," Emily said as she entered the morning room. Placing the tray on the table in front of the sofa, she continued, "Fresh cinnamon muffins. I thought the cinnamon might help calm your stomach."

"Oh, they smell heavenly," Allison said.

Emily handed her half a muffin on a plate. "Take small bites to see how your stomach feels," she warned her. "I also have some special tea for you that I hope will keep your stomach settled." She poured the tea through a small strainer into the teacups and then handed Allison a cup of the delicious smelling brew.

Allison took a tentative sip of the hot liquid. "Mmm, this tastes wonderful." She took another sip. "What is it?"

"Green tea with ginger root," Emily told her. She sat down in a chair by the fire and sipped her own tea. "The ginger is supposed to settle your stomach. I would have brought some sooner, but I had to special order the green tea and it took forever to get here."

The color in Allison's cheeks grew rosier. "How did you learn about this tea?" Allison asked as she took small sips.

"Oh, a very sweet older woman in…" Emily paused. She was about to say "in Chile" when she realized her mistake and stopped. She had no way to explain why she'd been to South America, so she knew it was best not to mention it.

"At the convent?" Allison finished for her. "One of the older nuns?"

"Yes," Emily said, relieved that Allison assumed she was going to say that. "One of the nuns gave me some of this tea to help settle my queasiness when I was expecting Harry."

Allison wriggled up a bit more into a sitting position, interested in Emily's past. "What was it like, living at the convent?"

"Very different," Emily answered. "But very nice. I had nowhere to go and the nuns welcomed me. I helped them by teaching the children who lived in the orphanage and they returned the kindness by giving me and Harry a place to live."

"Did you already know your husband had died when you started living there?" Allison asked.

Emily sat a moment, deep in thought about that time in her life. No, she hadn't yet known that Harry and Butch might be dead, just as she was still not sure. It hadn't been until January of this year that she had received any confirmation at all about the possibility of both men having died in a shoot-out in San Vincente, Bolivia. However, there was no definitive proof. Yet, it was difficult for Emily to believe that they had been alive all these years and hadn't tried to find her.

Allison took Emily's silence as sadness and apologized profusely. "I didn't mean to bring up a sad memory," she said quickly. "I'm so sorry I asked."

"No, don't be. You didn't do anything wrong. I was only thinking about the past," Emily told her. "Actually, it wasn't until after Harry was born that I knew he'd died," Emily said, trying not to lie to her friend.

"It must have been hard, losing your husband and being alone as a new mother," Allison said sympathetically.

Emily sighed. "Living at the convent helped me through the tough times."

"I'm happy you and Harry are here with us now," Allison said. "The entire town adores you. We can be your family now."

Emily smiled her appreciation to the young woman. She also hoped that her new-found life in Pine Creek would continue and she wouldn't have to leave. She was so tired of running. It would be nice to stay here and settle for good.

For a time, the women sat in silence, sipping tea. Emily warmed her feet by the fire and hoped her wool skirt would dry before she set out for home. She gazed around Allison's beautiful morning room, with its feminine décor. The home reminded her of Edward's house outside of town, and she wondered if Edward would ever live there again. It had been so long since

Emily lived in a nice home. She couldn't help but wonder what it would be like to have a home of her own.

Allison's color was much better and she was able to eat some of the muffin without being sick. She thanked Emily for being so thoughtful and bringing the tea. It seemed to help.

"There's more tea in a tin in the kitchen, but only drink two cups a day," she warned the young woman. "One in the morning and one in the late afternoon should help your stomach."

Emily stoked the fire again and helped Allison lie down so she could nap. "I'll see you tomorrow afternoon," she told her, then gave her a quick kiss on the cheek. After picking up the tea cups and plate, Emily headed back to the kitchen to check on the stew before leaving. She was surprised to find the sheriff standing over the stove, staring into the warmed pot.

"Oh, I didn't know you were here," he said, looking a little sheepish at being caught. "Sorry. It smelled so good, I had to take a look."

"I just came in to check on the stew before I left," Emily told him, opening the pot and stirring the food inside.

"How's Allison?"

"She seems better tonight. She's napping on the sofa right now."

Sheriff Neilson walked over to the table and picked up the tin that held the tea. He opened it and sniffed the contents. "This smells good. What kind of tea is it?"

"It's a special blend I made for Allison to soothe her stomach. It's green tea with ginger root. Please make sure she only drinks two cups a day, no more. Ginger is safe for the baby, but in small doses."

He nodded.

Emily reached up into the cabinet and pulled down a fresh

loaf of bread. She sliced several pieces and placed them on a plate, covering it with a towel. After placing the bread by the stove to warm, she put the remainder of the loaf away. The entire time she worked, she was aware of the sheriff's eyes upon her.

"Supper is ready whenever you and Allison feel like eating. I'll be leaving now," she said, hoping to slip out of the kitchen without any more conversation.

"Thank you for your help with Allison," Sheriff Neilson said. "I know she appreciates it."

Emily turned to face him. "I can't take all the credit. All the women are helping out. Evy made the stew and Anna sent over the loaf of bread. Everyone adores Allison and wants her to feel better."

The sheriff walked the short distance between them and stopped directly in front of her. "Yes, I understand that. And I do appreciate the help of all the women in town. However, it's you who Allison is the fondest of." He glanced over at the tea tin on the table. "And it's you who goes out of her way to help the most." He looked down into Emily's eyes. "I hope you aren't trying to butter me up so I forget who you really are."

Emily looked up into his steel gray eyes, eyes that reminded her so much of her husband's that it made her heart ache. Lifting her chin in defiance, she said, "I care about Allison and that's why I help. Good evening, Sheriff." With that, Emily turned to leave.

"Mrs. Pleasants," Sheriff Neilson said to her back. She stopped but didn't turn to face him. "Thank you," he said, his tone sincere.

Emily nodded her head slightly and continued down the hall to the front door to leave.

* * *

The Saturday evening before Christmas, after the store was closed, Edward, Harry, and Emily piled into a borrowed wagon and rode out to Edward's property to choose a tree. It was cold, and a dusting of snow was falling to the ground, but this made no difference to the little group of three. Harry had never decorated a Christmas tree before and he had been excited when Gertie had announced that they would all decorate a tree at her house, after they went out to chop one down. So, as Gertie stayed home to make hot chocolate and string cranberries and popping corn, the others ventured out to find the perfect tree.

Edward was in a merry mood as they trudged through his woods and selected a tree. He quickly cut down the chosen spruce and with some help from Emily, loaded it into the back of the wagon. The three snuggled under a blanket on the bench seat as they rode back to town, laughing and giggling at the fun they were enjoying together.

Emily was thankful that some of the animosity Edward had felt toward her had melted away, although he still kept his distance. At least he was spending time with little Harry again, and had even resumed eating meals with her and Harry at Evy's. Even if they never renewed the close relationship they'd once had, she hoped they could at least remain friends for Harry's sake.

Red-cheeked, damp, and smiling, the trio returned to Gertie's small home and after setting up the tree, began decorating it with all manner of items. Gertie had glass ornaments that had been passed down in her family for generations as well as some beautiful new ones she'd bought over the years. Gertie also surprised everyone with a homemade stocking for each of them to hang above her brick fireplace. Emily fell asleep that night feeling grateful for the friendships she had, and hoped to keep.

Edward, Emily, Harry, and Gertie all attended Christmas Eve service together on Sunday and Emily was thrilled to see Allison well enough to attend also. Although still weak and pale, she said she felt better each day after drinking the ginger tea and hoped to build her strength up before the baby was born. The children's Christmas play was also presented that evening, with little Harry playing a shy shepherd during the Nativity scene.

After church services, the group went back to Gertie's house where they enjoyed a delicious meal of roast duck, sweet potatoes, glazed carrots, and pumpkin pie. Both Emily and Gertie had worked together that morning to make the supper and also bake the special cut-out sugar cookies that Harry devoured.

After supper, they sat around the tree and exchanged gifts. Harry was delighted when he opened his present from Edward—a small, metal train engine with an attached cargo car and caboose. Gertie had given him a bag of marbles and a hand-knit scarf while Emily had given him a felt cowboy hat he had admired in the store and a new pair of shoes he so desperately needed. There were also handfuls of candies in his stocking as well as an orange, a treat which he planned on saving for breakfast.

The adults exchanged gifts as well. Gertie gave each of them a set of handmade scarves and mittens, which Emily thanked her for profusely because she made such beautiful, knitted items. During her hours sitting with Allison, Emily had embroidered a gorgeous pillow for Gertie and also gave her a decorative pottery bowl she'd seen the older woman eyeing at the store. When it was time for Emily and Edward to exchange gifts, Gertie not-so-subtly suggested Harry help her cut and serve the pie so as to leave the two alone.

Edward handed Emily two boxes, one containing a beautiful silk scarf and another which held brown leather riding gloves.

"They're beautiful," Emily told him when she opened the box of gloves. "And the scarf is lovely. Thank you." She then handed him a small box.

When Edward opened it, he looked up in surprise. "It's extraordinary," he told Emily. He lifted a gold money clip that had inlaid opal on the front. Edward stared at it in amazement.

"I hope you like it," Emily said, feeling a bit shy about the gift. "I noticed that you didn't have a money clip and I thought you might like one."

Emily had ordered the clip before Edward had become upset with her, when she still thought they might be heading toward a relationship. Now, while it seemed a bit extravagant, considering how their relationship had cooled, she was still happy she'd bought it for him. No matter what happened between them, she would always think of Edward as a dear friend.

"I do like it," Edward told her. "But it's much more than I ever expected."

Emily moved closer to Edward and spoke softly. "You've been more than kind to both Harry and me since we've come here. I wanted to give you something that reflected how much we appreciate all you've done."

Edward looked to be at a loss for words. Behind them, Gertie and Harry entered the room, handing out plates of pie. As they sat eating their dessert, Gertie looked pointedly at Edward.

"Wasn't there something else you had for Emily?" she asked.

Edward's eyes darted up at her and he shook his head as if to say, "Not now, Gertie." Gertie let out a long sigh. Politely, Emily ignored the exchange, although she did wonder what it was about.

It had been a wonderful Christmas holiday and Harry fell fast asleep that night hugging his new train engine with his cowboy hat perched safely on the bedpost. Emily was about to crawl into bed when she heard a light tapping on her door. Wrapping her robe around her, she opened the door slightly to see Edward standing there in the hallway, also wearing his nightclothes and robe.

"I'm sorry to bother you," he whispered. "May I speak with you a moment?"

She nodded and slipped out into the cool hallway, softly closing the door behind her. It was dark in the hall, with only the light from Edward's open door spilling out. Edward appeared to have something in his hand, but Emily couldn't make out what it was.

He looked nervously from Emily to his room and back. "Would you mind terribly if we stepped inside my room where there's more light?"

Emily smiled at his shyness. Even after all the evenings they had shared together and also the few intimacies, he still behaved as if he might insult her by defying propriety. She nodded and walked ahead of him into his room, lit up by the soft glow of an oil lamp.

When she turned to face Edward, he handed her a small box. At first, she thought he was returning her gift, but then she realized the box was not the same as the one the money clip had come in.

"I have another gift for you," he told her, his voice wavering. "I didn't know if it was appropriate to give this to you after the way I've acted these past few weeks, but I want you to have it."

Emily glanced between Edward and the small box. Slowly, she lifted the lid and pulled out the leather box that lay inside.

She drew in a breath. The last time someone had given her a gift in such a box, it was a ring.

"I hope you like it," he said, sounding unsure.

Emily gasped when she saw what was inside. Lying on red velvet was a lovely oval rose-gold brooch with an amethyst stone in the center. The amethyst was a rich, deep purple of the finest quality and the rose-gold filigree that surrounded it looked like gold lace. "It's beautiful. I love it."

Edward looked relieved. "I thought that after the way I've been acting, it was too forward of me to give you such a personal gift. But I truly wanted you to have it."

Emily smiled up at him and he seemed to grow braver.

"I've noticed the amethyst ring you wear and thought that it must be your favorite gemstone." He looked sheepish. "It also reminded me of your eyes."

Emily's heart swelled. She looked down at the ring she wore on her right hand, and the wedding band she still wore on her left. Long ago, Harry had said the same thing to her, and she saw it as a sign that this man, who was so different from her husband, could tug at her heart in the very same way.

"I will absolutely cherish it because it came from you." Emily reached up and hugged him close, tears filling her eyes.

Edward wrapped his arms around her, his voice thick with emotion. "I'm sorry I behaved so terribly to you these past few weeks," he whispered into her ear. "You deserve much more than I've given. I was so scared that I wasn't man enough for you that I backed away. Please forgive me."

Emily pulled away, looking up at him. "There's nothing to forgive. I realize that there's much you don't know about me, or about my past."

"None of that matters to me," Edward told her with certainty.

"It makes no difference to me who you were or what you've done or where you've been. All that matters is that you're here now, and I'd be a fool to ever push you away again." Edward's expression grew serious. "I'm in love with you, Emily. Is there any way you could ever love me?"

"Oh, Edward." She had deep feelings for this man standing before her, deeper than she would ever have thought possible. Although there would only ever be one man who held her heart completely, that man was gone from her forever. "Loving you would be very easy," she told him.

They kissed, a kiss that started out warm and loving, growing more passionate as their need grew too. Edward pulled away, breathing heavily. "We should stop. This isn't proper."

Emily, however, felt a deep desire for Edward. A desire that had been dormant a very long time. "It's all right," she said, her voice husky.

Edward held her tightly. "No. I won't ruin this night by taking advantage of you. We'll do everything right. The way it should be. I can wait a little longer."

Emily sighed. Although she knew he was being a gentleman, she silently wished he'd push propriety aside and make love to her. She wanted to hold someone close again, and feel loved again. She needed to know that she could love him as she had loved her husband. But she would wait, as Edward had said, a little longer.

Chapter Eighteen

San Antonio, TX
August 1898

Etta sat at the piano in the parlor of Fannie's house, softly playing a sad melody on the ivory keys. It was late afternoon and so hot in the room that she could hardly breathe. Soon the girls would be awake and the parlor would be full of patrons, so she enjoyed what little quiet time she had.

It had been a few days since she'd returned to San Antonio and Fannie's, where the older woman had welcomed her with open arms. "What did he do?" the Madame had insisted.

Etta's emotional dam had burst as she cried in Fannie's arms.

"It's his loss," Fannie had told her when she'd heard what had transpired.

"Do you have any room for me here?" Etta had asked her.

"No one has touched your room above the kitchen," Fannie said. "It's yours for as long as you wish, which I hope will be a long time."

Fannie had admitted she'd missed her young ward and said she hoped the wanderlust was out of her system and she'd stay in San Antonio. Just the other night, she'd mentioned to Etta that maybe she could find a teaching position in the area or go back to teaching piano lessons as she'd done before. Etta contemplated this now as she sat at the piano. She had truly believed she would be with Harry forever and it tore at her heart to consider a life without him.

As Etta played, she heard the front door open and close behind her and the scrape of boots on the entryway floor. She ignored the newcomer and continued playing, figuring the cook or Fannie would tell them to come back later in the evening when the girls were ready for business. Suddenly, from behind her, a husky voice spoke.

"Need some help there, miss?"

Etta froze, her heart pounding as she recognized the voice.

"Don't stop playing on my account," the male voice said, coming closer. "It's been so long that I forgot how beautifully you play the piano."

Slowly, Etta turned and there stood Harry, hat in hand, smiling down at her. Behind him, she saw Butch in the hallway, watching them.

Butch smiled and winked, then cleared his throat. "I think I'll go into the kitchen and see if the cook still makes those delicious corn muffins." He took off down the hallway.

Harry sat down beside Etta on the bench. "Seems to me we've been here before."

Etta stared at him, not knowing if she should be happy or angry that he had followed her here. Harry fingered his hat nervously.

"Etta, I know I don't deserve even a moment of your time, but I was hoping we could talk."

She lifted her chin in defiance, but when she saw the warmth in his eyes, she softened. "I'm listening."

Harry glanced around the room. "Is there somewhere private we can go?"

Etta nodded and led him through the kitchen, past Butch, who was sampling a cake the cook had just finished frosting, and up the stairs to her room. After closing the door, she folded her hands in front of her and waited for him to speak.

Harry walked around the bedroom, which was small but cozy and held a bed, bureau, a small sofa, and a pot-bellied woodstove. He chose to sit on the sofa instead of the bed and asked Etta if she'd sit with him. After a moment's hesitation, she did.

"I'm an idiot," Harry announced.

Etta raised her brows in surprise. It wasn't what she'd expected him to say.

"I had everything a man could want and I let it slip right through my fingers." Harry reached for her hand and lifted it to his lips. "Please forgive me, Etta. I know I treated you badly and I promise, if you give me another chance, I will make it up to you."

Etta's heart melted. Right or wrong, she loved Harry and she couldn't help but give in. "Oh, Harry, what happened? Why did you act that way? I thought you were unhappy with me, and that you no longer loved me."

Harry shook his head. "Oh darling, no. It had nothing to do with you. I've always loved you. It was me, my problem, my ego getting in the way." He stood and walked across the room, staring out the window a moment before returning his gaze to Etta. "I've been such a failure. I was afraid you'd no longer want me, so I pushed you away. You deserve so much more than I've given you and I felt as if I'd let you down."

Etta moved to stand in front of him. "You've never let

me down. I understood the type of life I would have when I followed you."

"You deserve better, though. You should have a nice home, children, and a husband who isn't being chased all over the country, wanted by the law. I wanted so desperately to give you all those things, but I don't know if I ever can."

His words tore at her heart. Etta hadn't realized Harry had been mad at himself all this time. Just because he thought he'd disappointed her. "Honey, don't you understand? My home is wherever you are. As long as we're together, we are home."

"Oh, Etta." He pulled her close, kissing her gently. "I love you. More than you could ever know."

"I love you, too," she responded, relieved to be in his arms again.

After a time, Etta drew away from Harry, her eyes filled with tears. "There's something I need to tell you."

He placed his hand under her chin and tipped it up to look into her face. A tear fell down her cheek. "What is it?"

"I lost our baby while you were away," she said, sorrow filling her voice. "I hadn't told you I was expecting because I wanted to make sure everything was going well. But then I lost the baby, just like the last time."

"Oh, sweetie." Harry rocked her gently. "I'm so sorry I wasn't there for you. I promise, someday we'll have babies, as many as you want."

He pulled out his handkerchief and wiped away her tears, then guided her to the sofa to sit. "I have something for you." Harry took a small leather box from his vest pocket and handed it to her. She lifted the lid to reveal an elegant gold ring with an oval cut amethyst stone that was the deepest purple she'd ever seen.

"Harry, it's so beautiful!" she exclaimed.

He took it out and slid it on the ring finger of Etta's left hand. "I know that promises should be made with diamonds," he said. "But this ring reminded me so much of your eyes that I couldn't resist it."

"What promises?" she asked in a whisper.

"I promise never to treat you badly again. I promise to care for you and love you forever. And I promise that someday, very soon, we will be married and have a real life together, if you will take me back."

Etta's heart filled with love for this man who she'd thought she'd almost lost. She knew she couldn't live without him. "All I ever wanted was you. I don't need anything else as long as we're together."

"Will you come back with me to the ranch?" Harry asked.

"Yes," she said, happy to have her Harry back.

He pulled a silver dollar from his pocket and placed it in her hand.

"What's this?"

"It's the silver dollar you shot the morning you left," he said, grinning. "I'm going to carry it with me for the rest of my life as a reminder of two things."

"What two things?"

"First, that I will always love you and treat you like you deserve," he said, kissing her forehead. "And second, never to make you angry again because you're one hell'uva shot."

They both laughed and Harry returned the coin to his pocket. True to his word, he kept his promise and the coin with him every day.

W S Ranch, TX
June 1899

The trio headed back to the W S Ranch where they lived for nearly a year in peaceful bliss. Harry kept his promise and stayed close to the ranch and home, no longer going into Alma to drink and gamble. Sometimes, Butch would be gone for several days at the horse camp twenty miles from the ranch, where the horses could graze on prime land. This gave Etta and Harry an opportunity to be alone.

It was during this time that the idea of moving to South America sprouted. Butch had researched the possibility of them earning a prosperous living there. The little family of three talked often of moving there, buying a ranch, and settling down for good where they were not known as outlaws. They knew that this was no longer possible in the States, so they began to make a plan on where they might live in South America. At this point, it was just talk, but after a time it grew more serious.

Slowly, their lives began to change. Unlike Etta, who was resigned to the fact that Harry might forever be an outlaw, Maude was not so inclined. She tried at every turn to talk Elzy into going straight so they could live a peaceful life back in Utah near her family. Elzy resisted, so Maude packed up little Marvel and moved back to Vernal, Utah to live with her parents. Elzy was heartbroken, and often left for weeks at a time to visit his family. Etta missed having another woman around to talk to, but her life was wherever Harry was. She had her men, Harry and Butch, and that had to be enough for her. She couldn't imagine a life without them.

The talk of moving to South America grew more serious as the months passed. Soon Butch was thinking about how they would finance such an adventure. His thinking turned into planning and he, Harry, Harvey, Lonnie, Flatnose, Will, and Ben Kilpatrick were ready to go to work again.

* * *

In the early morning hours of June 2, 1899, the Union Pacific Overland Flyer #1 was stopped by two men just outside of Wilcox, Wyoming. The outlaws, Harvey and Sundance, instructed the engineer to cross the bridge, and when he moved too slow, Harvey hit him heavily on the head with his six-shooter. Sundance gave Harvey a dark look at the violence of his action, but said nothing. The train crossed the bridge, and then the outlaws destroyed the bridge with dynamite to deter another train from following. Harvey and Sundance ordered the passenger cars uncoupled from the engine, leaving only the baggage, mail, and express cars connected. They then told the engineer to pull ahead on the tracks toward Medicine Bow where, two miles down the track, four more outlaws were waiting.

Butch, Will, Flatnose, and Lonnie joined Sundance and Harvey and proceeded to blow the mail car door off when the clerk inside didn't open the door fast enough. After another round with the express car clerk, Charles E. Woodcock, the outlaws blew off that door and then set dynamite to the safe. Too much dynamite was used. The money flew up in the blast and began raining down upon them.

The outlaws scrambled to collect as much money off the ground as they could. By the time the robbers rode away, they had managed to secure several pieces of gold jewelry as well as over $30,000 dollars in bank notes, some singed on the corners from the explosion.

The six outlaws rode hard to the first relay point where Ben Kilpatrick was waiting with fresh horses and supplies. Here they split the money seven ways, then Sundance, Harvey, and Butch headed south toward Brown's Hole while the other men headed north to Hole-in-the-Wall.

* * *

Etta had come along this time, and was waiting for the men at Brown's Hole. Sitting in a valley in the northwestern corner of Colorado, Brown's Hole had fertile land that was perfect for raising cattle and horses. It was also an excellent hideaway for outlaws, especially since the Bassett family who lived there had a long history of helping Butch and the gang. Here, staying in a small cabin not far from the Bassett ranch, Etta waited for the men with more supplies and fresh horses. She didn't worry this time as she had before. She was getting used to their escapades. She would have gladly joined them at the robbery scene had Harry let her, but he was adamant she stay away.

Two days after the hold-up, Harry, Butch, and Harvey rode into Brown's Hole and after only a few hours of sleep, the three men and Etta mounted the fresh horses and headed first to Cortez, Colorado to visit Harry's cousins, then south, back to the W S Ranch. They thought they had eluded the authorities, but soon the trail of singed money would eventually lead the Pinkertons to Alma and the ranch.

In late August, two months after they had returned to the ranch, Butch burst into the cabin. "Elzy's been captured!" Frustration lined his face.

Etta looked up, stunned. The thought of any of the men being arrested terrified her. It could just as easily be Harry or Butch.

"Where's he at?" Harry asked. He'd just returned from a long day's work.

Butch took off his hat and ran a hand through his hair. "He's in New Mexico, in Raton. Harvey just got here last night with the news after riding hard for two days straight. Dammit!" Butch yelled, throwing his hat on the floor.

He sat down heavily on the chair by the fireplace, the spot he'd sat in all winter long enjoying books and Etta's company. Elbows on his knees, Butch continued in a frustrated tone. "I told Elzy not to go off with Sam Ketchum and Harvey and to definitely not do a job with them. He knew better. Harvey and Ketchum are loaded pistols. They shoot anything in their way and don't care who they kill. Elzy's going to end up paying for them killing that sheriff in New Mexico after the robbery."

Etta took in a breath, which echoed in the quiet room. "Tell us what happened, Butch."

Butch looked tired. He told them he'd been up since midnight when Harvey had ridden into camp to report about Elzy and he'd spent the better part of the day working on a way to help his friend.

"Elzy, Ketchum, and Harvey were the ones who robbed the train over by Folsom last month," Butch said. "They got away fine, but the next day a posse caught up with them and took Elzy unaware and shot him twice in the chest. At that point, Harvey and Ketchum drew weapons and began firing. It was two men against ten or twelve, but you know Harvey. He's a good shot and ruthless, and he shot down several of the men, killing the sheriff. Ketchum was shot in the arm, but Harvey paid him no never-mind. He got Elzy onto his horse and the three rode off."

Etta's hand flew up to her mouth to hold back her gasp. She was afraid for Elzy, hit twice in the chest. And the killing of the men in the posse upset her too. Even though she lived with outlaws, she didn't believe in violence to gain money. Neither did Harry or Butch. She could live with their being outlaws as long as they weren't murderers. But hearing how Harvey gunned down a group of men, and killed the sheriff, made her blood run cold.

Butch continued his story. "A few miles down the road, Ketchum claimed he couldn't go any further and Harvey left him behind. Harvey's only concern was to get Elzy to safety where he could hopefully heal from his wounds. They ended up at a friend's cabin and hid out for over a month, giving Elzy time to heal so they could make the trip back here to the ranch. While Harvey was off getting ammunition and supplies for traveling, a sheriff and group of men came upon the cabin and found Elzy. Once they realized who they'd found, they took him into custody. That was two days ago. Harvey came directly here after Elzy's capture to secure our help."

"What do we do now?" Harry asked Butch, sounding ready for action. "Are we going to break Elzy out?"

Butch slowly shook his head. He was dusty from being out at the horse camp and there was several days' worth of stubble on his face and dark circles around his eyes. Etta had never seen Butch look so weary, so beaten. Butch, the eternal optimist, seemed to have lost his spark, lost his drive to move forward.

"There's nothing we can do," Butch said. "I've already been up to see Captain French and Harvey told him the entire story. There's more than enough money from the robbery to pay Elzy's bail, if he's given bail. We asked the captain if he could take the money and get Elzy out. But he said he couldn't risk it. He's already been questioned once by a Pinkerton detective about harboring outlaws and he can't risk them thinking he knows who we really are. Says he'll put in a good word for Elzy with the judge and at the trial, if necessary, but that's all he can do." Butch sighed. "The captain has been good to all of us and has stayed out of our business so far. We owe it to him not to bring anything bad to his good name and the name of his ranch."

"Can't one of us post bail for Elzy?" Etta asked hopefully. "Or get in touch with Maude and have her do it?"

"Sorry, Etta dear, but none of us, or even Maude, can walk in with stolen bank notes and use them to post a bond. We'll just have to see what happens to Elzy after the trial."

"But Butch." Etta's eyes filled with tears. "The punishment for train robbery in New Mexico is death. And so is killing a sheriff. We can't let that happen to Elzy. From what you say, Harvey shot the sheriff."

Butch wrapped his arms around Etta, holding her close as her tears spilled onto his dusty leather vest. "I know, Etta," he said softly.

"There must be something we can do." Harry placed his hand gently on Etta's shoulder.

"If it comes to that," Butch said sternly, "we'll get him out, come hell or high water."

Harry nodded his assent. Etta continued to hold Butch tightly as he rocked her gently back and forth and Harry's hand caressed her back.

"Our time's almost done here, boys and girls," Butch said sadly.

Even as she held her men tight, Etta felt a chill of dread run up her spine from Butch's words.

Chapter Nineteen

Pine Creek, MN
1911-1912

After Christmas, things changed for Emily and Edward. While their daily routine stayed the same, with Edward joining them for meals at Evy's and still driving them to church each Sunday, the tone of their relationship was different. Edward began inviting Emily to accompany him to social gatherings. Where once Edward would have gracefully turned down an invitation to a small dinner party, musical soirée, or an evening playing parlor games with other couples, he now accepted these invitations and invited Emily to join him. The town was no longer guessing at the relationship between their school teacher and Edward—it was common knowledge that the two were a legitimate couple.

"He's courting you and doing a fine job of it, if a do say so myself," Gertie said to Emily one Saturday afternoon when they were both working at the store.

Emily's felt her cheeks flush. "Courting sounds so serious. He's only inviting me to a few social gatherings."

"Funny, isn't it, that he hasn't accepted an invitation in years until now?" Gertie teased.

Emily didn't respond and continued dusting a case with glass shelving.

"By the way," Gertie said. "I never told you how pretty your new brooch is. Was it a gift?" Gertie winked and bustled off to help a customer with dress fabric, leaving Emily to shake her head in her wake. Emily didn't doubt one bit that not only did Gertie know it was a gift from Edward, but she'd probably helped him pick it out.

To be honest, Emily knew that Gertie was right—Edward was courting her. People in town were now thinking of them as a couple and everyone, so far, seemed to approve. Attending the New Year's Eve dance that evening would seal the deal with the townspeople when the couple entered together.

Emily wore the only fine dress she had left from her old life—a royal blue velvet gown with a full skirt, sweetheart neckline, three-quarter length sleeves, and gold piping along the hem of the dress, sleeves, and neckline. The bodice fit perfectly and tiny buttons ran down the back of the gown. She piled her auburn hair upon her head much as she usually did except for allowing a few tendrils to escape at her forehead and neck. A string of pearls her husband had given her was the finishing touch. Gertie helped her dress, fastening all the tiny buttons on the back, not once questioning who would unfasten them at the end of the night.

The last time Emily had worn that gown was several years before and thousands of miles away at a banquet she and her husband and their friend had attended. They'd been the guests of honor at a dinner and dance hosted by the mayor of the town they'd lived in then. But that was before things began crashing down around them, before they realized they were near the end of that peaceful existence.

Before leaving her room to meet Edward that evening, Emily stopped in front of her bureau and opened the drawer, pulling out the carved box which held the treasures of her past. Slowly, deliberately, she slipped off her wedding band and placed it gently in the box. It was a night for new beginnings, and it was time for her to let her past go. While it pained her to give up her ring, she knew it was the right thing to do for both her and little Harry.

As she was about to close the lid, she saw a twinkle from inside the box. Moving aside the photos, she lifted out the gold stickpin with the small diamond on it. The memory flooded back of the man who had handed it to her on the last day she'd seen him, telling her to keep it safe for him. Her husband's best friend, her best friend also. It was a reminder of all things good from her past life and all things lost. She held onto the stickpin as she closed the box and tucked it away, and then walked down the stairs to Edward.

* * *

Edward, resplendent in a deep navy suit and top hat, gasped when he saw Emily. Never had he dreamt she could be even lovelier than he'd already believed her to be. "You astound me," he said in a hushed whisper.

She smiled warmly at his reaction.

"You are the most beautiful woman I've ever known." Edward placed a kiss on her cheek. "I will be the envy of every man this evening."

"As I will be to every woman for being escorted by you," she told him. "Except for one small thing." She stepped closer.

Edward looked down at his suit, confused. "Is something wrong with the way I'm dressed?"

She chuckled. "No, nothing is wrong. If you will allow me, I'd like for you to wear this tonight." She lifted his left lapel and slid the stickpin into place, fastening it tight. Stepping back she said, "I'd like you to have this."

Edward looked down at the pin then back at Emily. "It's lovely, but I just couldn't. This is too valuable for you to give away."

"I want you to have it," Emily insisted. "A good friend gave it to me for safekeeping and now I want you to enjoy it."

"Oh, no, no, I just couldn't," Edward repeated. "You should save it for Harry. It should be his one day."

Emily placed a gloved hand on his chest as she looked into his eyes. "It will be Harry's someday, but until then, I'd like you to have it. Please accept it. My friend would want me to share it with someone I care about."

"Then I will treasure it," Edward said, honored by the special gift. "And I will take good care of it until the day we give it to Harry." He helped Emily on with her coat and reached for her left hand. "Shall we be off?" he asked, holding her hand firmly in his. It took only a moment before he felt she was no longer wearing her wedding band. He looked at her, his brows raised.

"To new beginnings," Emily said softly.

Edward smiled brightly. "Yes, to new beginnings."

That evening Edward and Emily swept into the town hall amidst gasps of pleasure by the men and women alike and danced all evening until midnight struck. They welcomed 1912 as a couple, with a soft kiss.

Chapter Twenty

W S Ranch, TX
August 1899 – 1900

Butch was right. When things began to change for the trio, they did so rapidly, and decisions had to be made quickly. Two months after Elzy was captured, he was sentenced to life in prison for his part in the train robbery. While they were all relieved to hear he wouldn't be put to death, a dark cloud seemed to hover over them, especially Butch. Elzy's fate reminded them, as well as the rest of the Wild Bunch members, of what could happen to any of them. Many nights after long days of work, Butch would return to the cabin, no longer carefree and joking but now looking tired and beaten down.

"We're coming to the end, guys," Butch said sullenly one evening as the three sat in front of the fire. Days were still warm, but a chill bit the air in the evening, prompting Etta to start a fire each night.

Harry, who was sitting at the kitchen table cleaning his pistol, glanced up at Butch looking annoyed. Etta was on the sofa darning a sock. She chose to stay quiet in the hope that the two men wouldn't go at it again. Of late, Harry lost his temper with Butch regularly, mostly over his morose state of mind.

"We all knew the risks!" he'd yelled at Butch the night before. "Stop acting like it's the end of the world when one of us gets caught."

Etta would rather avoid another confrontation like that one. She could tell Harry was fearful, too, but he chose to hide it behind anger.

Butch sighed loudly as he stared into the fire. His posture reminded Etta of a very old man, and her heart went out to him for the weight he seemed to carry for his men, his gang, his Wild Bunch. Even though Butch actually had no control over the large group, she knew he still felt a sense of responsibility for them even when they did stupid things he warned them against. They were his friends, and in the case of the W S Ranch, they were his co-workers and some of them, like Elzy and Harry, were like brothers to him.

"Okay, old man. What's the problem now?" Harry asked gruffly as he continued polishing his pistol. Harry rarely used his Colt, but he wore it daily out in the dusty pastures and it was always covered in grime. He cleaned it nightly, wanting it ready for use at a moment's notice.

"They know we're here and it's only a matter of time before they come for us," Butch said.

"What the hell are you talking about?" Harry asked.

"Pinkerton men," Butch said.

At this, Etta and Harry both stopped what they were doing and stared at Butch.

"The detectives hired by the railroad companies to find you?" Etta asked.

Butch nodded.

"Tell me what's going on," Harry insisted, moving over to the sofa, closer to Butch.

"I bought one of them a drink last night in the saloon in Alma," Butch told them. "After you yelled at me last night..."

"Forget that," Harry growled. "What happened?"

Butch continued. "I headed over to the saloon and had a couple of beers with Harvey. In walked a man in a dark suit, asking the barkeep a few questions, showing a photograph around. I knew who he was right away so me and Harvey went up to the bar and bought him a drink."

Etta held back a smile. This was exactly the type of thing Butch would do, but Harry didn't find it amusing at all.

"Are you insane?" Harry yelled. "If that was a Pinkerton man, he knew exactly who you and Harvey were. Hell, you may as well have just turned yourselves in!"

Butch grinned. Etta knew he enjoyed driving Harry crazy. "Oh, settle down, you old woman. He wasn't after me. He was showing around some of the singed money from the Wilcox robbery. It's been traced to one of the guys down here at the W S."

"He told you this?" Harry asked.

"No, he told the captain this morning when he showed up at the ranch. The captain had a nice chat with the detective then called me up to the house for a talk."

"So, what happened?" Etta asked, moving forward on the sofa. Butch and Harry had known not to pass along any of the money from the train robbery locally, but apparently some of the other men involved weren't as smart.

"The captain had the man who'd passed the money in town talk to the detective. It ended up that he'd gotten it from one of our men a few months back. Luckily, that man isn't here any longer and the ranch hand who passed it didn't know anything about it being stolen."

"What about us? Does the captain know who we are?" Harry asked. His faced creased in a deep frown.

"The Pinkerton man showed an old photograph of me and one of Harvey to the captain and told him he knew we were here because he'd run into us at the bar. When the captain asked if the detective was going to try to round us up, the man said no, that wasn't his job. He was only here to trace the money. Said he wouldn't have a chance trying to capture us here and wouldn't even try."

"Well, that was kind of him," Harry said, dripping in sarcasm.

"Yeah, but that doesn't mean a whole group of them won't be coming after us soon," Butch said.

Fear coursed through Etta. The Pinkertons knew Harry and Butch were here. It meant their quiet life was over. "What did the captain say about you and Harvey being here?"

Butch grinned. "He said he didn't have any problem with either of us staying on as long as we wanted to. He likes our work, and he doesn't care what we do on our own time as long as it doesn't involve the ranch. He doesn't know who you are, Sundance, or if any of the other men are part of the Wild Bunch—and he doesn't care. So, I guess we're okay for a while."

"You're right, though," Harry said. "It won't be long before they decide to send a whole group of Pinkertons to try and get us." He sighed, suddenly looking just as tired and worn out as Butch. "So, what's the plan, Butch?"

"I don't want to bring any trouble to the captain or the W S," he said. "I think it's time to go home."

"Where, Butch?" Etta asked, downhearted at the thought of leaving the ranch. Living here had been as normal as their life had ever been and she was afraid it would never be this way again.

"Back to Hole-in-the-Wall," Butch said. "It's time we make a plan for our future and that's as good a place as any."

Two weeks later, the group set out on horseback for home. Winter was fast approaching so they didn't have the luxury of taking their time. Etta and Harry stopped in Cortez to visit Harry's cousins while Butch made a stop to see Maude Davis to deliver Elzy's share of the Folsom robbery. Harry and Etta didn't stay in Cortez long because the Pinkerton men had already visited the cousins and made it clear they were watching the ranch for any sign of Harry. The law was closing in and their world was getting smaller. The outlaws had no idea how much longer they'd be able to ride between hide-outs unnoticed.

Throughout the winter at the Hole, Butch and Harry devised a plan for the three of them to leave for South America the next year. The southern continent was fast becoming as the American Old West had been in its heyday. Copper, silver, and tin mines were booming, and land in Argentina was being touted as a rancher's paradise. Butch, who was an avid reader, learned all he could about the land there and the best place to settle down. The trio felt that this was the ideal location to start over, where the lawmen wouldn't follow them and they could settle down to a respectable life. However, moving so far away was going to cost a lot of money, and Butch knew exactly what needed to be done to finance their trip.

Tipton, Wyoming
August 29, 1900

Butch crouched by the train tracks beside the fire he'd set to indicate where to stop the train. He could feel the rumble of the engine and cars through his boots as it drew nearer. It was 2:00 a.m., and the sky was dark as coal, but the headlight on the train shone brightly. Butch knew that Sundance and Ben Kilpatrick had jumped onto the engine car as the train left its stop in Tipton, and they'd be directing the engineer to break by the fire. Harvey and Bill Carver stood with Butch, waiting.

"No shooting this time," Butch told the men, although his comment was more for Harvey than Bill. "If we're chased, shoot over their heads or at their horses, but not at the men. I won't have any blood on my hands."

Bill nodded agreement while Harvey grunted. Butch wasn't happy with Harvey and his latest escapades. In March, Harvey had killed three men, part of a posse that had chased him and Bill in Arizona. In May, he'd shot Sheriff Jesse M. Tyler down in cold blood as revenge for the sheriff killing Flatnose Currie in April. Butch didn't want any part in killing. He might have been an outlaw, and he took money that didn't belong to him, but he'd never killed a man and he meant it to stay that way. He had no tolerance for bloodshed.

The train slowed to a stop and the gang went into action. They ordered the trainmen to uncouple the engine, baggage, and express cars and move them down the tracks away from the passenger cars. Butch didn't want anyone hurt when they blew the safe, especially after what had happened in Wilcox. When Butch ordered the express car messenger to open the door, he was surprised to find it was the same man, Charles E. Woodcock, who had refused to open up at Wilcox.

Butch asked Woodcock how he was and told him he'd hate to have to blow the door again with him inside. It wasn't until the train conductor, Kerrigan, told Woodcock that they were ready to dynamite the door that he finally opened up and the outlaws jumped inside. It took the men three tries to blow open the safe, which resulted in blowing out the walls of the express car and the baggage car next to it. Within an hour, the gang was done with their work and on the road heading east as the train took off to the west to Green River. With a two hour head start, it wasn't difficult for the outlaws to get far enough away from the posse that would eventually be sent after them. To Butch's relief, no one had been hurt or killed.

* * *

Etta waited anxiously for the men near Baggs, Wyoming where they had a third relay of horses and supplies stashed. Close to noon the following day, much to her relief, they arrived. The gang split the cash five ways, a little over $10,000 for each man, then rode as a group southwest to Brown's Hole where they could rest and change horses again.

For the first time ever, Butch had planned back-to-back robberies. Within ten days they would be at their next job. While several posses searched for the gang all over Wyoming and Colorado, Butch and the gang were already scoping out their next robbery site in Northern Nevada. This time, Etta rode along, staying close to her men. She wasn't going to be left behind.

Chapter Twenty-One

Pine Creek, MN
February 1912

Emily stood in the nursery in Allison's home, admiring one of the many baby gowns folded neatly in the bureau drawer. The room had been painted a soft yellow and held a lovely spindle rocking cradle, a matching dressing table, a bureau, and a Bentwood rocking chair with cane back and seat. All the items were new, Emily knew, because she had been in the store when Allison and Ted had ordered them from a store in St. Paul. A pile of soft cotton diapers was stacked on the shelf under the dressing table along with diaper pins, powder, and an array of creams and lotions.

Allison was sitting in the rocker, her hands resting on her rounded belly, as Emily admired the gowns. She had begun feeling stronger in December, allowing her to move about the house and do light chores as well as cook dinner some evenings. She claimed it was Emily's special tea that had helped her, but Emily shrugged off her praise. Emily was sure it had more to do with Allison being near the end of her pregnancy.

"These gowns are lovely," Emily told Allison as she pulled out one, then another, to inspect. Some had ruffles on the yolk and others had beautiful embroidered stitching. Emily knew that many of the church women had made these for the baby as well as knitted booties, hats, and blankets. Emily had also contributed to the baby's layette by hand-stitching a small quilt with embroidered circus animals on the panels. The quilt was displayed prominently over the rail of the cradle.

"I'm blessed to have so many caring friends." Allison sighed happily as she leaned back in the rocker. "I could never have done all of this on my own as sick as I've been."

Emily nodded agreement. The townspeople did take care of their own and everyone had pitched in to help Allison. It was easy to want to help her. She was so sweet, gentle, and kind, and also expressively grateful for the help. Recently, Ted had hired a local girl to assist Allison around the house in the mornings so as not to take advantage of the women who had volunteered over the past months. They planned for the girl to stay on after the baby was born as well so Allison could get her strength back slowly and not wear herself out.

Emily carefully folded the baby gown and placed it back in the drawer. Seeing all these beautiful, brand new baby items reminded her of when Harry was born and how little they'd had. Poor Harry, wearing hand-me-down gowns that were brought to the convent for the orphans. He'd also had used blankets and a scratched cradle with a stained mattress that one of the local women had given to Emily.

The nuns had been wonderful to Emily and had worked together to make a beautiful baby quilt. A few local women had also given her much needed necessities, but for the most part, little Harry had less than Emily had ever intended for him.

When Emily had sailed away from Harry and Butch, she'd thought it would be only a few weeks before she'd see them again. He'd given her a large sum of money to ensure she could afford all she needed while they were apart. But as the weeks dragged by and he didn't come for her, when Emily began to suspect the worst, she was careful how she spent the money. After Harry was born and it was obvious she might never see her husband again, she knew she couldn't spend too much money in case she and the baby had to flee in a hurry. So, she depended upon the charity of others and the generosity of the nuns in return for her teaching services.

Allison sighed again, bringing Emily out of her thoughts. When she turned to face her, Allison was smiling sweetly.

"It's been nice, seeing you and Edward together these past couple of months." Allison's blue eyes twinkled. "Do you think someday you and he will be married?"

"Oh, my," was all Emily could manage, having been taken off-guard. "I'm not sure how to answer that."

Allison blushed. "I'm sorry. I shouldn't have pried. I only thought that the two of you look so perfect together, so happy, that maybe a future was possible."

A future, Emily thought. A future with Edward. The idea was plausible, but she hadn't dared to think that far ahead. At the moment, they were enjoying each other's company and getting to know each other better. And there was still the threat of what Sheriff Neilson might do. Emily knew he could change his mind at any moment, and she'd have to flee.

"Edward has never looked happier," Allison continued in her dreamy voice. "And it's so obvious he adores little Harry. I always knew he'd be good with children and it seems he is."

"Yes, he is and Harry enjoys spending time with Edward

also." Emily smiled as she thought of the many times she'd found Edward on the floor playing marbles with Harry or pushing along the train engine while making chugging noises. Seeing him that way warmed her heart. He didn't care if he looked foolish—he enjoyed entertaining Harry.

"Do you think, if you do get married someday, that you'll want to have a little brother or sister for Harry?" Allison asked.

Emily laughed. "Now we are placing the cart before the horse." But Allison's question did make her wonder. Would Edward want to have children? She wasn't sure she could even conceive another child.

"I just want happiness for you, Emily," Allison said seriously. "You're such a kind, sweet person. You deserve it."

"Thank you." Emily was grateful for her friendship with Allison. Through the years, she had missed that. Her friends had been few, and they'd moved around so often, she'd no sooner make a friend and then have to leave. She was happy she'd met Allison.

Emily helped Allison down the stairs and onto the sofa where she could lie down a while. As Emily walked through the snowy streets back to the store, she couldn't help but wonder if, after the way she'd lived her life, she deserved any more happiness.

Winnemucca, Nevada
September 19, 1900 - 12:00 p.m.

Etta stood in the alley behind the First National Bank of Winnemucca, holding the reins of four horses. Harry, Butch, and Harvey had walked around the front and entered the bank while Bill had casually tied his horse to a post across the street and stood just outside the bank to prevent anyone from entering.

Etta's presence at the robbery had been the subject of a heated argument between Harry and Butch the night before. Originally, it had been decided that she would stay at the Silve Ranch, thirty miles northeast of Winnemucca, where the relay horses and supplies were waiting. However, when Butch was going over the details of the robbery, he'd said he wasn't comfortable leaving the horses unattended behind the bank. Harry had scowled at him when he realized what Butch was hinting at.

"Absolutely not!" he'd told Butch.

"Aw, come on, you old grouch," Butch said. "She's as good a rider and shot as any of us. Besides, she'd be safe behind the bank, and we'll be out of there long before anyone knows what happened."

For over two hours, Etta sat quietly by as Harry had refused while Butch continued to praise the merits of her watching the horses. When asked, both Harvey and Bill agreed that having Etta along would aid in pulling off a smooth robbery. Ever since Etta had planned the escape of the men from the Deadwood jail, the outlaws, especially Harvey, felt she was as much a member of the gang as they were. Finally, Butch asked Etta if she'd be willing to help out and she readily agreed, but only if Harry approved.

Outnumbered and tired of fighting, Harry finally agreed. "If anything happens to her," he'd growled at Butch, "I'm holding you accountable."

Butch had rolled his eyes, but made sure Harry didn't see him do it.

So now, Etta stood there, dressed in men's clothing with her hair hidden under a hat, a bandana tied around her neck. She was surprised at how calm she felt, despite the danger she could be in. But she trusted Harry and Butch. They'd protect her no matter what.

It took only five minutes and the men were back. While Bill casually stepped away from the front of the bank and slipped out of town on his horse, unnoticed, Harry, Butch, and Harvey ran quickly to where Etta waited, each man tossing a heavy bag of gold coins over their horse's saddle. All four rode off in a sprint down the alley. Harvey led with Harry close behind. Etta rode directly behind Harry and Butch took up the rear.

Adrenaline pumped though Etta as she rode with the men. She now understood the excitement they felt from pulling a job. She kept her eyes trained on Harry ahead of her and maneuvered her horse expertly.

A revolver fired several times from the front of the bank as the outlaws rode down Second Street. Suddenly there were people running out of buildings, chasing the riders on foot. Butch fired warning shots over their heads to scare them off to no avail. Finally, the outlaws turned onto Golconda Road which would take them to the Silve Ranch. Unfortunately, Butch hadn't planned on the Deputy Sheriff commandeering a Southern Pacific switch engine that took off after the bank robbers, following them on the train tracks that ran parallel to the road. Townspeople, as well as the deputy, drew close and fired shots at the gang.

Etta felt a sharp stab on her left thigh and a burning sensation followed. Galloping fast to keep up, she looked down and saw that she'd been hit by a bullet. A red stain seeped through her pants. Trying to focus on riding, she pulled off her bandana and pressed it down hard on her leg. Blood soaked through it quickly, but she didn't have time to worry. She had to keep up with the men.

The road turned away from the train tracks and the outlaws were no longer being followed closely. Dizziness enveloped Etta, and she tried desperately not to faint. Butch caught up to her as her horse slowed and his eyes grew wide when he saw the bloodied bandana. He grabbed her reins, stopping the horse, then grasped hold of Etta before she nearly fell off.

Quickly, Butch dismounted and pulled Etta off her horse, then slapped its hind quarters so it would keep running, following the men to the ranch.

"Let me look at it," he told her, laying her on the ground and pulling off his own bandana.

"I'm okay, Butch," Etta said faintly. "I've just lost some blood. It made me dizzy."

Butch peeled away the blood-soaked fabric and inspected the wound. He ripped the hole in her pants wider. "A bullet must have nicked your leg, but it's deep," Butch said. "Hang on while I wrap it."

Etta watched, dazed, as Butch tore cloth from his flannel shirt, placed it over the wound, and tied his bandana tightly around her leg to help staunch the bleeding. Her leg throbbed with pain.

"We've got to get out of here, dear," Butch said. "That posse could catch up at any moment."

Butch help her up onto his horse and held on to her as he pulled himself up behind her. "You okay?" he asked.

She nodded, still feeling light-headed.

"I'll be hanging on to you tightly." He placed a soft kiss on the side of her cheek. "I won't let anything bad happen to you, Etta. Just don't faint on me, okay?"

Etta knew she was safe with Butch. She leaned into him and tried hard to resist the urge to close her eyes.

Off they rode at a steady pace but much slower than they had been riding on separate horses. Between the weight of two people and the heavy sack of gold coins, the horse struggled as they made their way to the ranch.

Harry ran up to them as they rode in, reaching up to help Etta down off the horse and into his arms. "What the hell happened?" he snarled at Butch.

"Etta's been shot," Butch told him, looking guarded as he waited for Harry's reaction.

"What?"

"I'm better now. I just lost a little blood," Etta said quickly, trying to defuse a fight between the men. Harry carried her to the shade of a tall tree and set her down into a sitting position against the trunk. He pulled away the bandana and scrap of fabric to inspect her wound. Butch ran off and brought back a canteen of fresh water. Etta drank it thirstily.

"Goddamn you, Butch!" Harry bellowed. "I told you we shouldn't bring Etta. I swear, if anything happens to her, I'll kill you!"

"Well, you'll have to kill me later. Right now we have to tend to this wound and get the hell out of here." Butch left again, this time returning with clean fabric to wrap Etta's wound, and a flask of whiskey. "This is going to hurt like hell, darling," he told her. Butch poured a little of the alcohol onto Etta's leg.

She clutched Harry's arm and drew in a sharp breath but didn't cry out. She knew if she made a big deal about the pain, it would only fuel Harry's anger at Butch.

Butch covered the wound with the clean cloth and once again tore off a strip of fabric from his shirt to secure the make-shift bandage.

While Butch and Harry were attending Etta, Harvey and Bill

transferred Butch's saddle and supplies onto a fresh horse.

"Etta will ride with me," Butch instructed when the men began preparing a horse for her. "We'll see how she's feeling when we reach the next set of relay horses."

"To hell with that. She's riding with me," Harry told Butch. "I'm not trusting you with her anymore."

"Please, don't fight," Etta said weakly, but the men ignored her as they glared at one another.

Harvey and Bill had been standing to the side, watching the men argue. The thunder of hooves could be heard coming their way.

"I don't care who the hell she rides with!" Harvey yelled, cutting them off. "We have to get out of here. Now!"

"Listen, Sundance. We've no time for this. Tie the other sack of money onto your horse and I'll ride with Etta. It only makes sense. There'll be less strain on the horse if Etta and I share."

Harry pursed his lips, his eyes mere slits.

Etta held her breath, waiting for Harry's response. Butch was right, of course. Butch was always right, which made Harry even angrier. Harry was taller and broader than Butch and weighed more, so it would be a strain on the horse if he and Etta rode together. She could see in his eyes that he understood this, and reluctantly agreed.

"Fine," Harry said. "But don't think this is over—not by a long shot."

Etta felt a little stronger now that she'd rested, although her leg still burned. Blood wasn't seeping through the bandage, thanks to Butch's care.

Harry helped her up into Butch's saddle and Butch pulled up behind her. She smiled down at Harry, trying to reassure him she'd be all right. It seemed to work, because he finally saddled up and the group was off again.

They rode east to Tuscarora where they had their last set of relay horses stationed. Etta rode her own horse from there as they traveled north. She was clear-headed now, but her leg throbbed and burned. The men rode at a slower pace, which helped, but as dusk fell, she was exhausted. Right before dark, the men set up camp and split the money between them. Relieved to stop riding, Etta crawled into her bedroll that Harry had laid out for her and fell fast asleep.

In the morning, Harvey and Will readied their horses to go northeast toward Hole-in-the-Wall.

Butch announced he'd be staying with Sundance and Etta. "I want to make sure Etta is okay."

Harry glared at him and Etta wasn't sure his being along was a good idea.

"Maybe you should go ahead with the guys as planned," Etta whispered to Butch so Harry wouldn't hear. "It'll give Harry a chance to cool off."

Butch looked down tenderly at her. "It's my fault you're hurt. I couldn't live with myself if something happened and I wasn't there."

His words touched Etta's heart. She adored Butch, even if he got on Harry's nerves sometimes. She only hoped the two men wouldn't fight throughout the trip.

The trio saddled up and rode north into Idaho. They were heading to Pocatello where they planned to board a train that would take them to Salt Lake City and then on to San Francisco to visit Harry's older brother, Elwood.

The trip to Pocatello was long and tense as the two men alternated between cold silence and fierce arguing. Nothing Etta said helped calm Harry down. He blamed Butch entirely for her getting wounded and wouldn't let it go. After days of riding with the men, Etta was ready to shoot them both.

The road they followed paralleled the Snake River, which ensured they had fresh water for the horses and to fill their canteens. Etta had changed out of her bloodied pants into lighter, baggier trousers that felt cooler and didn't aggravate her wound. Although it still throbbed after long days of riding, it had scabbed over and no longer bled. She felt lucky that the gash hadn't become infected, and she had Butch's fast thinking to thank for that. The whiskey had burned painfully, but it protected her leg from infection.

The evening before the trio reached Pocatello, they camped along the riverside. After collecting firewood, Butch stripped off his clothes and made for the river to cool down and wash off the dust from the road. Etta, also feeling dirty from days of riding, decided to do the same. Wearing only her chemise, she slipped into the water. It felt deliciously cool on her skin. She wasn't self-conscious about Butch seeing her in her underclothes; the three had been sharing living quarters for years and she knew she was safe with him. She assumed Harry wouldn't mind either. He'd never been jealous of Butch, only irritated by him. Harry had already gone off to hunt up a rabbit or grouse for supper.

Etta lay back and wet her hair, hoping to wash off the dirt and dust. When they'd left the W S Ranch, she hadn't packed any of her skirts and blouses because she didn't need them for the road. Harry had promised to buy her new clothes for traveling after their work was done. She hoped to find some decent clothes in Pocatello and a few nicer outfits once they were in San Francisco. Etta wanted to feel clean and fresh when they rode into town and went shopping.

As she lay floating in the water, Butch snuck up from behind and splashed her. She turned around and splashed back, and suddenly they were in a friendly water fight. Etta finally called a truce. They were both laughing and wiping water out of their eyes. Butch came up closer and stood in front of Etta in the waist-deep water.

"How's the leg healing?" he asked.

"It's fine. It scabbed over and is a little swollen, but it doesn't look infected."

"Let me have a look." Butch reached down and lifted Etta's leg out of the water. She placed a hand on his chest for balance. Slowly, tenderly, he ran his thumb over the scabbed area.

"Looks ugly, but it's healing fine," Etta told him, smiling up into his brilliant blue eyes.

"There's nothing ugly on you, darling." Butch bent down and kissed the wound on her leg. "I'm so sorry this happened to you," he whispered.

Touched, Etta gently caressed Butch's face. "I know."

Looking past Butch, she saw Harry standing on the shoreline, watching them. From his vantage point, she could only imagine what he was thinking, and the fierce look he was sending Butch said it all. Anger that had been simmering the entire trip was now written all over his face. She watched in disbelief as he dropped his gun belt and ran into the water with all his clothes on.

"You son-of-a-bitch!" he yelled. He grasped Butch's arm and pulled him away from Etta. Then Harry took Butch by the throat and shoved him under the water. "I'm going to kill you!"

Etta fell over backward into the water when Harry pulled Butch away. She struggled to get her footing and shook the water from her face. Etta watched in horror as Harry held Butch underwater and Butch struggled to get up.

"Stop it! You're drowning him!" She tried pulling him off Butch but he swatted her away like a fly. With his boots still on, Harry had trouble keeping a foothold in the water. It gave Butch a chance to knock him over and come up for air. But no sooner would Butch come up then Harry had him down again.

Helpless to stop them, Etta looked around and saw Harry's gun belt on the shore. She waded quickly over to it, picked up the Colt revolver, and aimed it over the men's heads. Two shots went off, echoing throughout the silent woods.

Both men froze in the water, Harry's hand clinging to Butch's hair as he was about to dunk him again. They gaped at Etta with the revolver pointed at them.

"Stop it now or I swear I'll shoot you both dead!" Etta screamed hysterically.

Harry let go of Butch's hair and Butch sputtered and coughed, clearing his lungs of water. Both men continued staring at Etta.

"I don't think I'd trust her not to shoot us," Butch said to Harry as he wiped the water from his eyes. "She's shot at you before."

Harry nodded. "Yeah, she's pretty deadly with a gun. And she looks really angry."

Butch chuckled. "She looks really wet, too."

Etta stood there, dripping wet, her hair falling in tangles around her face, holding the Colt straight out in front of her. She glared at the men as they spoke. She was fuming, and there they were, making fun of her.

Butch was the first to start laughing out loud, then Harry started in, too.

Etta slowly lowered the gun. "What's so funny?" she yelled.

"I mean it! I'm sick of your fighting. I'll shoot you both and leave you right there in the river."

This only made the men laugh harder. They fell down in the water, laughing until tears ran down their faces.

Butch turned to Harry. "We really shouldn't let her have a gun. One of these days, she's going to hurt one of us."

"You go ahead and tell her that," Harry said. "We'll see how it goes over."

Etta stared down at herself and realized just how silly she looked. The guys didn't look any better. She couldn't help but see the humor in it all, but forced herself to stay serious. Walking to the edge of the river, she yelled, "Are you two going to behave now?"

Butch laid his hand on Harry's shoulder. "I didn't mean anything by what you saw, Sundance," he said sincerely. "You know I love Etta, but I would never betray our friendship."

Harry nodded. "I know."

"And I'm sorry she was shot on my watch. It scared me as much as it did you, believe me."

Harry nodded again. "I know that, too."

"So, are we over this shit? Can we stop fighting?"

"Yeah, it's over."

Butch smiled wide. "Good, cause I wasn't looking forward to spending a lifetime together in South America with you being so damn mad at me."

Harry grinned back, and the two men shook hands.

Etta waded out into the water and joined them. "Are you two done fighting?" she asked. "Or do I have to shoot you?"

"We're all done, darlin'," Butch placed a kiss on her forehead.

"All good," Harry replied, pulling her close.

The next day the group rode into Pocatello where they rented two rooms in a nice boarding house. While Butch went off to sell two of the horses and saddles at the livery stable, Harry and Etta went shopping. At the general store, they found ready-made clothing for both of them as well as other personal items they needed. They each purchased a valise as well for traveling.

Etta was excited to have the robberies behind them and a new life to look forward to. While she enjoyed buying new clothes as well as any woman did, she was more excited about the idea of her, Harry, and Butch leaving the outlaw life behind and beginning anew. She would go anywhere with her men, as long as they were together.

That night, as they undressed for bed in their room, Harry surprised Etta with a small box.

"What is this?" she asked. For once, he was smiling, his eyes sparkling with excitement. Her serious Harry was enjoying a rare moment of happiness.

"Open it," he urged her.

Etta opened the box and gasped. Inside lay a gold wedding band. She lifted it up and admired the intricate carvings on the band that, when touched by light, glittered. "Harry? What does this mean?"

He took the ring and slipped it on the third finger of her left hand. It fit perfectly. "If I could legally marry you right now, I would. But I don't want to leave a paper trail that will somehow lead the detectives to you now, or in the future. So, I hope you'll take this ring as a reminder that I love you, and I promise to take care of you forever."

"I love you, too," Etta said, tears filling her eyes. "In my heart, we are married, and that's all that matters."

Two days later, Harry and Etta boarded a train that would take them to San Francisco to see Harry's brother. Butch, satisfied that all was well, rode off to Hole-in-the-Wall to meet up with Harvey and the rest of the gang. They all planned to meet in Fort Worth in November for their final goodbye before Etta, Harry, and Butch left for South America.

Chapter Twenty-Two

Pine Creek, MN
February 1912

Emily kept a close eye on Allison as she was due to have her baby near the end of February. Even though the weather was brisk, sometimes snowy, she visited almost every day after school let out. Often, little Harry went along with her, or sometimes spent time in the shop with Gertie. Although Allison was stronger, Emily knew she appreciated her visits and the small ways she helped her. Emily often brought grocery items that Allison needed or dropped off a warm meal from Evy's or fresh bread from the bakery.

The third Sunday in February, Edward drove them all, including Gertie, to church. After the service, as they drove her back to her home, Gertie invited them to eat Sunday supper with her. They happily accepted, and planned on returning to her house after checking in Edwards home.

As Gertie alighted from the buggy, she asked little Harry if he'd like to stay with her. "You can be my helper baking cookies." Harry readily agreed and followed Gertie inside, leaving

Edward and Emily to ride out to his house alone.

It was a sunny, calm day and although the temperature was only in the mid-twenties, the sun made it feel much warmer. Emily sat up next to Edward in the driver's seat, wrapping a heavy wool blanket around them to stay warm. Both were also bundled in wool coats, gloves, and thick scarves around their necks, so the cool air didn't bother them.

Once they arrived at the house, they split up to walk through it as they had so many times before. Emily went upstairs to check on the bedroom windows while Edward examined the rooms downstairs. Finding everything in order, she walked back down the stairs and met up with Edward.

"Everything looks fine," she told him and he nodded agreement. When they'd first entered the house, Emily had loosened her scarf and taken off her hat, setting it down on the table in the entryway. Her hair was still piled high upon her head but the sunlight coming from the parlor windows shone upon it. She saw Edward staring at her, smiling, as if in a dream and wondered what he was thinking.

"Is something wrong?" she asked, self-consciously.

"Oh, no. Nothing is wrong," Edward replied, looking embarrassed at having been caught staring at her. His expression turned serious. "I was thinking about moving back into the house this summer."

Emily's brows rose. "You mean, you'd no longer be living above the store?"

He nodded. "The house has been sitting empty far too long. I think it's time to bring it back to life."

Emily nodded slightly. Looking around, she couldn't blame him for wanting to move back into the house. It was quite cozy, yet had plenty of room, much more space to move around in than his one room above the store. "That sounds like a lovely idea," she finally said.

"Of course, it needs a little work, maybe some updating. The rugs and curtains may need changing and even fresh paint and wallpaper. I'm not sure if I'd be very good at decorating."

"I'd be happy to help you," Emily offered. "And I'm sure Gertie would also love to help."

Edward smiled mischievously, his brown eyes crinkling in the corners. "Actually, I was hoping you and Harry might also like to come live here with me."

Emily was stunned as he pulled a small, velvet box from his coat pocket. He opened the box, then held Etta's hand as he showed her what lay inside. A ring was nestled in the black velvet. It was a rose gold filigree setting surrounding a large, square-cut diamond that reflected a rainbow of colors in the sunlight.

Her heart pounded as she stared at the ring, completely taken aback.

Edward bent down on one knee as he continued holding her hand. "Emily, I fell in love with you the first day I met you and since then my love for you has only grown. I want to spend the rest of my life taking care of you and Harry. Will you please do me the honor of marrying me?"

She was so astonished that she would have fallen over backward if Edward hadn't been holding her hand. Her eyes traveled back and forth between the diamond ring and Edward's eyes, not knowing which to settle upon. "This is so unexpected. I don't know what to say."

Concern creased Edward's face as he slowly rose from the floor. "I know you weren't expecting this today, but I had hoped you thought we might marry someday. Was I wrong?"

He looked so crestfallen that Emily's heart went out to him.

She moved closer to him and looked up at him tenderly. "Please don't be hurt, Edward. It's just that you surprised me completely. There's still so much you don't know about me, or I of you. Is it right for us to marry when we know so little of each other?"

Edward smiled down at her. "I know everything I need to know about you. I know you're kind and caring and that you're a good and loyal friend. I know you're a wonderful mother to little Harry and a patient teacher to all the children in this town. I know you're intelligent and a hard worker. I also know you're an excellent shot if I ever need protection." He chuckled. Growing serious again, he said, "I love you for all those reasons and I love little Harry too. I want to have a life with both of you and be a family."

Family, Emily thought. Would Edward want children of his own? Was she able to have more children? "Edward, you're so sweet and kind and loving that it is very easy to love you, but there are things we should discuss first. Like..." she hesitated before continuing. "Like children. I had trouble conceiving before finally having Harry. I'm not sure if we could ever have children of our own."

"Then we won't," Edward said matter-of-factly. "If we do, that will be wonderful, but if we don't, we will always have Harry. All I want is you, and Harry, and a life together no matter where that may lead. I don't care about your past or where you've been or what you've done. All I care about is now and how much I love you." Edward wrapped his arms around her, looking deeply into her eyes. "All I care about is how much I need you. I was so empty before you came along and you changed my life completely. Please, marry me, Emily."

His words touched her heart. She closed her eyes and searched deep within her soul. Emily knew that she cared deeply for Edward and she could build a meaningful life with him. He would be a wonderful father for Harry and he'd take good care of both of them. She could stop running away, stop worrying that her past might come back and take her happiness away. Her husband was gone. She had to accept that. And her past was over. It was time to look ahead, let him go, and build a different future than the one she had once longed for.

"Marry me," Edward whispered into her ear, kissing her neck. "Make me the happiest man alive."

She opened her eyes and looked up at the man who just asked her to change the course of her life. "Yes," she told him as tears filled her eyes. "Yes. I'll marry you, Edward."

Edward hugged her close then pulled back to slip the ring on the third finger of her left hand. It sparkled in the sunlight pouring in from the windows, much as the other ring she'd once worn. But this was a new beginning, a new start to her life with a man of integrity, honor, and who had a good heart. And although she knew that a large part of her heart would always belong to her first husband, she truly believed she could give Edward all the love he deserved.

* * *

Gertie must have known Edward was planning to propose because as soon as they returned to her house for supper, she gave Edward a questioning look and quietly asked, "What happened?"

Of course, Emily heard and smiled at her as Edward whispered back, "She said yes."

Gertie cheered and gave hugs all around before admiring the ring Edward had given to Emily.

Before supper, Emily and Edward explained to Harry that they planned to be married and become a family. Being so young, Harry accepted it readily. He enjoyed spending time with Edward and the idea of eventually living together as a family sounded like fun to him.

After enjoying the delicious supper Gertie had prepared and complimenting Harry on the sugar cookies he and Gertie had made, they retired to their rooms above the store. It wasn't until Emily was alone in her room, and Harry had fallen asleep beside her, that second thoughts began to creep in.

She thought of her past, of how much she had loved her husband, and of all the adventures they'd shared. Her love for him had been strong and passionate, a love that did not die easily even though he was no longer with her. Could she love Edward the way she had loved Harry? Was she cheating Edward of true love if she wasn't able to completely let go of the man she'd once loved?

Emily struggled with these thoughts until she could stand them no longer. Quietly, she slipped out of bed and threw her robe over her nightdress. Stepping out into the dark hall, she stopped a moment to look at Edward's closed door. Light filtered through underneath, so she knew he was still awake with a lamp lit.

Tentatively, she knocked. "Edward?"

Edward quickly opened the door. He stared at Emily, and she suddenly felt self-conscious about her appearance. She wore only a thin, white cotton nightdress under her woolen robe, her hair falling loosely around her shoulders. Edward's reaction was to take in a sharp breath, and she suddenly felt nervous.

His face creased with worry. "Emily, are you all right? Is something wrong with Harry?"

His concern touched Emily. "We're both fine. I had to talk to you. Do you mind if I come in?"

He waved her in and hurried to light another lamp. He then placed a log on the woodstove fire to ensure the room stayed warm.

Emily sat on the side of the bed and was looking at the book he'd set down on the nightstand. When Edward saw her there, his face reddened, which she found amusing.

"I'm sorry to bother you," she said. "I saw your light was still on. Were you reading?"

Edward nodded. He looked unsure as to what to do. Finally, he sat in a chair across from Emily and pulled his robe tighter around him. "You aren't bothering me at all. And yes, I was reading. It seems that after the excitement of today, I couldn't fall to sleep."

Emily nodded. "I understand. I couldn't sleep either." She smiled over at him. His hair was tousled, and he still had his reading glasses on, which made him look far less proper than usual. Seeing him this way made Emily feel closer to him than she'd ever felt before.

Realizing Emily was staring at him, Edward self-consciously raised a hand to his face and felt the glasses. "Oh, sorry. I forgot I had these on." He pulled them off and slipped them into the pocket of his robe. "They make me look like an old man, don't they?"

Emily chuckled. "I think they look charming on you. I like seeing you this way."

"Disheveled?"

"No. Comfortable." Emily stood and walked over to stand in front of him. Edward looked up at her curiously.

"I was lying in my room, worrying that I might not be able to be the wife you wish me to be. But now, seeing you as you really are, I feel much closer to you."

Edward stood and held out his arms and she gratefully stepped into his embrace. He felt good—solid and strong, warm and loving. She raised her face and he lowered his lips to hers. Their kiss started out tender, but soon grew more urgent. Edward ran his hands through her hair as he kissed her deeply. Emily's desire grew. She hadn't realized that she could desire another man so completely. His touch brought dormant parts of her back to life.

Edward pulled away first with a choked gasp. "I'm so sorry," he said between breaths. "We shouldn't be doing this."

But Emily no longer cared about propriety. All she knew was that Edward had awakened the woman in her for the first time in years and she didn't want him to stop.

Reaching for him, holding him close again, Emily whispered into his neck. "Please hold me, Edward. I need your touch."

"We shouldn't. It isn't proper," Edward said softly, although his body denied his words and he didn't let her go.

Emily gazed up at him and smiled. "Oh, Edward. We are not young innocents. We've both been married before and we're engaged to be married. Would it be so terrible if we show our love now instead of waiting?"

Edward looked torn. "Are you sure?"

She answered him with a kiss. There were no more words. Edward carried her to his bed and made love to her with a tenderness and passion she hadn't thought he possessed. Finally, she was able to let go of her doubts and see a glowing future ahead of her.

Chapter Twenty-Three

Pine Creek, MN
1912

Once the door to their passion was unlocked, Emily and Edward were unable to resist its urge. After their first time together, they spent almost every night in each other's arms. The glow that stained Emily's cheeks during the day was thought by the townspeople to be the glow of new love as everyone congratulated the couple on their engagement. Had the town known they were spending nights together, it would have been scandalous. But the couple kept their private moments to themselves. They shared secret smiles, touches, and kisses in the store and held hands in the restaurant during meals. Edward mellowed and became less rigid and proper and Emily basked in his attention and outright adoration.

Each night, Emily put little Harry to bed and made sure he was fast asleep before quietly slipping out of the room to spend a few blissful hours with Edward before returning to her own room by dawn. Some nights they just held each other and talked about their future together, but most nights were spent exploring new ways to satisfy one another until their bodies were tired and fulfilled.

Edward was in awe of Emily's beauty and her appetite for lovemaking. Her body was soft and round in all the right places yet firm and slender where it should be. He loved her smooth, creamy skin and the way her silky hair fell over her shoulder when she laid on her side and smiled down at him. But it was her eyes that continued to enchant him. The unique lavender-blue color he'd noticed that first day he'd met her sparkled brighter when she laughed or deepened in color in her most passionate moments. They were like a mystical stone that changed color with her moods and charmed him to his core.

He couldn't believe how lucky he was to be with a woman who was so proper and respectable by day yet willing and eager to please, and be pleased, by night. Never had he thought lovemaking could be this exciting. He thought back to his first marriage with his lovely Lily and how shy and complacent she'd been in their marriage bed. While he had loved her tenderly, and would always have love in his heart for her, he felt a different kind of love for Emily. Theirs was one of mutual respect and fiery passion as he had never known.

One evening, as Emily lay on her side facing Edward, her left leg and arm slung familiarly over his body, he ran his fingers slowly over the smoothness of her waist, hip, and thigh. She was nearly asleep, looking warm and satisfied after their lovemaking. The oil lamp flame flickered, sending light and shadows over the two bodies under the quilt. As Edward continued to run his hand along her bare skin, he became aware of a small bump on her upper thigh. Slowly rubbing it with his thumb, it felt rougher than the rest of her skin.

"Did I hurt you?" he asked, afraid that their passionate and sometimes very physical lovemaking had caused her skin to bruise and swell.

"Hmm..." was all Emily managed as she lay sleepily in the warmth of his arms.

Edward grinned at how relaxed and content she looked but was concerned about the spot on her leg. He pulled back the quilt and inspected it. In the lamplight, he saw a faint scar on her leg, its color a shade or two lighter than the rest of her skin. It was almost two inches in length and at least an inch wide and was slightly raised. "What is this?" he asked, more to himself than to the sleeping figure beside him.

The raised quilt brought cool air over Emily's body and she woke slowly, looking over at Edward. "It's just a scar," she said. She wiggled, trying to snuggle closer to him.

Edward loved how completely comfortable Emily was with him and how she didn't mind the lamp being lit when they were together or him looking at her beautiful body. He'd never felt as close, both physically and emotionally, to anyone as he did with Emily. "How did you get this scar?" he asked, still running his thumb over it.

Emily closed her eyes again, as if thinking about her answer. "It's from a bullet," she finally told him, opening her eyes as his grew wide. "I was accidently shot in the leg a long time ago."

"Shot?" Edward sat up. "How in the world did that happen?"

Emily remained calm. "It was an accident. The bullet only grazed my leg."

Edward relaxed a bit. "Tell me."

"It was nothing, really. I was out hunting with my husband, our good friend, and a few of the ranch hands. One of the men shot his gun and it ricocheted off a rock or a tree and hit my leg."

"How badly did it hurt?" he asked curiously. Edward couldn't imagine being shot.

"At first all I felt was a stinging sensation and I didn't even realize I'd been shot until it started to bleed. It was a pretty big gash, and it bled profusely. Our friend thought quickly and poured whiskey over it and bandaged it up tightly to stop the bleeding." She glanced over at Edward, who was shaking his head ever so slightly.

"Hunting? Shot by a bullet? Whiskey? What kind of life did you lead?" he asked.

"A very dangerous one," she teased.

"Was your husband angry at the man who shot you?"

Emily nodded, chuckling. "Oh, yes. Mostly, he was mad at our friend because it was his idea for me to join the group. It all worked out, though."

Edward's eyes twinkled. "I can almost guarantee that you will never have to fear being shot while you're with me. Although, if I remember correctly, you're an excellent aim yourself, so perhaps I should be the one who is worried."

"I have no need of carrying a gun or shooting one here," she assured him.

Edward lowered his head and kissed the scar on her leg ever so gently. He continued placing soft kisses slowly up her leg, on her hip, in the crook of her waist then gently in the hollow of her neck. When he reached her lips, he was surprised to see tears trailing down her cheeks. "What is this?" he asked, wiping a tear away.

"Nothing. I was just remembering something from long ago. But it's all in the past now." Emily reached up and drew his face to hers. "I never thought I could love anyone again like I love you."

He replied by showing her how much he loved her with each intimate touch to her warm and willing body.

Fall 1900 – Winter 1901
San Francisco ~ Fort Worth ~ Pennsylvania

Etta's bullet wound healed and she and Harry enjoyed visiting San Francisco and his brother. Elwood Longabaugh was ten years older than Harry and had a calm, quiet, almost shy nature that belied the fact he worked among whaling men with salty language and rough ways. Elwood worked at the Laguna Honda Home for Sailors, a place where seamen lived while the whaling ships waited out the long, cold winters before taking off again to icy waters. The home was also an almshouse, a place for people who had fallen on hard times or who were sick and had nowhere to go. Elwood, with his caring ways, fit in perfectly working among the people who lived there.

Etta liked Elwood immediately and he seemed quite taken by her.

"How did you ever manage to make this beautiful, cultured woman your wife?" Elwood teased Harry.

Harry grinned. "Just lucky, I guess."

Etta wore the gold band Harry had given her and it was assumed by Elwood that the two were married. Harry hadn't wanted his family to have a reason to shun her, and since she felt they were married already, Etta was fine going along with the small deception.

The couple stayed at a charming boarding house with a beautiful view of the bay. They used the alias' Mr. & Mrs.

Harry Place. Place was Harry's mother's maiden name and it was untraceable by Pinkerton agents and any other lawmen that might be searching for him, so it was the perfect cover.

Etta and Harry shopped at some of the finest places in San Francisco and bought clothes for the trip they would soon take out east to visit the rest of Harry's family. Before they left for South America, Harry wanted to reconnect with his family and let them know he was planning on going straight. He would no longer be the outlaw they knew he'd become.

The couple said goodbye to Elwood in early November and took a train to Fort Worth, Texas. They met up with Butch, Harvey, Will, and Ben Kilpatrick for one last reunion before heading east. The entire gang had rooms at the Maddox Hotel on Main Street, where they partied the nights away. This was their final goodbye and the men certainly made the most of it.

Etta steered clear of the men and their rowdy parties. She spent her days shopping or enjoying quiet time reading books in the room she and Harry shared. When Will married his long-time sweetheart, Lille Davis, a woman who had once worked for Fannie, Etta joined in on the celebration. She hadn't known Lille, but she was happy for Will.

"I can't believe you tied the knot," Butch told Will the night of the celebration. "All the Wild Bunch men are becoming domesticated. Except me, of course."

Harry wrapped his arm around Etta's waist and grinned at Butch. "You just haven't found the right woman yet, Butch. Someday, some beautiful filly will turn you to mush. You just wait and see."

Butch shook his head and took another shot of whiskey. "Not ever going to happen. You already took the best woman I've ever known." He winked at Etta.

Etta smiled as Harry glared at Butch. It was all in fun, though. Etta adored Butch, but Harry held her heart and he knew it.

Butch came up with the idea that the group should have a photo taken wearing their finery and looking like prosperous gentlemen, not notorious outlaws. The gang gathered at the Swartz Portrait Studio just down the street from their boarding house and took a group photograph. Looking dapper in their suits, watch chains, and bowler hats, the five men posed for the photograph that would prove to be their downfall. Soon, the Pinkerton agents would be carrying this photo to identify the outlaws, but they had no idea this would happen as the shutter snapped and the photo became history.

In December, Etta, Harry, and Butch headed to San Antonio for a quick visit with Fannie. Believing Harry and Etta were finally married, Fannie happily greeted the couple and Butch. She agreed that their plan to move to South America to go straight was a good one, although she admitted she was sad to see them go.

"I'll miss you terribly," she told Etta when they were alone. "I know we rarely see each other, but I always knew where you were. Now, I won't ever see you again."

"I'll write to you," Etta assured the older woman, giving her a warm hug. "And Harry says that we'll be able to come home from time to time. Eventually, the lawmen will stop looking for us."

Fannie didn't look convinced.

"Please be happy for me, Fannie," Etta said. "I'm thrilled to be going. Now, we'll have a normal life where we can settle down and maybe even start a family. It's what I want."

The flamboyant madame smiled at the girl she once took care of. "If it's what you want, then I am happy for you, dear. Just know I'm always here if you need me."

Etta knew she'd miss her beloved friend. She would always be grateful to Fannie for everything she'd done for her mother and her. Fannie was like family to her, and she'd always adore the kindhearted woman.

The threesome stopped long enough in New Orleans to celebrate the New Year of 1901. Afterward, they headed to Pennsylvania to visit Harry's family.

Etta was excited about seeing Harry's family, but a little nervous about meeting his older sister, Samanna. Harry talked little of his other siblings, but he praised Samanna incessantly. She was eight years older and had been married and starting a family of her own by the time he left Phoenixville. Because Harry had been the youngest, he'd spent a lot of his time with Samanna and her husband, Oliver, and even helped out often at Oliver's wrought iron business. Harry described Samanna as kind, sweet, patient, and extraordinarily beautiful. Etta hoped she wouldn't be too much of a disappointment to his sister.

"Don't worry," Harry assured her on the train trip to Pennsylvania. "Samanna is going to adore you."

"How could she not?" Butch added. "You're everything Sundance says she is, so you're two of a kind."

Etta appreciated Butch's sincere assurance, but she still secretly worried. She wanted Harry to be proud of her and make a good impression on the entire family, especially Samanna.

When they finally pulled into the very same train station that Harry had left town from at the tender age of fourteen, and she met Samanna for the first time, Etta found her fears had been unwarranted. Samanna was just as sweet, kindhearted, and beautiful as Harry had remembered. She greeted Etta with a welcoming hug and said in a joyous voice, "I'm so happy to have you as my sister, Etta."

Etta fell in love with her immediately.

Samanna and her husband lived in a large, three-story home and although there was enough room for the trio to stay there, Etta, Harry, and Butch had decided to rent two rooms at the nearby Mansion House Hotel. Being the kind soul that she was, Samanna welcomed Butch into her home as graciously as she would any family member, although everyone called him James, for James Ryan, the alias he was using. Samanna knew exactly who he was, but since he was such a close friend of Harry, she chose to ignore his reputation.

Samanna and Oliver's three children were grown, two of whom Harry had last seen when they were only babies. The children were as welcoming and kind as their mother and enjoyed spending time with Etta and Harry, and even Butch. Harry's other older sister, Emma, who was unmarried and owned her own dressmaker's business, did stop by to visit, but her displeasure at Harry's notorious outlaw life showed clearly on her lined face. She had little to say to her long-lost brother or to Etta and mostly sat with a sour, disapproving expression.

Harvey, Harry's brother who was older by only two years, also visited bringing along his wife Katherine and their three young children. Harvey had an easy-going manner and a mischievous twinkle in his eyes. He loved teasing his baby brother, and got along well with Butch, too.

The more time Etta spent at Samanna's, helping her in the kitchen or with laundry, despite Samanna's protests, the more she grew to love and admire her. Samanna's dark hair, caught up in a bun, blue eyes, and petite frame so resembled Etta's that the two women could easily have been mistaken for sisters. And Etta could see that Samanna loved her younger brother dearly, no matter what his lifestyle was. She teased him mercilessly when he gave her a serious frown and told stories of when he was a little boy and the mischief he got into. Then she'd smile or wink at him, making him grin, bringing out the boyish charm in his smile that Etta had loved that very first day she'd met him.

Harry transformed into a different man at Samanna's home with family all around. He was carefree, laughed easily, and smiled often. He joined in with the children as they played and he and Butch even started a snowball fight in the backyard with Harvey's children and a few neighborhood kids. Etta marveled at the change in Harry and she gave credit completely to Samanna.

"Is this how it will be when we're finally settled in South America?" Etta asked Harry one evening as they sat quietly on the porch swing at Samanna's house. "Will you be this carefree and happy?"

Harry smiled down at her. "I can't promise it will be like this," he told Etta, kissing her sweetly on the forehead. "But I do hope it will be. Maybe, with the stress of the outlaw life behind us, we can finally be truly happy."

Etta prayed that they would be.

Chapter Twenty-Four

Pine Creek, MN
February 1912

The snow began falling on a Friday morning the last week of February and continued throughout the day. It was light and fluffy at first, and the children had fun playing in it, building snowmen and throwing snowballs during their lunch break. But by the time school let out, the snow had become heavy, piling up on the streets and sidewalks.

Emily's skirt hem was caked with snow by the time she and little Harry walked the short distance from the school to the store. The sky was thick with clouds and the day was a dark gray. Harry begged to play in the snow, but Emily thought it was best to get him dry and warm and for him to stay inside. Once they had both changed, they went downstairs to the store where Harry found a corner in the back room to play with his toys.

"It's still coming down out there," Gertie said, staring out the front window. There were no customers in the store. "Everyone must have decided to go home and wait out the snow."

"We might as well close up and do the same," Edward said.

"Let me walk you home, Gertie, before it gets dark. I don't want you trudging through this heavy, wet stuff alone."

"Don't be silly. I can walk home on my own." She tossed an impatient look Edward's way. "But I think I will leave. It doesn't look like the snow is stopping anytime soon."

Emily grinned as Gertie went in back to put on her coat and boots. She loved how feisty and independent Gertie could be at times.

The door opened and in walked Arnold Townsend, snow-covered and carrying a basket with a towel over it. "Hello, all," he said, beaming. "It sure is a bugger out there. So much snow!"

"My goodness, Arnold." Edward walked up to him. "What are you doing outside? Come over by the stove and warm up."

"I'm fine." He handed Edward the basket. "I just came to deliver this. Evy wanted to make sure you and Mrs. Pleasants had your evening meal before we closed up early. There'll be no customers tonight, not with this blizzard. The roads are impassable now, and the sidewalks are becoming treacherous."

"That was so kind of you, Arnold," Emily said. "Please send our appreciation to Evy for her thoughtfulness."

"I will," he said, smiling at her.

"Arnold. What are you doing out in this weather?" Gertie asked, coming out from the back room.

"Just bringing over some supper. It looks like you're headed home, Gertie. I'll walk with you since we're going the same way."

"Sounds fine," Gertie agreed. "Goodnight," she called to Emily and Edward before heading out the door.

"I'm happy Arnold is walking with her," Edward said. "I'd hate to see her fall. I know he'll insist on taking her the entire way home."

Emily nodded and looked inside the basket. There was a

crock of soup, bread, butter, crackers, and three slices of apple pie. "Well, at least we won't starve."

"With a store full of food supplies, I'm sure we could have come up with something to eat." Edward chuckled. "But it was very thoughtful of Evy to do this."

They closed the store and pulled the shades, then the three sat near the woodstove in the back room and ate their supper. Harry grew drowsy after his long day of school and playing in the snow. Emily readied him for bed and tucked him in. He was asleep in no time. After changing into her nightclothes, she made sure the stove had plenty of wood in it to stay warm then went across the hallway to Edward's room.

* * *

A pounding sound woke both Emily and Edward with a start.

Edward quickly lit a lamp and glanced at the clock. "It's three in the morning! What on earth?" He slipped on his dressing gown and slippers, then went out the bedroom door to investigate.

From inside the bedroom, Emily heard a man calling out Edward's name as he pounded. She realized it was someone at the outside door. She slipped out of bed and put on her robe and slippers, but stood inside the bedroom door, listening.

"Edward! Please, let me in. It's Ted!" the voice called through the door.

Edward quickly unbolted the door and opened it. Ted stepped inside, shaking the snow off his boots and hat on the rug.

"What's wrong?" Edward asked, concern creasing his brow.

"I'm sorry to wake you," Ted said. "I came to get Mrs. Pleasants."

"Whatever for?"

Ted's voice sounded anxious. "Allison is having the baby. She's having a difficult time. The doctor is out at the Albright's farm, stuck there in this snowstorm. There's no way to get him. The pastor's wife is with Allison and has been all day, but she's getting worried. And Allison is asking for Mrs. Pleasants. I wouldn't bother you if I didn't think it was important."

Before Edward could respond, Emily stepped out of Edward's bedroom and into the hallway.

"Just give me a moment to dress and we can go," she told the sheriff.

Ted nodded, looking relieved. If he thought it strange that she'd come out of Edward's bedroom in the middle of the night, his expression hadn't revealed it. "I have my horse out front. It was the only way to get through the snow-covered streets."

"That's fine," Emily said. She walked quietly into her own bedroom and lit an oil lamp. Miraculously, Harry had slept through the noise. Her heart beating rapidly, she quickly dressed in a split-skirt, warm stockings, and ankle boots. She put on her wool coat and wrapped a thick scarf around her neck. It mattered little to her how she looked. She was worried about Allison and wanted to get to her as quickly as possible.

As Emily left the bedroom, she heard Edward speaking quietly to the sheriff.

"I hope I can count on your discretion about what you saw here tonight," Edward said, sounding nervous.

She saw Ted place a hand on Edward's shoulder. "I would never judge you, my friend. What happens behind closed doors is no one's business."

"I'm ready," Emily interrupted.

"Come this way." Edward walked through the doorframe

leading down to the shop. "There's no sense in you trudging in the snow down the alley."

The trio hurried downstairs and through the store to the front door. Emily saw the sheriff's horse tied out front. The snow had grown deeper throughout the night. It was up to the horse's belly.

Emily turned to Edward. "Will you please keep an eye on Harry?"

He smiled at her. "Of course. Don't worry about him. Put all your energy into helping Allison."

She raised up on tip-toe and kissed his cheek, then followed the sheriff outside.

* * *

Edward watched as Ted pulled himself up onto his horse while Emily waited on the boardwalk. Then, extending his arm, Emily grabbed hold of it and he pulled her up onto the horse behind him in one smooth motion before they took off down the road at a fast clip.

Edward's heart swelled with pride at how expertly Emily had jumped onto the horse. It was as if she'd done it a hundred times before.

"Maybe she has," he said aloud into the quiet store. She never stopped surprising him. He had a feeling she never would.

* * *

Emily slipped off the horse before the sheriff even came to a complete stop in front of the house then made her way up the porch stairs and into the entryway. Quickly, she pulled off her boots and coat and shook the snow from her skirt. Then she ran up the stairs to Allison.

Pastor Johnson was sitting on a bench in the upstairs hallway. He glanced up, his eyes tired and worried.

"Pastor," Emily said, grasping his hands in greeting. "How is Allison?"

"Poorly, I'm afraid," he said. "My wife will be relieved you're here. Allison has been asking for you."

Emily nodded. The pastor squeezed her hands as if to reassure her. She turned and gently opened the door to the bedroom. Allison lay on the double bed, looking exhausted. Her face was pale and her hair was damp with perspiration.

"You're here," Allison said, her voice weak.

Emily hurried to her bedside and took her limp hand. "Yes, sweetie. I'm here," she said soothingly. Emily ran her hand gently across Allison's forehead, brushing her hair away. It frightened her to see Allison looking so pale and her eyes glazed over. "Everything is going to be fine," she whispered to her friend. She prayed her words were true.

Millie, the pastor's wife, was standing on the other side of the bed, also looking relieved. "I'm happy you came," she said. "Allison so wanted you to be here."

Suddenly, a contraction seized Allison's body and she squeezed Emily's hand as she cried out in pain. Emily spoke softly to her until the contraction slowed and Allison once again went limp on the bed.

"Let me speak with Millie a moment, dear," Emily said to Allison calmly. "I'll be right back."

Emily and Millie moved to the far corner of the room and spoke quietly.

"How long has she been in labor?" Emily asked.

Millie sighed. "Since around eight o'clock in the morning—yesterday. Almost twenty-four hours. For anyone else, I wouldn't worry about the first baby coming so slowly. But Allison was so sick and weak to begin with. And she is very slight in size. She has also lost a lot of blood. I've helped bring many babies into this world, but this is not running the course of what I'm used to." Millie placed a hand on Emily's arm. "I'm afraid for her," she said in a whisper. "Something isn't right."

"Let me have a look. I helped the nuns deliver a few babies at the convent. Maybe there's something we can do to help her."

Millie nodded. She looked tired and worn, and Emily's heart went out to her. The poor woman had been at Allison's side all this time and Emily knew she must be exhausted.

Emily quickly checked to see how far along Allison was, and was surprised to see she was fully dilated. Yet, when the next contraction came, she couldn't see the baby's head crowning. Instead, she saw what looked like the baby's shoulder. Fear gripped her. The baby wasn't in the right position for a proper birth. Both Allison and the baby were in a dire situation.

Quickly, she pulled Millie aside. "The baby is in the wrong position," she said. "Not breech, but the head isn't positioned properly. We'll need to turn the baby."

Millie's eyes widened. "I've never done that. Nor seen it done."

"I watched a nun turn a baby once," Emily said. "If we don't at least try, we'll lose the baby, and maybe even Allison."

Fear filled Millie's eyes, but she nodded agreement.

"Please comfort Allison while I find the sheriff," Emily said. She walked calmly out of the room, despite the fear she felt. She had to stay composed or she'd scare Allison. That was the last thing she wanted to do.

"How is she?" Ted asked, anxiously.

"She's in need of some help," Emily said truthfully. She turned to the pastor. "Would you please bring up more clean, warm water to wash my hands with? And any clean rags or towels you can find."

"I've been keeping water heated on the stove," the pastor said. "I'll hurry back."

She turned back to Ted. "Allison needs your help. The baby is sideways and needs to be turned. Strong, large hands are needed."

He gaped at her, shocked. "Me? In there? I can't."

"Yes, you can," Emily insisted. "Your wife needs you."

The pastor came back up the stairs with a pail of warm water and strips of cloth. "I'll heat up more," he said. He hurried downstairs again, obviously sensing it would be needed.

Emily took a deep breath to calm her nerves before entering the room again, carrying the pail. Ted followed her inside and shut the door, looking everywhere except at his wife in the bed.

"Why is he in here?" Millie asked, looking horrified.

"We need him to turn the baby," Emily whispered to Millie so as not to scare Allison. Emily poured the clean water into the basin on the dresser and began to wash her hands.

At that moment, another contraction hit Allison and she cried out. Millie held her hand and wiped her brow with a wet cloth that Emily had handed her. Ted watched his wife, the color draining from his face.

"She's fine," Emily told him. She walked over to the side of the bed and talked softly to Allison after the contraction was finished. "Allison, dear. The baby isn't in the right position to be born, so we're going to give it a little extra help. We need you to be strong for a little longer."

Allison looked up at her with glazed eyes. She nodded that she'd heard. "Just save my baby," she whispered.

Tears threatened to fill Emily's eyes, but she forced them back. "Everything is going to be fine," she told her. Emily wished she felt as certain as she sounded.

Pulling Ted aside, Emily whispered, "I need you to focus and do as I say. During the next contraction, you're going to gently move the baby as I try to move it from inside. Do you understand?"

Panic filled Ted's eyes. "If we have to choose between the baby and Allison, please save Allison."

Emily's heart went out to this man who so obviously loved his wife. She placed her hand on his arm. "We're not making that decision today. Both will survive."

Ted gave her a pained look.

Emily guided him over to the other side of the bed. Lifting Allison's nightgown to expose her stomach, she showed Ted what he needed to do. "When I say, you have to place your hands here, and here." She showed him exactly where to position his hands around the baby bump. "Then, you will press against the baby and move your hands to the left. Firmly, but gently."

He looked terrified but nodded. Emily hoped he wouldn't pass out from fear.

She positioned herself at the foot of the bed and Millie stood on the other end, clasping Allison's hand. A contraction began and Allison tensed.

"Now! Move the baby," Emily ordered Ted. She could see more of the baby's shoulder and part of its arm. She reached inside the womb and tried to guide the baby into position as Ted slowly moved the baby from the outside.

Allison screamed from the pressure, causing Ted to stop and pull away.

"We're hurting her!" he yelled, his face contorting with fear.

The contraction subsided. Allison lay there, whimpering, tears seeping from her eyes.

Emily grabbed Ted's arm and pulled him across the room. "If you want to save your wife's life and your baby's, you will do as I say," she said sternly. Her fear had been replaced by anger. She had to save Allison and the baby.

He glared at her. "I won't do it. I can't hurt her like this."

"Yes, you will!" Emily insisted. "Now go back and do what I've told you to do."

He stared at her, looking shocked at the fierceness of her tone. Their eyes met and clashed. He must have seen her determination to save Allison, because he finally did as he was told.

Another contraction seized Allison, and they worked together to move the baby. It took all the courage Emily had to reach inside Allison's womb again and maneuver the baby, knowing it caused her pain. She had to disregard her friend's screams, and she could see Ted's jaw tighten as he also tried to ignore them. On the third contraction, Emily pushed the baby's slippery body in and over as Ted turned it. She was rewarded when she saw the head crowning. Relief flooded through her.

"We've turned it!" she yelled joyously.

Ted heaved a great sigh, as did Millie.

Once it was in position, the baby came quickly. Ted held his wife's hand while Millie assisted Emily. With one last push, the baby fell into Emily's arms. Tears of relief filled her eyes as she held the newborn. Millie handed her a towel to wrap around the damp child and Emily quickly wiped the mucus from its nose and mouth. The baby let out a wail, and everyone in the room seemed to sigh in unison.

"It's a girl," Emily told the new parents, tears trailing down her cheeks. "A beautiful, perfect girl."

Allison cried, relieved, as Ted leaned over the bed and held her. Emily cut the umbilical cord and Millie took the baby over to the basin to wash it with the warm water the pastor had brought up again. Once the baby was cleaned and wrapped in a blanket, Millie laid the child in the crook of Allison's arm. Mother and father stared down at their baby in awe, and the look on their faces warmed Emily's heart.

Millie helped Emily clean up Allison once the afterbirth was delivered. They shooed Ted out for a few minutes to change the bed and dress Allison in a fresh gown. Ted looked crestfallen about leaving his wife's side.

"Take the baby with you and show my husband." Millie lifted the little girl and handed her to him.

Beaming, Ted held the newborn as if she were made of glass and left the room.

Once all was cleaned up, Allison fell back against her pillows and sighed. "Thank you," she said softly, all her energy spent.

Millie kissed her forehead. "You rest now. The baby will be hungry soon and you need your strength."

Allison nodded.

Emily placed a hand on Millie's shoulder. "It's your turn to rest now. You must be exhausted. Let your husband take you home so you can sleep. I'll stay a while to make sure all is well."

Millie sighed. "I won't fight you on that. I am tired." The two women hugged. "That was an amazing thing you did tonight. You saved a life, maybe two," she told Emily.

"We all did it together," Emily said.

After gathering up the bloodied sheets and rags, the women went out to the hallway.

"You can join your wife now, Ted," Emily said. "She's almost asleep."

Ted was rocking the baby back and forth in his arms. "Are you leaving?"

"Millie is, but I'll stay and keep an eye on Allison for a bit."

He nodded, then walked carefully into the bedroom.

"A fine baby," the pastor said, yawning. "I think we're all ready for a good sleep."

Emily walked downstairs with them and saw them out. She found a washtub in the kitchen, set the dirty items in it, and filled the tub with the hot water from the stove, leaving them to soak. Then she went about making fresh coffee and some tea for herself. Doing these mindless chores kept her from thinking about what could have happened had it all gone wrong. Thankfully, all went well.

As she glanced out the kitchen window, she saw the sun coming up. She smiled. It was going to be a beautiful day.

"Can I help with anything?" Ted asked, coming up behind her.

Emily shook her head. "You should be upstairs with your wife and new daughter."

"Allison fell asleep and the baby is curled up in her arm. I'll go back up in a minute."

Emily offered him a fresh cup of coffee and he accepted it thankfully. They both sat at the kitchen table and sipped their warm drinks.

Ted looked at her intently. "Thank you for saving my wife and baby."

"I'm thankful I was able to," Emily said, looking up at him.

"You know how much I care about Allison."

"You amaze me, you know that? You were so calm and collected in there while I was scared out of my wits. If you hadn't kept your focus like you did, I'd hate to think of what could have happened to Allison."

"I've had experience with a few tense moments in my life," she said, then grinned at him. "Keeping calm is the only way to get through them."

Ted chuckled. "I bet you have."

They sat in silence, both in their own thoughts. Emily no longer feared being alone with the sheriff. After what they'd just done together, nothing else seemed as important.

"Allison said she wants to name the baby Emily, after you," Ted announced, breaking the silence. "Emily Ava Neilson. Ava was her mother's name."

Emily raised her brows. "That's very sweet. But how do you feel about it?"

"If it makes Allison happy, then I'm happy. I didn't have the heart to tell her that your real name isn't Emily. She must never know who you really are."

Emily looked into Ted's eyes. "Emily is my real name. I'm not lying about that. And I'm honored that Allison chose to name your baby after me."

He nodded. "I guess that means we're forever tied together, almost like family," he said, then laughed. "It wouldn't do for me to arrest the woman my very own daughter is named after."

Emily watched him, staying silent.

He sobered. "What I'm trying to say is you saved Allison's life, and I will forever be in your debt. Anything that has passed between you and me in the past is over."

Emily couldn't believe what she'd just heard. It was over. She looked up at the sheriff and saw in his eyes that he meant what he'd said. Relief flooded through her. She was safe. She and little Harry could live out their lives here without worrying about her past catching up with her.

"Thank you," she said softly.

Ted smiled and nodded.

A knock on the kitchen door startled them both. Ted stood up and answered it.

"Has the baby arrived?" Edward asked, stepping inside.

"Yes. We have a little girl," Ted said, grinning proudly. "We've named her Emily Ava."

Edward's face lit up. "That's wonderful! Congratulations! You couldn't have named her after a more deserving person." He patted Ted on the back.

"I couldn't agree more," Ted said. He left then to check on Allison.

Edward walked closer to Emily. "Did everything go okay?"

All the stress of the morning hit Emily. She reached up and hugged Edward, relieved that all had gone well and he was here with her.

"My goodness. What did I do to deserve that?" he asked as she pulled away.

"I'm just so happy you're here. It was a difficult birth, and I was scared for a time, but both the baby and Allison are fine now," she said.

"I'm sure she was in good hands with you." He placed a kiss on her cheek.

"Where's Harry?" Emily asked.

"He's with Gertie. She came to the shop early and I asked her to take Harry to Evy's for breakfast. The snow has stopped and the streets are being cleared. It's going to be a beautiful day.

Are you ready to go home?"

Emily nodded. Home. It had been a long, tense night, and so much had happened. For years, she'd wanted a place to settle down, a place to call home. Now, she finally felt free. Free to move ahead with her life without the shadow of her past following her. Free to call this lovely little town home.

"Yes," Emily said. Let's go home."

Chapter Twenty-Five

New York City
February 1901

Etta, Harry, and Butch checked into Mrs. Catherine Taylor's boarding house on West Twelfth Street in New York City on February first. They signed in as Mr. and Mrs. Harry E. Place, and Butch used the alias James Ryan, posing again as Etta's brother. They rented the entire suite of rooms on the upper floor where they planned to stay for three weeks.

Before they'd arrived in New York City, Etta and Harry had visited Buffalo, New York where they'd checked in to Dr. Pierce's Invalid Hotel, a renowned medical facility that advertised the treatment of chronic diseases. Harry suffered from chronic sinusitis and also had a leg wound he wanted them to treat. Etta saw a doctor for her inability to become pregnant. She worried that she had a medical condition that kept her from either becoming pregnant or carrying to term. After spending time at the facility, both were given a clean bill of health.

"You're a healthy young woman," the doctor told her.

"Perhaps, once you're settled, you will be able to conceive and carry to term."

Etta hoped he was right. She wanted so badly to start a family with Harry once they were settled in South America.

Etta loved New York City. Smartly dressed people walked the crowded sidewalks and new automobiles filled the streets. At night, the street lamps shone brightly, and people bustled to and fro. After having lived out west where life was simple and crude, it was exciting to be in a new, modern city.

The trio took in a play and ate at the fanciest restaurants. They played tourist, taking carriage rides in Central Park and shopping all over town. Dressed in the most fashionable attire themselves, Harry surprised Etta with a stop at Tiffany & Company jewelry store.

"Pick out something you'd like," he said. "Anything at all."

Etta was overwhelmed by the choices, but eventually her practical side won out, and she chose a beautiful lapel watch made of rose gold with an intricate leaf design on the cover.

"It's perfect for you," Harry told her as he helped her pin it on her dress. He lovingly kissed the tip of her nose. "You are a lady through and through."

Etta smiled and Butch chuckled. "Yeah. A lady with a great aim," he teased. Butch wasn't as practical. He chose a gold stick-pin with a diamond on it. "I have to keep up with the rich folks," he said as he stuck it through the knot of his necktie.

Butch paid for the purchases. Harry trusted him to carry their money. Being an avid gambler, Harry knew it wasn't safe for him to hold large amounts of money.

As they walked out into the chilly day, Butch smiled widely. "You two are pretty enough for a picture." His eyes lit up. "That's where we're headed next. To have your photo taken."

Harry frowned at Butch. "Whatever for?"

"To remember our time in New York City. To commemorate how lovely our Etta is. To celebrate!"

"Our Etta?" Harry asked.

"Okay, okay. Your Etta. Come on, you old grouch. Let's celebrate with a photo."

They entered the DeYoung Photography Studio and Harry and Etta posed for a picture together. The photographer handed Harry a top hat to hold in his hand and posed the couple to best show off Etta's long, full skirt and the lovely sleeves of her dress that were trimmed in gold thread and pearls. As the camera flashed, the couple looked handsome and dignified. The photographer was so enraptured by the serene look in Etta's eyes, he later displayed the photo in his shop's window to show off his work.

The trio spent three glorious weeks in New York City before boarding the British steamship *Herminius* for Buenos Aires, Argentina on February twentieth. They were determined to change their way of life and go straight. No more robbing trains or banks. They wanted to start a ranch far away where no one knew who they were and live out their lives on the right side of the law. With high hopes for their future, the little family of three sailed away to their new life.

Chapter Twenty-Six

Pine Creek, MN
March 1912

As spring came to their small town, Emily grew excited over the changes in her life. She finally felt free. Free to love again and free to live her life without the threat that her past would catch up with her. Pure happiness swelled inside her, a happiness she hadn't allowed herself to feel in years. She looked forward to a wonderful future with Edward and, most importantly, for her son.

She and Edward were planning their wedding for mid-June, when the weather would be warmer and the flowers would be in bloom. School would let out in mid-May, and that would give her time to prepare for the small ceremony. Allison was delighted that her dear friends were getting married and wanted to host the reception at her house. Over the past month since she'd given birth, Allison was feeling stronger and enjoying her role as a new mother. She and Emily had formed an even stronger bond since little Emily Ava was born. Emily visited the new mother and baby often, and Harry went along too, intrigued by the rosy little infant.

Throughout March and April, Edward, Emily, Harry, and Gertie went to Edward's house on weekends and worked at tidying it up. They cleaned, painted, stained, and wall-papered. Gertie measured and sewed new curtains for nearly all the rooms from fabric Emily and she had chosen from catalogs at the store. The smaller bedroom upstairs was given to Harry, and his eyes grew wide when he learned he'd have a room all to himself. Edward insisted he have a new bed and bureau set, and placed a large toy chest in the room which he added new toys to every time they went to the house.

"You'll spoil him," Emily admonished him, but Edward just laughed.

"That's the point. To spoil him and you. I've waited a long time to fill this house with love again."

Edward gave Emily full reign over every decision for the house. He encouraged her to choose new furniture where she felt was necessary, and they also updated the kitchen and added a water closet on the main floor. Emily was frugal with her purchases, but Edward told her she needn't be. He'd earned a good living for years from the store and bank, and he'd saved most of it. He could afford to give his wife-to-be almost anything she wanted. But Emily was used to being careful with money. In her past life, when money was plentiful, it was spent too quickly, leaving months in between with little to live on. Now, she couldn't allow herself to spend money recklessly.

As they were deciding what to change in the parlor, Emily saw Edward glance at the unfinished tapestry on its frame, then look away quickly. She placed a hand on his arm and he looked at her. She could see pain in his eyes.

"We can keep whatever memories you wish," she said gently.

Edward glanced away. "No. We should start anew. It won't

do for there to be memories of the past haunting my new life."

"Happy memories are welcome in our new life, Edward," she told him. "Your Lily was a happy memory. I'd be more than willing to have her things around."

Edward turned to her. "You know about Lily?"

"Not much. Gertie mentioned her name once, but it's obvious, looking around here, that a woman once lived here."

He nodded. "I've never mentioned her before, because I didn't want to burden you with her memory."

"Oh, Edward," Emily hugged him close. "Your past life would never be a burden to me. I'd love to hear about your first wife. I have no doubt she was a lovely woman."

"She was." Edward took Emily's hand and led her to the sofa by the fireplace. "Lily and I were married when we were young. She was only eighteen and I had just turned twenty-one. She was the most beautiful girl I'd ever met, and the sweetest." He smiled, then looked into Emily's eyes. "Except for you, of course, my dear."

Emily patted his hand. "You're sweet. Tell me more about Lily."

Edward took a deep breath, as if bracing himself to let the memories come through. "I fell for her the very first time I met her, at a church function. She had the most beautiful, pale blond hair and sparkling blue eyes. Her skin was like porcelain. And when she smiled, it warmed my heart. The first time she smiled at me, I fell fast." He smiled, and Emily couldn't help but kiss him sweetly on the cheek.

Edward continued, "Her family had just moved here. Her father was a tailor and opened a shop in town. We married a year after we met, and I had this house built for her. Lily chose all the decorations, and she also worked in the store with me. People adored her. She was warm and kind to everyone."

He stopped then, and his smile faded.

"What happened?" Emily asked.

"We'd been married for about five years when she suddenly grew quite ill. It was after the fall harvest when there had been an influx of temporary workers in town. The doctor thought she may have contracted something from one of the many people she'd had contact with at the store. Her symptoms grew worse. There was nothing the doctor could do. Five days after becoming ill, Lily died in my arms." Edward choked on the last words and tears filled his eyes.

Emily wrapped her arms around him. "I'm so sorry, Edward."

He turned to her. "She was carrying our child at the time. I lost them both."

Emily's heart broke for him. She hadn't expected such a tragic ending. "How devastating. I understand now why it hurt you so much."

He wiped his tears with a handkerchief. "It was devastating. But I couldn't wade too long in my grief. Several other people lost their lives from the outbreak. Gertie's husband died that year, too. I pushed my grief aside and tried to help others. I knew that was what Lily would have done."

Emily brushed her hand across his cheek in a comforting gesture. "You have a big heart. That's just one of the many things I love about you."

He took her hand and brought it to his lips, kissing her palm. "I feel so lucky. I've loved only two women in my life, and both are incredible."

Emily smiled at him. His kiss to her palm reminded her of her Harry and how much she'd loved it when he'd done that. It opened her heart up to Edward even more.

"I closed up the house and moved above the store," Harry continued. "My father died the next year, then my mother two years after that. The store became my life. And it's been that way for nearly twelve years. Now, I have you and little Harry. You both fill my life with so much happiness."

Emily kissed him sweetly on the cheek and stood, walking over to the unfinished tapestry. Three completed ones decorated the walls. They were beautiful, made with a loving hand. "I want to keep the tapestries," she said. "They are a beautiful reminder of a wonderful woman."

Edward stood and walked over to her. "I think that's a wonderful idea." He gently took her in his arms. "You are a kind, generous woman."

She smiled up at him. "And you are a dear soul. We're going to bring this house to life again, and make happy memories."

"I know we will."

With her promise in mind to make happy memories, Emily decided to quit her teaching job after the spring session ended. Instead, she'd help out in the store and spend more time with Harry. She'd have a house to keep and a family to care for now. Emily didn't mind quitting her job. She enjoyed working in the store and wanted to be as helpful to Edward as she could. So the school board went to work immediately searching for a new teacher.

"And I refuse to hire any more beautiful widows," Edward teased Emily one evening as they ate supper at Evy's with Harry by their side.

Emily raised an eyebrow. "Why? It worked out well for you." She grinned.

He chuckled. "And no handsome, single schoolmasters, either. We want a stern, plain-looking teacher who will not attract any attention. I don't want to lose my new wife to a younger man."

Emily laughed. She reached across the table and took his hand. "You have nothing to worry about." As she watched Edward beam with delight, she knew what she'd said was true. She'd finally found home.

South America
March 23, 1901 – October 1904

After sailing for a month, Etta, Harry, and Butch arrived in Buenos Aires, Argentina. They settled into the Hotel Europa near the harbor, signing in under the aliases Harry "Enrique" A. Place and James "Santiago" P. Ryan. After depositing money in a bank, instead of withdrawing by gunpoint for a change, Harry and Butch set out in search of land they could settle on and raise horses and cattle.

The trio enjoyed their stay in Buenos Aires for the month they were there. They felt more relaxed than they had in ages, knowing that they wouldn't be recognized in this bustling city so far from where they'd come. Etta felt especially relieved. The men were talking seriously about ranching and living a quiet life. No longer would she have to sit and worry while they held up a bank or a train, wondering if they'd come home to her. Now, they could live a normal life like everyone else.

Butch had done his homework and k new where he wanted to settle. He set his sights on the western edge of Argentina where a beautiful, fertile valley was surrounded by the Andes Mountains with the Rio Blanco, running through it. It would be much like the areas where they'd lived in the United States, and far enough away from big cities not to be bothered by the authorities. Or so, they hoped.

Once it was settled on where they'd homestead, the trio began the long, arduous trip in mid-1901. From Buenos Aires, they took two separate trains inland. There, they bought a wagon and supplies to drive four-hundred miles to the Cholila Valley in Chubut Province. It was a long, and sometimes treacherous, ride to their land, crossing the mountains on a bumpy, narrow road. But Etta didn't mind. She was used to roughing it. She tried imagining what their new home would look like, and wondered if any other settlers would be nearby. Starting a new life was exciting, and scary. But she wasn't going to let that get in the way of enjoying their adventure.

After traveling over the mountains, then through scrub brush and desert that reminded Etta of Wyoming and Utah, they finally arrived at their land. Stopping at the crest above the valley, Etta gazed at it, in awe of its beauty. With the snow-capped Andes Mountains as a back drop, the lush valley below was spell-binding. They'd finally found their paradise—their home.

"Well, what do you think, Etta, dear? Can we make this valley our home?" Butch asked, coming up alongside her to also admire the view.

She looked from Butch to Harry, and beamed. If anyone could tame this wild land, it was her boys. "I think it's going to be an amazing adventure." She grinned at Harry, who'd wrapped his arm around her waist.

"I think you're right," Butch said.

They settled on their property in cloth tents—much like the ones they'd spent the winter in at Robbers Roost—and the trio went to work building a log home. They used the local cypress trees for their house, and Butch made several long trips with the wagon for supplies. They put in real glass windows and bought furniture, a woodstove for cooking, and many other necessities. Etta made curtains for the windows and papered the walls with pictures cut from magazines. By the time winter had arrived, their little four-room cabin was ready to live in and the men set about building barns and planning their livestock purchases.

Etta pitched right in beside Butch and Harry. She helped in building the house and barns, putting up fencing, and caring for the livestock when it came. Harry built a chicken coop, and Etta tended the hens. The next spring, she planted a garden so they'd have fresh vegetables and canned ones for the next winter. When she rode alongside the men, she wore pants and a gun belt with a pistol on each hip. While at home, she was everything a lady should be.

The local ranchers marveled at these strange North American settlers. When at home, Etta was always dressed nicely, and served meals on fine bone china brought all the way from town in a wagon with their other supplies. They had built shelving for their many books, since all three enjoyed reading, and were always generous in loaning them out to neighbors. Butch and Harry hired two local men to help with their herds. By the summer of 1902, they had nearly thirteen hundred sheep, five hundred cattle, and thirty-five horses. Harry planned on breeding the best horses around, possibly to be used as racehorses.

They soon earned the respect of the local ranchers, and would often get together with them for dinners or dancing to music around a campfire. The people were intrigued by the beautiful Etta who could serve tea like a queen and shoot and ride better than most men. Butch was also a favorite among the locals. He was generally jovial and good-natured, and flirted with the single ladies. He established a small store filled with supplies most needed in their remote location and hired a local boy to run it. He'd bring back supplies for his small venture on his many trips to town which was several days ride away.

Harry was more reserved, but the people grew to respect him as well. He was a hard worker and knowledgeable in many things, especially horses. Harry had learned tricks as a young man—like running and jumping on a horse from behind, or standing up on the saddle while the horse trotted. Sometimes he'd show off his skills to the neighbors at a gathering, and they were delighted by the show.

Etta loved her new home. She felt welcomed by the locals and often visited with the ranchers' wives or played with their children. She spoke Spanish very well, having grown up in Texas, and was able to communicate easily with the other women. There were also European settlers nearby who spoke English. Although it was a life filled with hard work, she felt it was a good life. They were free here to live their lives without having to constantly look over their shoulders.

What Etta loved most, though, was that Harry had relaxed, despite his long days of hard work, and was happier than she'd seen him in years. He was doing what he loved, training horses, not for a heist, but for a good purpose. Harry was excited about the possibility of eventually racing them. When they would lay in bed at night, he'd hold her close and talk about his dreams for the ranch. Dreams of a future, not of constantly running away from the law. It filled her heart with joy for this man she'd given herself to so willingly. She'd loved him as an outlaw, but she thought that perhaps, she loved him more now, as a hardworking rancher.

While the summers were beautiful and rarely uncomfortably

hot because of the mountain air, winter was damp and cold. They didn't have the snow and ice they'd been used to back home, but it rained constantly, and sometimes would freeze. Spring was the worst, with snow melting down the mountains and rain falling, causing the ground to become soggy and muddy. So it was in the spring that Etta and Harry took trips away from home to get out of the terrible weather.

In March 1902, Etta and Harry returned to the United States by steamship passage from Buenos Aires to New York City. They visited Samanna and her family again then traveled to Atlantic City, New Jersey to see his brother Harvey and his family. Butch didn't travel with them this time. He'd gone as far as Buenos Aires to see them off, then had to tend to business. Even though they had homesteaded acreage in Cholila Valley, they still had to file for ownership. Butch went to the Colonial Land Department and filed for the first right to buy the land.

While still in the United States, Etta and Harry took a train to Chicago where Harry checked into a hospital as a patient. He still suffered from sinus issues and his leg wound hadn't healed well. After a month in the Chicago area, they headed back to New York City and by July tenth, the couple was on a steamship sailing back to Buenos Aires.

Etta loved that they were free to come and go as they pleased. It seemed as if the Pinkertons were no longer actively searching for them, especially since Butch and Harry hadn't robbed a bank or train since 1900. She knew that Harry enjoyed being in touch with his family again, too. As long as he lived an honest life, his family accepted him back in the fold.

The couple returned to the United States a second time in the summer of 1904. While there, they attended the St. Louis World Fair and sent a post card to Harry's sister Emma. After that they went to Fort Worth and San Antonio to visit friends. Much to Etta's dismay, her dear friend, Fannie Porter, had closed up the house and moved away. No one in the area knew of her whereabouts. Some told her she'd married a wealthy man and left town. Others said she'd left the country. Etta was saddened that she wasn't able to say a last goodbye to her friend, and hoped Fannie was happy wherever she ended up.

Upon their return to the ranch in late summer of 1904, their quiet, ideal life was on the brink of ruin. Earlier, in 1903, unbeknownst to the trio, a Pinkerton agent had traveled to Buenos Aires in search of Butch and Harry. The agency had learned of their whereabouts from intercepting letters that were sent to known family and friends of the outlaws. The agent spoke with a man who identified Butch and Harry as the men who'd homesteaded in the Cholila Valley under the names Harry A. Place and James Ryan. He discouraged the agent from going after the outlaws because of the many miles of rough terrain. The Pinkerton agent took his advice and instead distributed posters with pictures and descriptions of Harry, Butch, and Etta to all the local police stations, banks, and shipping offices.

While visiting Buenos Aires in late 1904, Butch saw one of the wanted posters and tore it down, bringing it back to the hotel where he was staying with Harry and Etta.

"Do you believe this?" he bellowed, throwing the poster on a table in the room.

Etta stared at it, stunned. They had used the photo of the men from Fort Worth and of her and Harry from New York City. "How did they get copies of these photos? Especially this one from New York? No one knew who we were."

Harry scowled at it. "Those sneaky bastards! They must have been one step behind us the entire way. And now they're here!"

Harry looked at Butch. "Now what do we do? We've made a home here. Are we going to let them run us out of the country?"

"No!" Butch insisted. "They can't do anything to us here. We haven't committed any crimes. And as long as we keep our noses clean, there's nothing they can do."

Etta sat down in a stuffed chair and folded her hands in her lap. They shook, despite clasping her hands tightly. "Are you sure about that, Butch? Are you certain they can't arrest us here and take us back to the States?"

Harry placed a protective hand on her shoulder. "They know who Etta is now. That wasn't supposed to happen. I couldn't care less if they find us, but what about her?"

A long sigh escaped Butch. "I'm almost positive they can't do anything here. We can't go back to the States now, but we should be safe here. Especially at our ranch." He looked at Etta, his blue eyes softening. "You know we'll always protect you, darling. And if we can't, we'll make sure you go somewhere safe. I promise."

Etta glanced from Butch to Harry, then back to Butch. "It's not me I'm worried about. It's you two. Can you promise me that you both will be safe?"

Butch dropped his eyes and Harry squeezed her shoulder. Etta knew then, without their having to say it, that there was no guarantee their perfect life here would stay that way.

Chapter Twenty-Seven

Pine Creek, MN
April – May 1912

Spring slowly came to their little prairie town. Emily continued to enjoy sharing breakfast each morning before school at Evy's Restaurant with Edward and her son. Daily, friends and local shop owners dropped by their table with cheerful greetings. It felt so good to be a part of a community without fearing someone would find out who she really was. She would never be known as Etta Place here. She would always be known as Emily to the townspeople, and that made her very happy.

Like the rest of the world, Emily had read about the tragic sinking of the RMS Titanic in the newspaper in late April. It reminded her of the many ships she'd traveled on throughout the years and how lucky she was to have never experienced a tragedy. How different her existence was now compared to then. She led a simple, quiet life and she was thankful for it. She had her son, and now she had Edward, who loved her dearly. Everything seemed almost too perfect in her life. As if at any moment, her luck could fail.

School let out in mid-May and Emily worked in the store most afternoons alongside Gertie while Edward managed the bank next door. Little Harry spent time over at friends' houses or in the back room, playing with the many toys Edward had bestowed upon him. He also willingly helped out in the store with small chores, like dusting or taking out the trash. He was still very young but loved assisting his mother with big-boy chores.

It was on one such day as the spring breeze blew gently through the shop's open doors that fate twisted the tide of Emily's happy life. Edward had stopped by the post office and brought the mail back to the store, handing Emily a letter that had come from California.

At first, Emily's heart leapt with joy when she saw the return address. It was from the convent where she'd lived before coming to Pine Creek. She had written the nuns when she'd first arrived to tell them she and Harry were safe. Emily had never expected to hear from any of the nuns again, and hadn't, until this letter arrived.

Edward watched her reaction to the letter. "Is everything okay?" he asked.

She smiled up at him. "Yes. It's from the nuns at the convent."

The strain on his face softened. "Sorry. It's just that the last time you received a letter, you had to leave. I was afraid that might happen again."

Emily kissed his cheek. "Hopefully, this is a happy letter." But she wasn't making any promises. She had no idea why the sisters would be contacting her.

After Edward had returned to the bank, she went into the back room to read the letter privately. Harry had his small train set on the floor and was pushing the locomotive around in a circle. Small soldier figures were set up all around the tracks and he was quietly speaking for them.

"My, what have we here?" Emily asked him, bending down to inspect the scene.

"The train is being robbed and the soldiers are helping catch the bad guys," Harry said.

A chill ran through Emily as her son's words sank in. She quickly regained her composure. "How do you know about train robberies?"

"Arthur told me about train robbers. His dad talks about them. We play sheriff and robbers all the time. It's fun."

Emily's mind spun. She knew it was just child's play, but it still worried her. Arthur was Ernie's son. Of course Ernie might speak of robberies since he worked with the trains daily. Still, it was sobering hearing of her son playing those games.

Harry, however, hadn't noticed how still his mother had become. Realizing he was still busy at play, she walked over to the staircase and sat on a step. She couldn't stop the real world from touching her child any more than she could protect herself from it. Taking a calming breath, she opened the letter.

Inside was another sealed envelope along with a single sheet of paper. She opened the letter first, and smiled when she saw who had written it. Sister Mary Frances had been one of the younger nuns whom she'd worked with teaching the older children. She'd been a sweet, kind soul who Emily had connected with easily. Even though Emily had gotten along well with the other nuns, Sister Mary Frances had been her favorite.

"Dear Emily," the letter read. *"Mother Superior has given me permission to write and pass along this note from a visitor who came in search of you. He was a pleasant man with a kind smile, although Mother*

Superior was very stern with him despite how polite he acted. I believe she feared he wasn't a friend of yours as he'd said. But she did allow him to give her a note to send on to you, and in turn, he gave her a very generous donation for our orphanage.

"I do so hope all is well with you and our beloved little Harry, and you are flourishing in your new life. We all would enjoy hearing from you and how you've fared. We are all fine. Sister Agnes Theresa grew very ill over the winter months, but is feeling much better now. The children are all fine and miss you so very much.

May God bless you and young Harry,

Sister Mary Frances."

Emily carefully folded the letter as memories of her time at the convent washed over her. The sisters had been wary of her at first, although the Mother Superior had agreed to let her live there in return for her services as a teacher. As time went by, the sisters began to warm to her, and after Harry was born, they seemed to accept her more willingly. Elwood, Harry's brother, had found her the place to live. A sailor he knew up in San Francisco had a sister in the convent. At first, Emily had been unsure about living at a convent, but Elwood had talked her into it. It was a safe place for her and the baby when he was born. Now, as she thought back on it, Elwood had been right. The convent had been the perfect place for her to stay while she waited for her husband's return.

But Harry never came for her.

Now, sitting on the step, she looked at the envelope that had been inside the letter. Her heart began to beat faster. Who could the man looking for her be? Sister Mary Frances said he'd been a pleasant man with a nice smile. Her Harry wasn't always quick to smile, but she knew one man who was. Butch. And, where Butch was, Harry should be also.

But if this note was from Butch or Harry, her entire life would change.

Taking a deep breath, she opened the sealed envelope, then slid out the note. She recognized the familiar script immediately.

"My darling Etta," it began. Emily's heart swelled. She already knew this letter was from Butch. Harry had loved her, she knew that, but he wasn't the type to use endearments often.

"I write to you now as a very stern Mother Superior stands over me, so excuse the short letter. I had hoped to find you here, as our mutual friend in SF said you'd be. But of course, I shouldn't have expected you to wait four long years to hear from me or the third member of our trio. I am happy to know that you are safe, and that there are those willing to protect you, like these very diligent nuns. There is so much to tell you, and can't be told in a note. Please find a way to come see me. As always, I have landed on my feet in a pot of gold that wasn't given to me this time by a deceased uncle. Ha Ha. I'm living quite comfortably just outside of Spokane, Washington. Below are the directions to my place. Please come and visit. I have news of the third member of our family of three that I must share.

All my love to you, dear Etta, JR."

James Ryan. She knew that this letter was truly from Butch. How would anyone have known she was at the convent if they hadn't been told by Elwood? He would have only told Butch or Harry. And the writer's reference to money not given to him from a deceased uncle was telling. Only she, Harry, and a small handful of friends knew that was how Butch described the money he'd get in a robbery.

Butch was alive. After all this time, she could hardly believe it. She'd worried for months when he and Harry hadn't come for her. A year after she'd left South America, she'd begun contacting people they knew there, looking for any clue as to what had become of her men. No one had any information.

There had been rumors, but nothing concrete. All rumors led to their demise. But she knew they were smart. She knew Butch was cunning.

Dying in a shootout would never have happened. Unless they'd been caught unaware. Unless…she'd never let herself think it. But by the time three years had gone by, she had to accept that something had happened to them.

Now, she knew at least one of them was alive.

Emily read the instructions on how to find Butch's ranch. It was a train ride away, a long one, but doable.

She turned her gaze to her son, playing quietly with his train set. He made chugging noises for the engine and whistle sounds when it rode into the station. She would do anything for her little Harry. She'd already moved half-way across the country to keep him safe. Did she dare search out Butch to learn what he had to tell her? Would it jeopardize her safety, and that of her son?

And if she did find that Harry was alive, what then? She'd loved Harry enough to follow him across another continent. But now, could she give up the safety of her new life to go back to Harry? Could she leave Edward behind? Her heart ached just thinking about hurting sweet Edward.

"Here's where you're hiding," Edward said, chuckling as he walked across the back room. He ruffled Harry's hair as he passed the boy, then came over to where Emily sat on the stairs. "Are you playing trains, too?"

She shook her head as she returned the letter to the envelope. "I just took a moment to read the letter from the convent."

"Good news, I hope?"

She nodded. "They are all fine."

Edward studied her. "And?"

Her eyes flew up to search his. "And what?"

"The tone of your voice tells me there is more to it," he said softly.

Emily felt weak. She was so tired of keeping secrets. She placed her head on his shoulder and he draped his arm around her. "You know how much I love you, don't you?" she asked, not daring to look at him.

Edward kissed the top of her head. "Yes. I do. And I love you, too." After a moment, he said, "You can tell me anything. You know that, don't you?"

"Yes, I know." She rose and patted his arm gently. "We'll talk later. I should go help Gertie."

Edward nodded, but concern etched his face.

As Emily walked toward the front, she turned and caught sight of Edward taking off his suit jacket and laying it over the stair rail. She stopped at the curtain that separated the back room from the store and watched as Edward sat on the floor beside Harry. "So, Conductor," Edward said. "Where is our train heading today?"

Tears filled her eyes as she watched Edward play alongside her son. He was a wonderful man—and he wanted to spend the rest of his life doing nothing more than please her and Harry. How was she going to tell him she had to leave? If only for a while. And what if she found out that her Harry, the man she'd loved all those years, the man who'd fathered her child, was still alive? It was all more than she could bear.

* * *

That night, after putting little Harry to bed and making sure he'd fallen into a deep sleep, Emily slipped out of the room and went across the hall to Edward's room. When she opened the door, she was surprised to see he wasn't there. Taking a small blanket from his rocker, she wrapped it around her shoulders and walked to the back porch. She glanced out the window and saw Edward sitting outside, smoking his pipe, an oil lamp on the table lighting up the darkness.

She went outside, and Edward looked up at her expectantly.

"We should talk," Emily said quietly.

"Let's go inside where it's warm." He began to rise, but Emily shook her head.

"No. It feels good out here. Please, sit and relax." She moved her chair closer to his and sat, wrapping the blanket tightly around her.

"It's hard to relax when I sense something is wrong," he said.

Emily sighed. The air was cool, but it felt good after a long winter of being cooped up indoors. The businesses on this end of town were all closed, but across the train tracks, she could hear music coming from the saloon. She'd lived on both sides of the tracks, and she understood how fortunate she was to be with a man like Edward. Was she willing to give that up?

He bent forward in his chair and reached for her hand. "Whatever it is you have to say, please just say it. I don't think I can wait another minute."

She squeezed his hand. "If I told you I must go away for a short time, would you understand?"

He let go of her hand, looking hurt, and sat back, taking a puff of his pipe. "Does this have something to do with the letter you received?"

She nodded.

"Where do you need to go? California?"

"No. Spokane. But only for a quick trip. There is someone I need to see. Something I need to clear up before we're married."

Her heart ached as she watched his face, seeing the pain in his eyes as he imagined all the reasons she would say this. Emily didn't know how else to tell him without laying bare all the details of her life. But maybe that wouldn't be a bad idea after all.

"Is this about your husband?" he asked.

"Yes. Part of it. It's also about my past. There are things I need to know."

"Is your husband still alive?"

Emily closed her eyes. For the past four years, all she'd done was hope and pray Harry was still alive. But now, after having accepted that he was most likely dead, it was difficult for her to believe anything else. Butch hadn't said one way or the other. She had to find out, though, no matter how it hurt Edward, or her.

"No," she answered, feeling a twist in her heart for lying. "I have to see my friend to make sure everything is taken care of. It's more like I will be settling his estate."

Edward's face relaxed a bit. "Must you go? Can't you do that from here?"

"I have to be present. They want to make sure it's legal. A friend of the family is helping with it." Lies. Too many lies to a man who had been nothing but kind to her. Emily hated it, but she had to go. She had to see Butch one last time. She needed to know about Harry.

Edward leaned in closer to her. "Let me go with you," he urged, sounding desperate. "We'll make a vacation of it. We can even bring little Harry. I'd like to see that part of the country."

Tears burned in her eyes as she saw how anxious Edward was. "I have to do this myself." When she saw his disappointment, she caved. She couldn't live with the lies any longer. "Edward, I'll tell you anything you want to know about my past. I don't want to have lies between us. Ask me what you want to know, and I'll tell you the truth."

He took a breath, as if he were going to ask her a question, but then he let it out. "I realize you have a past. I also realize there is much more to you than just being a schoolteacher and a mother. I've never seen a woman ride as expertly as you, nor handle a gun as well. But…" He paused as his eyes met hers. "But, I don't want to know anything about your past. I want you to leave it behind you as we begin our future. If going away will help you settle your past so that we can build our future, then you must go."

Emily moved closer and took his hand in hers. "This will be the last trip without you," she said. "After this, we'll travel wherever you wish, together. As a family."

Edward smiled. "I'd like that." He stood and she did also, and they walked into the hallway, his arm encircling her waist. When they stopped at the end of the hallway, by his door, he looked down at her. "Will you stay with me tonight?"

She nodded, and they went inside his room to share the night together.

Two days later, Emily left on the train heading west. Little Harry stayed in Edward's care, much to his relief. Emily knew that if she left her son behind, it would prove to Edward that she was coming back. No matter what lay ahead of her in Spokane, she had to believe that she'd return to her new life with Edward. Because now, no other life would be safe for her son—and little Harry was what mattered most to her.

Chapter Twenty-Eight

South America
February 1905 – April 1908

No matter how determined Harry and Butch were to build a new life at their ranch, events beyond their control caused everything to fall to pieces. On February 14, 1905, the Banco de Londres y Tarapacá in Rio Gallegos was robbed of 7000 pesos by two English speaking bandits with descriptions similar to Butch and Sundance. The fact that they also used Butch's strategy of relay horses to get away made the two former outlaws look guilty. When word got to the trio in Cholila, they knew their peaceful days of ranching were over. Between the Pinkertons tracking them down and now the warrant out for their arrest for the bank robbery, they had to escape.

Etta's heart broke as they sold their property to an English gentleman who had settled not far from them. It was the only home she'd ever had with Harry where they'd felt safe and lived a normal life. After all the hard work they'd put into it, and all the love, it was now gone.

Leaving their livestock in the hands of good friends, she, Harry, and Butch hid out in the mountains around Cholila to avoid being arrested. It didn't matter that they weren't guilty of the bank robbery. The authorities had decided they were, due to speculation, and there was no way to prove otherwise.

Hiding out in the mountains for several weeks was rough on the three who'd become used to their comfortable life. Harry and Butch argued often, and Etta found herself playing moderator, which only irritated Harry more. It brought back memories of the days after they'd robbed the Winnemucca bank, and all the animosity between the two men. Etta hated it. They were regressing and she desperately missed their life at Cholila. It didn't help that they lived in a small cabin that was generally used for hunting. Their trusted friend, Dan Gibbons, brought them supplies and also handled the sale of their property and possessions.

In June 1905, once the sale of their property had transpired, they traveled over the mountains and into Chile, settling for a time in Valparaiso. Their money was running low, and they had two options: return to the States or return to a life of crime here.

"We can go to San Francisco," Harry suggested as he and Butch discussed their situation in their small hotel room. "It's a big city. No one would even think we'd go there."

"Except that your brother lives there and they've been tracking our relatives and friends," Butch said, sounding disgusted. "The Pinkertons would figure it out quickly."

"We can't stay here," Harry shot back.

Etta sat in the corner of the room, watching the men as they argued. She no longer knew what she wanted to do. Her dream of living peacefully in Cholila had vanished. It seemed there was nowhere they would be safe from the law.

"We could go to Europe," Butch suggested. "Or Australia. It's like the wild west there now. Lots of open territory for us to roam."

Harry glared at Butch. "And do what? Rob banks? Then what? We'll be wanted there, too. And where will we get enough money to take us there? We've barely got enough to see us through next winter here."

Butch sighed. "We've tried going straight," he said sadly. "Now what?"

Once Butch and Harry had resigned themselves to the fact that they had nowhere to go until they could acquire money, Harry decided that Etta should return to San Francisco on her own.

"I will not!" Etta said, shocked that he'd even consider her leaving them after all they'd been through together.

"Yes, you will!" Harry insisted. "I will not risk your life. You can wait for us there."

Anger burned inside her. Hadn't she proven, after all this time, how valuable she was to them? She'd followed Harry down here, and she wasn't about to leave now. "I won't go. We're in this together—all three of us. No matter what."

"Are you crazy?" Harry yelled. "It was bad enough you worked alongside us in the States. I won't have you pulling jobs with us here, in a foreign country. God only knows what they'd do to you, a woman, if you were caught. I just won't allow it!"

"You don't own me, Harry Longabaugh!" Etta yelled back. "I'll do as I want."

Butch sat quietly in the corner of the room, watching his two friends.

Harry ran his hand though his hair and sighed. He finally spoke in a calmer voice. "Etta. I don't own you. But I love you and I want to know you're safe. You can't do jobs with us. Not here. Please. Go home. I can't control what will happen to any of us the longer we stay here."

She walked over to Harry and pulled him close. "Without you, I have no life," she whispered in his ear. "I can't leave you."

Harry gave in and let her stay, but Etta knew that she'd only won temporarily. Harry would continue to dog her about leaving. He loved her, she knew that, and was afraid for her. But she really didn't know what she'd do if she couldn't be with Harry and Butch. If something terrible happened, at least they'd be together.

* * *

In the early morning hours of December 19, 1905, Etta stood with three horses outside of the Banco del la Nacion in Villa Mercedes. She was disguised as a man in pants and a shirt with a hat pulled down low, hiding her hair. No one on the street paid any attention to her until shots rang out from inside the bank. Moments later, Butch and Sundance rushed outside and the three hopped on their horses and rode out of town as shots rang out.

Butch had planned this robbery exactly like the ones in the States. He had fresh horses waiting for them farther up the road and they changed onto them quickly. That was when Etta saw the blood stain spreading on Harry's sleeve.

"You've been shot." She quickly sprang into action. Tearing his shirt sleeve, she saw that he'd only been grazed by the bullet, but he was bleeding profusely.

"Leave it," Harry said impatiently. "We have to go."

She ignored him. Etta pulled off her bandana and tied it tightly around the wound to stop the bleeding.

"Let's go!" Harry yelled, and they all jumped on their horses and took off. Not far behind, they could see the dust flying up from the posse following them.

They headed west toward the mountains where they could easily hide out, but they had a long way to go. The posse stayed close behind and when the outlaws stopped for the second time to change horses, gunfire erupted between them and the posse.

"Aim for the horses only!" Butch called out. The last thing they needed was a murder added to their crimes.

One of the lawmen's horses went down and Butch, Sundance, and Etta took off. The posse gave up after that, and the trio was able to escape.

That night while sitting around a campfire, Butch counted the money. They'd stolen nearly 12,000 pesos. It wasn't a fortune, but it was a start.

They all sat quietly as the fire crackled and sparked in the humid air. Etta knew the men felt the same as she did. This was not a victory—they'd gone backward. What did life hold for them in the future? She couldn't bear to think of it.

* * *

Butch, Harry, and Etta didn't stay in one place for very long after that first bank robbery. They moved from town to town, hotel to hotel. Butch was always scoping out the next job, while Etta and Harry just followed along. After the robbery in Villa Mercedes, posters of the North American trio went up all over the country. Soon, they were being credited for robberies that they hadn't committed. Other outlaws were using their technique, and it was assumed by all that it was them. To stay one step ahead of the law, they were constantly on the move.

It was a tiresome existence, and Etta grew weary. She missed their ranch and the friends they'd made. This was worse than when they were wanted in the States. There, they could go to known hideouts and spend months on end feeling relatively safe. Here, they weren't familiar with the land and were always looking over their shoulders. She grew to hate it as much as she knew the men did.

By early 1906, Butch had secured a job with the Concordia Tin Mine in the Santa Vela Cruz range in Bolivia. Harry had returned to their Cholila ranch to sell off some of the livestock they'd left behind tended by their friend, Dan. Etta stayed in a small house they'd rented in La Paz, not far from the tin mine.

Etta disliked being left behind, but she couldn't follow Butch or Harry. Butch had devised a plan where he and Harry would work regular jobs so they wouldn't be suspected of being outlaws. Then, from time to time, they'd pull a robbery out of the area, and no one would be the wiser. Butch still dreamed of owning a ranch, somewhere they could live without the fear of being detected. All the money they stole was to go toward that dream.

Harry, on the other hand, was tired of South America. He wanted to save money that they could use to leave. He didn't care if they went back to the States or Europe, or even Australia. He just wanted out. He was tired of the outlaw life. He and Butch argued constantly about what decision to make. The long trip back to Cholila for business was the perfect escape for Harry. He'd told Etta that time away from Butch would be good for him.

While Etta waited for his return, she found a job working in a local mercantile store. The owner was an elderly man whose wife had passed away and his children were grown and gone. He needed help now that he was alone. Etta liked working for the man, and also got to know many of the area people well. The ability to speak Spanish helped her to blend in.

When Harry returned from Cholila, he signed on to work for the mine alongside Butch. The acting manager at the time, Clement Rolla Glass, had found he could trust Butch (under his alias James "Santiago" P. Maxwell) and had placed him in charge of guarding the payroll. He also trusted Butch's recommendations, so he hired Harry (under the last name of Ingersoll) without question.

The two outlaws found it amusing that they were in charge of protecting such large sums of money, but Butch and Sundance were outlaws with integrity. Neither would have ever thought of stealing from their employer. This was the reason the men had been friends for so long, despite their bickering. They agreed on terms that most outlaws would find ludicrous. Never steal from your friends, family, or employer, never shoot to kill, and always treat a woman like a lady. It seemed incongruous that the pair had those rules, but that was what made them different from all the rest. They had never set out to hurt anyone. They robbed banks. They robbed trains. And now, they robbed payrolls that didn't belong to their employers. But there was a limit to the crimes they'd commit.

That was how Etta was able to live with the fact that she loved an outlaw.

Harry lived up at the mine with the other employees but often rode to La Paz to be with Etta. As they lay in bed one night, wrapped in each other's arms, Harry spoke sadly. "I've failed you. This isn't the life I planned for us when we came here. I loved our life at Cholila and thought that was where we'd raise a family and grow old. Now, I don't know what the future holds."

Etta kissed him sweetly. "It's not your fault, dear. It's no one's fault. I'm here because I want to be with you. We'll figure it out as we go, and hopefully things will get better."

"I wish you'd go home. To San Francisco, or maybe out east to stay with Samanna. Somewhere I'd know you were safe. I could come for you when we've saved enough money."

"I'm not going anywhere without you and Butch," she told him. "I love you, Harry. I don't want to be anywhere you aren't."

"Then promise me one thing," Harry said, pulling her tighter to him. "If anything happens to me, you'll take the money we have hidden and go. Don't wait for Butch or anyone else. Just go back home."

"Harry…"

"Promise me this, Etta," Harry insisted. "I have a bad feeling about being here. I need to know you'll leave here if I'm gone."

Etta didn't like the way Harry was talking. He sounded broken, and that was not the kind of man he was. "I promise I'll leave if anything happens," she said. She hoped it would give him enough peace of mind to no longer worry.

Later that year, a new manager took charge of the mine and Butch, Harry, and Etta met him for the first time at a special Christmas party for the employees, held at Grand Hotel Guibert in La Paz. Percy Seibert was a young man who came from the States but had worked for the Concordia mine for quite some time. He liked Butch immediately and seemed charmed by Etta's beauty and grace. Harry didn't always make a warm first impression, but Seibert grew to like him as well. The trio became such good friends with Percy that they often dined at his family's home on Sundays.

Etta, Harry, and Butch had once again settled into a quiet life for a couple of years. Occasionally, Butch and Harry would leave the area for a week or two, then return to the mine. Seibert never asked them where they'd been, even when there was news of another mine's payroll having been stolen. They were good workers, and good friends, so the manager ignored the fact that his employees might be the bandits everyone was talking about.

In early 1908, in his frustration over still living in South America, Harry got drunk in a bar in La Paz and bragged to fellow workers that he and Butch were the ones who'd robbed the local mine companies. Butch was furious with Harry, but Etta was only disappointed. She understood that Harry had started drinking again out of frustration. But this time he'd threatened their safety with his drunken bragging. She was afraid they'd never settle anywhere for very long.

Feeling they were no longer safe in the area, Butch quit his job and the trio moved on to Chili, then northern Bolivia, then the coast of Peru. It was while they were there in March of 1908 that Etta told Harry she was pregnant.

"You're what? Are you sure?" he asked. They had all three been sitting in the hotel's restaurant when she'd dropped the news on them.

"Yes, I'm sure." She'd been nervous about what Harry would say. But a moment after she'd told him, he smiled broadly, stood up, and pulled her into a hug.

"That's wonderful!" He kissed her sweetly on the cheek.

"That is good news," Butch said, kissing her too. "How long have you known?"

"It's been four months," she admitted, a bit sheepishly. "I didn't want to get excited until I knew this baby would be fine." She also hadn't wanted to tell Harry too early because she knew he'd want her to leave. She had mixed feelings about that. But now that the baby was growing inside her, she knew what her answer would be.

"You can't stay here," Harry said, his tone serious. "Not with a baby coming. We don't have a steady place to live and we're always on the run. It's not safe for you here."

Etta agreed with Harry. She wanted to go where she could have her baby and not worry about her husband being arrested at any moment. "But I want to be with you," she told him. "Where can we go together?"

"Let's leave for San Francisco. It's a big city. We can get lost in the outer area," Harry said.

"I agree that it isn't safe for Etta here," Butch interjected. "But what about our idea for a new ranch? Remember how much you liked that property in central Bolivia, Sundance? We could build it up, just like we did in Cholila."

Harry shook his head. "I can't do it anymore, Butch. I'm sorry. I want to leave, and I want Etta back in the States where she's safe. We've been gone for seven years. There's no reason anyone would still be looking for us."

Butch gave up easily. Etta thought he must be tired of the vagabond life as well. "I agree with you about Etta. Her safety is the most important thing right now."

A month later, Harry and Butch saw Etta off on a ship headed to San Francisco. They'd written to Elwood to help find her a place to live once she arrived. Harry and Butch were staying behind to travel to Cholila one last time to sell off the remainder of their livestock, then they'd be on a ship to San Francisco too.

Etta held Harry close as tears clouded her eyes. She didn't want to leave without him, but she knew she should go. The baby was growing larger every day and she wanted to be somewhere safe by the time their child was born.

"Promise me you'll be careful," she begged Harry. "I want our baby to have a father."

"I promise," he said, then grinned. "I want to be around to

teach my son how to be a good cowboy."

"What about your daughter?" she asked, smiling through her tears.

"If she's anything like her mother, she'll be a good cowboy too," he teased.

Butch hugged Etta tightly. "Take care. We'll miss you like crazy."

"I will. Please bring Harry home to me," she whispered. "Promise me that."

"I promise I will, Etta, dear," Butch said.

As the ship left port, Etta waved from the deck. Their dream of a quiet life in South America was over. Etta placed her hand on her rounded stomach, deciding she was only going to look forward now, for her baby's sake. She prayed the man she loved would come to her very soon.

Chapter Twenty-Nine

Spokane, WA
May 1912

Emily arrived at the station in Spokane three days after departing from Pine Creek. Stepping off the train with help from the porter, she carried her suitcase down the wooden platform as she looked all around her. People milled about, and both motorcars and horse-drawn buggies stood by the side of the road, waiting for passengers.

Emily tried to get her bearings as the late afternoon sun beat down on her. She'd worn her traveling suit, and grew warm from so many layers. Emily hadn't written to Butch to announce she was coming, so there'd be no car or buggy waiting for her. She'd been afraid to write. There was always a chance that this was a set-up by the Pinkertons to trap her, even after all these years. While in her heart she felt the letter had been written by Butch, she couldn't be one-hundred percent certain. She was taking a risk coming here, but she'd had to. If it was Butch, she needed to know about Harry.

"May I help you, ma'am?"

Emily turned and saw a middle-aged man wearing a tweed jacket and cap. He looked like one of the many men who were waiting for passengers.

"Perhaps," she said. "I need someone to drive me to my…" She hesitated. She was about to say friend's house but she decided otherwise. "My brother's home. I believe it's a ranch, outside of town."

"Well, then, I'm your man," the driver said, beaming. "I've got my motorcar waiting right over there. Just tell me where you need to go."

"I'm not sure, actually." Emily opened her small handbag and pulled out a slip of paper. "These are the directions he sent me."

The man squinted as he read the note. "Ah, yes. I know exactly where this is. You must be Mr. Ryan's sister. Well, I'm pleased to meet you, ma'am."

"You know James?" she asked, surprised.

"Ah, yes I do, ma'am. Most everyone does in these parts. About the nicest fellow you could ever meet, that's for sure. And generous to a fault. But you already know that, being as you're his sister."

Emily smiled. She did know how generous Butch could be.

"Let me carry your bag, ma'am," he offered, taking it from her. "My motorcar is over here."

Emily followed him to his Model T. He had the roof up over the back passenger seat. He helped her step in, then ran around and placed her suitcase on the floor in the spot next to her.

"My name's Ray, ma'am." He tipped his hat. "Now, you call out to me if you need me for anything during the ride."

"Thank you, Ray."

Ray maneuvered his motorcar through the busy streets

around the station, then headed west, out of town. They turned onto a dirt road, and continued driving.

Emily gazed out the window at the surrounding landscape. There were fields of blond-colored wheat for miles around. It wasn't tall yet, but it colored the landscape with a golden hue. Occasionally, she saw cattle and sheep, and a few horses. But mostly, she saw open land that was either waiting to be planted or already growing wheat.

They bumped and bounced down the road until Emily began to wonder how far out Butch lived. Finally, Ray turned up a driveway and passed under an arch that read Gilbert Ranch. Farther down the driveway, a house came into view. It was a big Victorian, three stories high, with turrets on either side, and a large, covered, wrap-around porch. It sat on a square of lush, green lawn amidst all the golden fields, and had sprouts of colorful flowers growing along the front of the porch.

Butch had said he'd landed on his feet into a pot of gold. Gazing at the house, Emily understood now what he'd meant.

Ray pulled the car up to the front of the house and set the brake. He ran around to Emily's door and opened it, helping her out. "Here we are, ma'am. I'll knock on the door for you and let them know you're here." He hustled away quickly, before she could tell him that wasn't necessary.

The house was white with dark green trim, and the door was also green. There was a large stained-glass window on the door as well. When it opened, a middle-aged woman, conservatively dressed, gazed out at Emily as she listened to Ray. She nodded, then leaving the door open, she disappeared.

Ray returned to the car and pulled Emily's bag out. He carried it to the front porch and she followed, not quite sure what to do. Suddenly, the door opened wider and there was a familiar face smiling down at her.

"Etta," Butch said, walking to her and pulling her into a warm embrace.

Emily's heart leapt at seeing her old friend. She hugged him tightly, afraid it wasn't real and she'd lose him if she let go.

"You're really here," Butch said. "After all this time. Are you sure I'm not dreaming?"

"I'm here," she said, beaming up at him.

"I bet it's nice to see your sister, Mr. Ryan," Ray spoke up, interrupting their long-awaited reunion.

"Sister?" Butch glanced from Emily to Ray. Then he nodded. "Yes. My beautiful sister," he said. "It is so nice to see her." Butch patted Ray on the back and walked him to his motorcar, pulling out his money clip.

Emily watched as Butch spoke a few words to Ray, then handed him a wad of bills. Ray grinned and waved to Emily before getting back in his Model T and driving away.

Butch came back to Emily, his blue eyes sparkling mischievously. Picking her up in a bear hug, he twirled her around and they both laughed. She remembered the first time he'd done this when they'd first met, so many years ago. Now, it felt as if it had only been a moment ago. Time had passed so quickly.

Once he'd stopped, he sobered. "Sister? Really?"

"Well, you are James Ryan, aren't you? I believe in New York City years ago that James Ryan was my brother."

"You have a mind like a steel trap." He grinned.

Butch wrapped his arm around her, picked up her suitcase, and they both entered the house. The woman who'd opened the door stood in the entryway, her hands clasped patiently in front of her. She wore a white button-down shirt with a high, frilly collar and a long, tan skirt. Her hair was pulled up into a chignon much like Emily's. Emily thought she looked very respectable.

"Mrs. Harrington," Butch said gleefully. "I'd like you to meet my sister." He paused and glanced at Emily. She realized he wasn't sure what name she was using.

"Emily Pleasants," she said, extending her hand to Mrs. Harrington.

The woman smiled kindly and shook her hand. "It's very nice to meet you, Mrs. Pleasants. I'm assuming you're married since you don't carry the Ryan name."

"Yes," Emily answered but didn't add that she was a widow. Since she wasn't sure about Harry's whereabouts, it would be odd to Mrs. Harrington if suddenly her dead husband appeared.

"Shall I show her to the guest room?" Mrs. Harrington asked Butch.

It was then that Emily noticed Butch was wearing his work clothes, although he wasn't dirty in the least.

"That would be fine," Butch said. "The room on the second floor should suit Emily well."

Mrs. Harrington nodded.

"I'm so sorry, dear," Butch said. "But I must go out and finish helping the men with some work, then I'll clean up for supper. It will give you some time to rest before we eat. We have much to discuss tonight."

Emily nodded. "Of course. You had no idea I was coming, so you go along and get back to work. I'll be fine. I'm a bit tired after the long train ride. One doesn't sleep well on a train, even in a sleeper car."

Butch's eyes twinkled. "Aw, I see you're traveling in style these days."

"I'll explain later," she told him.

The two stood, staring at each other as if memorizing each other's faces, hardly able to believe they were once again under the same roof. Finally, Butch bent down and kissed her cheek. "Until this evening," he said softly, then he was gone.

Mrs. Harrington had discreetly stepped aside and lifted Emily's suitcase. "Shall I show you to your room?"

"Yes, thank you." Emily followed her up the wide, carpeted staircase that curled around to the second floor landing. Down the hall, Emily noticed another staircase that she assumed led up to the third floor. The house was elegantly decorated, and family portraits hung on the wall going upstairs and in the hallway.

"I noticed that the arch entering the property said the Gilbert Ranch," Emily said to Mrs. Harrington as they stopped at a bedroom door.

"Yes. The Gilberts have owned this ranch for almost a century. That is, until Mrs. Gilbert passed away and left it to Mr. Ryan." She cocked her head. "I'm sure your brother has told you that, though."

"I'm afraid we've been out of touch for a while," Emily said. She realized she shouldn't ask too many questions until she and Butch get their stories straight.

Mrs. Harrington showed Emily into a luxurious room and she had to stop herself from gasping as she entered. It had a large, four-poster bed with nightstands on either side. A heavy dresser with a mirror stood against one wall and a dressing table was on the other. The closet was built in, and very large. Plush rugs had been laid on the floor and heavy draperies hung over the two large windows. A sofa and chair were across the room, next to the brick fireplace.

"It's lovely," Emily said. The room was bigger than any she'd stayed in over the past few years. Even bigger than the master bedroom in Edwards beautiful house. A woman could get spoiled here very quickly.

"I'm sure you'll be comfortable in here," Mrs. Harrington said. She set her suitcase on the floor. "Would you like me to hang up your clothes now, or later?"

"That won't be necessary, but thank you. I can do it myself," Emily said.

"As you wish. I could draw you a bath, if you'd like," she offered. "It might be relaxing after your long train ride."

"Oh, that does sound nice," Emily said, thinking how much she'd love to sit in a hot bath and soak. "But I wouldn't want to put you to any trouble, bringing up a tub and hot water."

Mrs. Harrington gave her a small smile. She walked over to a door on the other side of the room and opened it. "It wouldn't be any trouble at all."

Curious, Emily peeked through the doorway and couldn't believe what she saw. The small room held a large bathtub, a commode, and a sink. Emily had stayed in expensive hotels with luxurious water closets that had running water, but never in a house.

"We can heat the water right in here and fill the tub," Mrs. Harrington said.

Emily beamed. "Then in that case, I'd love a bath."

Chapter Thirty

Spokane, WA
1912

Emily was just stepping out of her bedroom when she saw Butch coming from the direction of the third-floor staircase. She smiled at him, and he at her.

"You look as lovely as the last time I saw you." Butch pulled her into a hug.

She laughed. "I was expecting the last time you saw me."

"And you were beautiful."

He escorted her down the stairs and they turned left toward the formal dining room.

"This house is gorgeous," Emily said as they walked into the room. "And the furniture is stunning. I'm certain you didn't have a hand in choosing it," she teased.

"I can't take credit for any of it." Butch pulled out her chair from the mahogany Queen Anne table large enough to easily seat twelve guests. Tonight, there were only two place settings, with candles flickering in silver candlesticks. The gas lights on the wall had also been lit, enveloping the room in a golden glow.

"The woman whose family owned this house had decorated it years ago. Even the portraits on the wall going up the stairs belong to the Gilbert family."

Mrs. Harrington brought out a bottle of wine and set it on the table. Butch poured as she returned to the kitchen and carried out a tray with two china bowls of steaming soup.

"I hope you're hungry," Butch said with a wink. "The cook insisted we have a large meal, since we rarely have guests."

"The soup looks delicious," Emily said. "I'll do my best to eat as much as possible so as not to insult your cook."

As they ate, they made small talk but didn't delve into topics that could be overheard by others. Emily was anxious to ask about Harry, and to also tell Butch about her life in Minnesota, but she refrained. She wasn't sure how much Mrs. Harrington knew of Butch's past, and she didn't want to give him away.

After the soup course, they dined on roast beef with rich gravy, small potatoes, and peas. Dessert consisted of a rich, creamy cheesecake with cherry topping.

"Oh my," Emily exclaimed after a few bites of cake. "I'd be as round as I am tall if I ate like this every night."

"I've put on a pound or two." Butch patted his stomach. "But we usually don't eat like this, since it's generally just me."

He escorted her past the stairs once more to the library and Mrs. Harrington brought a tray of coffee and tea for them. Butch thanked her and told her she could take the evening off. She nodded and left, closing the door behind her.

Emily walked around the large room that held floor-to-ceiling shelves of books as well as a large desk that she assumed was where Butch sat to work. A fireplace was lit, to ward off the evening chill.

"You've done quite well for yourself," she said. "I can't

imagine how you ended up here, but I'd love to hear the story."

"We're finally alone now," Butch said. "We can talk in private."

Emily sat on the sofa and poured herself a cup of tea. She glanced around again, and her eyes fell to Butch as he sat in the chair opposite her. They both looked refined and dignified, dressed in nice attire and sitting in this proper room. She almost laughed. She remembered the tent the three of them had shared with only a curtain between them. The suites they'd stayed in hotels across the country. And the log cabin in Cholila, where they'd sat in the living room together in the evenings, Butch with his stocking feet up on the table while he read a book in his favorite chair. They'd come a long way since then, but in her heart, he was still the same old Butch she'd always known.

"You're remembering, aren't you?" he asked. "I can tell by the smile on your face. We've lived rough and we've lived high. But it's still us, isn't it? We've not changed a bit."

Emily grinned. "No, we haven't. Just older, maybe wiser."

"Huh! Speak for yourself," he joked.

The room fell quiet again, as though neither wanted to start the conversation that they knew they must have. Finally, Emily asked, "Harry?"

Butch closed his eyes, and Emily held her breath in anticipation.

"I'm sorry, Etta, dear," Butch finally said. "He's dead."

The words were as hard for Emily to hear as she could tell they were for him to say. Her Harry was dead. Gone, forever. Of course, she'd already accepted that fact a year ago, but after finding Butch, there was a glimmer of hope. She should have known, though. If Harry were alive, he would have come and found her sooner.

"How?" Emily finally asked, wiping away the lone tear that had fallen. "I had heard from our friend down in Chile, Frank Aller, that you had both been killed in a shootout in San Vincente. He even obtained death certificates for me last year. I could never fully accept that was how you both died, but I didn't know what had happened."

Butch shook his head. "It wasn't us. I've heard that story too. There were a couple of other North American outlaws down there who copied our way of pulling jobs. I'm sure it was them who died there in '08. But our friend Percy Seibert saw an opportunity to help us, and spread the word that the bandits who died were us. No one questioned it."

"Then how?" Emily asked again. "What happened to Harry?"

"After you left, we went to Cholila just as we'd planned and sold the last of the livestock. Then he and I made our way to Chile. There was still a price on our heads, so we had to be careful. All this took months, of course, and we sought a couple of opportunities to earn a little money." He gave a small grin. "A couple of uncles left us some cash. Then we tried to find a ship on the Chilean coast to take us to San Francisco, but they required official papers to buy tickets. With everyone on the lookout for us, we didn't dare use the papers we had for our former aliases. So we took a train up into Peru and were able to finally get on a ship as crewmen, but it only went as far as Mexico. We figured we'd be able to get on another ship once we were there, so that's what we did."

Butch stopped a moment and took a sip of his coffee. Needing something stronger, he stood and went to the bar, pouring himself a shot of whiskey. He returned to Emily, sitting down beside her on the sofa.

"Once we made it to Mexico, we had to wait for a ship that was going to San Francisco. We rented a room not far from the harbor and stayed there a month before our ship was to leave." He sighed. "Well, you know Sundance. He liked to play cards whenever he could find a game, and there were always games down in the harbor saloons. So he'd take a little money each night and go off to gamble. I found my entertainment elsewhere." Butch winked at Emily.

Emily listened intently, trying to digest what he was saying. They had tried to get to her. She dreaded what Butch would say next, but she let him continue.

"We were due to board our ship in two days when Sundance didn't come back to the room that night. I didn't think much of it until it got to be around four in the morning. He hadn't stayed out that late before, so I became worried. I headed down to the saloons and walked the streets and alleys, looking for him. Most of the places had closed down for the night. Finally, I found him. He was beaten up pretty badly and had been shot."

Emily's hand flew to her mouth. Tears blinded her eyes as she thought about her Harry lying in the street, hurt and alone. Her heart clenched.

"Etta, dear," Butch said softly, handing her a clean handkerchief from his pocket. "Are you sure you want to hear this?"

"Yes," she said. She had to know what had happened.

"All right," Butch conceded. "Sundance was still alive, but barely. I found someone who helped me carry him and that person knew of a doctor. The doctor was a kind man, and he did his best, but it wasn't enough. Sundance passed away the next day."

Butch took a breath, then continued. "Before he died, he told me who the two guys were and that they'd only gotten two-hundred pesos off of him. Can you imagine? Killing someone for that amount? They must have thought Sundance carried money with him, but he never did. You know that he always let me keep ahold of the money. He didn't trust himself not to gamble it away."

Emily nodded as she wiped her tears. Harry knew his strengths, and he'd known his weaknesses, too. He'd always trusted Butch with the money.

"I buried him in a cemetery on a hill, under a shade tree. The doctor and his wife came to pay their respects, and I even got a preacher to say a few words. I bought him a nice headstone, too. He's buried under his alias, Harry A. Place, but I suspect that God will know who he is when he gets there."

Despite her tears, Emily smiled at Butch's words. Both Harry and Butch had been raised by very religious families.

He squeezed her hand. "I'm sorry, Etta. I should have been with him when he was at the saloons, but I never thought that anyone would jump him like that. But don't you worry. Those guys got theirs. I made sure of that."

It didn't surprise Emily that Butch would get revenge. He and Sundance were close, like brothers. She just didn't want to know what Butch had done to them.

"I know you'd do anything for Harry," she said, a lump forming in her throat. "Thank you for taking care of him."

"He was family to me," Butch said. "The three of us were a family."

Those words were more than she could take. Emily dropped her head in her hands and wept. Her Harry was gone. He'd died such a terrible death. And he'd tried to come for her. They would never be the little family of three again.

Butch wrapped his arms around her and hugged her close.

Finally, her tears subsided. She looked up at Butch. "How did you end up here?"

"I stayed longer in Mexico because I'd missed the ship to San Francisco. About a month later, I was on a ship to Seattle. I figured it didn't matter anymore, and that was the only ship I could get on. Once there, I rented a nice hotel room and thought about my next move. I thought I could work on the docks and no one would ever know who I was. But that didn't sound too enticing to me. I contemplated going down to Oregon, but didn't know what I'd do there, either. And I knew I had to get word to you, but it wasn't something I wanted to put in a letter. Plus, I knew that Elwood's mail was being watched. That's why it took so long for me to find you."

"I never told Elwood where I'd gone," Emily said. "I also knew his mail was being watched. And I guess I figured it would be best if he didn't know. I wanted to start fresh, without any ties to the past. I had more to protect than just myself."

"The baby," Butch said. "I can understand why."

"Your story first, though," Emily said.

Butch nodded. "One night, I was eating supper in the hotel restaurant, sitting all by myself, when I overheard an elderly lady say she was having a terrible time finding a ranch foreman. Well, my ears perked up and I listened a while. She was talking to another woman, a friend of hers. After I'd finished eating, I walked over to her table and introduced myself. Told her I had overheard her conversation and that I was an experienced rancher who'd recently sold his ranch, and that I was in-between jobs. Well, you know the ladies can never resist my baby blue eyes and smile." He laughed. "Suddenly, I was sitting at the table with her and we were talking about ranching. She had a good head on her shoulders about the business, and she could tell I had experience. The next thing I knew, she offered me the job."

"And that was Mrs. Gilbert?" Emily asked.

"It was. Her husband had died a few years back and she'd entrusted her ranch to her then-foreman, but the guy cheated her. She needed someone who was trustworthy and could manage the other hands. I was her man."

"Well, you've always said that you'd never steal from an employer," Emily said.

"That's for certain," Butch said proudly. "And I never took a thing from her. I ran the ranch carefully, increased the cattle and sheep, brought in the best horses for a good price, and managed the wheat and hay fields as well. Mrs. Gilbert's ranch made a good profit that first year, and she trusted me completely by the end of the second. I never took a dime I didn't earn."

"How did you end up owning the place?" Emily asked. "Don't tell me you seduced Mrs. Gilbert." Emily gave him a sideways glance.

"Heavens no!" Butch said, laughing. "Why, she was in her late seventies! I'm no spring chicken, but I'm not that desperate."

Emily laughed too. "Then how?"

"Well, Rose—that was her name and she insisted I call her by it—began inviting me up to the house for supper every night after that first year, to fill her in on the day's work. I think she was just lonely and enjoyed the company. She'd never had children, and she had no nieces or nephews she wanted to leave the ranch to. So, we became good friends. Then, last spring, she became very ill. We had the doctor out here several times and she had a full-time nurse, but it was too much for her. Right before she died, Rose told me she was leaving the ranch to me. You can imagine how flabbergasted I was. She said I was the closest thing to a son she'd ever had and wanted me to have it.

She also gave generously to her most trusted employees, like Mrs. Harrington and her husband who works with the cattle. All of a sudden, I went from ranch foreman to gentleman rancher. It really was crazy."

"It could only happen to you." Emily gave him a mischievous grin. "But I'm so happy it did."

Butch chuckled. "Me, too." Sobering, he continued, "This past year I could finally get away and go down to find you. I visited Elwood, and that's when he told me you were in Southern California at a convent. You can imagine how surprised I was to hear that." Butch made a face which made Emily laugh. Butch always could cheer Emily up.

"So I hopped a train and headed down there. And, well, you know the rest. That very stern Mother Superior refused to tell me where you'd gone, but finally gave in and said they'd send my information on to you. It seems they really liked you there, and miss you, too."

His words warmed her heart. "I miss them, too. They took me in when I needed a place to stay and were like a family to me for three years. Then, Mother Superior told me that I shouldn't hide out from the world any longer. That, and the fact that I'd received information that you and Harry were dead, prompted me to move on."

"I'm sorry we put you through so much," Butch said, once again squeezing her hand. "We had thought we'd only be two or three months behind you. All that went awry, though."

"I'm grateful that Harry made me leave when I did. I was in a safe place by the time I had our baby, and I'm thankful for that."

Butch's eyes lit up. "The baby! Now it's your turn. What did you have? A boy or a girl?"

Emily smiled just thinking of her son. "A boy. One who looks very much like his father." She pulled a photo out of her skirt pocket and handed it to Butch. It was a recent one of Harry, dressed up in a new suit that Edward had bought him just for the picture. Edward had insisted they have their photo taken for their engagement, and he'd also wanted one of Harry.

Butch stared at the small, framed photo and his eyes softened. "Well, look at that. Such a handsome boy." He glanced up at Emily. "You're right. The spitting image of Sundance. Wouldn't he be so proud?"

Tears threatened to fill Emily's eyes again and she forced them back. Yes, her Harry would have been proud. He would have enjoyed teaching little Harry to ride, and he would have taught him how to care for horses, too. Of course, he'd have insisted on teaching him to do riding tricks, like he could, and shoot a gun. Emily wouldn't have been so sure about that. But still, Harry would have been a good father.

"Yes. He would have been proud," she agreed.

"What's his name?" Butch asked.

Emily grinned. "Harry Robert Pleasants. I've been using my maiden name. But I named him after my two favorite men in the world."

Butch straightened proudly and beamed. "Well, I'll be. I have a namesake." He stared at the photo again before handing it back to her, but Emily shook her head. "It's yours to keep. That's why I brought it."

"Thank you," he said softly. He slipped the small photo into his jacket pocket. "I'll place it on the bureau in my room. That way I can see him every day when I wake up."

They talked well into the night. Emily told him about her time at the convent, and how she'd moved to Pine Creek to teach school. She told him about Edward, Gertie, Allison, and the baby girl named after her. She also told him about her scare when Sheriff Neilson figured out who she actually was.

"But you charmed him out of arresting you," Butch said, grinning wickedly. "No one is immune to your charms."

Emily laughed. "Not quite. After I delivered his baby, he had no choice but to give in. We're friends now."

Butch snorted. "Friends? With an ex-Pinkerton agent? Well, that's incredible."

"I wouldn't believe it either if it hadn't happened to me," she said.

"It sounds like you've made a bushel of new friends out there," he said. "I'm happy for you, Etta. I really am. But what about this Edward? Is that his ring you're wearing?"

She nodded, serious now. "He's asked me to marry him, and I've accepted. He's a good man, and he adores little Harry. I'm very lucky to have found him."

Butch's smile faded. "But do you love him? I mean, really love him?"

Emily dropped her eyes to her lap and was quiet a moment before raising them to his. "I'll never love a man as I did Harry," she admitted. "I followed him everywhere, because he was the one man I felt was worth following. But as you've told me, he's gone now. Edward will be good to me and my son. He's warm and loving, and he doesn't care at all about my past. He'll make a good father, too. I love him. In a different way, but yes, I do love him."

Butch's face dropped, as if disappointed. "I'm happy for you then," he said. "You deserve to have a good life."

Emily reached up and touched the side of Butch's face, making him look into her eyes. "I would have stayed with Harry forever. You know that. I would have followed him around the globe. But now I have little Harry to think of. Edward will give us a good home and I won't have to worry about being chased by the law anymore. Our son will grow up to be a good man. That's the most important thing for me now."

"Of course it is," Butch said sincerely. "I've never had to think of anyone but myself. What you're doing for your son is right."

She smiled warmly at him. "Butch. Don't sell yourself short. You always thought of me and of Harry, and of others. You've given money to widows of outlaws, or wives of friends who needed to feed their families. You've never been selfish a day in your life. You're a good man, well, despite getting your money in questionable ways." She grinned.

"Have I ever told you how much I love you, Etta Place?" Butch asked.

"Only about a hundred times," she said.

"Well then, I'm telling you again. I love you, Etta. You've been the bright light in my dismal existence. Why, if I could have found a woman half as good as you, I'd have married her in a second."

"Oh, of course you wouldn't have," Emily said, shaking her head. "You know you're not the marrying type, Butch."

He shrugged. "Maybe someday. Who knows?"

Emily yawned. It was late, and she was weary from the emotions of the night. "I think I'll go to bed now," she announced. "I should see if there's a train to take me home tomorrow."

"Don't go yet," Butch said, sounding desperate. "Stay one more day, at least. We can ride the ranch tomorrow, and spend a little more time together. I fear I'll never see you again after this visit, and I want to spend more time with you."

"I'd like that. One more day." She stood to go upstairs, but Butch stopped her.

"I have something to give you," he said.

Emily watched as he crossed the room to a large painting of a regal-looking gentleman. Butch took hold of the frame and pulled it out from the wall. Behind it was a safe. She watched in amazement as he opened it and pulled out a large envelope. Closing everything up again, he came back to stand next to her.

"My goodness," she said, her voice teasing. "A hidden safe. You are the gentleman rancher now."

Butch chuckled. "I'm no longer breaking into them. I know the combination." He sobered as he handed her the envelope. "This is for you, Etta dear. Sundance entrusted me to give it to you, and I've held on to it all these years to do just that."

Emily looked at the envelope in her hand. It was thick and felt heavy. She knew there was money in it, just not how much.

"It was his take on the sale of the livestock, along with his half of the last two jobs we did. He planned on starting his new life with this money. His life with you and his child. Before he died, he made me swear to give it all to you. There's twenty-thousand dollars in there. Enough for you to start a new life with little Harry, if it is ever necessary."

Twenty-thousand dollars. That sum stunned Emily. After all the years of worrying about money, she no longer had to. She decided right then that she'd let Edward help her invest it for her son.

"Thank you, Butch. You're a good friend. I have a wonderful life now, and this will make it even better. I just don't know how I'll ever be able to explain to Edward where it came from."

He winked. "Just tell him an uncle died and left it to you."

Emily laughed. "Yes. That story seems to work well for you. Maybe it will work for me, too."

Butch placed his arm around her waist and they walked toward the staircase. The house was very quiet with the staff gone or already in bed. Butch blew out the oil lamp sconces along the staircase as they ascended.

"You know, I'd give all the money back just to have my friend alive and well," Butch said. "He could sure be an old grouch, but I do miss him."

"I miss him, too," Emily said quietly. And she did. Harry would always be the love of her life. But now, the most important person in her life was her son.

They stopped at her door and Butch kissed her on the cheek. "Goodnight, Etta dear. I'll see you in the morning." Then, he was off to the staircase that went up to the third floor.

As Emily lay in bed that night, she thought of all the things Butch had told her. It was hard to believe that after all they'd been through together, her Harry had died at the hands of ordinary bandits. He and Butch had always been so careful, and both carried knives and guns at all times. Harry had always been keenly aware of who was around him, and what their intentions were. For him to be beat up in an alley in a strange town made little sense to her. Maybe he'd had too much to drink and his reflexes had been slow. Or his instincts had been off. She didn't know. It was a terrible way for a man as able and cunning as Harry to die. And it broke her heart that she hadn't been there for him when he'd needed her most. But she'd left to keep his baby safe, and that had been what Harry had wanted—insisted—she do. She thanked God she at least had her son to remind her of the man she'd loved so dearly.

In the stillness of the night, she thought she heard voices in the distance. Emily strained to listen, but only heard a low rumble of sound. Getting up, she opened her door and listened. The voices were still not clear, but she could tell they were coming from the third floor. She went back to her bed, too exhausted to investigate. It might just be Butch giving instructions to one of the servants for the next day. Or maybe he'd invited one up to his room for a game of cards. She smiled. That would be more like Butch. He'd always been a night owl. Without another thought about it, she finally fell into a deep sleep.

Chapter Thirty-One

Spokane, WA
1912

Butch hurried up the stairs to the third floor after having bid Etta goodnight. Striding past his own door, he made his way to the end of the hallway and knocked softly on the door before opening it and stepping inside.

The room was dark, except for one oil lamp flickering by the bed. Butch walked around the room, lighting wall sconces and lamps, until the man lying in the bed said gruffly, "Are you trying to burn the place down?"

Somberly, Butch went to the bedside and sat heavily in a chair. Butch usually sat there next to the small table where they played cards.

"I did what you wanted," Butch said, sounding miserable. "I lied and said you were dead."

With great effort, the man pushed himself up higher in the bed. He started to speak but coughed instead. His coughing grew worse until he sounded as if he were choking.

Butch quickly poured a glass of water from the pitcher on

the table and held it to his lips. The man took a few sips, and slowly, his hacking fit subsided. Butch handed him a clean handkerchief from the drawer to wipe his mouth.

"You okay?" Butch asked, frowning.

"I'm fine," the man said, annoyed. He stared at Butch. "Did you give it to her? The money?"

Butch nodded. "Yes, I did. But I felt terrible, lying to her. She doesn't need the money, Sundance. She needs you."

Sundance turned away. His face was thin and covered in thick scruff because he'd only allow Butch to shave him once or twice a week. His hair was long and thinning. His gray eyes could still glower, but they no longer sparkled with excitement as they once had.

"As long as I know she's taken care of, that's all that matters," Sundance said.

Butch shook his head and began pacing. "I should have told her the truth. I should have told her that we nearly didn't make it out of that last payroll heist in Chile and were shot up all to hell. That a local family helped us and nursed us back to health so we could get on a ship back to the States. Instead, I told her an entire story of lies."

Sundance glared at him. "Nursed *you* back to health. Not me. There was nothing to help me," he spat out.

"You're alive, aren't you?" Butch asked.

Sundance pointed to his useless legs under the blanket. "What's the point of being alive if I'm only half a man?" he yelled. "Is that what you want Etta to have? A cripple who she'd have to take care of the rest of her life?"

Butch stopped pacing. "You have a wheelchair. You can get around a little."

"Yeah. Right," Sundance said. He coughed again but brushed

away Butch's attempt to help him. He covered his mouth with the handkerchief to catch the blood he spat up. Looking up at Butch, he finally said, "We both know there's more wrong with me than just my legs."

Sitting down again beside the bed, Butch's tone softened. "She still loves you, Sundance. She'd stay in a heartbeat if she knew you were here."

"Then we're going to make sure she doesn't find out," Sundance insisted, staring hard at Butch.

Butch sighed. Then he remembered what was in his pocket. He pulled out the photo of little Harry and handed it to Sundance. "You have a son," he said gently. "And he looks just like you."

Sundance gazed at the photo, and his expression softened. "I have a son. All this time, I've wondered. And here he is. He does look just like me." Sundance gave a small smile when he looked up at Butch.

"His name is Harry, too. Harry Robert Pleasants. Our name is tied together for another generation," Butch teased.

"She's using her maiden name then."

"What did you expect? We've been using aliases for so long, she didn't dare use your real name, or Place. I think it suits her fine. She's going by Emily. A beautiful name."

Sundance nodded. "That's her middle name. Her real name is Ethel, and that's why Fannie and everyone else called her Etta."

Butch's brows rose. "I had no idea. She's always just been Etta to me."

Sundance stared at the photo of his son for a little longer, then awkwardly moved to place it on the nightstand. Butch helped him, turning the frame so Sundance could see it while lying in bed.

"Don't you want to be that little guy's father?" Butch asked. "Imagine the fun we could have, teaching him to ride here at the ranch. It could be the three of us again, plus one. I could call us our little family of four." Butch smiled just thinking about it.

Sundance shook his head. "No. That's just a nice dream. I could never be the father I'd want to be. Or the husband Etta needs. You told me earlier that she has a new life in Minnesota. She should stay there."

"But what I didn't tell you is that she's engaged. To a banker, no less." Butch watched for Sundance's reaction, figuring that would be enough to make him jealous and reconsider.

"Well, isn't that a twist of fate?" he said wryly. "Good for her. She can live a nice life and provide for our son." He looked up at Butch. "Is he good to little Harry?"

Butch nodded reluctantly. "She said he is. He adores the young boy. And he loves Etta. He told her he didn't care about her past—doesn't even want to know about it. He sounds like a good man."

Sundance's eyes dropped, but he nodded. "Good. She'll finally have the nice life she deserves. The life I could never give her."

"But she won't have you," Butch insisted. "Or ever be with us again. Don't we deserve the chance to finally give her every-thing? We're in the position to give her a nice life now, too."

Sundance shook his head. "You know I appreciate all you've done for me, Butch. Don't you? It wasn't easy, bringing me all the way from Chile, finding work that allowed you a place where I could stay too. And now, living in this nice house. You never once considered abandoning me, and that makes you a damn good friend. And I know I haven't always made it easy."

Butch snorted. "That's for certain."

A rare smile formed on Sundance's lips. "I appreciate all you've done. And that you were able to find Etta and give her the money. But that's the end of it. We'll let her go and live her life. She deserves that."

Butch sighed heavily. He glanced up at the clock on the wall. "It's after midnight. I should let you get some sleep. Do you want to take some medicine?"

"No medicine," Sundance growled. "But I'll have a shot or two of whiskey and a couple rounds of poker. Unless you're too much of a coward to play a hand or two against me."

Butch grinned as he poured whiskey for both of them. "I'm not afraid of you." He handed Sundance a shot glass.

"We'll see about that. Deal the cards."

* * *

The next morning, Emily arose early and took a bath, luxuriating in the warm water and lilac scented bath salts. Afterward, she pulled her hair up in a chignon, dressed in her usual shirtwaist and skirt, and stepped out into the hallway. A girl who had helped serve dinner the night before was just about to walk up the stairs to the third floor with a covered tray.

"Is that for Mr. Ryan?" Emily asked the girl.

She turned to Emily, a worried look on her face. "Oh, no, ma'am. It's for his friend."

Emily stopped short. "Friend? Is there another guest staying here?"

The young girl shook her head. "No, ma'am. He lives here. I best get upstairs now. Mrs. Harrington said I was to bring up the tray and get back to the kitchen." She had gone up the first step before Emily stopped her.

"Wait! I'll take it up for you," she told her.

The girl looked unsure. "I'm not sure if I should."

"It's fine," Emily told her gently as she took the tray from her. "What is your name, dear?"

The girl swallowed hard. "Florence. But everyone here calls me Flo."

"It's nice to meet you, Flo. Don't worry about the tray. And if you get in trouble, I'll be sure to let Mrs. Harrington know that I insisted on bringing it up."

Flo nodded, then turned to leave.

"Flo?"

"Yes, ma'am?" she asked, turning back.

"What room is the friend in?"

"It's the last room at the end of the hallway, ma'am."

Emily smiled at her reassuringly and Flo smiled back before heading down to the kitchen.

As she walked up the stairs, Emily wondered about the voices she'd heard last night. Why hadn't Butch told her he had another guest? Was he hiding something? Or someone?

Her heart pounding with each step, Emily walked up the stairs and down the hallway until she came to the door at the end. Taking a deep breath, she balanced the tray with one hand and reached for the knob with the other. Just as she turned it, a voice startled her from behind.

"Good morning, Etta, dear." Butch's voice boomed through the hallway. "Is that tray supposed to be for me?"

Emily jumped, almost dropping the tray. She let go of the doorknob and turned to face Butch. "I offered to bring it up to the other guest you have here," she said, watching Butch's face closely for his reaction. "I was surprised you didn't tell me you had a friend staying here."

Butch's expression remained calm as he took the tray from her. "That's because he's not a guest, my sweet Etta. He's an elderly gentleman, a lifetime servant of the Gilbert family who has grown too old to work. He's quite ill, and has been for some time. Before she died, I promised Rose that I'd take care of him in his old age and he'd always have a home."

Emily studied him, not completely sure if he was telling the truth. "Well, I'd love to meet him. I'm sure he'd enjoy having company for a change." She turned back to the door, but Butch interjected.

"He's an ornery old man, Etta. He really doesn't want any company, besides me. Not even a beautiful woman like you. Why don't you go downstairs, and I'll be with you in a few minutes? I can smell our delicious breakfast all the way up here."

Emily considered arguing with him, but decided against it. She didn't want to barge in on someone who wanted to be left alone. "I'll see you downstairs, then," she told Butch.

After breakfast, Butch loaned Emily a pair of his trousers and found her riding boots that had once belonged to Rose. When she emerged from her room in her new attire, Butch laughed. "Just like old times. All you need is a six-shooter on your hip."

Two horses were already saddled and waiting for them when they went down to the stables. They took off through the pasture where the cattle were grazing, then wound around fields that would soon be tall with wheat. They came upon a river, and followed it for a time.

"What river is this?" Emily asked with interest. She'd been enjoying their ride. No matter how refined she generally acted, at heart she was a rancher's daughter and an outlaw's wife. She loved the outdoors, and being on the back of a horse was second nature to her.

"The Spokane River," Butch replied.

"I remember a river long ago where I almost shot you and Harry." She grinned mischievously at him.

Butch broke out laughing. "Those were the days, weren't they?"

"They certainly were."

They reminisced as their horses walked slowly along a well-worn trail. They talked about the winter they'd spent in Robbers Roost with Elzy Lay and his wife, Maude, and laughed over Emily having the nerve to talk Lonnie Logan and Flatnose Currie into helping her break Sundance, Harvey, and Walt out of the Deadwood jail.

"My goodness but you were a tough one," Butch said. "Those hardened outlaws were too afraid of you to say no."

"Oh, they said no," Emily told him. "But I threatened to tell Harvey Logan that his own cousin wouldn't help spring him from jail. That's what made Lonnie agree to go."

Their talk turned to their travels around New York City and the day Harry had bought Emily the gold lapel watch.

"I've worn it every day since then," she told Butch. "And do you remember the stickpin you bought for yourself? The one with a diamond on it that you gave me to take care of?"

"Ah, yes, I do," Butch said. "What happened to it?"

Emily smiled warmly. "I hope you don't mind, but I gave it to Edward to wear. He said he'll give it to little Harry when he's grown. Edward was touched when I offered it to him."

"Well, that's sweet," Butch said. "I'm glad you're keeping it in the family."

"Me too," she said.

The day grew warm, but they hardly noticed. They were both wrapped up in the past, enjoying being able to share it with each other after all their time apart. Butch was her last connection to memories she couldn't share with anyone else. She loved talking about the past with him. And she missed the old days, too. But she had a good life now, and she couldn't give that up because of memories.

Finally, they rode back to the house. As it came into view, Emily glanced up at the third-floor window. She could have sworn she saw the lace curtains moving.

"Are you and the old servant the only ones who live on the third floor?" she asked casually.

"Yes. I have a large room up there. He has a smaller one. Why?"

"He must be able to get around easily. I just saw the curtains in his room move."

Butch looked startled, which piqued Emily's interest. But he caught himself and said, "Mrs. Harrington must be up there opening the window. It's a warm day."

Emily nodded. She felt uneasy, though. It seemed as if even the mention of the old servant unnerved Butch. She had a nagging feeling that Butch was lying to her, but she brushed it aside. After all, why would he?

They ate dinner together that night in the dining room and relaxed in the library afterward. They continued to reminisce about past memories at Hole-in-the-Wall, the W S Ranch in New Mexico, and their time at Cholila.

"I miss those days most of all," Butch said. "We were anonymous there. Running the ranch, spending time together at night, relaxing in the cabin, getting together with the other ranchers and their families. It was as close to normal as we ever got."

Emily nodded. "It didn't last nearly long enough. I'd have been happy there for the rest of our lives."

Butch gave her a warm smile. "Me too."

As the hour grew late, Emily yawned. "I'm afraid that long ride tired me out. I'm not used to riding all day like that anymore."

"Lightweight," Butch joked. "I sent a hand to town to buy you a ticket on tomorrow's train back to Minnesota. Ray will be here in the morning to pick you up."

"Thank you," Emily said.

"Unless I can talk you into staying longer," he said, looking hopeful.

"As much as I've enjoyed being here, I really should get back," she told him. It would be so easy to say yes, I want to stay. Butch was familiar. She adored him, and always would. But staying would mean putting her son at risk. Butch would always be a wanted man, just as her Harry would have been. Emily was tired of running. With Edward, she wouldn't have to.

Butch took her hand and walked her up the stairs. He looked like a lost boy, trying so hard to cling to the past. When they were in front of her bedroom door, he turned to her, his eyes serious.

"Stay here, Etta. Please? Marry me. You know I've always loved you, and I know you have a tender spot in your heart for me. I can take care of you and your son, and I'd make a great daddy. I adore children, you know that. Please. Stay."

Emily widened her eyes; she was so taken aback by Butch's sudden proposal. "Oh, Butch," she said gently, pulling him into a hug. "I do love you, you must know that," she whispered in his ear. "But I can't stay. I'm sorry." When she stepped away, she saw pain in his eyes.

"But we get along so well," Butch said, sounding heartbroken. "We could have a wonderful life."

Emily slowly shook her head. "I have to protect my son. As long as I'm with you, I'll always be looking over my shoulder, wondering if someone recognizes me or you. I don't want little Harry growing up that way. We're safe in Pine Creek, with Edward. I care deeply for him. It's time I stop being alias Etta Place, and be myself, Emily Pleasants."

Butch dropped his eyes. He looked defeated and it broke Emily's heart seeing him that way.

"You're right. I can't be selfish. You deserve to be the woman you were before you met Sundance, and live a good life. And so does your son."

Emily hugged him once more, then kissed him softly on the cheek. "I'll miss you, though," she said, a lump forming in her throat. "So very much." Then she went inside her room and let the tears fall. Tears for Butch, for Harry, and for losing the men she'd love most of all.

* * *

Early the next morning, Butch saw Emily off. They stood on his front porch as Ray loaded her bag into his Model T and waited for her by the car.

"Goodbye, Butch." She held him tightly. "Please stay in touch with me, now that we've found each other again."

"I will. I promise," Butch said. "And send me pictures whenever you can. Of you and the boy."

She nodded. "I will." She glanced up at the third-floor window and Butch's eyes followed her gaze. The curtains fluttered. Emily turned back and looked Butch in the eyes. "Tell him I love him. That I'll always love him. And that I'm doing this for his son." Her voice cracked as tears fell down her cheeks.

Butch gasped. "You know?"

She smiled sadly as she wiped her tears. "Yes, I figured it out.

You've never been a very good liar, Butch Cassidy. At least not to me." She stood on tiptoe and kissed him one last time, then walked to the car with Butch right behind her. He held her hand as she stepped into the backseat.

"Please keep me informed about him," Emily said. "And about you. You know I love you both so very much."

Butch nodded, still unable to believe that she'd known the truth all along. With one last hug, he closed the door and stepped back. Waving to Ray, the car took off, bumping down the dirt road.

Butch watched the car until it disappeared from view. *She knew,* he thought as he stared out at the stretch of road. *She knew that Sundance was alive, yet she left anyway. That's how much she loves her son.*

With a burst of adrenalin, Butch rushed into the house and up both flights of stairs. He hurried down the hall and went directly into Sundance's bedroom. Butch found him sitting in his wheelchair by the front window, looking drawn.

"She's gone," Butch said.

"I know."

Butch locked eyes with Sundance. "She knew I was lying to her all along. She knew you were still alive. Yet, she still left."

Sundance pushed the wheels of his chair closer to the bed. "She was always a smart woman. And you've always been a terrible liar."

"I proposed to her last night," Butch blurted out. "I asked Etta to marry me and stay."

Sundance's face turned red with rage. "You what? Are you crazy?"

"Well, you didn't want her anymore!" Butch shouted. "I've always loved Etta. I'd do anything to make her stay."

"Why, you worthless skunk! Taking my woman!" Sundance tried to reach the nightstand which held a six-shooter. "I'll kill you right here, right now!" he bellowed.

Butch slumped into the chair on the other side of the bed. "Lot of good that would do you. Besides, I unloaded the gun while you were sleeping. I didn't want you to get any ideas about using it."

Sundance glared at him, then his anger abated as quickly as it had begun. "She turned you down, I see."

"Of course she turned me down. It's you she loves. It's always been you."

"I'm glad she left," Sundance said. "She deserves a good life. I was never able to give her that. Now, she and my son will have it."

Butch heard the pain in Sundance's words. "She still loves you, Kid. She told me so. If you weren't so pig-headed, she'd be staying here for good. Tell me you don't love her anymore, and I'll let it go. But you have to say the words and mean it."

Sundance raised his eyes to Butch's, his face creased with pain. "I don't love her."

"Who's the terrible liar now?" Butch asked.

They sat in silence, each in their own thoughts. Butch couldn't stand the thought of Etta leaving forever and never seeing her sweet face again.

"It's not too late to stop her." Butch shot up with a final burst of energy. "Come on, Sundance! Let me go after her. Let me bring her back here and we can all be a family again. Just say the words."

Sundance dropped his head in his hands. Butch thought he might have finally gotten through to him. But after a moment, Sundance raised his head and shook it. "No, Butch. Let things be as they are. If you truly love Etta, you'll let her move on. I'm willing to do that for her. You should be too."

Butch wasn't used to giving up, but he gave in for Sundance's sake. Still, the pain of losing Etta tore at his heart. It hurt deeply.

Both men sat there, defeated. They had once been the wiliest outlaws the west had ever seen. Railroad companies paid thousands to try to capture them; bankers feared them. Now, here they were, nearly broken by the one thing in their life they loved the most. Etta.

"Help me up on the bed," Sundance said gruffly.

Butch helped him get settled, stacked pillows behind him so he could sit up, and placed a blanket over his withering legs.

Sundance reached for a tarnished coin that sat in a small bowl on the nightstand. He rolled it through his fingers several times, as he did often, rubbing his thumb over the bump in the middle.

Butch watched him and grinned. "She was one hell'uva shot, wasn't she?"

Sundance stared at the coin and nodded. He carefully placed it back in the bowl. "Why don't you pour us each a shot of whiskey and I'll beat you in a game of poker."

Butch glanced at the clock. "It's only nine-thirty in the morning. Don't you think it's a little early for whiskey?"

"You getting soft on me, Cassidy?"

Butch chuckled. "I could drink you under the table any day." He poured the whiskey and started dealing the cards. "Well, at least we still have each other, right, Kid?"

Sundance snorted. "Yep. We're stuck with each other."

The two former outlaws drank and played cards the rest of the day while the woman they both loved left on the morning train.

Chapter Thirty-Two

Pine Creek, MN
1912

Emily stepped off the train at the Pine Creek Station and the porter handed down her bag. She glanced around the now familiar landscape. She remembered how, less than a year ago, she'd stepped onto this same platform, anxious to begin a new life for her and little Harry. Today, she felt almost the same as she'd felt then. Confronting her past had helped her finally choose her future. She was confident in her choice now—satisfied she'd made the right decision.

Not that it had been easy. Leaving Butch that morning had been one of the hardest things she'd ever done. Especially after realizing the truth. She'd suspected Butch was hiding something from her, and when she'd played her hand, his expression had proven her right. Her Harry was still alive, and living at the house with Butch. But he hadn't wanted to see her. Or maybe, he hadn't wanted to be seen. She suspected that part of Butch's story had been true and Harry had been injured badly. He was a proud man. He wouldn't have wanted her to see him if he'd been weakened in any way. And he wouldn't have wanted her to take care of him.

In that moment on the porch when all this was running through her mind, she had to make a decision. She'd decided to honor Harry's wishes. Even though her heart had been heavy, and she'd cried nearly the entire trip back to Pine Creek, she knew she'd made the right choice. This town was where she now belonged.

And hadn't Harry taken care of her and little Harry after all? The money he gave her was his way of showing how much he still loved her and ensured she was safe and secure. It was his final act of love.

And dear, sweet Butch. He'd proposed just to try to stop her from leaving. She knew he'd asked her out of desperation, but she'd found it heartwarming just the same. Emily would miss her boys, her tough, outlaw men, every day of her life. But she was ready to begin her new path in life.

The sun was unusually warm for May and Emily felt perspiration gather under her layers of clothing. Despite the heat, she decided she could easily walk the distance to the store. Turning in that direction, she stopped when she saw a man wearing a brown suit, a gold pocket watch chain stretched across his vest. He looked like a banker, which made her smile.

"Are you in need of a ride?" the gentleman asked.

"That depends," Emily said, drawing closer to him. "Are you going to give me a difficult time? After all, I'm a widow with a son. And I hear that wasn't what the school board was expecting." She grinned.

He chuckled. "I think the school board got much more than they were expecting. At least, this board member did."

"Then I guess I'll accept that ride," Emily said.

They stood close, each smiling at the other.

"You came back," Edward finally said, sounding relieved.

"Of course I came back. You didn't think I'd let you out of your promise to marry me, did you?"

"Did everything get settled?" he asked.

"Yes." She looked up at him and saw all she needed to see in his eyes. Edward truly loved her. It was a love she felt honored to accept for as long as she was on this earth.

"In fact," she said with a sly smile. "I seem to have come into some money. I was told an uncle died." She couldn't help herself. It was her last homage to Butch.

His brows rose. "Really? I'm sorry to hear that. You weren't close, were you?"

Emily slipped her arm through his. "No, not at all. Strange, isn't it? How someone you hardly knew could leave you so much money."

"Yes. Very odd." He lifted her suitcase and they walked toward his buggy.

Edward helped her up then went around and pulled himself up on the other side.

"How did you know I was coming today?" She hadn't sent word that she was.

"I've been coming to meet the train every day since you left," Edward admitted sheepishly. "I didn't want to miss seeing you when you returned."

She smiled. "You're a good man, Edward Sheridan. I'm lucky to have you in my life."

"And I'm very lucky to have you, too," he said. "Shall we go home? There's a little boy waiting impatiently for his mother."

She placed her hand over his. "Yes. Let's go home."

Chapter Thirty-Three

San Francisco, CA
1972

S usan Sheridan stared open-mouthed at Grandma Em before finally catching herself and clamping it shut. She was stunned by all that her grandmother had told her. "Grandma. Sundance was alive, and you walked away? But he was the love of your life!"

Grandma Em nodded. "I had to. It was what Harry wanted. Harry died two years later, and Butch wrote to me and told me the true story. Harry hadn't wanted to be a burden to me and he wanted his son to grow up to be a respectable man. As hard as it was to walk away, it was the right thing to do."

"What happened to Butch?" Susan asked.

"He passed away years later. He stayed at the ranch all that time, and even though there had been rumors he was the famous Butch Cassidy, no one ever did anything about it. He left the ranch to the employees and the Harringtons to do what they wanted with it. They ended up selling it and splitting the money. He also made sure to include me in his will. He's buried under his alias, James Ryan, next to Harry in a little cemetery outside of Spokane. I've never been there, but I was informed of it by Mrs. Harrington."

Susan stood and began pacing the small living room. "I still can't believe it. You were Etta Place. Do you realize how famous you are? Why, just by disappearing into thin air, you became more famous than if everyone had known what happened to you."

Grandma Em shook her head slowly. "Who knew that anyone would care who Butch, Harry, and I were after all these years? I disappeared to protect my son, not to become famous."

"Wait!" Susan said, suddenly coming to a halt. "How could you legally marry Grandfather? You were married to Sundance, and he was still alive."

Grandma Em glanced down at her hands and touched the wedding band on her ring finger. "I was never legally married to Harry," she said. "He didn't want there to be any way for the law to connect me to him if he were ever caught. But we were as committed to each other as if we were married."

"Grandma…" Susan said, shocked.

Her eyes darted up to her granddaughter. "It really wasn't uncommon in those days not to be legally married, dear. Especially in the west. Many couples lived as husband and wife without a piece of paper. Most marriages were just written down in the family Bible, not at the courthouse."

Susan nodded. "I've never thought of it that way. But what about Grandpa Edward? Did he ever learn about your past?"

"No," the older woman said. "He never asked. Edward only cared about the future. He was a good man."

"And Dad? Does he know who his real father is?" Susan asked. It seemed so strange to her to think that her blood grandfather was the Sundance Kid.

Grandma Em shook her head. "He knows his real father's name was Harry, like his own, but honestly, he never asked about him. He was so young when Edward came into our lives that he accepted Edward as his father."

"That's kind of sad, isn't it?" Susan asked. "It's as if Sundance—Harry—never existed other than as a famous outlaw. But he has a son, and a granddaughter. And no one knows that."

"That's why I told you the story, dear." Grandma Em reached for the wooden box. She slid it across the table to Susan.

Susan stared at it a moment before realization hit her. "Is that the box Butch made for you that one Christmas?"

Grandma Em smiled. "Yes. Open it, dear."

Susan sat down and lifted the box into her lap. It was lighter than she thought it would be. Opening the lid, she peered inside. There was a pile of old, sepia-tone photographs, her grandmother's lapel pin watch, an antique amethyst ring, and a wedding band. Susan pulled out the photo that was on top. She gasped when she realized the young woman in the beautiful dress was Grandma Em.

"Is this Sundance standing next to you?" she asked, looking up expectantly.

"Yes, dear. That's my Harry."

"It's amazing. He does look exactly like Dad."

The older woman nodded. "Yes. He does."

Susan set the picture carefully back into the box. "Why are you telling me all this, Grandma? You've kept it a secret for so long. Why tell it now?"

"It's time the story was told," she said. "I couldn't leave this life without sharing it with someone, and I decided who better to share it with than you? You are a young woman on her own, supporting herself. I thought that in some small way, you'd understand my story better than anyone else."

Susan thought about that a moment. True, she was single and living on her own. She'd never thought of her grandmother that way, even though she'd known her grandmother had been a teacher when she'd met her grandfather. It just never occurred to her that this woman who'd spent her life as a volunteer at schools, a member of the local school board, and the once-head of their local community center, could have such an interesting past.

"How did you end up in San Francisco?" Susan asked. She'd never even thought to ask that before.

"A few years after Edward and I married, we took a train trip out west and he fell in love with this town. We waited another year, then made the move here. He sold his store in Pine Creek and his holdings in the bank there, so we had enough money to build our house up on the hill, and for him to invest in an up-and-coming bank." Grandma Em smiled. "Well, you know how well that investment has done. Your father is chairman of the board there and our family still owns the majority of the stock."

Susan nodded. She'd grown up in a family of privilege, and she'd never given it a moment's thought to how they'd become so wealthy. But she'd also been taught a great work ethic, and she'd been successful on her own as well.

"What happened to the money Sundance gave you?" Susan asked.

"I gave it to Edward to invest. I trusted him completely. Some was invested in the bank; other was put into stocks. He did well, and we didn't lose much during the crash of '29 because Edward was always careful. He was a smart man."

"Did he know where the money came from?"

"I eventually told him the truth—my husband left it to me.

It wasn't that hard for him to believe. He'd already suspected we had money, because of the clothes I owned and the traveling we'd done. He just assumed it came from the sale of a ranch we'd owned."

Susan shook her head, still trying to digest what she'd been told. "This is so much to take in, Grams. You're a completely different woman from the one I've known my entire life. You participated in bank robberies. You rode with outlaws. You were even shot once! It's all so crazy."

"It's all true, though, dear. I'm not saying I'm proud of some of the things I've done in the past. But it is what it is. I've spent all of these years trying to live a respectable life. I can only hope the good will outweigh the bad I've done."

Susan quickly moved over to her grandmother's rocker and knelt beside her, taking her hand. "I didn't mean to say you were a bad person. You've done more good over the years than most people do in a lifetime."

"I know you didn't mean anything by it, dear. I've tried to make up for it. But still, I don't regret those days. I loved Harry. I really had no other choice but to follow him, no matter where it led me."

"That's the most amazing thing of all about your story," Susan said. "To love someone that intently, and be loved back as much. How lucky you were. I'd be happy if I found someone who loved me even half as much as Harry loved you."

Grandma Em patted her hand. "You will find that. I found it twice. Surely there is one man out there who will love you deeply too."

Susan stood and kissed her grandmother's soft cheek. As she did, she noticed how tired her grandmother looked. As if telling the story of her life had drained her.

"Well, dear," Grandma Em said, pushing herself up to a standing position. "I've taken up enough of your time. I think I'll go lay down until dinner."

"Of course." Susan linked arms with her grandmother and walked with her into her bedroom. The room was tiny but held a queen sized bed, an antique bureau and nightstand, and her grandmother's old Singer sewing machine. Susan remembered the days when her grandmother would sew her frilly dresses for her dolls and stuffed animals. Susan had always marveled at how easily her grandmother could create beautiful items out of scraps of fabric.

She helped Grandma Em onto the bed and pulled a light blanket over her.

"Take the box with you, Susan," Grandma Em said. "It's yours now. As is the story. Do with it as you wish. Tell it, or don't. I'll leave it up to you."

"Oh, Grandma. I could never do your story justice. There's so much I still don't know."

Grandma Em smiled. "You're the writer in the family. You would do just fine with it. I entrusted it with you for a reason. Now, it's up to you to decide. Does Etta Place go down in history as the woman who disappeared? Or do you give her the final word? It's up to you, sweetie."

Susan wasn't as sure as her grandmother. While the idea of it sounded enticing, it felt daunting as well.

After tucking her grandmother into bed, Susan went out to the living room. She picked up her tape recorder and the wooden box, and quietly left the apartment.

* * *

Two hours later, Susan entered the noisy newspaper office and headed for her desk. She'd stopped by her appointment despite being late and was relieved that the person she was supposed to interview understood she'd had a family emergency. She had an article to write up quickly before her work day was over.

Susan set her grandmother's wooden box on her desk. She couldn't resist looking through it again. Opening it up, she carefully began pulling out the photos. There was the one of Grandma Em and Sundance, dressed in their best clothes. Her grandmother looked so young and beautiful, it was difficult for Susan to make the connection between the woman she once was and the woman she was now. Setting that aside, she looked at the other photos. They were postcard style, the type that were common in the early 1900s. One was of Grandma Em, Sundance, and a man who Susan believed must have been Butch, sitting outside a rough cabin in nice chairs. They held tea cups and Grandma Em held a teapot. Two dogs sat in the photo also. On the back someone had written: *"Tea Party."* Susan smiled. She wondered if this was taken at their ranch in South America.

The noise in the office seemed to fade away as Susan gazed at her grandmother's belongings from so long ago. She pulled out another photo of a group of people standing with horses in front of the same cabin. Sitting in the bottom of the box, Susan saw her grandmother's lapel pin watch again. Reverently, she lifted it up and placed it in the palm of her hand. She remembered as a child how much she loved looking at the watch her grandmother wore daily. Turning it over, she was surprised to see engraving on the back. Susan lifted it up to the light, and read: *"To my dear Etta. Love, Harry."*

Her eyes filled with tears. The love between her grandmother and Harry had been epic. Almost unreal. But here was proof. Proof that Sundance loved Etta.

The phone on her desk rang, startling Susan from her trance. The noisy newspaper office filled her senses once more. She'd been so intent on her grandmother's keepsakes, she'd ignored what was going on around her.

The phone shrilled again, and she hurriedly lifted it from its cradle. "Susan Sheridan here," she answered.

"Miss Sheridan? Hello. I'm sorry to bother you at work, but I couldn't get ahold of your father. They said he'd already left work and he didn't answer at home."

Susan frowned at the phone. "Who is this?"

"I'm sorry. I should have told you right away. My name is Cathy Rhonedale. I'm the head nurse here at Shady Gardens. I'm so sorry but I have bad news."

Susan clutched her grandmother's watch that was still in her hand. "What's wrong?"

"I'm afraid your grandmother has passed on. A nursing assistant went to her room a few minutes ago to escort her to dinner and found her in her bed. It appears as if she passed quietly in her sleep."

Susan was stunned. She pictured her grandmother lying in bed right before she'd left. Her eyes had been closed and she'd looked so peaceful. It was hard for Susan to believe that she'd gone so quickly.

"Miss Sheridan?" Cathy said. "Are you still there?"

"Yes, I am. Sorry. I'm just trying to absorb the news. I was just there this afternoon, visiting with my grandmother. It's difficult thinking that she's gone now."

"I understand. You have my deepest sympathies. Mrs.

Sheridan was such a kind soul and well-liked among the staff and residents here. She will be greatly missed."

"Thank you," Susan said.

"I see that there are arrangements written in her file in the event of her death. Shall we call the mortuary listed?" Cathy asked.

"Yes, please. I'll contact my father. Thank you for calling," Susan said, still feeling dazed. She hung up the phone, and stared at the wooden box Grandma Em had given her.

It was as if she'd known, Susan thought. She looked once more at the watch her grandmother had worn every day. Then she set it back in the box and picked up the phone to call her father with the dreaded news.

Chapter Thirty-Four

Three days later

The somber black sedan pulled up near the gravesite which sat on a hill, with an old, oak shade tree above it. The minister stood beside it, waiting patiently.

Susan and her father, Harry Sheridan, stepped out of the sedan, linked arms, and walked over to the gravesite. Harry nodded to the minister, and he said a few words and a prayer. Shaking hands with both Harry and Susan, the minister left them alone.

Susan watched as her father stared at the casket that held his mother. Her heart went out to him. He'd always been close with her, which in itself was a testament to what a kind and loving mother she'd been. Susan studied his face, trying to see the resemblance between him and his father, the man in the photos that Grandma Em had given her. There was a genuine likeness, although her father, at age sixty-four, had lived much longer than his own father had. Yet, even though her father had gray running through his dark blond hair, and lines around his eyes and mouth from smiling broadly throughout his life, she could still see Sundance in him, especially around his gray-blue eyes.

Harry lifted those eyes to his daughter's. "So, this is where my biological father is buried?" he asked, looking a bit lost. Susan felt bad for her father. He was a man who was used to being decisive and in control. But today, he was a man who had lost his mother, and only recently learned more about his birth father than he ever could have imagined.

"Yes," Susan said gently. "His plaque is right there." She pointed to the grave that was on the left side of her grand-mother's.

"Harry A. Place," Harry read aloud. "Place? Was that my real last name?"

Susan shook her head. "That's where it gets complicated. From what Grandma told me, his real name was Longabaugh. But Butch couldn't bury him under that name. Place was his mother's maiden name, and an alias he and Grandma used when they were together. Thus, Etta Place."

"There's so much I never knew," he said, shaking his head. He glanced at the grave on the other side of his father's. "So, who is James Ryan?"

"That would be Butch Cassidy," Susan explained. "James Ryan was the name he was using when Grandma last saw him. He used it until his death."

"It all seems so strange to me," Harry said. "I can't believe my mother didn't want to be buried beside my father, er, I mean stepfather, Edward Sheridan. Why here? In the middle of nowhere, beside these men she hadn't seen in decades?"

Susan looked around the little cemetery that sat beside an old church in a field outside of Spokane. It seemed odd to her too, to bury her beloved grandmother here where no one knew who she was. Especially since her grandmother had requested her gravestone be marked with her real name: Ethel Emily Pleasants. But it was what she'd requested in the letter Susan had found in Grandma Em's box. She'd wanted to spend eternity with the man she'd loved first. The man she had followed to the middle of nowhere and back again. The man who she'd let go out of love for her son.

"It's what she wanted," Susan told her father. "But she did also request a headstone be placed beside Grandfather, under the name Emily Sheridan. She loved him, too."

Harry nodded. "And we should all be so lucky to have our last wishes respected."

They stood there until the men came to lower the casket into the ground. Turning, both unable to watch, they made their way back to the car.

"I'll arrange for fresh flowers to be placed on mother's grave every week," Harry said. "I don't want her to be forgotten."

Susan smiled. "Believe me, Dad. Grandma Em will not be forgotten."

He looked at her quizzically. "Well, maybe you can tell me more about her story on our trip home. I'd really like to know about her life before I was born."

Susan nodded. As her father slid into the car, Susan turned and glanced at the cemetery one last time. The sky was a pale blue with streaks of white clouds floating through it. In the distance stood a large Victorian house surrounded by open fields. She wondered if that had been Butch's house, in his later years when Etta had finally reunited with him. It was such a wonderful story. She couldn't wait to listen to it again on the tapes and make notes. But write it? She wasn't sure if she could do it justice.

"I hope you and Sundance will be happy again," she said

aloud to her grandmother, knowing she couldn't hear her, yet wishing she could.

Turning back to the car, Susan was just about to step inside when she thought she heard the sound of hoofbeats in the distance. She scanned the horizon, expecting to see a group of horseback riders. But there were none. Suddenly, she heard the soft laughter of a woman. It sounded carefree—happy. Susan smiled. Then she slipped into the car and she and her father drove away.

Epilogue

2018

Susan Sheridan Riley stood in her closet on tiptoe, reaching high above her head for the item she was searching for. Her fingertips could barely reach it.

"Grams. Let me get that for you," Brooke, her fourteen-year-old granddaughter, offered. Brooke was taller than Susan by two inches, maybe more now since Susan had probably shrunk a little at the age of seventy-four.

"Thank you, dear," Susan said, accepting the wooden box from her granddaughter.

"What is that, Grandma?" Brooke asked, looking at it curiously with the same lavender-blue eyes as Susan's. Brooke looked much like Susan had in her younger years, with long blond hair and those incredible eyes. Even though Susan adored all four of her grandchildren, she and Brooke had always had the closest relationship.

Susan smiled. "You'll see." Carrying the box out to the dining room, she set it down carefully on the table. "This is very old and very delicate. Like me," she teased.

"Oh, Grandma," Brooke said. "You're anything but delicate. You know that even I have a tough time keeping up with you."

Susan laughed. She was fortunate to have good health at her age, and still took long walks around her hilly San Francisco neighborhood. She also biked at times with her grandchildren, and enjoyed taking trips to places where she could hike trails in quiet, secluded areas. Of course, she knew each year that she was slowing down, but she intended to keep moving as much as possible for as long as she could.

Brushing back a tendril of gray hair that had fallen from the clip that held it away from her face, Susan lifted the lid of the box. It had been years since she'd looked inside, and even more since her Grandma Em had given it to her for safekeeping.

Brooke gasped when she saw the old photos inside. "Are these of Great-Great-Grandma Emily?" the young girl asked.

"Yes, dear. They are. And her first husband, Harry. And their good friend, Robert LeRoy Parker. They called him Butch."

Susan carefully lifted the first picture from the box to show her granddaughter. It was the one with Emily and Harry, alias Etta and Sundance.

"She was so beautiful," Brooke said, looking awed.

"Yes, she was. And you have her eyes."

Brooke grinned. "I know. So do you."

Together, they looked through the other pictures and items in the box as Susan told Brooke a little about Grandma Em's exciting life.

"That's amazing!" Brooke's eyes danced with excitement.

"When I was younger, there were several books and movies out about Butch, Sundance, and Etta. To this day, no one knows what ever happened to the three of them. Well, no one except me."

Brooke's eyes grew wide. "So, I know a secret that no one else knows?"

"Yes, dear. Now you do."

"Grams? Why didn't you ever write Grandma Em's life story? You wrote for a living. You even wrote a few books. Why not about her?"

Susan thought back to the day Grandma Em had entrusted her life story and the box of memories to her. At the time, Susan hadn't known what to do with all that knowledge. Would anyone believe her if she did write a book? Would anyone even want to read it? She'd put it aside as her life grew busy, first with marriage, then having two children of her own. She'd worked off and on at the newspaper, and had even managed to acquire a publishing contract for several romance novels that she'd written through the years. But in all that time, she'd never let herself believe she was capable of writing her grandmother's life story. Until now.

"It's taken me all these years to feel I could write her story," she told Brooke. "It will be a big job, researching all the pieces of information that I don't know. But I think I'm ready now. After all, it's really now or never."

"I can help you research," Brooke said excitedly. "It can be a project for both of us."

Susan smiled. "I'd like that. You know, your great-great-grandmother was a teacher. I think she'd love your helping me and learning history in the process."

Brooke beamed.

Susan looked down at the lapel pin watch she'd worn every day since Grandma Em had given it to her. Snapping it open, she saw that it was already lunch time.

"Why don't we have a bite then get started on this project? We have a lot of work ahead of us," Susan said.

"I can't wait," Brooke told her.

Susan couldn't wait either. She'd waited too long already. It was time the world learned what had really happened to Butch, Sundance, and Etta Place. And she was honored to be the one to tell the story.

-End-

Author's Note

The Real Etta Place

Etta Place was a real woman who followed Harry Longab-augh, alias the Sundance Kid, on his exploits between the years of 1895-1907. No one knows her real name or where she came from. There is speculation that she was one of Fannie Mae Porter's girls or that she was a schoolteacher or music teacher. She was a young, beautiful woman who was said to be refined and mannered, but she could also shoot and ride as well as any man. No record of their marriage has ever been found, but the lovely photograph of them in their finery was said to be their wedding picture.

Etta, Harry, and Robert LeRoy Parker, alias Butch Cassidy, were known to be friends. The trio did travel out east together in 1900-1901 before heading off to South America and settling on a ranch in Cholila, Argentina. In a letter to a friend, Butch described the trio as "our little family of three." Butch and Harry seemed to get along well enough to run the ranch together for nearly five years, until the law began moving in on them.

Sometime between 1906-1908, Etta disappeared. Some

say that during that time, Etta died in a Denver hospital and Sundance went on a drunken binge and shot up a bar before returning to South America. Others say she died in childbirth. Stories persist that she left Sundance for someone else, that she came back to America alone, or that she was killed in the final shootout in San Vincente, Bolivia where it was believed that Butch and Sundance died. In reality, no woman was killed during that shootout, and there has yet to be any evidence that Butch or Sundance died that day.

What became of Etta Place? No one knows. And that is what makes her story so interesting. Using a timeline of true events that I put together from my research through reading multiple books on all three characters, I created her life with Butch and Sundance, while giving a fictional version of her life after she disappeared. Etta was an interesting woman with an incredible life. I hope you enjoyed her story.

Book Club Questions

1. When Etta first meets Harry Longabaugh in San Antonio, she opens up to him about her father's tragic death and how that experience, as well as her close relationship with the "Madame" Fannie Mae Porter, changed how she viewed the concepts of right and wrong. Do you think that her experiences in her younger years were what made her able to accept Harry's outlaw life?

2. Both Butch and Sundance turned to a life of crime after having been wronged by being honest. Have you ever had an experience where being honest held you back and didn't benefit you?

3. Wherever Etta went with Sundance, she always tried to make their dwelling, be it a rough cabin or a tent, as homey as possible. Do you think she was trying to make up for not having a stable home or did she really believe that her home was where Sundance was?

4. When Sheriff Ted Neilson confronted Emily about being Etta Place, she never admitted or denied she was her, she

only said that she was no longer the woman in that picture. In what ways had Emily changed from her days with Sundance and Butch to make her statement true?

5. By the time Harry met Etta, he was already a known outlaw. Yet, he pursued a relationship with her, and stayed loyal to her for the twelve years we know they were together. Knowing that he'd been raised the youngest child in a Christian family and that his favorite sister was the sweet, kind Samanna, why do you think he was drawn to Etta and to having a lasting relationship?

6. Some historians believe that Etta was in love with Butch as well as with Sundance. In fact, some say she was Butch's girl-friend first. What did you think about the close relationship she had with Butch? Do you think she may have loved him too? In what way?

7. Emily/Etta got her happily ever after, just not the one the reader may have expected she'd have. Were you satisfied with her choice at the end of the novel, or would you have wanted Emily/Etta to have a different ending? What would that ending be?

About the Author

Deanna Lynn Sletten is the author of *Maggie's Turn, Finding Libbie, One Wrong Turn, Night Music,* and several other titles. She writes heartwarming women's fiction and romance novels with unforgettable characters. She has also written one middle-grade novel that takes you on the adventure of a lifetime. Deanna believes in fate, destiny, love at first sight, soul mates, second chances, and happily ever after, and her novels reflect that.

Deanna is married and has two grown children. When not writing, she enjoys walking the wooded trails around her home with her beautiful Australian Shepherd, traveling, and relaxing on the lake.

Deanna loves hearing from her readers.
Connect with her at:
Her website: http://www.deannalsletten.com
Blog: http://www.deannalynnsletten.com
Facebook: http://www.facebook.com/deannalynnsletten
Twitter: http://www.twitter.com/deannalsletten
Visit Deanna's Amazon Author Page to see more of her books.

Made in the USA
Middletown, DE
23 May 2019